SIX SAVAGE THRONES

By Holly Race

The Queens of Elben
Six Wild Crowns
Six Savage Thrones
Six Broken Realms

SIX SAVAGE THRONES

HOLLY RACE

orbit

orbit-books.co.uk

ORBIT

First published in Great Britain in 2026 by Orbit

1 3 5 7 9 10 8 6 4 2

Map illustration by Viv Mullett, The Flying Fish Studios

A CIP catalogue record for this book is available from the British Library.

HB ISBN 978-0-356-52269-2
C format ISBN 978-0-356-52270-8

Typeset in Electra LT Std by Aptara
Printed and bound in Great Britain by Clays Ltd, Elcograf, S.p.A.

Papers used by Orbit are from well-managed forests and other responsible sources.

MIX
Paper | Supporting responsible forestry
FSC® C104740
www.fsc.org

Orbit
An imprint of
Little, Brown Book Group
Carmelite House
50 Victoria Embankment
London EC4Y 0DZ

The authorised representative
in the EEA is
Hachette Ireland
8 Castlecourt Centre
Dublin 15, D15 XTP3, Ireland
(email: info@hbgi.ie)

An Hachette UK Company
www.hachette.co.uk

orbit-books.co.uk

For my friends; my own found family

"Soul of my Soul, my Joy, my Crown, my Friend"
from *To Mrs M Awbrye* by Katherine Philips, 1631–64

The Kingdom of Elben
Pkolack
Mathmas
Sigelburh
Brinlaw
Brinhafn
Uuvek & Alpich
Heahmore Mountains
Forest of Braeden
High
Sweillan
Plythe
Kyttle River
SWEGAN SEA
Kywsa Bay
Kyttle Falls
Gemæres
Cnothan Town
Cnothan
Perfugi

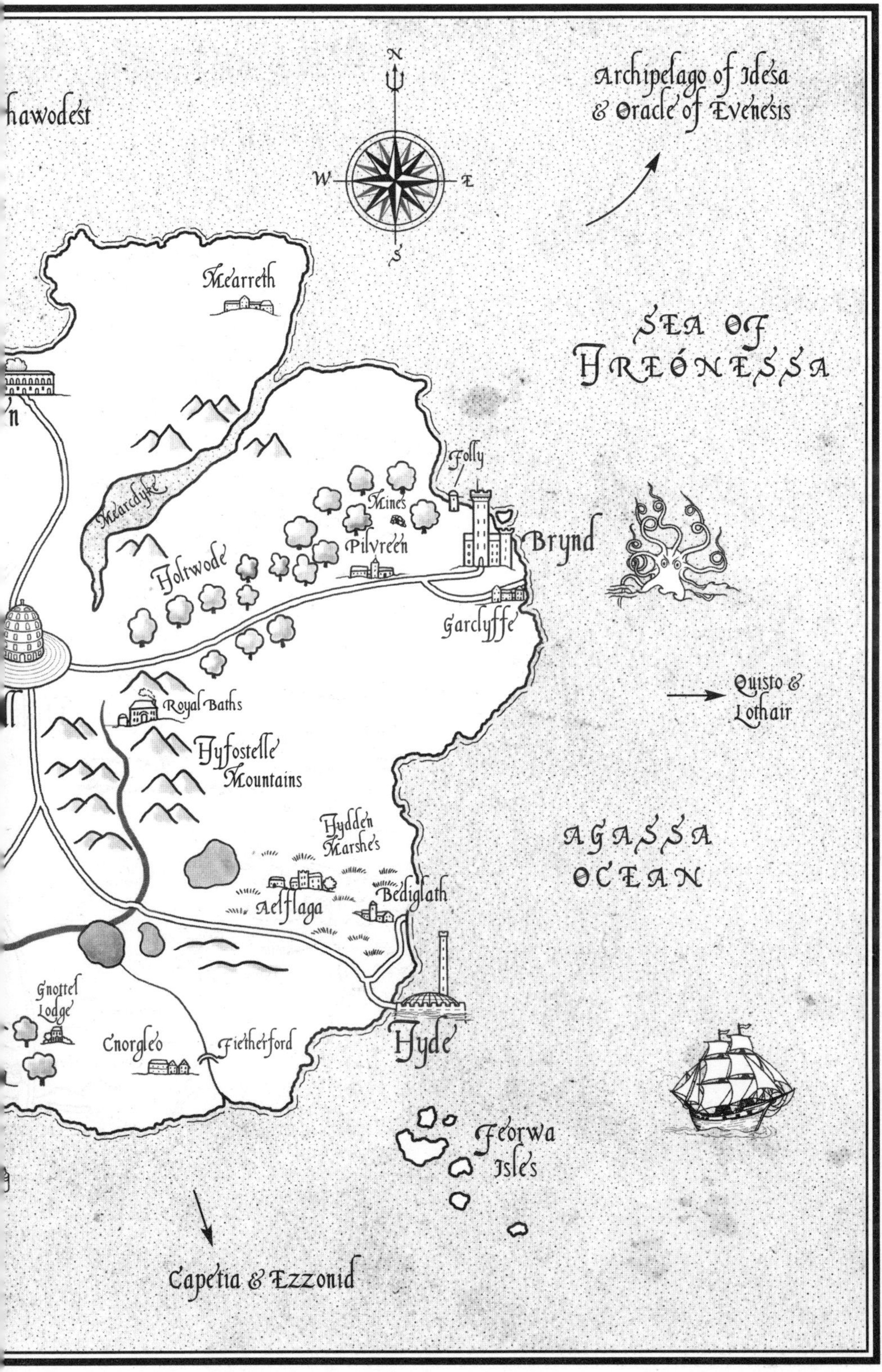
N
W
E
S
Archipelago of Idesa
& Oracle of Evenesis
Mearreth
SEA OF
HREÓNESSA
Folly
Mines
Bryndd
Pilvreen
Holtwode
Meardyke
Garclyffe
Royal Baths
Hyfostelle
Mountains
Quisto &
Lothair
Hydden
Marshes
AGASSA
OCEAN
Bediglath
Aelflaga
Gnottel
Lodge
Cnorgleo
Fiethertord
Hyde
Feorwa
Isles
Capetia & Ezzonid

TRIGGER WARNINGS

Despite the best efforts of Boleyn and Seymour in *Six Wild Crowns*, the world of *Six Savage Thrones* remains deeply patriarchal. This book contains scenes of violence, sexual assault and abuse, and features two adult/minor relationships. Multiple characters are navigating war- and relationship-related trauma.

AUTHOR'S NOTE

Six Wild Crowns ended at the start of a religious revolution. If you have not read the first book in this trilogy, I urge you to do so before starting this one, as otherwise very little will make sense to you!

Many of the characters in *Six Savage Thrones* will be familiar to those with a working knowledge of Tudor history. However, there are two authorial liberties that I particularly wish to flag. The first is that Dowager Queen Cecilia is very loosely based on Henry VIII's youngest sister, Mary Tudor. While her history and trajectory may feel familiar, I have markedly altered her personality from what we know of Mary Tudor, and I chose to change her name to make this distinction. Likewise, while I like to think that "my" Cleves has more than a touch of the real Anne of Cleves about her, and the "Unrest" in Ezzonid is inspired by the Guelders Wars (which affected the Low Countries in the early 1500s), Anne of Cleves was not affected by them in the way she is in this novel.

Six Wild Crowns touched upon and referenced multiple real historical moments, such as Henry VIII's "romances" with Anne Boleyn and Jane Seymour, and those queens' subsequent pregnancies, as well as the arrests of Anne and Thomas Wyatt, among others. However, as a result of Boleyn and Seymour's choices in the first book, *Six Savage Thrones* diverges a little further from the historical record. I have chosen to give my leading ladies an agency and a sorority (and a lapdragon) that they were not afforded in real life. I hope you enjoy seeing how the choices they subsequently make spin their stories, and the story of Elben, in new directions.

PART ONE

CHAPTER ONE

Cecilia

Cecilia takes great delight in her needles, and has in her collection seven hundred and something of all kinds and lengths. Gold, pewter, plain, jewelled, long, stubby. Some add glitter to fabric; some turn the thread invisible for the channelling of messages between women. And one, her favourite, bought at great cost (many thousand coins and the life of her lover) holds in its slender form a poison that will kill at the slightest touch of bare skin and leave no trace. Yes, Cecilia loves needles very much, partly because she enjoys embroidery, but mostly because she enjoys death.

Cecilia is taking great care over a new piece when her confidante Lorena Consego arrives, striding into her room without even the most perfunctory knock. The tapestry is intended for Lorena's bedchamber – when finished it will cover the wall opposite her bed so that she can see it before she falls asleep and as soon as she wakes. The woman in the piece is unmistakably Cecilia: each hair picked out with long threads of gold; the same pale body, constellation-freckled with beads, long-limbed and round-stomached.

"You are ruining the surprise," Cecilia says. Lorena's hair is bound in two long, black plaits knotted tightly around her scalp, revealing skin so richly brown it makes Cecilia quite jealous. There are fine wrinkles around her eyes and forehead that make her look a few years Cecilia's elder, even though they are of an age.

"My apologies, Your Highness," Lorena says, barely glancing at the cloth. Cecilia does not like that. She thought it would elicit a reaction from Lorena: either disapproval at the hint of bare leg on the portrait, or at the very least false gratitude.

"What is it?" she says, trying to keep the petulance from her voice.

"A letter from the bishop. I thought you would want it immediately."

Cecilia does not like this either. Lorena knows her too well.

"Read it to me," Cecilia says.

She selects a new needle – a thicker one, designed to give height – and loops deep pink thread into the tapestry, directly above the line of the gown. A hint of nipple, standing erect and proud from the canvas. Surely this will shock Lorena. She is tempted to lick it, but that is going too far, even for her. Besides, it wouldn't taste nice and she makes a point of not putting anything in her mouth that she doesn't find pleasant.

Lorena has not seen the addition yet; she is too busy breaking the wax seal – the two horns of Cernunnos indicate the letter comes from a religious man. Bishop More is the only man of God who would ever write to Cecilia.

Lorena clears her throat.

"Your Highness, dear Cecilia,

"Your most recent missive gave me great joy, and I must admit made me smile – it is rare to hear so quickly from you. While I do not condone your interest in worldly gossip, it is difficult to resent it if it means our correspondence is more frequent.

"Your shock is understandable – while it has been several months since the death of the Boleyn traitor and the disappearance of the Seymour girl, the reverberations of their actions are still felt across your home country. Your brother, I believe, takes it very hard. As you know, he is a great romantic and the betrayal of two loves has been a heavy blow. I can only be thankful that Lady Boleyn perceived her end was inevitable and made the choice to take her own life – in that at least she spared Henry the pain of executing her. May she and her lover be tormented for eternity by the wælcyrge of hell. To commit treason for the sake of a poor and, if I may say so, barely talented poet is unthinkable to me.

"But enough of my verbosity. I can picture your expression at this moment: you will be rolling your eyes. 'Enough moralising, you tiresome old man!'"

Cecilia snorts. She lays her needle just so next to the others, then straightens, cracking her aching shoulders. She goes to the fireplace and throws another acelath rock into the cold flame. A chill gust blows around the room, leaving icy patterns on the marble walls as Lorena continues:

"The king has this very day returned from Capetia with Queen Parr. I believe his discussions of an alliance between the two countries was fruitful – your brother could charm a fairy from its nest if he set his mind to it. And I bear further news still. Indeed, this is news that may pertain directly to you, if you are so inclined. I do not think that Lords Cromwell or Wolsey shall mind me sharing this with you (whichever of their servants are reading this letter – is it you, Oswald? Or is it Nicholas this time? – I direct you to send it immediately to the Lady Cecilia, and if your masters take issue with the contents, I pray you direct them to me).

"My news is that the surviving traitor, the Lady Seymour, is rumoured to be travelling to Perfugi. The king, as you can imagine, is keen to see her arraigned for her crimes. As to her motives for coming to Perfugi – who knows? But if you are the same girl I once knew, full of curiosity and spark, who caused me so much trouble before you married your late royal husband, I think you will be just as eager to find the Lady Seymour as your brother. You must know that the reward and gratitude of the king would be great indeed should you manage to find her. I would only warn you that she may have with her a great beast: a black panther, which is large and dangerous. Be sure that you do not fall foul of the creature, for I would never wish to see you harmed.

"Yours, in fondness,

"Bishop Thomas More of Pilvreen."

Cecilia thrums her fingers on the mantelpiece. The cold fire makes her gown – thin silk, unlike the heavy articles worn in Elben – move like water.

"So she is alive after all," Cecilia says.

Lorena passes the letter to her with a dipped curtsey.

"I wonder how she has survived for so long," Lorena says.

"The Feorwans, I imagine," Cecilia replies, examining More's handwriting. "They helped her to escape Elben. They must have been helping her all this while."

"Your brother will not like that."

"No."

This explains the tales she has heard of Elbenese raids upon the Feorwan Isles. She rarely pays attention to matters of international politics, which are too broad and impersonal to hold her interest, but that she did find curious. The Feorwan Isles have been under Elbenese rule for a century or more, and it is unlike her brother to exact punishment needlessly. Now it makes sense – Henry is ensuring their loyalty.

Lorena edges closer to Cecilia. "Would you like me to rub your shoulders? You have been long at your work; your back must be aching."

"Do not fuss over me," Cecilia says, striding past Lorena and sitting back in front of the tapestry, tossing her hair over her shoulder. She throws Lorena her most scornful look. "You are being a mother. You know what I did to my mother."

"Yes, Your Highness," Lorena says.

"What did I do to my mother?"

Cecilia wants to hear her say it.

"You killed her, Your Highness."

"I did. I killed her."

Lorena bites her lip. If she says what Cecilia knows she wants to say – you were a baby, she would not resent you her life – Cecilia will drive the needle into Lorena's arm. There is a litany of pinprick scars across Lorena's skin from many years of displeasing her queen. Cecilia would rather like to see whether there is a point at which Lorena will break. She has not found it yet. One day. One day, when she no longer desires her company, she will find that point.

Cecilia picks up her needle once more. Her shoulders *are* aching.

"You may rub me, I suppose," she says.

Lorena stands behind her, studiously not looking at the tapestry. She begins to rub Cecilia's shoulders, just the way Cecilia enjoys. Cecilia sighs, then she groans, knowing the sound will make Lorena uncomfortable.

"Would you like me to engage the doctrini?" Lorena says.

"Six."

"So many for one woman?"

"Are you ignorant? Do you not recall what More said about the panther?"

Lorena increases the pressure on Cecilia's shoulders.

"I am a little afraid for her," she says.

"You know as well as I that people are far better weapons than swords. In my hands, at least."

"And now I am very much afraid for her."

Cecilia holds up a hand. Lorena stops and moves to one side so that she can be seen.

"You have not commented on your present," Cecilia says, angling her head towards the tapestry. Lorena looks reluctantly, and Cecilia takes the opportunity to reach out and flick the embroidered nipple, watching Lorena's reaction all the while. Nothing. Even worse – a flash of boredom.

"It is beautiful work as always, Your Highness. I am fortunate indeed to be the recipient of such generosity," Lorena says.

Heat rises in Cecilia. "You are in my space," she says. Lorena steps backwards and sinks to the floor. "Forgive me, Your Highness."

Anyone else and Cecilia would have cut off their hands, or hobbled them. But then Lorena has always known how to appeal to Cecilia's softer instincts; has done ever since Cecilia met her on her first night on foreign soil, days before her wedding to the strange, ailing king of Capetia. He had gifted Cecilia seven ladies-in-waiting, and Lorena with her purring accent, not quite Capetian, not quite Perfugian, had understood immediately how to wrestle with Cecilia's wit. Lorena, the widowed Duchess of Giralve, with her voice like steel and her posture like the ancient oak trees that line High Hall's pathways.

Cecilia flicks her wrist, dismissing the woman. Lorena backs out, her eyes lowered. By the time she reaches the door, Cecilia has thought of another way to needle her.

"Send your brother to me," she says.

The ploy works, no matter how hard Lorena tries to conceal it. In the little flash of her eyes, Cecilia reads hatred, disappointment, fear and resignation. But Lorena only says, "Of course, Your Highness," before excusing herself.

Cecilia examines the tapestry. Days of work, and now when she looks at it, all she can see is Lorena's boredom. She selects the one knife in her collection of needles. She punctures the tapestry in silence, first the face, then the nipple and the hint of bare leg. It isn't enough. Her stabs turn to slashes, until the whole piece is fluttering ribbons.

By the time the boy Florin slides into her room and bows, she has worked up an appetite.

CHAPTER TWO

Cleves

She is far too busy to attend to the artist. A queen's territory is like the innards of a clock: intricate, each part relying on the other to work correctly. And the queen must be at its centre. So it is with Cnothan: her pile of correspondence is extensive.

The artist sighs.

She has another letter from Ezzonid: *I am already at the docks, cousin, so there is no point in telling me to turn around. Your missives will not reach me. With a fair wind, I shall reach your little castle . . .*

She bites her lip to keep from swearing. Any guest, even family from her homeland, is unwelcome. She does not need people scurrying around her castle peering into her business. She sets the letter aside, since it requires no reply, and casts her eyes over the next.

I have something of a cough at present, and have been forced to take to my bed. I find my mind wandering to the past as I lie here . . .

Lady Paston – her first and, for a long time, only vulnerability. She must give her response proper thought.

The artist sighs again.

Cleves pulls her glasses from her nose and leans back in her chair, observing the man who sits with charcoal-sooted fingers in the corner of the room.

"Is my pose not to your liking, Master Holbein?" she says.

The man smiles apologetically. "I simply cannot draw you flatteringly at such an angle, Your Majesty."

"And what makes you think that I would concern myself with flattering angles?"

"Everyone prefers to show the best of themselves, do they not?"

She supposes she must give him credit for saying "everyone" rather than "every woman", but then again the people of Avahuc do not concern themselves with gender, so perhaps it is merely cultural.

"I believe that actions, not appearances, show the best of a person."

Master Holbein offers a little seated bow, and his canvas – a piece of blue-washed paper secured over a wooden board – dips with him, offering a tantalising glimpse of his sketch. "And the best of my action lies in the mastery of my art, Your Majesty."

Cleves laughs. She puts her glasses down upon the pile of parchment – accounts, correspondence, pleas and offers. She studies Holbein more carefully.

"You know I have no desire for this portrait. My husband is the one who commissions you," she says.

"This is true." There is a frown line between his eyes which grows deeper as he speaks. He is stocky, clean-shaven, and the only mark of status he wears is a single gold chain around his neck. His skin is a warmer brown than hers.

"*Correan aspa pir esperido*," she says, stumbling over the lisp of the accent.

Holbein gasps, then grins. "Her Majesty knows my language?"

"A very little," she says.

What follows is a stream of words in Avahucian. She barely recognises two of them, and can no sooner guess at his meaning than she can guess at the notion of enjoying lovemaking with a man. She laughs again. "Stop, sir, I beg of you. Do you mean to humiliate me to my face?"

Holbein covers his eyes with one hand. This she finds curious too – is his over-gesticulation nature or performance? The former, she decides.

"My humble apologies," he says. "My homesickness made me eager for conversation in my native tongue."

"If you answered my question in your native tongue, I am none the wiser," she says.

Holbein licks his lips. The question she asked him in his own language – "has my husband not commanded you to make me appear ugly?" – should make him nervous. He cannot very well admit to it if those were Henry's instructions.

"I believe His Majesty wishes to circulate a variety of portraits of his queens for the pleasure and education of the people," Holbein says.

Nobility and royals across the known world have always done as much. It is a way of offering a connection between subjects and their rulers. It cements status, for if one is deemed influential enough to have a portrait – and to have that portrait replicated in multiple great houses – then one must be influential indeed. Recognition is power.

Artists like Master Holbein have amassed fortunes on their ability to take a likeness that flatters while reflecting the subject's true features. She doubts that many of his patrons have ever requested that he make his subject less attractive.

"You take pride in your work," she says.

"I do." He hesitates, and she leaves him space to talk. Cleves has several talents, but one of her greatest lies in being able to put anyone at ease, no matter their rank. "There is a moment in the process where I know – aha, I have got them. Captured their essence. It might be a little fold in the chin, or a certain sharpness to the eye, or the texture of the skin. But once I have that, all else flows from there. The sensation when that happens . . . it is glorious, Your Majesty."

Cleves leans forward, her elbows on the table. "And what if that is denied, or you never get that feeling?"

"Then I am very unhappy. I do not like those portraits to be seen."

"But sometimes they must be. Sometimes I imagine your employer prefers the portrait that does not contain the . . . essence."

Holbein juts his chin. "I have never permitted that to happen across my whole life."

She sees the conflict in his eyes – he does not need to confirm his instructions from Henry. It is imperative to Elben's king that Cleves be perceived as a joke, a failure, an abomination. Such humiliation is designed to keep Cleves in line, to remind those loyal to her that she can never be taken seriously as a ruler. A woman scorned can harbour no thoughts of rebellion or defiance.

Here, in Holbein, is a man who wishes to reflect the truth of her, but whose paymaster wishes him to tell a lie. Which shall it be? Integrity or survival? Cleves knows which she would choose, but Holbein is one of those rare humans who will stake all on integrity. There are more of them around of late. Queen Boleyn. Queen Seymour. Look where it led them – death and exile. Strange, poor creatures. She will never be one of them.

Her eyes land on the papers before her. The one on top is a report, in her master of horse's scrawl, on the latest additions to her menagerie and their associated costs.

"Follow me, Master Holbein. I have a scheme that will make all parties contented," she says.

She has never had a throne – the royals of Ezzonid have not settled for such things for nigh on twenty years – but she has her servants carry a sturdy wooden chair from the banqueting hall into her receiving chamber. The space is, like the rest of Cnothan, a mishmash to its core. She has adopted the Ezzonid manner of painting elaborate murals onto the ceilings. She looks up at skies of palest blue and pink, rimmed with clouds and fharah – the many-coloured, troublemaking birds that are a common sight in the wildernesses of her home country. But the floor is Elbenese terracotta, made by artisans in the neighbouring town of Cnorgleo from clay taken from the riverbanks of the Fietherford.

Holbein sets up his easel in the centre of the room, facing the chair. Cleves settles into the seat, plumping the cotton sleeves of her blouse and smoothing her burnt-ochre gown. She pats her hood, making sure that her hair is tucked beneath it properly. She does not usually wear hoods, the informal nature of her castle not demanding it, and her hair rarely cooperates when she attempts to cover it. She perches the glasses on her nose. She does not require them unless she is reading, but they will contribute to the look.

"This is excellent," Holbein is muttering. "Straight on, so you are looking at me directly. No games. This might be it."

"Not quite, sir," she says, and gestures to Fergus, her master of horse. He is leaning against the door frame, watching the affair with his usual sardonic smile. He moves aside and ushers in an assortment of animals. A single hunting dragon, a handful of small pigs, two greyhounds, a horse and six or so ferrets.

"Come to me, friends," Cleves says, patting the bottom of her skirts. Holbein watches, eyes wide, as one of the pigs and a few ferrets settle themselves in her lap. The horse nuzzles her shoulder from behind, and the rest gather around her on the floor.

"Where is Lelij?" she asks Fergus.

"Behind me. He's shy today."

From the doorway, a snout appears, sniffing the room. Cleves clicks her tongue several times and holds out her hand. A servant places a segment of orange onto her upturned palm. The snout sniffs again, and then a head follows, and then the whole creature. It is a lopsided, crooked-limbed beast, with a tongue so large it lolls out of its mouth. It lollops into the room and swipes the orange segment, before licking the remnants of juice from Cleves's hand.

"Here, Lelij," she says, gently drawing the creature by its collar to sit at her feet, displacing one of the greyhounds.

Holbein stares at it.

"What is such a beast?" he says, kneeling so that he is at the creature's own level.

"Come now, Master Holbein, surely you have drawn many gargoyles in your time," she says, raising an eyebrow. He looks between her and Lelij, and then both he and she begin to laugh.

"Oh, very good, Your Majesty," he says, patting his chest. "Very good indeed."

He begins to work, his fingers deftly swiping the charcoal this way and that, taking a brief likeness of her and her pets for reference. When he returns to his studio, he will work the sketch up into a full painting. Cleves will look like the foreigner she is, in her Ezzonid fashion, her glasses rendering her bookish. Her animals will make her an oddity, will conjure the smells of unwashed fur and moulting hair. Henry will be able to overlook the fact that Holbein has painted her as she truly appears – clear skin, eyes like flint, regal posture – because he will be able to point to the gargoyle, that ugliest of beasts, at her feet. And he and his friends will laugh and compare the two. *I would rather marry the gargoyle,* they will smirk. And in their ridicule, Cleves and Holbein will both be safe.

"Yes," Holbein mutters, his fingers moving faster. "I have you, Your Majesty. I have you."

CHAPTER THREE

Howard

The fabrics cover the gallery floor, turning the wood to shimmering pearl. Howard kneels beside them, runs her fingers over them one by one. Damask and velvet and fine lace woven from the tiny silkworms of Thawodest.

"This one is like a cloud," Ursula Askew says. She rubs the velvet against her face, her eyes closed, her smile mischievous. Howard forces herself to laugh.

"You should have it," Howard says.

Ursula opens her eyes. "What?"

"What, *Your Majesty*." Howard picks up a piece of lace and holds it to the light of the gallery windows, admiring the intricacies of the pattern. "I have many such pieces. My lord father used to bring them back for me from his posts abroad."

She avoids looking at her half-sister, Legh, who knows that their father never gifted anyone more than scraps.

Ursula hugs the bolt of velvet to her bodice and stares at her shadowy reflection in the glass of the windows. "May I really have it? Truly?"

Howard lowers the lace. "It will suit you well. Pair it with your green sleeves and it will make a beautiful gown."

Ursula does not need to be offered a third time. She laughs, spins, letting the velvet whirl around her like one of the Elbenese flags atop Plythe's turrets, buffeted by the wind from the Swegan Sea. Howard's laughter is real this time. She does so love to please her ladies.

"Which one will you choose for the new queen's gift?" Lady Tylney asks, ignoring Ursula's squeals.

Howard forces herself to study the fabrics with Mary Boleyn in mind. The very thought revolts her: that she must offer something extravagant to the woman who betrayed Howard's friend and protector, Mary's own sister. And yet everything dictates that Howard must play the part of the pleasant queen, welcoming another into the fold.

"The silk," she replies at last, stroking the fabric in question. Cool, smooth, expensive and inoffensive. Very fit for one such as Mary Boleyn, she thinks, and then worries that she is becoming uncharitable, and then worries that she is worrying, for if anyone deserves an uncharitable thought it is that bitch.

Oblivious to Howard's thoughts, Tylney sighs. "Your judgement is impeccable, Your Majesty."

"Let us order several bolts, and then we can begin the embellishments," Howard tells her steward, who bows silently as he takes the silk. Howard notices the look he gives her ladies as they twirl around the room, trampling upon the rejected samples in their gaiety. She claps, then cocks her head to one side so they know she isn't rebuking them. "Come now, you are making my steward frown."

They all laugh, flocking to one side so that the servants can collect the fabrics. The little gold clock that sits at one end of the gallery chimes midday, and Howard detaches herself from her ladies. "I must to my lesson," she tells them.

She is followed by a chorus of "Nay, do not leave us!" and "We shall be so dull without you!" but she does not believe them. When she rejoins them, they will be laughing, in the middle of some joke or jape. And she will have to join in with them, even though her heart will be breaking.

Voda Kelaverinn is the only one left in Plythe who knows the truth of her. Who knows that treachery has taken root in her soul. He alone knows that she is both more and less than her kingly husband thinks of her. He is her compass, and she must cast him out. It cannot be put off any longer. Every day that he stays at Plythe calls her loyalty to the crown into question, for he was secured as her tutor by Queen Boleyn, who is disgraced and dead.

Kelaverinn is sitting in his study, at the far side of the room that was once the palace's library. Its long shelves are in a state of flux: half ancient, moulding tomes, half fine, new leather bought from the craftsmen in the towns surrounding High Hall or from masters on the continent. There are few windows here, to prevent the sunlight or any sea-salty draughts from ruining the books, and Voda reads by candlelight despite the sun being at its zenith outside.

He looks up at her entrance, a smile spreading across his kindly face. Warmth spreads through her, as it did when her father ruffled her hair on one of his rare visits.

She is going to lose him. Unthinkable. Inevitable.

"I must confess myself excited to see what you make of this new poem I have found for us to study," he says, seeing her to her chair. He has arranged them so that they are next to each other – no stuffy table between them. He tells her this is the way students are taught in Uuvek – where teacher and pupil can bend over a text in shared discovery. It is scandalous, but Howard has never attempted to create distance. She likes being close to him.

Her hand flutters over the manuscript. She picks out a few words – *passion, fate, union* – as if the poem is giving her permission. Her eyes fall upon a gathering of paper lying next to the manuscript.

"Are all of these poems for us to study?" she says.

Kelaverinn glances at them, then rests a hand upon the stack.

"These are from my family. My wife writes to tell me that our youngest is beginning his riding lessons."

He goes on and on about his children back at home, and his wife and how wonderful she is. Howard doesn't want to hear it.

"I must send you away," she says, interrupting him.

He looks at her, suddenly quiet and still.

"I am sorry," she continues. "But given . . . everything . . . it would not be prudent for me to . . . that is to say . . ."

"I understand," he says. "I should have anticipated this. To be truthful, I should have suggested it myself, long ago, but I did not wish to leave you when you were just starting to gain confidence. My apologies for placing you in such an awkward position."

She latches onto those words: *I did not wish to leave you.*

"It has been my honour to serve you and teach you these past several moons," he says. His voice is so gentle, his eyes so kind.

She leans forward and kisses him, her mouth open, her tongue reaching for his. He stiffens then pulls back with an "Oh" barely breathed. They stare at each other. His hands are curled into fists against his chest.

"I thought . . ." she begins. Tears spring to her eyes, and she does not know what hurts the most: his rejection, or the realisation of her foolishness. Kelaverinn stands, putting distance between them.

"You are a very kind queen, Your Majesty. I am a grateful teacher."

"Do you not think me beautiful?" she says.

He pauses, and his eyes are full of pity. "I think myself old."

The unsaid hangs between them: *And I think you young.* He does not use his wife as a shield. That smarts more than anything else – she cannot tell herself that he is merely faithful. He simply does not see her as a match.

He is saying more, but she does not hear anything else, her head and heart thumping. She scrambles to her feet and runs out of the room, and does not stop until she is in her bedchamber. The room is hexagonal, and but for the door, the windows and a single large mirror, it is all softness. Cushions, throws, rugs and curtains, all of them thick and warm, the kind of fabrics one wishes to lose oneself inside.

How dare he refuse her? She is beautiful, she knows she is. It is all she is, all she has. *It is a good thing you're pretty*, her father had told her when she was twelve. Good, but not enough.

And now he is not only leaving her – she has ruined his impression of her. She cannot fathom why she kissed him. It is not even that he is terribly handsome. He was, in that moment, an echo of a dream.

Howard bangs a fist against the closed door. It feels good. She does it again and again, until her fists are sore. She reaches behind her back and loosens her bodice, pulling at the stiff front until she can breathe properly.

There is a mirror at one side of the room, wide and tall. Henry sometimes fucks her up against it, so he can feel as though he's fucking two Howards at once. She stares at herself. Her cheeks are wet with tears. A droplet hangs from the tip of her nose. All she can think is: *Henry will not like me. He will no longer think me beautiful.*

She presses a hand against the mirror and stares at the place where real joins fiction. In the seam between the two, she sees the truth. She has spent her whole life wrapping a vision of herself for others, making a gift of her body and voice, until she had nothing left for herself. And ever since Boleyn rode into her life, she has been unwrapping the layers of tissue. So many layers, so much wrapping, so much concealment to entice, to seduce, to please please please please please please please please please . . .

Where is she?

CHAPTER FOUR

Cecilia

Cecilia wakes from her slumber with the suddenness of prey. Lorena is standing over her.

"They have found her," Cecilia says.

Lorena nods. "The messenger arrived moments ago."

The boy, Lorena's brother, stirs on the other side of the bed and looks blearily at them, the moonlight glancing through the window and off his face in a way that makes him squint unbecomingly. His black, curled hair is messier than she'd ever allow in public. Cecilia throws off the coverlet and slides out of bed, walking naked to her clothes, which are pooled across the floor.

"Where?" she asks, as she pulls a linen shift over her head.

"They have traced her to the Fontis veh Noyt district. They have a string of doctrini surrounding her from a distance, and they're awaiting your orders."

"Good."

Cecilia attempts to shrug her silk dress on, and gets stuck in the bodice. Lorena helps to tug it over her shoulders and lace up the back. That done, Cecilia takes Florin's breaches and pulls them on, tucking the bottom of her dress into the waist.

"What are you doing?" he protests.

"I cannot very well go hunting through the city with a train, can I?"

"But what will I wear?"

"You can stay here until I return or make your way to your own room. It is not as if the servants haven't seen you naked before," Cecilia says. He grimaces, his boyish face even younger than usual.

"Don't pout at me, or I'll cut off your lips," she says.

As she strides from the room, Lorena mutters something to her brother. Cecilia does not much care to know what it is – perhaps some pathetic attempt to stop him from coming to Cecilia's bed again. As if Lorena could hold any sway over him. Cecilia is his drug. Even when his nubile body and heady stamina has grown tiresome and she has stopped calling for him, he will haunt her because the very thought of her haunts him. The inexperience of boys is outweighed by the power they freely give her.

Her palace here in Perfugi is more vertical than the sprawling buildings of Elben or Capetia. It took her some time to get used to the stairs. Now, though, she relishes her muscles' movement as she descends white stone steps to the lower levels. The passages are not as cool as her chamber was: acelath is expensive, even for a dowager queen, so it is used sparingly and only in the rooms she frequents. Before long, she is sweating.

She and, behind her, Lorena, slip out into the scorched streets of Perfugi, where the network of bridges across the lava is made of the same whittled dragon horn that adorns the windows of the palaces, to keep the city's inhabitants from burning.

The trees of Cecilia's childhood and married life – the oaks and cedars, elms, silver birches and graceful willows – cannot survive here. Only the hardiest and most interesting of flora thrives on this mountain: venomous vines wind through the molten lava, their many-coloured flowers perfuming the air; leafless piwis trees that seem to be made from the volcanic rock, their roots fed with fire; the rare lossova plant, whose fruit, once plucked from its flaming bed and cooled in ice, produces a juice sweeter than any strawberry.

"This is a circuitous route," Cecilia says, as Lorena leads her left through the night markets which line Perfugi's eastern bridges.

"It feels that way, but I swear it will be quicker," Lorena says, ushering Cecilia around a corner.

"Ah yes. Your mother grew up on these streets, didn't she, before she married into wealth?" Cecilia says.

Lorena stiffens momentarily at the reference to her lowborn background, then recovers. "And are you not glad that she did, now I can whisk you to your target more quickly?"

"What was she again? A trader's daughter?"

"A fugitive, like most in this city," Lorena says.

"I was a fugitive too, in a way," Cecilia says. Lorena does not respond. "I was," Cecilia says again.

"Yes, Your Majesty."

Cecilia reaches out and pinches the hard little arc between shoulder and neck. Lorena hisses, but gives no other indication of pain. She needs to understand that simply because Cecilia moved to Perfugi with a dowager queen's pension does not mean she is any different from the other souls who sought new lives here.

They take a quieter road east, towards the districts where those not involved in trade but not wealthy enough to live in the south, pass their lives. A little beyond them is the Fontis veh Noyt. It is an unusual bridge, made of the same dragon bone as the others in the city, but instead of being sculpted into gargoyles or salamanders, the bone has been dyed many colours. Each one represents a different religion practised in Perfugi, for Fontis veh Noyt is a religious district. The district of a thousand naves. Cecilia has never understood the need to cleave to a religion. The gods are many; why can her worship not be also? It is inhibiting, tiresome, small-minded.

"There," Lorena says, pointing to a shape secreted behind a wine barrel on one side of the cobbled street. They tiptoe over to the shadow, which reveals itself to be a youth dressed in the black robes and inconspicuous sigil of the doctrini; those who seek, for a price.

"She is heading further into the district," the youth says. He leads them to another figure, an older man this time.

"What are your orders, Your Majesty?" the doctrini leader asks. "Shall we take her now?"

"No," Cecilia says. "Let us follow her until I am certain of her destination."

The man opens his mouth to protest, but Lorena silences him with a minuscule shake of her head. Once he has nodded and turned away, Lorena leans towards Cecilia.

"She may be seeking sanctuary. It would be difficult even for you to extract her once a church has taken her under its protection."

"Difficult but not impossible. This way I gather information that she may not give up if we capture her. It is worth the risk."

They follow the doctrini as they creep up the street, their hand signals their only method of communication. Cecilia and Lorena move with them. It is some time before Cecilia spots the woman. She wears a hood, despite the heat, and although her gown is of a lighter fabric than the heavy wools and velvets of Elben, the cut still seems old-fashioned compared to Perfugian clothes. She appears to be travelling alone. Her gait is ephemeral. Cecilia cannot decide if it stems from fear, grace or caution.

From time to time, Seymour pauses, listening, and the group following her stills. The streets here are quieter than in the trading district, but Perfugi is never entirely silent at night, for it is the only time when the temperature is bearable. This makes it easier for Cecilia and the doctrini to track Seymour, for they can blend in with the watchmen, the midwives, the vagabonds and knackers.

They follow her past the Sanctuary of Cernunnos, where a statue of the horned god of Cecilia's youth eyes her with contempt.

They go deeper, beyond the most common religions practised in Perfugi. It is, after all, a city of fugitives – what began as a group of homeless Lotharians fleeing religious persecution ended as a haven for all, irrespective of beliefs. The occasional skirmish has never marred the core tenets of the city and its motto: *composiru an flira, liberu anas* – forged in flame, we are free.

Seymour stops, finally, at a door in one of the narrower streets of the district. A rudimentary symbol is painted upon the varnished wood – six orbs arrayed in a circle. There: an answer. Cecilia nods to the doctrini leader, and he raises his fist in signal – Cecilia is ready. She does not want Seymour to enter that house.

As Seymour knocks upon the door, a dozen shapes seem to fall from the sky, landing in a neat horseshoe. One of them pulls her arms behind her back, while another covers her mouth to stop her from screaming. Through it all, she makes no move to escape. Cecilia thinks she hears someone speak, though Seymour's mouth does not move. Hen-flesh rises along Cecilia's arms despite the heat from the mountain and its rivers of lava. She is forgetting something. It is enough to make her remain in her hiding place when the doctrini leader and Lorena step out of the shadows and into the woman's line of sight.

Lorena signals the doctrini covering Seymour's mouth to step aside and pushes the prisoner's hood back, revealing a tall woman of around Cecilia's age. Her skin is the colour of the Quistoans or the Avahucs, and her blank expression suggests either stupidity or veiled intelligence.

"Queen Seymour, I presume," Lorena says. What is Cecilia forgetting? She wracks her memory for the words of More's letter.

She had escaped Elben by ship. Her and her servant and . . .

"There was a panther," she whispers. Before she can warn anyone, Seymour utters a single word – "Haltrasc" – and a shape of death leaps from the shadows.

Cecilia may have been told of this creature but she could never have imagined it in action. The panther springs from doctrini to doctrini, ripping out a throat here, slashing a neck there with steel-tipped claws. It is so beautiful that Cecilia almost forgets what she must do. The doctrinis' screams echo through the street, the wet sounds of their dying an undercurrent. No one comes to help – people tend to mind their own business if it means the difference between life and death. Cecilia advances at a crouch from barrel to barrel.

One by one the doctrini fall, their knives no match for the beast. Cecilia cannot take her eyes from the spectacle, even when lifeblood sprays across her face like a lover's slap. At last, the panther turns to Lorena. Cecilia steps from the shadows and rests her knife just beneath Queen Seymour's ribcage, hard enough for her to feel its blade.

"Haltrasc," Seymour says again, and the panther stills. The master of the doctrini steps behind the beast, rope wound around his hands. They must make an interesting tableau: two women frozen with the blade between them; the third woman trembling on the ground beneath a panther's bared teeth, and the only man there awaiting his orders from a safe distance.

"We appear to be at an impasse," Seymour says, the tremor in her voice belying her otherwise calm demeanour.

"My people outnumber yours," Cecilia says.

"Less than they did a moment ago."

Cecilia smiles despite herself.

"Call your beast off and come with me now and I will not slit your throat," she says.

"I have a better bargain," Seymour says. "Allow me and Haltrasc to go and we will leave Perfugi and not return, nor will he kill your servants."

"He may take my companion's life, but he will not escape those ropes," Cecilia says, indicating the doctrini.

"Very well. Allow us to go and he will not kill your companion."

"Your Majesty?" Lorena says, her voice lighter than usual, her face softer than it has been in many years. It reminds Cecilia of the way Lorena used to treat her, before she took Cecilia's mercy for granted. She has been growing above her station.

"I shall miss you," Cecilia tells her.

Lorena's face barely has time to crumple before the panther lowers his muzzle and, with a single bite, rips out her throat.

CHAPTER FIVE

Cleves

A narrow bridge is all that connects Cnothan castle to the mainland of Elben. The town that serves the castle and its environs perches at the mouth of the bridge, and there's a clear view along the coast to Cnorgleo, sitting on the glittering Fietherford. Cnothan Town is unusual among the six palaces of Elben in that it serves as both a port and a castle town. This conflagration of uses makes Cnothan all the dearer to Cleves: despite her royal upbringing, she has never been one to require two objects when she can make do perfectly well with one. It is one of the many reasons she has never understood the Elbenese fashion for taking multiple spouses, if one has the money.

As she rides through the settlement, with its market stalls on each side of the main road, her people dip their heads and call out in pleasure at the sight of her. She enjoys playing up to their expectations. She never leaves the castle without a retinue of animals: lifting a piglet onto the front of her saddle to make the children laugh; sending Lelij the gargoyle to carry coin to a few of the stallholders in exchange for pastries. It makes them love her, and if her kingly husband has taught her anything, it is that earning the love of one's people can never be considered too costly. If portraying herself as a harmless eccentric will gain their loyalty, she will play the part.

The docks are on the far side of the main thoroughfare. As she alights from her horse, she can already see a flotilla of smaller boats bumping across the waves from the larger ship, anchored further out.

"*Maharron, malingi!*" A figure shouts from the prow of the foremost boat, before vomiting into the sea. *Greetings, stranger.* She cannot see him clearly yet, but she would recognise the burr of his voice anywhere. She raises a hand in response, knowing that the wind would carry her words away from the figure, not towards them.

As the boat reaches the dock, Cleves strides towards it, signalling to the workers to help the occupants climb onto land. Johana embraces her with a broad smile. Everything about him is broad and comforting.

"The sea does not agree with you, cousin," she says, hoping that he will follow her lead in speaking Elbenese, not Ezzonidian. She belongs to this country now – in public, at least. While many foreign languages are spoken here, especially in the port towns, it would raise suspicion to have a queen be seen consorting in strange tongues.

"Alas, it does not. I agree with it, though. And I agree with this excellent country you now call home. Show me all of it, I beg you."

Cleves pats him on the shoulder. "Should we embark upon the grand tour immediately, or shall I fill your newly empty stomach first?"

Johana bows, and a trace of vomit falls from the corner of his mouth. "Perhaps some sustenance."

Behind Johana, a group of men swathed in brown cloaks kneel, awaiting her acknowledgement.

"Your friends are less colourful than they once were," she says.

"Not my friends. Merely my companions upon the voyage," Johana says, watching the men with distaste. Lelij sniffs them. The one closest to him leans away from the gargoyle, and Lelij rewards him with a long, damp lick.

Cleves addresses the men. "Rise, good sirs, and make yourselves known to me."

The one who Lelij licked peers up at her while surreptitiously fending off the gargoyle's further affections. Several pendants hang among the folds of his cloak. Cleves spies the crooked horns of Cernunnos among them. "We are most honoured to have been invited to your fair country by His Majesty the King," he says.

"Ah, you are the great leaders of our religion across the sea," she says. Not for the first time, she is glad of the correspondence she has received from her butterflies, for it would not do to reveal that the king does not communicate on such matters with her.

"His Majesty wishes to consult us," the man says.

"Of course. You must take supper at my castle. You must be weary after your long journey."

Some of the other men look up at that, clearly eager for food. But their leader shakes his head. "We must travel directly to High Hall. The king has arranged transport for us."

Cleves says nothing of the rudeness of turning down a queen's invitation, for she has no desire to host these men. She nods graciously and turns her back on the lot of them, summoning Lelij to her side with a click of her tongue.

"Come, cousin," Cleves says, sweeping back up the dock and climbing onto her horse. Johana is given his own steed and takes his place by her side as they make their way back through the town. He exclaims loudly at everything he sees: "What a wonderful town! These fruits, they look so sweet! Your Elbenese weather, it is quite charming!"

When they reach the castle, Cleves goes directly to her presence chamber, taking with her a pack of animals. She settles them around her feet – the pigs on one side, Lelij on the other and a lapdragon upon her gown. Servants bring delicacies from both Ezzonid and Elben, and some that take inspiration from both in a fusion that Cleves rather enjoys. Rye bread smothered in soft Elbenese goat's cheese and peppered with dill. Local apples poached in spices from Ezzonid's southern markets. Johana presses his hands together in thanks, exclaiming over the delicious smell and the way everything is presented. Cleves' people, won over by his effusions, bow and titter and angle the plates towards his end of the table.

As soon as the servants have retired and Cleves and Johana are alone, his smile drops. "This country is a *biskizan*. A shithole. Let me assist you in escaping, cousin."

"What happened to everything being so charming?" Cleves says.

"I am a diplomat. I would say that your king's piss was the height of fashion if it would help our country." He grows thoughtful. "Do kings with divine powers piss?"

"He would have us think not," Cleves says, offering him a platter of apple fritters. Johana spears one on his knife. He bites it and grimaces.

"The apples are delicious," Cleves says, feeling oddly defensive of the island she now calls home.

"Too sweet," is all the reply she gets.

Cleves stares at Johana. He grins. "I jest. This is an excellent fritter. I merely enjoy teasing you."

"I had forgotten how much my family enjoy their jests."

"Do not tell me you have grown serious in your old age?" Johana says. Cleves plucks the half-eaten fritter from his knife and takes a bite in reply.

As Johana selects more food, Cleves feeds the remains of the fritter to one of her pigs, then crosses her legs, musing how to approach the meat of the conversation.

"I shall not keep you in Elben for long, cousin," she begins.

Johana frowns laconically. "You shall not keep me anywhere I have no wish to be. Indeed, I was the one to invite myself to join you."

"Indeed? I had quite forgotten."

"Six years and not a single summons, cousin. It is outrageous."

Cleves shrugs. "It was my duty to acclimatise to my new country."

"And have you? Acclimatised?"

She does not like the way he is studying her.

"What do they say of me in Ezzonid?" she asks.

"You did not answer my question."

"You did not answer mine," she counters. "And I think that tells us both everything we wish to know, does it not?"

Johana smiles as he cuts a slice of cheese and dips it in lavender-kissed honey. They allow the silence to stretch, like a rousing cat.

Eventually, Johana says, "Are you not lonely? When we were pups, you were the centre of every ball. You could charm the magic from a witch and the faith from a priest. You could make even your lady mother laugh. Your spirit could conjure company from the quietest of forests. The palace ever rang with the sound of your merriment."

"And much good it did us," she snaps. She hears it then, in the soft puffs of Lelij's breath, and the shouts of the servants in the courtyard outside her window. Other shouts, other huffs; needles from the past.

"Ezzonid is secure now, you know, should you ever desire to return," Johana says, leaning across the table to select a bread roll. Cleves hands him one that she knows he'll enjoy – stuffed with fruit and nuts.

"Would my brother permit me to dine with my animals at my feet?" she says, indicating the many mouths upturned, hoping for scraps.

"That I think he may object to."

Cleves shrugs. "Then there is nothing for it. I must remain in Elben."

"Then that is why I will stay on this awful, rainy little island in this miserable, damp castle to keep you company, cousin." Johana takes a bite of another apple and looks round the receiving chamber. At the murals on the ceiling, the tapestries on the walls; anywhere but Cleves. "It surprises me though, cousin."

"Why should that be?"

"We heard that perhaps Elben was going to see its own . . . upheaval."

"Indeed?"

Johana cocks his head. "Perhaps you felt some kinship with certain sister-queens."

Cleves sighs. "My dancing with the traitor queen at the Moon Ball."

"It has been commented upon."

Cleves adopts the "you should know better" attitude that has served her well for much of her life. "She may be a traitor, but she was wearing a very fetching gown, cousin. Did they comment upon that as well? I may be faithful to my husband but my fondness for a pretty figure has not faded with time."

Johana does not laugh as she intended. He leans further forward. "I am with you, cousin. You know this, yes? You can tell me the truth."

Cleves gets up, feigning boredom, and goes to the sideboard to pour herself a cup of wine. "You are being very strange, Johana. I am neither a schemer, a rebel or a heretic. I merely wish to live my very comfortable life in my very comfortable castle with my very delicious apples."

And that is not so far from the truth. She may not know what made her don the gossamer overgown at the Moon Ball, or why she joined that dance with Seymour and Boleyn. She has pondered it often. But she is committed now, and if she is going to take Cnothan and the power of the bordweal for herself, then she will gather knowledge around her like so many bricks. They will form a fortress against her husband and his allies every bit as strong as the many walls of Cnothan castle itself. And part of that fortress lies in not revealing more of the truth than is absolutely necessary, not even to the cousin she trusted most as a child. As far as she is concerned, too many people already suspect the truth. A secret shared is a danger increased.

Johana grunts and nods, all business at last, and pats his pockets down before producing a thick packet of letters. He hands them to her. One bears her brother's seal, one her mother's and one her sister's. She fingers the letter from her mother. The Dowager Queen Sidonia hardly ever writes to her.

"I suspect you will mostly find questions inside those letters, rather than news," Johana says.

"Ah. There has been gossip."

"Gossip. Rumours. Scandal. I cannot think of more words just yet but I'm sure they will come to me."

"You had better be careful, cousin. The very air has eyes in this country," she says.

Johana puts down his cup. "Speculation. There's another. And I do not think they expect a response by letter."

"You are to be the vessel."

"I am." He nibbles on one of the cakes. "This is dry. I do not like it."

"How strange. I think that about you all the time."

Johana pulls a face at her. "I have missed you, cousin."

"And I you," she says.

Outside, a bell tolls. Cleves wipes her mouth on the napkin draped over her shoulder and rises.

"I must go now. My people will see you to your chamber. You must be tired after all that vomiting."

He bows as she sweeps from the room. She must think of a way to return him safely to Ezzonid without raising the suspicions of those at High Hall. She will give him anything but the truth. It is safer that way. It is why she has shaped Cnothan the way she has, why she rarely keeps ladies-in-waiting. The walls must grow thicker and thicker.

CHAPTER SIX

Howard

On the day Voda Kelaverinn is due to leave Plythe, Howard sits in her receiving chamber with her ladies all around her. Goldfoot, her little dragon, is nestled in her lap, his hot breath curling a few stray threads of her silk gown. She idly scratches at a patch of bare skin on her scalp, hidden by her curls. Lord, but it itches.

Her receiving chamber is not as dramatic as Boleyn's was at Brynd, but it brings Howard an immense sense of peace. It sits at the side of the palace, and the windows are in the newer style: a series of arches that bounce across the room, each one looking out upon the River Kyttle and, beyond, the Swegan Sea. In the mornings, like now, the sun skates over the water below instead of assaulting the windows. In the few pauses between her ladies' conversations, the songs of the Swegan whales vibrate through the stone, filling the space with a mournful tune that undercuts the laughter.

"What think you, Your Majesty?" Ursula says.

They are looking at her expectantly, hands paused over their needlework or prayer books. Howard shakes her head. "My thoughts flew away with me. What were you discussing?"

Lady Tylney leans forward from her window seat and pretends to whisper in Ursula's ear. "She was thinking of His Majesty," she says, and the others grin.

Howard strokes Goldfoot. "Am I truly so predictable?"

"You are in love," Lady Tylney says. Howard hopes her smile does not betray the sudden clench of her stomach. It is true that she owes

Henry everything. She may be a nobleman's daughter, but the king plucked her from obscurity nevertheless. She should be his: heart, body and soul. Until Boleyn, that was the truth around which she had shaped her queenly self.

"We were talking of the strange religions gaining traction abroad," Ursula says, her eyes wide and earnest.

"What strange religions?" Howard says.

Ursula closes her prayer book, covering the title with the palm of her hand. "Their preachers are women, Your Majesty. They speak of ancient goddesses."

The women fall silent. Howard and her ladies have never spoken of such matters before. They do not have a map for how to navigate such subjects. Howard must be the mapmaker.

Lady Tylney's nervous laughter cuts through the hush. "I told her not to talk of such things," she says. Ursula blushes. The other women continue to stare at Howard.

"I am mistress of Plythe alone, not of anyone's soul," Howard says eventually. "I am glad that we can all speak freely within these walls. We are old friends, are we not? We love each other through all."

There is general agreement, and the conversation moves on to safer subjects. A love scandal in a foreign land, impropriety at court and shared girlish memories of girlish shared bedchambers. Adjusting Goldfoot so that his sleeping form is draped over her shoulders, Howard rises and goes to the window. If she stands right at the edge, she can see the courtyard. There is the carriage, all arranged to take Kelaverinn to Sweillan. She wonders whether he will take all of the books he made her commission. It is not as though she will ever read them. They were all for him.

"I heard that the King of Capetia greeted Mary Boleyn *very* warmly," Howard's half-sister, Legh, says. She is lying on her back on the floor, like she used to do when they lived with their aunt. Howard wants to tell her to sit up, but she does not wish to unbalance the easy company they all keep.

Susanna Horenbolt looks up from her easel in the corner. "That is old news. When I served Queen Cleves, we heard tell she was his mistress for a time."

Legh sits straight up, covering her mouth in shock. "Did you serve Queen Cleves, Susanna? Really? You have never before mentioned it!"

Susanna dips her head behind her easel as the other ladies laugh.

"Let us be kind," Howard murmurs, but they do not hear her.

There he is. Voda Kelaverinn walks slowly towards the carriage. He carries a single bag made of tired brown velvet; the same one he arrived with. Howard tries to spy whether he has any servants with further belongings, but she can see none.

"Your Majesty?" Lady Tylney says.

"What?" Howard is sharper than she should be.

Tylney motions towards the steward hovering in the doorway. He picks his way around Legh, who is back to lying on the floor, and presents Howard with a letter. Howard does not need to ask who it is from. The Voda is the only person who has ever formed a handwriting style solely for her ease of reading.

"Is it a love letter?" Ursula says, more to the other ladies than to Howard herself.

Howard breaks the seal, hoping that her pointed silence will indicate her displeasure.

Your Majesty,

I take my leave of you with all the fondness and gratitude in the world. Teaching you has been an honour: your remarkable memory and open spirit are every tutor's treasure. If I may be so bold, you have made being separated from my family bearable, for you put me in mind of my daughters.

I shall pray for your present and future happiness, dear queen.

V. Kelaverinn

"Are you quite well?" Lady Tylney says. She places a hand upon Howard's forehead, as if she were her mother when she is only ten years Howard's senior and barren besides.

"Stop it," Howard says, swatting her away. Tylney cowers. "Stop that too; I'm not going to hit you."

Their eyes are all fixed on the floor. Goldfoot, woken from his slumber by her movement, nips her ear. Howard removes him from her shoulders and stands. She gathers her skirts so they fall properly, and steps right over Legh as she stalks from the room. Behind her, Goldfoot lets out a mewl of rebuke.

The gallery that forms Plythe's spine stretches right across the Kyttle Falls. It is the polished glory of her reign, for she redesigned it herself when she was made queen. Her footsteps are crisp upon the wooden floor. Its patterns of cedar and rosewood swirl around her, like the tumbling water beneath the palace. Like her thoughts. It is not as though she shouted at them.

She starts to run.

The ivory doors to the west courtyard open at her approach, tied by a mechanism linked to the palace's spirit stone, which awakens at her footfall. Voda Kelaverinn's carriage is nearly at the gatehouse.

"Stop!" she shouts, tearing down the steps and across the courtyard. Her shoes are not made for cobbles. The driver has not heard her.

"Stop!" she shouts again, raising a hand. The guards at the gatehouse spot her and step in front of the carriage.

By the time she is level with the vehicle, her curls are flying across her face and she is damp with sweat. Plythe has ever been a humid territory, and not even her fine silk and taffeta gown can withstand exertion in this climate.

"Your Majesty," Voda Kelaverinn says, peering out at her with a frown. She steps back, not wishing him to feel uncomfortable in her presence. He opens the carriage door and steps out.

Only, once they are facing each other, Howard finds she does not know what to say. In the corner of her vision, she sees the driver shrug at the guards.

"You did not take the books," she says eventually.

"My wish was that you would make your way through them yourself, in time."

He folds his hands over his stomach. She fixes her gaze on the set of painted bangles that she has never seen him without: the black a symbol of his marriage; the orange, yellow and red symbols of his children.

She cannot say what she knows she must in front of the guards and driver who are watching them. To do so would be to admit to thoughts of infidelity and treason.

"Shall we take one final walk along the escarpment?" Kelvarinn says. She nods, watches as he speaks a few words to the driver and passes the man a coin for his time. She should compensate him for that.

They make their way to the edge of the courtyard, where high walls muffle some of the sound of the waterfall. They have taken many such strolls before, and Howard cannot help but notice that he keeps more distance between them than in the past. She remembers her failed kiss, his startled breath, and closes her eyes against the shame.

"I had intended my letter to comfort you, Your Majesty, but I fear it only troubles you further," he says.

"It was a kind letter. You are very kind."

They come to a natural halt before a gap in the wall which affords a view across the river. Howard swallows. She does not look at him when she says, "You likened me to your daughters, Voda."

"Yes. You are of an age with my eldest."

"The Princess Tudor is older than me."

"Yes, Your Majesty."

She places a hand on the stone sill. Is he being deliberately obtuse? The irony that she must be the one to spell this out to him.

"My husband still desires me, despite me being of an age with his daughter."

Kelaverinn remains silent. She darts a look at him. Perhaps he is realising that it need not be a barrier, her being so much younger than him. Perhaps she could whisk him back into the palace for a farewell tryst. She turns to him fully.

"I am very beautiful, sir."

"You are as beautiful as any young woman can be, Your Majesty."

She swallows again. Dare she admit to her adventures before her marriage? Well, she has pushed this far.

"No man has ever turned me down when I have taken a fancy to him."

She waits for him to admit his mutual attraction, to renounce his moral nonsense. He sighs, and his features soften further.

"I am sorry that it is so," he says.

The heat takes her fully, but there are still guards and workers watching them from a distance.

"You profess to be open-minded, yet you presume to judge me?" she says.

"My judgement is not for you."

Howard huffs. She has seen the way Lady Tylney wrinkles her nose when Howard kisses her husband, or when he takes liberties with her in company. This is the province of prudish elders, who think that a woman of Howard's age cannot know her own mind.

"Your lectures grow tiresome, Voda," Howard says, putting a hand upon her hip to soften the jibe.

"Then my departure is for the best."

She cannot crack this patient shell of his. It almost makes her want to try to kiss him again, to prove that he feels something towards her.

She may be working against Henry now for Boleyn's sake, but how can she make Kelaverinn see that before the king plucked her from the lice-infested hole of her aunt's estate, she was a nothing? Theirs was an equal transaction: she gave him her youth; he gave her the highest consequence that a woman can possess.

"I am so fortunate. I have lived a dreamer's life, sir," she says.

"Have you? I will tell you this, now that we are no longer beholden to each other. It is not the dream I would dream for any of my daughters."

"You would not wish them to be queens of your land?"

"Some jewels are not worth the cost, no matter how brightly they shine."

That is nonsense too. She fingers the rings upon her hand, the cobalt spinels at her throat.

Across the courtyard, the driver of Voda Kelaverinns's carriage coughs loudly. Perhaps he has deemed the single coin no longer sufficient for this delay. Kelaverinn glances at him, then looks back at Howard with an intensity she does not like.

"May I ask you a question, Your Majesty?"

"Of course."

"Have you ever told the king what you enjoy?"

"The king is very generous to me."

Why is she so defensive of the man she is trying to topple? Kelaverinn cocks his head, waiting for a direct answer.

"He has very good taste. His gifts always suit me well."

Still, he waits.

"Very well. No," she says. She rolls her eyes, taps her foot. Why did she leave her ladies' company for this? At least *they* never ask her such tiresome questions.

"Then may I suggest that this be your final study under my tutelage? Tell him, when next you see him. Tell him what *you* enjoy."

Howard smirks. "What do you suppose I will learn?"

"Well, at the very least it will bring you and your husband, as attentive as he is, closer, will it not?"

Suddenly she understands: this is his way of tempering her disappointment. He hopes to direct her affections back towards Henry instead of upon him. He is defending himself, poor man. And while his refusal hurts, goodness knows she has refused certain men in her time. It had to happen once in her life.

"I am sorry to have behaved inappropriately towards you, sir," she says.

Inexplicably, Kelaverinn sighs again. "All is forgotten. Now, I shall return to the carriage and allow this poor man to deliver me to Sweillan."

They walk peaceably back to the gate, and Howard watches as her tutor climbs awkwardly into the carriage. Once he is seated, he peers out at her and presses his hands to his chest – the Uuvek way of showing respect, as the Elbenese remove their caps.

"You are an excellent student, Your Majesty," he says, as the driver cracks his whip. "You always learn. Always."

CHAPTER SEVEN

Cleves

When the moon is high and full, Cleves pulls a chamber robe over her nightshirt and checks that no one is skulking outside her room. She keeps a lean court, more animals than servants, and her guards accompany her only when she leaves Cnothan. Still, one cannot be too cautious.

Her *sunscína* is never far from her. She will never know whether she discovered it by accident or by the design of a former monarch of Cnothan. She had been queen for two years when she spied the loose floorboard in one corner of her bedchamber. Inside it was a box of no worth or significance, and had it not been in her chamber she would have dismissed it as the worthless treasures of some servant, keen to keep their meagre wealth a secret from their spouse. But when opened, she found a small bag of silk that would once have been very fine, though now it was worn and the colour faded. Inside was a brooch far heavier than it should be by its size. It was a simple piece by Ezzonid's standards; certainly not of the modern fashion. Thin gold wire plaited around a large stone of mesmerising depth. Cleves was not generally one to fawn over material goods, but she had spent many an hour, in those first weeks, staring at the brooch, even stroking it like one of her pet dogs. She grimaces to think of it now.

It was during one such night that she understood the brooch's true power. The face of Henry's most favoured queen, Queen Blount, had appeared before her. They had met before, of course, at High Hall, but in the tradition of Elben's queens had exchanged nothing but empty pleasantries.

Blount had startled and then smiled: "I was wondering whether Cnothan's *sunscína* had been lost, like Brynd's. But here you are."

Cleves misses Blount, as much as Cleves can miss anyone. She was a harmless woman, but like all the queens of Hyde she possessed many secrets.

Enough. It will not do to dwell on the queens of Hyde too much before she is due to speak to one.

She goes to the window seat and draws her knees up to her chest for warmth. The light of the full moon reflects strangely upon the bruised depths of the brooch, and Cleves has the dizzying feeling of . . . what? An ending and a beginning, like the snakes of the ancient empires that ate their tails.

Howard is the first to appear. Her beauty always shocks Cleves, even though they have met each other several times. On closer inspection, though, Howard looks tired. Her youthful skin does not glow as it usually does, and there are crescent moons beneath her eyes. But Howard smiles when she realises it is just the two of them.

"Sister!" she says. "I was so hoping it would be you first."

"Oh? Do you mean to say you do not enjoy Aragon's scathing insults or Parr's relentless silence?"

Howard gasps, looks away in delighted shame.

"I find them difficult to talk to. You are always so kind."

"It is all an act, sister," Cleves says. "Do you not see my expression whenever Aragon boasts about her nephew as if she birthed him herself?"

Howard is hovering in her music room – Cleves can see the exquisite wood panelling and vibrant tapestries behind her. They are a far cry from what Howard must be able to see of Cleves's bedchamber: all cold stone with crumbling plaster and dreary candlesticks. Cleves cares not what others see: she alone knows that she is warm beneath fine fur blankets, and that her mattress is made of the softest wool, sheared from the wild Imizen sheep of the nameless meadows beyond the Garzac Sea.

Before Howard can reply, Parr and then Aragon appear. Using the *sunscína* is akin to dreaming, for Cleves feels that they are in the room with her, those other queens, and that she is in their rooms too – the little closet behind Aragon's bedchamber, and Parr's turret study. It is only right, then, that they choose to meet at night beneath the moon at its brightest and most powerful.

"Have you heard from Seymour?" Howard asks Cleves before the other queens can speak.

"I have not. Have you?" Cleves says. That damned dance at the Moon Ball. Can a queen not take a passing fancy to another woman without people assuming love and other such nothings?

"My nephew's ambassador tells me she landed in Perfugi a sennight hence," Aragon says.

"And who is your nephew again, sister? I do not believe you've told us," Cleves says. Howard attempts to suppress a snort of mirth.

"Perhaps she cannot find the privacy to use her *sunscína*," Parr says. Cleves agrees, although she cannot stop a seed of disquiet lodging in her stomach. If Aragon's spies can find out that she has landed, perhaps Cleves's can discover whether she is safe. Still, it will not do to admit her concern.

"We are well able to discuss our plans without her," Cleves says, forcing herself to smile.

"Indeed. I cannot talk for long tonight," Aragon says. "Wolsey is staying at Daven and you know how he is prone to working late into the night."

"We should talk first of the king,' Parr says. His plans will affect our own."

"Did you receive his summons to Gemæres?" Howard asks Cleves.

"Yes," Cleves replies. In truth, she had forgotten about the letter from Cromwell in the flurry of entertaining Johana. She must remember to respond.

"I received no invitation," Aragon says. "Did you, Parr?"

Cleves stops herself from rolling her eyes. "Do not feel left out," she says. "It is merely to unveil new portraits of myself and Queen Howard at the border of our territories. The king wishes to demonstrate how beautiful our youngest sister is compared to myself."

"That is not true, I'm sure," Howard says.

"Do not worry for my feelings; I have born his humiliations for six years now. I can bear another in the knowledge that I shall have the final laugh."

Parr stirs – she talks so sparingly that Cleves is never quite sure whether she is half asleep in their meetings. "He is a fool," she says. "If you are present at the unveiling, it will be obvious that you are not the woman he seeks to portray you as. People may once have convinced themselves to his way of thinking, but his power is waning."

Cleves shifts in her seat. She is comfortable playing the fool. Parr may be paying her a compliment, but she does not like the thought of people knowing the truth of her. "It matters not either way," she says. "Tell us – what happened in Capetia?"

Parr smiles grimly. "He signed a new treaty with them. The Capetian king was a most attentive host to us all."

She emphasises that *all*, so that they know that she means Mary Boleyn, the woman who will shortly take her sister's place as Queen of Brynd. So much for Capetia's supposed loyalty to Boleyn. Cleves is not surprised – kings and courtiers will always serve their own interests above anyone else's – but Howard flinches.

"Surely he made some reference to Boleyn?" Howard says.

Parr shakes her head, not unkindly, as Aragon says, "Of course he did not. Do you wish Capetia to start a war with Elben for the sake of your dead friend?"

Howard stammers. "I'm sure I did not mean . . ."

"It is merely good foreign policy," Cleves says. "If it makes you feel better, sister, he'd have behaved the same way if any of us were in Boleyn's place."

Howard tugs at her hair, mortified. Cleves tries to imagine what it must be like to be raised from minor nobility to the queen of a nation. Not merely a queen, but one who must also hold her own alongside women such as herself and Aragon, who were born into royalty, and alongside Parr and Boleyn, who spent their formative years in royal courts. Poor girl. It is a wonder she strings two words together at all in their presence. Aragon alone is intimidating enough to silence all but the boldest of women.

"So Henry is fearful," Aragon says. "A few years ago he would never have sought an alliance with Capetia. He fears that Quisto will come down on our side – and perhaps Ezzonid too – and seeks to bolster his own defences."

Cleves considers this. To her chagrin, it makes sense. She remembers the men who came to Elben on Johana's boat. "He and Cromwell are brewing something, I am sure of it," she says. "He has summoned foreign religious men to High Hall."

Parr rubs her forehead. "He is likely doing as we are doing: searching for information. If I were him, I would be looking for ways to separate Medren's power from us queens entirely."

"But you are speaking as though Henry knows we are working against him," Howard says, her voice high.

Aragon rolls her eyes and says something rude in Quistoan.

"He does not know," Parr says. "At least, I had no indication that he knows. But he would be a fool not to put precautions in place."

"Indeed. Why do you think he has suddenly commissioned Master Holbein to paint us?" Cleves says. Aragon opens her mouth, ready to answer, but Cleves holds up a hand. Let the girl have a moment to think. Howard frowns, lines appearing on her smooth forehead.

"Because . . . because he wishes to humiliate you . . . and in doing so he seeks to ensure we remain divided."

"Precisely," Parr says, her voice honey.

"We should not be surprised if he attempts to test our loyalty," Cleves says. She shifts in her seat. The cushion is not thick enough; she must tell her steward to arrange for it to be re-stuffed. Her movement wakes Lelij from his slumber at the bottom of her bed. He crawls sleepily into her lap, crushing her against the windowpane.

"You are right," Aragon says. "I should have thought of that myself."

"Well, you must leave something for the rest of us to do, sister," Cleves says. She is suddenly very tired. Seymour's absence niggles at her, and there is something else – a memory that has been yawning from deep slumber ever since Johana came to Cnothan. Another time, long ago, when loyalties were tested and blood edged every deed.

The other queens are talking again, of possible tests that Henry might throw at them. It is all immaterial. The tests will come when they come. Why are they guessing when there is so much to be done that does not need to be guessed? Cleves holds up a hand again, and all but Aragon fall silent.

"I am not one of your mongrels to bark on command, Cleves," Aragon says, eyeing Lelij with disdain.

"Indeed no, Queen Aragon. You are a pedigree if ever I saw one," Cleves says, smiling sweetly.

Aragon hisses as she leans forward, and if she had free use of her legs Cleves could almost imagine her stamping her way across Elben to whip Cleves herself.

Parr sighs. "Must we exchange such barbs? Sisters, please."

Cleves catches Howard's eye, and to her surprise she sees no merriment there. She had half made the jape to entertain Howard, to make her feel more at home, for she has heard through her old lady-in-waiting how Howard's household is run on gossip and the trading of petty powers. But no. Howard's eyes are bright with tears, her lips pressed together. Cleves had thought that Howard must be intimidated by them, and the thought had pleased her passingly. But how can anyone be intimidated by spiteful insults? How can one hold such queens in esteem? Cleves has played right into Henry's hands for the sake of an easy joke.

Lelij stirs, nuzzles Cleves to stroke him.

"My apologies," she says, and after a moment Aragon nods stiffly.

"My own butterflies have been working on our behalf also," Cleves continues, keen to redeem herself.

"And?" Aragon says.

"And while Cromwell and Wolsey are working hard to conceal the truth of Boleyn and Seymour's betrayals, word is spreading both in Elben and out. There is scepticism, of course, but people are questioning now. In Brynd most of all. I do not think Mary Boleyn will have a happy reception there."

Aragon leans back, looking pleased with herself. "And my own spies have been busy also. I revealed the truth to my nephew's ambassador several moons ago. He will have seen to it that my right as Queen of Elben is known in Quisto."

"I am shocked, Queen Aragon," Cleves says.

"Why?"

"You consider it safe to reveal our secrets when you are not certain of the recipient's loyalty?"

Lelij begins to chew on Cleves's hair.

"You question that Quisto's ambassadors are loyal to me over our husband?"

"I question whether a man is loyal to a woman over another man. Has Capetia's willingness to enter into an alliance not taught us that?"

Aragon raises an eyebrow. "Yes, well your loyalty to women is certainly well known."

A dozen retorts clamour to be spoken, but Cleves catches Howard's eye once more and swallows them. "You are more trusting than I, and from a strategist like yourself that surprises me. That is all, sister."

Aragon softens a little. "In every game there comes a point where the hand must be shown. The trick lies in moving one's pieces into place in time. I merely see my nephew as one of those pieces."

Howard coughs. “Besides, is that not what Boleyn died for? To make us trust each other?”

Cleves smiles, swallowing bile. “Trust. Yes. I trust you, sister. I trust that you know what is right.”

But she does not. Trust is such a little word, but to Cleves it heralds death.

CHAPTER EIGHT

Cecilia

It's not that she wants to hurt the panther. She's not a monster. In fact, she had rather hoped to transfer the creature's affections to her, with time and food. She is adept at achieving such switches in loyalty: anything can be bought for the right balance of love and cruelty. But she never wanted it scarred. Scarred pets are so unsightly.

But she needs to understand the woman Seymour, and her usual methods are not working. The first day she brought Seymour back to her palace, tied and gagged, she attempted friendliness – their common ground as women, as queens. It did not work. She tried starving the girl of light as well as sustenance, locking her in an old well deep in the palace's cellars. Still, Seymour said nothing.

Then it was time to bring out the needles. Broad wounds, deep wounds, hot or ice-covered needles. Even one tipped with a poison that makes its recipient hallucinate horrors. Still, silence.

It would be admirable if it were not so frustrating.

There is nothing else for it. She has the doctrini bring the panther to the dungeon where Seymour is shackled. It struggles against its chains, thrashing like a demon. By the time the doctrini has secured it to the wall opposite Seymour, it has struck four lines across his face. As the man retires, straining beneath a bag of gold coin, Cecilia approaches the muzzled beast.

The panther bares his teeth at her. She bares her teeth back.

Cecilia goes to her needle collection, laid out on a simple wooden table in Seymour's view.

"You love her, don't you?" she says to the beast. It growls again, every muscle in its body tense.

"The more pertinent question is – does she love you?"

Seymour stirs, her bruises delightfully purple against her brown skin. One of her eyes is swollen shut; a regrettable loss of control. Cecilia is usually more delicate in her persuasions.

Cecilia selects a slender steel needle, one she sometimes uses for making kid gloves or hidden pockets. Then she opens a chest filled with bottles, each one stoppered and waxed.

"Did Henry ever talk to you of the games we played together as children?" She raises the needle so that Seymour can see it clearly. "My sister and I were taught embroidery, of course. From time to time, Henry would join us. He would bring me things that he wanted me to embroider. A mouse. One of his songbirds. A quiet little serving girl."

It is untrue, of course. Henry did no such thing, but it is useful to see how Seymour will take this information. Her lack of reaction is surprising. What an ingrate, to turn on the man who has only ever been generous to a fault.

"Did he embroider you from time to time, Lady Seymour?" she asks. "Or did he just prick?"

"Whatever he did, he never spoke of you," Seymour says, and though her voice is measured there's a spark in her eyes that Cecilia rather enjoys.

"No, I don't imagine he did. I am the family's shame, you see. Rather like you are your family's shame."

"The difference being that I killed my brother, and you are still ruled by yours," she says.

Cecilia laughs. She bounces on her tiptoes.

"Did you? No one told me that. Which brother? No, do not tell me; I will guess. It was the snivelling one, wasn't it? The eldest. Oh, what was his name?"

"Edward."

Cecilia points the needle at Seymour. "Edward. Yes. I only met him once but I wanted so badly to put my hands around his skull and just . . ."

She mimes cracking a man's head. Seymour's eyes shutter. Ah well, for a brief moment she provoked a reaction.

Cecilia holds up the bottle.

"This is an extract brewed from the leaves of the portesia tree. Do you know what effect it has when it is placed just beneath the skin?"

Seymour raises her head. "Have you not realised by now that hurting me gains you nothing?"

"Indeed I have." Seymour follows Cecilia's eyes to the panther. She pales, but says nothing. A pathetic attempt at pretending she doesn't care.

"Portesia sap has a curious effect when touched. It leaves no mark on the skin. Or fur. But an icy fire brews beneath. The kind where you feel as though you will never be warm again. Put enough on and it burrows deeper still, through every muscle and organ, gripping them in a deadly frost."

Cecilia goes to the window and pulls the shutter aside, holding the bottle against the bone window until the wax securing the cork drips onto the floor like blood, warmed by the lava outside. The other woman's panic fills the chamber like smoke. At last, she has found the key to unlocking the truth. It will just take a little more pinching of the heart, and the door will spring open.

She pulls the stopper from the bottle and, careful not to let any of the tincture touch her own hands, dips the needle into it, shaking gently to rid it of any excess. The panther, as if aware of what is about to happen, growls at her even as it cowers.

"Such a magnificent beast. I think the back of the neck to start, don't you?"

Seymour straightens. "If you hurt him, you will never be able to claim him as yours."

Cecilia continues to circle the panther. "You underestimate me at every turn. A good play, though, my lady. I applaud the attempt."

In one swift movement, Cecilia springs onto the panther's back, wedging one knee at the top of his neck, the other pinning him on his side. She takes hold of his scruff, readying the needle. The creature whimpers, his tail lashing ineffectively.

"What do you want to know?" Seymour says. "I will tell you. Please do not hurt him."

Cecilia is tempted to insert the needle anyway, just to teach the woman a lesson, but on this occasion her desire for knowledge is greater than her desire for power. She lifts the needle but does not yet rise. The panther continues to whimper beneath her.

"Why were you visiting the Hleaws?" she asks.

"I follow their religion."

"Is that why you left Elben? Because you turned heathen?"

"I would not expect someone like you to understand."

"Born royalty, you mean?"

"I mean Henry's sister."

"The king's sister, ordained by God."

Seymour smirks. The last time someone looked at Cecilia like that, she sewed their eyes shut.

"Have a care," Cecilia says, passing the poisoned needle between her fingers like a coin trick. "Tell me what you are not telling me."

The panther whines again, and Seymour's bravado is punctured.

"What have you been told about Queen Boleyn's death?" she asks.

"Many things." Cecilia doesn't want to admit that everything she has been told has felt wrong in some way, even in More's missives.

"Have you been told that she leapt to her own death?"

"I have." She does not say that of all the things she had been told – execution, magic, the power of Cernunnos, at Henry's hand – this had seemed the unlikeliest cause of death. Cecilia cannot fathom anyone throwing away their own life.

"She did so because she discovered something about the true nature of the bordweal."

"Tell me."

Seymour looks at her panther, lying submissive beneath Cecilia's knee.

"Boleyn and I came to understand that the god we'd worshipped all our lives – Cernunnos – was an imposter. The true power of the bordweal comes not from him, or any king, but from the goddess Medren and from the six queens. The palaces of Elben were built long before High Hall, and whichever women command them command the bordweal. Your brother is using the power of the goddess – through his queens – to wage war on the world and to make himself invincible. The truth is, without his queens he would be nothing."

Cecilia leans forward, examining Seymour's expression. She can find no sign of deception.

"Who knows about this?" she says.

"Only Boleyn and me," Seymour replies, a little too quickly for Cecilia to credit it. Still, she lets that lie go for now. She has greater questions to ask.

"You say my brother knows that his power is based on a lie."

"Oh, he knows."

Cecilia doesn't have to wonder how long Henry has known for. She knows precisely when he was told.

"So you went to the Hleaws because they worship this goddess you say is the true source of the bordweal's power?" Cecilia says, rising and going to the window, trying to think clearly.

"Yes."

"No." Cecilia rounds on the prisoner. "Do not mistake my getting up to mean that your beast is no longer in danger. You were seeking allies."

"Yes."

Cecilia comes close to Seymour now. Her heart is pounding in a particular way: the way it does when she fucks in the audience chamber, hoping for someone to see her; the way it does when she perfects a particularly difficult stitch.

"And this goddess. She contains the power of the bordweal. And whoever commands one of her palaces will command the power of a goddess? With no need to marry him?"

Seymour stiffens in understanding. She cannot bring herself to say yes, but she doesn't have to. Cecilia laughs. She tosses the poisoned needle into the air, not caring where it lands, and spins, arms outstretched, to the door of the dungeon. Flinging it open, she speaks to the guard outside: "Commandeer a ship immediately."

The guard bows. "To go where, Your Majesty?"

"To return to my homeland, imbecile."

She turns, drinking in the hunch of Seymour's shoulders. "I'm going to get myself a palace."

CHAPTER NINE

Cleves

The town of Gemæres is known only for what it lacks: fresh water. Originally a settlement built inland upon the borders of Plythe and Cnothan, it was intended to be a gateway between those two territories. When Cleves was studying her new home, she halted upon the history of the town. It made no sense: who would ever build such a place, where one must travel several hours to reach the nearest stream? Why was a gateway necessary?

When she reached Cnothan, she asked Wolsey over their first banquet. He told her nothing that the books had not already claimed: "Some dispute between the two queens. You will discover that Elbenese queens are rather territorial. If you will take an old man's advice, you will keep an eye on your borders."

Now, with what she knows of Medren, she wonders whether Wolsey was more correct than he realised. For if Elben was truly ruled by six queens of equal status, they must have had their disagreements. What might she do if she shared a border with an empire-builder like Aragon? Ironic, that the kings of Elben have always sought to sow discord between their queens, when giving them power could have the same effect.

She has visited Gemæres only once in her reign, for it is an impoverished town and has no residences fit for a queen of her heritage. This, undoubtedly, is one of Henry's tests – will his queens be obedient to his wishes despite the ignominy of the place?

Her expectations are low, therefore, when she and her entourage – Johana, a handful of servants and her animals – turn onto the road that leads over the Coltmar Hills, each one topped with a tired windmill.

"They look like the washerwomen on the banks of the Bhinozs," Johana says. He is steering his horse with one hand and eating an apple with the other. Cleves looks across at him from her own mare. "I do believe you are warming to my new country," she says.

Johana waves the apple dismissively. "I will concede that the fruit is edible."

"This is bread country," Cleves says.

"That explains why the air is so dusty."

The road dips into a valley, a muddy ribbon ending in the gateway to Gemǣres. An ancient wooden archway, perhaps an exact marker of where one territory ends and the other begins, stretches over the road. It must once have been elaborately carved, and even now Cleves can make out the burnished shape of a flower here, a stag head there, but mostly the details have been lost to time.

A small deputation waits on the other side of the arch.

"Lord Cromwell," Cleves says, jumping from her horse and approaching him with her hand held out. She likes to greet Elbenese nobility in the Ezzonid fashion. It solidifies her as an oddity.

"Punctual as ever, Your Majesty," Cromwell says, bowing first in the Elbenese way, and then shaking her hand. His message is clear: country before queen.

"Master Holbein's portraits must be wonderful indeed to bring you to Gemǣres," she says.

"I trust you will agree that they do justice to you and Queen Howard," he says, and with a sweep of his arm invites her through the gateway to meet the rest of his group. Introductions are made to the nobility of the town and to Johana, and more than once Cleves catches Cromwell watching her, and he catches her watching him, and every time they do so they smile as if they are sharing some marvellous joke.

Gemǣres has gone out of its way to welcome royalty. The streets are lined with townsfolk, all of them cheering and waving cloth or ribbon of home-dyed colours – oranges and ochres from meadow glædflowers, which before they run to seed look like little suns. Musicians play jaunty tunes at every street corner. Usually rundown towns such as these have a distinctive smell – shit, piss, rotten meat and decay – and Cleves has warned Johana not to press a handkerchief to his nose under any circumstances, but she need not have worried. The windows and archways are wrapped with garlands of ivy and honeysuckle, so that the air always smells sweet, and the streets have been swept with water.

Cleves begins her usual act of getting her pets to give alms to the crowd, but when the first child cries out in pleasure at the gold coin Lelij has delivered, she sees Cromwell tense and realises her error. This is all part of the test, of Henry's people as much as Henry's queens. He will not like that she is buying their affection. He will not like that at all.

She knows what she must do. Survival above all else. She cannot allow Boleyn and Seymour's notions to turn her soft.

"*Gritsch*," she says, loud enough for Cromwell to hear the curse.

"Your Majesty? Is all well?" he says, stepping right alongside her as they walk.

"I made a mistake, Master Cromwell. My eyes, they are not as good as they once were."

She casts a regretful glance back at the child with the gold coin.

"You did not intend to give him one of such value?" Cromwell says.

"Would you? I am not Daven; I do not have Quisto's patronage."

His lips purse, almost imperceptibly. He has picked up on her petty gripe at Queen Aragon and it pleases him.

"I do not mind reclaiming your gold, if you would like?" he says.

"It is mean and dirty work, Lord Cromwell."

"That is my life's work," he says, with a curious little bow to round off the joke that is not a joke.

Cleves watches as he strolls over to the child and his parents, their cheeks flushed with joy, and leans in to talk to them. All three adults look at Cleves, and she looks away, her stomach clenching. She will see them right in the end, no matter what they may think of her now. No matter what poison Cromwell is dripping into their ears about foreign stinginess and the ways of rich women.

Their procession comes to a halt in the town square, which is really more of a circle where four streets meet. At its centre is a fountain: something of a curiosity given the lack of fresh running water. As with the archway, much of the stone's detail has been lost. Two oval shapes – perhaps heads – adorn the apex of the monument, one on each side.

"Are those supposed to be breasts?" Johana says quietly, nodding to a pair of rounded shapes beneath the head closest to Cleves.

"I think they may once have been, yes."

"I may not be an expert, but are they usually so smooth? Do women not possess . . . how do you say it in Elbenese . . .?"

"Nipples?"

"Nipples, yes."

Cleves and Johana tilt their heads in unison, considering the mystery of the nippleless bosoms.

"I cannot speak for all women, but in general, yes, we do. I suspect that these have lost their nipples through centuries of puerile touching."

A cheer goes up from the other side of the town square.

"My god, what insanity is happening now?" Johana says.

There is laughter and whistles in the distance.

"My sister is here," Cleves says.

"Sybil?" Johana looks around for a woman who he knows to still be in Ezzonid.

Cleves smacks him gently. "Idiot. I meant my sister-queen."

And there she is. Howard is radiant in her customary gossamer and silk. Her gown has been embroidered all over with white and red roses – the emblems of the Tudor dynasty. Clever girl, to align herself so symbolically with her husband.

"Well, she was made to be a muse," Johana says.

"She was made to be herself," Cleves replies, and strides forwards, circling the fountain to greet Howard.

The women stop when there is still some distance between them – they must be friendly but not familiar. No one can suspect that they do more than exchange pleasantries in brief meetings and perfunctory letters. Cleves almost smiles at what Cromwell would think if he knew that they met magically beneath the new moon to discuss overthrowing the men of their land.

Howard's eyes are wide, poised between panic and purity, as she dips into a curtsey. Her ladies-in-waiting follow her lead, and Cleves spies Lady Susanna Horenbolt at the back, a little apart from the others. If Cleves could have been persuaded to keep any of the ladies-in-waiting granted to her upon her arrival in Elben, she would have kept Susanna. A sensible, steady woman with an artistic talent to rival Master Holbein.

Cleves curtseys too, although not as deeply, for she is of royal stock.

"Well met, sister," Cleves says, as Cromwell rejoins them, the gold coin Cleves had given to the boy glinting in his palm.

"It has been some time," Howard says, stuttering a little. Ever aware of Cromwell's presence, Cleves smiles. "Let us hope that this meeting is less eventful than the last."

There is a general silence. The nobility of Gemǣres are too lowborn to have attended the Moon Ball, but all of Elben knows by now that something happened there, and that it was followed by Boleyn's arrest. Cleves would have rather not referenced it at all, but since Howard did so clumsily, she must do so too, and hope that it will offer Howard some protection.

Cromwell steps back. Perhaps he wants to be able to keep both of them in his view to better assess their behaviour. Howard appears to be frozen.

Johana laughs, loud as a horn. He keeps laughing, until slowly the Gemæres nobility join in, and then Cleves, and finally Howard and her ladies and then, at last, Cromwell. Lelij presses against Cleves's legs, distressed by the noise. Her dragons take flight. And still she laughs.

"Indeed, let us hope so," Cromwell says, patting his chest as though he is out of breath from so much merriment. He nods to the Mayor of Gemæres, who holds up a hand in some prearranged signal.

Howard's eyes widen, if possible, even further at something behind Cleves. She swings around to see that a clumsily rigged mechanism attached to the base of the fountain is being cranked by several maidens.

A strange bubbling sound, and then, out of what once must have been the nipples of the stone women, pour thin streams of wine – white on one side, red on the other. Cromwell claps effusively, and the townspeople, clearly proud of their handiwork, applaud and cheer. Cleves joins in, although she hardly knows what she says as she congratulates the engineers. Johana does not clap, only stares in barely disguised horror at the statues. Cleves wants to rebuke him for his disgust of something that is, after all, only mirroring a perfectly normal bodily function. But then why can she herself not look at the statues? Why does she almost gag when someone holds a goblet beneath one of the streams and then passes it to her with a wink?

She and Howard are corralled to another corner of the town square, goblets still in hand. Two easels have been erected and covered with red velvet curtains. Men crowd around them, eager to witness the unveiling of the famous Master Holbein's portraits. Eager to witness the queens' reactions to their likenesses.

The sound of laughter rings in Cleves's ears. It melts into the sound of marching.

"Lelij, *heem*," Cleves says to the gargoyle at her feet. *Space*. Lelij shakes his ruffled neck and arches his scaled back. From his belly comes a guttural wheeze, and as it sounds, his stomach expands, making him seem far bigger than he really is. The pressing crowd backs away, alarmed by the strange creature. Space.

The movement pushes Cleves and Howard against each other momentarily, and momentarily their free hands touch. Cleves catches Howard's fingers in her own and squeezes. Howard darts a smile at her, and Cleves is reminded of another girl, long ago, who once looked up at her in such a way.

"Ready?" Cleves says.

"I do not know," Howard replies.

Cromwell takes his place before the easels. Johana tuts.

"Hush," Cleves says. She knows why he is displeased: it is inconceivable that a mere lord such as Cromwell should be acting as master of ceremonies for this occasion. The queens should be asserting their rights to unveil their own portraits.

There will be time enough for that, Cleves thinks. She must be sure of her footing first.

"Gentlemen, ladies, townsfolk," Cromwell says. His voice is like a burrowing animal, a badger. "We are honoured to greet your queens of Plythe and Cnothan to Gemǣres for a very special unveiling of two new paintings commissioned by His Majesty King Henry, eighth of his name. For the love between a king and his queens is alike to the love between a king and his country. When one is true, the other can never be broken. So without further delay, allow me to present to you the famous Master Holbein's new portraits of Queen Howard and Queen Cleves!"

He flings back the curtains. Red velvet snakes to the ground as the townspeople applaud before they have even seen the paintings. Cleves has practised her reaction already. She must be seen to be concealing her distress at how ugly she looks compared to Howard. She must be foreign in her mannerisms. This is the test that she must pass to ensure her safety.

She approaches the portrait and pulls her spectacles from a pouch at her belt. She perches them on her nose and peers closely at the rendering, examining the way in which Holbein has captured her direct gaze – too direct for Elbenese modesty – and her proprietary hand upon Lelij's head as the gargoyle sits, as regal as such a creature can be, beside her throne.

"Well done, Master Holbein," she whispers. "It is well done indeed."

She looks strange, true, but not ridiculous. She wonders whether Henry and Cromwell have realised this, or whether their own feelings towards her have coloured their view of the portrait.

She makes a performance of looking at the ground, as if trying to collect her emotions, and polishing her spectacles and looking at the portrait again. But she cannot force herself to hunch, as she had planned. It turns out that her pride does have limits. She is not ashamed of this portrait. She is not ashamed of herself.

She moves on to examine Howard's painting, and the queen in question joins her.

"Did he truly see me so?" Howard says, so that only Cleves can hear.

Holbein has captured her singular beauty. How could he fail to do so? In the portrait, she is wearing the same gown that she wears now – covered in white and red roses to mark her as Henry Tudor's property. She holds a rose too, its stalk slender and smooth, unadorned with thorns. But her fingernails are long and sharpened to points. Cleves glances down at Howard's hands – her nails are rounded. In the portrait, her eyes are wide, even larger than they are in reality. Where Cleves's expression is sharp, Howard's is vacant – she looks past the painter, not at him.

She can understand why Howard is so thrown by this reflection. Even Cleves is confused: what message was Holbein attempting, and to whom? Are the sharp nails a reference to the thoughtless cruelty that she has heard tell of among Howard and her ladies-in-waiting? Or are they a trumpet call to Howard herself, to turn her softness to blades?

"What do you see when you look at it?" Cleves asks Howard.

"I do not know," Howard says. Her hands flutter to her neck. "Henry thinks I am perfect. But – is that what the portrait says?"

She is asking Cleves so many questions in one: *Am I safe? Am I as I should be? Who am I?*

Cromwell joins them. Howard stiffens even as she turns a beatific smile upon him. Cleves likes to think she is a little more natural.

"Your Majesties, has our painter not done a wonderful job? The king is having these likenesses copied for houses across Elben and beyond. Even some of our foreign ambassadors have asked for their own copies to send back to their royal masters."

Cleves polishes her spectacles again. "If our husband approves of them, then what do our thoughts matter, Lord Cromwell?" she says.

Cromwell places a hand upon his chest. "You do not like yours, Queen Cleves?"

"Oh, I like it well enough. But you know me: I do not see the point of such frivolities."

She indicates Howard. "My sister may be very pleased with hers, though, I think. Do you not, Lord Cromwell?"

Cleves does not like the way he looks at Howard. She is reminded of a carrion crow. Howard evidently feels it too, because she takes a small step back.

"His Majesty likes it very much. *The rose without a thorn*, he said, when he saw it. Is that what you are, Queen Howard?"

Howard's mouth is open, but no words emerge. She laughs nervously. *Say something*, Cleves thinks. *Do not freeze.* But Howard is in the pit of her panic, and the silence stretches.

"For shame, Lord Cromwell," Cleves says, batting him playfully. "Any discussion of pricks should be between a husband and his wife alone."

She and Cromwell laugh. "My apologies, Queen Howard," Cromwell says, bowing, and Howard curtseys and laughs in turn, understanding that Cleves has given her an opening to pretend that she was merely shy.

"Thank you," she whispers once Cromwell has left them alone. Cleves tucks Howard's arm into hers as they walk back to their parties. "I am a fixed point now, sister. My paint is dry. But you – you are young. The oil has yet to set. I suggest you think on your self-portrait before it does."

And think on it soon, sister, or you will drag us all down with you.

CHAPTER TEN

Howard

She is only back from Gemǣres for a night before the king comes to Plythe, as though summoned by the scent of her treachery. She and her ladies watch from the window of her receiving chamber as the carriages and carts of the royal train stretch along the riverbank, the Tudor rose embroidered on the canopies and flags. As they watch, one of Henry's men relieves himself into the river far below. He spots the women and salutes them with one hand, the other holding his member as he thrusts his crotch in their direction. The women look to Howard for how they should react.

"It is a good thing he saluted with his hand. At least it is big enough for us to see," she says.

Her ladies laugh. She turns away from them as they continue the ribaldry, stumbling towards the door and out into the galleries. She must greet Henry with delight. His ancestors look down upon her as she moves, her shoes tapping on the tiled floor.

Henry did not tell her he was coming. He has been with Mary Boleyn at High Hall since returning from Capetia. She has not seen him since the Moon Ball. His letters have been brief but loving, and under Voda Kelaverinn's guidance she has responded with longer missives than she used to. She cannot help but wonder, though: he has never come with such a large retinue before. That must mean that he intends to stay for longer than two nights. Why? And why now? Is this because of her fumble at Gemæres? Was she not convincing enough for Cromwell?

She stands at the top of the steps which lead down from the palace, looking out onto the wide, golden cobbles of the courtyard. Henry dismounts his horse and looks up. "My love!" he calls.

Howard pastes on her most brilliant smile and shouts, "Henry!" before racing down the steps and flinging herself into his arms. She must forge the situation to her advantage as Boleyn and Seymour would have done. She must use this time to gain information that will impress the other queens. Maybe then they will like her. Maybe this is what Cleves meant by her paint not yet being dry.

Henry crushes her within his arms. She inhales his musk: charcoal and the faint sweat of travel. This has never failed to excite her before, and she waits for the desire to crawl through her body.

"You grow more beautiful every time I set eyes on you," Henry murmurs. She curtseys deeply to him, leaning forward so he can get a better view of her breasts. Then she rises, lifting her gown a little too high so that he can spy her bare leg. This is their ritual – a promise from her to him, a lesson taught to her when she was twelve that has stood her in good stead in her marriage.

Henry grabs at her.

"Come then, wife; I am tired after my journey."

She takes his hand and leads him towards the palace.

"Let me tend to you, my lord."

This is how it is between them. How it has always been. He is attractive and charming and she has never had trouble desiring him before. She has no doubt she will be able to enjoy herself once again. Sex is the natural way between man and woman, as easy as a conversation. Easier, far easier, than a letter or an argument.

Henry's rooms are adjacent to hers, sparser but grander. The canopied bed is enormous. When they married, he permitted her to redecorate Plythe to her liking but suggested a particular painter to cover his bedchamber in murals. She had agreed happily, not knowing that Henry had told the artist to paint her, naked, in various poses.

"It is so that I can only see you when we are making love," he told her when she first saw them. It is romantic. A sign of how much he desires her, and therefore of how much he loves her.

She does not look at the murals now as she leads him to the bed and begins to undo the fastenings of his doublet.

"You have missed me, my dear."

"Every day," she says.

"And I you."

She pushes his doublet back over his shoulders, then runs her hands over the thin shirt he wears beneath. Her hands go to his hose, tugging them down so she can take him in her mouth. He likes it when she does this as soon as he arrives. It shows how passionately she wants him, when his scent is less pleasant after so much travel. Usually if her desire has not come by now, the sound of his pleasure at her tongue is enough to make her wet. She squirms from her position on the floor, wondering why it is not working this time.

"What is it?" he says.

She hesitates. "I'm so happy to see you."

She pulls his hose down fully, and he winces as it catches on a bandage secured around his thigh.

"Oh," Howard says. She remembers that day, even though he cannot know she witnessed it: Boleyn shot him with an arrow. But the divine power should have healed him. And even if it did not, the wound should have healed naturally by now. Why has it not?

"It's nothing," he says, pulling her onto the bed and flipping her onto her back. She stares up at so many imagined versions of her body, splayed like a stuck deer on the ceiling. He fumbles his hose off and lifts her gown so it is over her face. She can't breathe, too stuffy on her top half and cold below her waist.

He enters her before she is ready. "Oh," she says again.

"Are you all right?" he says, starting to move. She cannot see him through the folds of her gown.

"Yes," she says, hoping that he will understand her reluctance from the tone of her voice. He keeps thrusting until it is no longer uncomfortable.

"You feel so good, my darling. You feel so good," he says, again and again.

Howard closes her eyes and tries to lose herself. He desires her, and that is enough. That is enough.

"You are very quiet," he says afterwards, his arms around her, her head on his chest. She likes to feel it rise and fall beneath her.

"I am worried about you. Your leg," she says.

"It is an irritant," he replies. "Nothing more."

"How did—?"

"It need not concern you," he says more firmly. Howard falls silent. He isn't holding her now. She must do something before his mood turns entirely. She sits up, wriggling her gown into place, and grins down at him.

"Where are you going, wife?" he says as she stalks across the room.

"You will see, husband," she shoots back over her shoulder. She is going to order oysters to be brought to the room. Oysters in sharp sauce are one of their shared favourites.

She flings open the door, and comes to a halt.

"Oh," she says, staring up at a stranger. He is leaning against the wall on the other side of the passage, somehow both bored and watchful, like a cat.

"Your Majesty," he says, bowing. His eyes are bright, his dark hair tousled. He cannot be much older than her. There is something familiar about him, and yet she is certain they have never been introduced – she would remember his name if they had. He stirs up strange emotions within her. A flitting feeling of power and dread. A sense of imminent danger, and Boleyn's scent.

Henry comes to stand beside her, still naked, supremely confident in his physique and the size of his cock. The bordweal power glistens in his sweat.

"Ah, Culpepper," Henry says. "Did you get what I was looking for?"

Culpepper makes a show of bringing something slowly from behind his back. Howard's fingers work the fabric of her gown. Where has she seen him before?

On his open palm sits a brooch. The setting is filigreed gold, and in its centre sits a golden topaz the size of a coin. It has been fashioned into the shape of a rose by craftsmen far more skilled than any that still work on Elben.

"It's beautiful," Howard says. Henry plucks the brooch from Culpepper's palm, and wraps his arms around her to pin the jewellery to her gown.

"A rose for my own rose without a thorn," he says. "Doesn't it suit her well?"

"I think it would suit any woman well." Culpepper's look pierces her then. She feels as she used to feel when attempting to read: that look is like the letters that would jumble on the page.

"I remembered my father's old queen wearing it," Henry says. "And it struck me that it wasn't accounted for in her will. I thought it must be hidden somewhere at Plythe and instructed Culpepper here to find it."

"I see," Howard says. "Where did you find it? I thought I'd discovered everything there was to discover about my palace."

Culpepper steps back and glances out of the window as though her question is a nothing.

"Oh, I found it in a box."

"A box?"

"Yes. A box full of fabrics, destined for Perfugi."

Howard stills. A box of fabrics, destined for Perfugi, was where she and Seymour had hidden Boleyn. And suddenly, she places him. The man who tried to stop the cart where Boleyn was concealed. The one whose position she threatened in order to ensure Boleyn's escape.

"Is that so?" she manages to say. Henry presses into her again, kissing her neck.

"Isn't it surprising what kind of things can be found in such places?"

She can barely breathe. She has not one but two wolves in her home, and she does not know how to get them out.

CHAPTER ELEVEN

Cleves

Everything has its place at Cnothan. It may not seem that way, on account of all the animals, but even the animals know where they are allowed and where they are forbidden. It is the same with things: each letter in Cleves's study is carefully stowed in a particular order.

It is the same with people. Johana belongs in Ezzonid. Cleves in Cnothan. Seymour in the *sunscína*: visible but untouchable.

It's always the people who cause problems with the order, never the animals. Johana has come here and is making no move to return to his proper country. And Seymour: Seymour has seemingly vanished. It bothers Cleves, in as much as she ought to know where Seymour is for her own safety. Not because she takes any particular interest in that woman's wellbeing.

"Something is troubling you," her lover says from her position between Cleves's legs.

"Forgive me," Cleves says, sitting up. Her lover, Lady Arundell, kisses her way up Cleves's body. Cleves tries to lose herself in the sweetness of it, burying her hand in the woman's hair.

"Your hair is the colour of the sun, did you know that?" Cleves says, letting her head fall back to provide easier access to her neck. Arundell bites her gently as thanks for the compliment. It is unexpectedly fierce for the usually pliant Arundell, and it makes her think of Seymour tearing and sawing at her own gown with a crone's tooth.

"I have lost you again," Arundell says, pulling away from her. She is not one for petulance, but her lips are pursed. Cleves grasps the back of her head and pulls her in for a kiss, enjoying the taste of her own desire on Arundell's tongue. But Arundell places a hand on her chest.

"Talk to me," she says. "Let me be your secret-keeper, Cleves."

"What could be more secret than our assignations?" Cleves says, turning her attention to Arundell's bare shoulder. She strokes the branch of bone that runs just beneath the skin. "Does it make me very strange that I can be so attracted to such parts of a body?" she says. "This bone here, and then here, and here . . ." She kisses the shoulder bone, then the rivets beneath Arundell's neck, and then down to the jut of her hips.

"Cleves," Arundell says. It is a command. Cleves sits up, ignoring the way Arundell reaches for her. They have always had an easy tactility, but Cleves has known this moment was coming. It always does.

"I have never misled you," she says.

"I know."

"We are both married."

Arundell fumbles her way through the coverlets to bridge the distance between them. "I am not asking for a proposal, my queen. You know that is not what I am asking."

Cleves hears laughter, then. Laughter and the stamp of armour, coming ever closer.

"You can tell me anything," Arundell says. She places a hand on Cleves's cheek, and for a moment Cleves is almost tempted. But friendship is harder, far harder, to extricate oneself from than lust.

"I have much business to attend to," she says, climbing out of bed and pulling on her stays. Arundell pulls the coverlets across her naked body. She tries to laugh, but it's a hollow sound.

"Cernunnos forbid you ask your court to do anything."

"You know how particular I am. Trust me, it is easier for everyone if I do it myself," Cleves says. She steps into her skirt and then pulls the bodice over her head. The strings are tangled, though, and even with her dexterous fingers she cannot find a way to pull it tight at the back.

"Let me," Arundell says. She climbs off the bed and stands behind Cleves, naked. Her breath is warm upon Cleves's arms as she works her way through the knots.

"It is safer this way," Cleves says into the silence.

"And that is all you want? Safety?"

Cleves almost laughs, except she knows that Arundell might take that as derision. The question is stupid. "Of course. Is it not what we all wish for?"

Arundell finishes undoing the knots and begins to pull at the strings. The boning tightens around Cleves's ribs and waist – plank after plank of scaffolding to prop her up, to protect her.

"There," Arundell says at last. "You are all armoured." The nightingale's song is inside her words.

"My thanks, my lady," Cleves says. She cannot turn around, though she knows she should. She must give her lover the respect of a proper farewell.

"My husband returns from the north tomorrow," Arundell says. Cleves smiles at the floor, closes her eyes. The sweet woman knows what she needs from her, and has given it to her as a final gift. She turns and takes both of Arundell's hands in her own.

"Will you be meeting him at High Hall?" she asks.

"Yes, I think he'll appreciate that."

Cleves casts around for something to give Arundell that is just for her; not something her husband can claim. She keeps a small chest on a cabinet in the corner of her bedroom. She unlocks it and surveys the jewels within.

"Have I told you of my country's superstitions around gems?" she asks, running a hand across the pieces.

"No."

"It is a remnant of our old religions. It was said that certain powerful creatures, sometimes even gods, lived in jewels, and their divine powers run through them. Protection for topaz, lightning in diamonds, and so on. The brighter the jewel, the stronger the godly power."

She lands upon a simple, large amethyst, set in a pendant surrounded by diamonds. Perfect.

"You do not believe it?" Arundell says.

"To believe it would be blasphemy against Cernunnos, would it not?" Cleves says. She drapes the necklace around Arundell's neck so that the pendant rests upon her clavicle.

"What godly power does amethyst have, then?" Arundell says, her hand resting on the jewel.

Cleves smooths her lover's hair over the chain. This is the last time she will perform such an intimate act with Arundell.

"Healing," Cleves says. "Healing and good health."

Arundell half sobs, half laughs. "Does it heal every ailment? Even heartbreak?"

"I hope so," Cleves says.

Johana is waiting for her in her study, his booted feet resting on her desk.

"*Grutzch,*" she curses when she sees him.

"Good morning to you too, cousin."

"No," she says. She slaps his feet off her desk. "I do not want you here, Johana."

"That hurts my feelings."

She pushes him out of her chair, which is no small task given he is so much larger than her.

"I do not care. I did not invite you to Elben. I did not invite you to Cnothan. I do not want this."

"What do you want, then?"

He is being infuriatingly calm with that little smirk he is so fond of wearing.

"I want to be *alone*. I just want—" She gestures at her surroundings, her perfectly neat study and the courtyards outside her window, populated by animals and as few servants as she can manage. "I want to be with my pets, and my work, in my castle, by myself."

Johana considers this. "Very well, cousin. I will give you some peace."

"Thank you."

"I merely came to deliver some excellent news," he says.

Her heart skips a beat. Has Seymour been seized?

"Enlighten me then," she says.

"Our two countries are to become closer than ever. Your husband and brother have signed a new treaty of enduring friendship between Elben and Ezzonid."

"I see," Cleves says. She eyes a bowl at the edge of her desk that she rather wants to throw at a wall. "That is excellent news indeed. And does this treaty involve more than pretty words of friendship?"

Johana waves a hand airily. "Oh, some warships and a few dozen war dragons. And in exchange we receive favourable trading routes through Elbenese waters and a good price on the exquisite crystal that is so prevalent in this meagre little island."

Warships and dragons. Henry is planning further conquest then – the question is: over his queens, or over other countries? Or both?

"You do not seem to be as happy as I might expect," Johana says, his head tilted.

"I am merely surprised that no one thought to inform me of these negotiations," Cleves says.

"Ah, the same way you do not think to inform your relatives of, well, anything?" Johana retorts. They are both speaking lightly, like children walking across ice.

"What do you suppose I should be informing you of? How large my prize sow's litter was last month? Where I source my wine?"

"Queen Aragon tells all to her country's diplomats."

Cleves bites her lip. She knows from her butterflies that Henry had made overtures towards Quisto – a new alliance between them – and that Queen Aragon's royal nephew had refused all negotiations. At the time she had assumed it was merely because Quisto believed it had the strength to take Elben when the time was right. Now she wonders: is it because Aragon, that damned prideful woman, had asked her nephew not to?

"We cannot stand by you if we do not know we must," Johana says, looking at her directly at last. Cleves's heart is pounding too fast, but she does not let her smile slip.

"I will keep that in mind, cousin, if I ever have something to share that might be considered of interest. Now, if you please."

He salutes her smartly, then shuts the door behind him. Cleves growls as she sits. His boots have left dirt on her lovely desk. Lelij mewls from his bed in the corner of the room, and she pats her leg so that he knows he can curl up against it as she works.

"Why does everyone want to be friends so suddenly?" she asks the gargoyle. He snorts.

"Precisely. It is tiresome," she says.

She tries to lose herself in her work: to push aside Johana's pointed comments, and the news that her kingly brother now has more reason to be loyal to her husband than he does to her. She tries not to think of the fallen queen who is missing across an ocean, and all the many treasons she might confess if seized.

For a while, she is able to forget. There are dozens of letters containing nothings that require answers containing equal amounts of nothings. There are accounts and receipts and invoices that must be paid, for she has never been indebted to anyone and is damned if she'll let a moon pass without paying her bills. The people she employs need the money far more than she.

There is a report from her master of husbandry into the crone that has taken up residence near the Fietherford, and another from her steward outlining the costs of renovating the castle's stables. She usually finishes reading her correspondence before inviting more, but this morning she lays a handful to one side to make space for her paper and inkwell.

She does not address the letter, for it will not be delivered by any of the usual methods, and it is better if no one knows the intended recipient, should it be intercepted.

Please you to set your butterflies upon Lady Arundell, as you did Lady Paston. I will compensate accordingly.

She pauses. Should she ask what she wants to ask? Surely the recipient will already be hunting for information. She would have heard if there was any news. To ask outright would be to show her cards.

She closes the letter and warms the wax to seal it. A single droplet falls upon the parchment before Cleves sets aside the heated wax in its brass cup, and opens the letter once more.

Have you heard news of our mutual friend from the east? I am concerned by their silence.

"You're a fool," she mutters to herself as she closes the letter once more and presses a blank seal into the wax with such force that it splatters.

Lelij grunts again at her feet.

CHAPTER TWELVE

Howard

Howard tries not to look at Culpepper over the following days, but she is always aware of his presence. He seems to be everywhere she goes. If there is dancing, he is requesting every lady's hand but hers. If there is music, he claps politely from the back row of seats, in accordance with his status. If there is hunting, he is the person who delivers the killing blow upon the boar. He never speaks to Howard unless she addresses him, although sometimes she feels his gaze upon her.

What would Boleyn do? It is her constant refrain. But she does not have Boleyn's strategic mind. She cannot see three or four steps ahead in a game of *beadulác,* so how is she supposed to see her way out of this trap?

The palace is mercifully empty during the day while most of Henry's court and Howard's servants are busy preparing for a dragon-baiting. Howard can see the arena from her bedchamber: the barriers being erected around a circular pit; the thrones on which she and Henry will sit. Culpepper, as the chief organiser, is in the centre of all of it. She watches him laughing with the workers as he directs them. One of her noblemen approaches him and he bends his head to the other man, at once showing deference to his superior status while also encouraging the earl to lean his head in too – an intimacy entirely engineered by Culpepper. She cannot decide if Culpepper knows the brilliant game he is playing, or whether it is instinctive, easy amiability. When the two men have finished talking, they part ways with a mutual slap on the back, and Culpepper turns to his task without any indication that he knows that he has just gained favour with one of the most influential men in Howard's territory.

In the afternoon, the whole palace trips across the gardens to witness the sport. Howard's arm is slipped through Henry's, and she turns her face up to the brittle sun that is never far from this side of Elben. She loves this about Plythe: how open it is, all wide windows and wider views. The trees and forests of Brynd or Mathmas, or the claustrophobia of the destroyed palace of Hyde are not for her.

Here, on the other side of the gatehouse, the narrow footprint of the palace widens to incorporate hunting grounds, herb gardens and jousting lawns. The cymbal sound of the Kyttle Falls is muted by a row of beech trees.

Howard looks back towards the palace. When she first saw it, she thought it looked like something chopped from the heavens, or raised by godly hands from the riverbed.

And she is set on a path that means she could lose it all.

"Here we are," Henry says. Howard turns her attention to the makeshift arena.

The two thrones have been set on the lawn, side by side, for the monarch and his queen. Her throne is almost as magnificent as Henry's: a mahogany seat carved with her emblem – a nightingale – entwined with the Tudor rose. Naked women and fauns frolic across the wood, so that when she sits on it, she is stuffed between an orgy. Henry seats her gallantly and cocoons her hand in his. She clenches the other in her lap.

The rest of the court takes their places at the barriers, the higher-ranking nobility sitting and the lower ranks standing behind them. Cromwell and Wolsey have seats affording the best view. They confer with each other in low tones, the least interested in the spectacle about to play out before them. Howard casts her eye across her inner circle, ensuring her ladies are behaving themselves. Ursula Askew stands a little distance from the others. It is unlike her to not be in the centre of a gathering, and Howard wonders whether there has been some disagreement.

Seated at the front, on account of being Howard's half-sister, is Legh. Beside her is Lady Tylney, and behind them stands Susanna Horenbolt. Susanna despises violence of any kind. They all joke that she is too soft for court. Lady Tylney reaches a hand over her shoulder and, without looking, takes Susanna's. Howard is very aware of the way in which Henry is holding hers. Is it loving? Is it caring, as Tylney's is? Or is it because Howard is his, and the ring upon her finger is not symbol enough of his possession?

She wonders what Voda Kelaverinn would make of all this bloodsport.

"Are you excited, little rose?" Henry says.

She startles, then covers it with a fluttering hand across her chest. Henry's eyes follow her fingers. She used to liken him to a wolf. Now she wonders if he is a vulture.

"Of course, my king."

"Have you laid a bet with young Culpepper yet?"

She doesn't let herself look at the man in question.

"A bet?"

Henry tweaks her cheek. "Is there any substance in that beautiful head of yours? A bet on the sport. On the winner."

Was that an insult or a compliment?

"Oh. No." Is she being too dull? Or does he enjoy her dullness?

She cocks her head and leans over the arm of her throne, letting her dress fall off her shoulder. "All I shall wager is that you could defeat any creature in that arena," she says. He stills, searching her eyes. Then he leans towards her, their foreheads touching. "You are quite ravishing, Howard, do you know that? I can hardly bear to watch the sport with you here and so tempting."

There it is – the ember of desire that has been so absent lately.

"I could be more tempting still, if it would not be so scandalous," she says. On impulse, she leans over even further and nips his earlobe. She feels sure of herself for the first time in many moons. She knows what she must do and say at last. She is the Howard she was raised to be, not the Howard that Boleyn and Cleves and all those other women want her to be.

The ember fades.

Henry lifts her from her throne and pulls her into his lap. She can feel his hardness through her gown, digging into her lower back. He holds her round the waist with one hand. The other he slips beneath her gown, letting its folds conceal his arm as he finds her core and dips a finger into her.

"Wet for me already," he whispers.

"Of course, my king," she says. She finds a fixed point – the apex of the trees on the other side of the arena – and stares at it as he pushes one, two, three fingers inside her. It is delicious and scandalous and she didn't ask for it, and yet she *is* wet and getting wetter, so it must be what she wants.

A stir goes around the arena, and for a moment Howard thinks that the courtiers have noticed what is happening on the king's throne. But then she sees movement from beyond the treeline, where Plythe's bestiary is situated, and she catches her breath.

Culpepper is leading a dragon across the lawn. Its front and hind legs are manacled, two by two, so it is forced to walk in an awkward, loping gait. There is an iron muzzle over its long jaw. A wild dragon. Tame dragons are bred for particular jobs – small to be lap dragons; large wings and eyes and smaller bodies for hunting dragons; cropped wings and muscled back legs for the dragons sometimes employed in labour in the fields or mines; pearlescent scales and more fat than muscle for the ceremonial dragons used in royal weddings. This dragon has none of those features. Its front legs are as long as its back legs, and its wings are in perfect proportion to its body, which is gnarled and covered with the scars that accumulate from a life of catching cattle and battling other dragons for territory.

Culpepper expertly lashes the dragon's hide, darting this way and that with a long whip. He has another set of chains in his other hand, ready to manacle the dragon to the stake embedded in the centre of the arena.

"Will it be a fair fight?" Susanna asks Lady Tylney, just loud enough for Howard to hear.

"It will certainly be entertaining," Lady Tylney replies, with a tight glance towards the king.

Culpepper fastens the dragon to its stake, and the beast utters a stifled roar at this further indignity. Culpepper lashes it again, then turns and grins at Henry. "Your Majesty, the creature is hungry!"

"Then let us feed it!" Henry replies, his voice sonorous with glee. He pushes deeper into Howard. She places both hands on the arms of his throne. Do they all know what he is doing to her? Do they all see? What must they think of her? Do they think she is enjoying it? *Is* she enjoying it?

With the skill of a hunter, Culpepper unshackles the dragon's legs, unclips the muzzle and steps back, out of the dragon's reach.

The creature roars full-throatedly at last, aiming to incinerate as many of its spectators as possible. But it has been fed iced meat and its fires are dulled. It would be too quick a fight if the dragon had all its faculties. At a signal, a pack of hunting hounds are produced, their ribcages showing from a long fast.

Culpepper ducks out of the arena as the hounds are released. Henry beckons him over with his free hand.

"An excellent entertainment you have arranged, Culpepper. The dragon's magnificent."

"He's a fine beast, Your Majesty. It almost makes me pity him for what is to come."

He bows to Henry, bows to Howard. She inclines her head towards him. Sweat prickles the back of her neck.

"He is a handsome creature," she says, hoping that entering the conversation will mask her confused desire.

"He is. I would say like yourself, except your beauty is without compare. And you have fewer scars," Culpepper says.

The hounds are circling the dragon, licking their lips and growling.

"Her bite is kinder too," Henry says, nuzzling her neck. He does not see the look Culpepper grants Howard: earnest and questioning.

A hound darts forward and snaps at the dragon's soft belly. The crowd cheers.

"First blood," Culpepper says. "It will go quicker now."

Henry is caught up in the sport, his fingers moving faster. Howard cannot shake the sense that she is not a full being but her husband's garland. A pretty star in the intense infinity of night.

The dragon catches one of the hounds in its jaws, snapping the little dog's body this way and that. Bones click and shatter, even above the cheers of the crowd. Susanna covers her mouth with gloved hands. Then the dragon tosses the broken hound up into the air and swallows it whole.

Culpepper laughs and, without warning, Howard climaxes around Henry's fingers.

"Good girl," he says, withdrawing his hand, wiping it on her silk gown.

"Thank you," she says, as she always does.

The rest of the hounds quickly follow the first. Some of them realise the futility of the fight and turn tail, only to be caught as they run, or even more cruelly caught by the men on the other side of the barriers and tossed back into the arena. As the crowd jeers, a great brown bear is lined up just beyond the barriers to be the dragon's next opponent.

Howard watches it all with the strangest feeling that she is not in her body. She watches herself watching the gore, and she watches

Culpepper cheering. He suspects her, she is sure of it, or why else would he have mentioned the fake shipment to Perfugi? Surely if he were going to tell Henry what he suspects, he would have done so already and her neck would be on the block. So why has he not? He must want something from her, but what can she give him that Henry could not give him more of? Sex? She is beautiful, yes, but he does not seem like the kind of man who would love someone to the point of self-destructive obsession. He is no Thomas Wyatt.

The bear is pushed into the arena, and the crowd leans forward as one, anticipating a more even fight, for the bear has iron spikes welded to its claws. The dogs were a trifle; the bear is the meat of the afternoon.

"Now we shall have sport," Henry says. He squeezes her thigh with such force she knows she will bruise.

But the dragon is in the throes of a blood famine, and the bear is not prepared. The dragon pounces upon the creature before it can raise its paws, rending the bear's head from its body and tossing it into the crowd, where a lesser lord holds it aloft, his mouth open to catch the blood as it drips onto his tongue.

"Shit," Culpepper mutters. He shrugs. "I did tell it to drag things out a little. It seems it did not listen to me, Your Majesty."

Henry laughs. "Shall I make it listen?"

Before any of them can ask what he means, Henry lifts Howard from his lap and stands, raising his arms like a conquering hero. Howard slinks back to her own throne, aware of the darkened patch of moisture on the bright blue silk of her gown.

The effect on the crowd is immediate, such is the power he radiates. Howard knows that part of that power rightly belongs to her, by dint of her divine connection to Plythe, but by god if he doesn't contain his own innate power of a different kind. She cannot look away from him.

Henry leaps over the barrier and into the arena. Howard and some of the other women cry out in alarm. Even some of the men cover their faces. Cromwell is gripping the arm of his chair. Legh and Susanna are among those who make the sign of Cernunnos, fingers shaped to form the God's antlers. Howard spies Ursula's lip curl.

The dragon slowly arches its neck towards this new assailant. Its bloodied jaws snap in warning, but it is limping and tired.

"Allow your king to entertain you," Henry says. As the dragon contracts its neck, ready to strike, Henry lifts one hand, stretching it out towards the creature. Howard feels a ripple of agony, sharp and brittle, beneath her ribcage. She gasps, clutching at her breast. A blast of bordweal light shoots from Henry's hand. It hits the dragon in the chest, and the beast roars the roar that is stuck in Howard's throat. She and the dragon are connected in their pain.

She knows she must not make a sound, must not display weakness or fear or knowledge, but her organs are being wrung out. She has felt this once before: at the Moon Ball, when she was the chosen victim of Henry's wrath. Then the other queens had used their combined power to defend her. She has no such saviours now.

"Your Majesty? Are you all right?" a voice is saying, a hand on her shoulder.

"Yes. Yes," she whispers, trying to make it so.

"Let me help you," the voice says. Culpepper. *Let me help you.*

"Wine," she whispers.

He returns within an instant with the wine, and helps her to straighten. Their fingers feather against each other as she takes the goblet. His hands hover, close to her agony but not touching. Respectful.

"Are you all right, wife?" Henry says. She didn't see him return.

The dragon is barely alive, slumped in a heap upon the ground. Culpepper steps back.

"Our entertainment is tired," Henry tells him. "Take it away. It will be healed by my next visit, and then we can enjoy more sport."

Culpepper does as he is told. She watches him whip the dragon to its feet. Its neck is angled strangely as it stumbles from the arena.

"Did you enjoy my power, darling?" Henry says.

"Mmm," Howard replies. He holds her chin. Makes her look at him.

"I said, did you enjoy my power? I did it for you, after all."

He laughs at her confusion. "Did I drive your memory from you with my fingers, sweetheart? You wagered, remember? That I could defeat any creature in that arena?"

It is a test. The other queens had warned her that he would do this. She slips into the Howard he wants her to be. It is as easy as slipping beneath warm sheets in winter. Her hand plays with the patch of darkened silk, drawing his eyes.

"You did, my king. Do I win?"

CHAPTER THIRTEEN

Cecilia

Not even Cecilia's threats can prepare a ship speedily. It takes weeks for her new stewardess – a pinprick of a woman given by an amorous Perfugian noble, tight bodice and tight mouth – to commission a crew willing to work for Cecilia.

"I am told that there was an incident on your last voyage," she says, curtseying deeply on the alabaster floor of Cecilia's receiving chamber. Her ashen hair is wound in tight braids around her head. The fashion is not for hoods in Perfugi, not since so many women were lost to fainting when the city was first established. From her throne, Cecilia eyes a curl that has escaped its plait. She wonders what sound the woman would make were she to pull it out at the root.

"That was twelve years ago; surely they cannot still remember," Cecilia says.

"Your Majesty is memorable."

Cecilia herself can barely recall the voyage that brought her from Capetia, where she had briefly been a young queen to a dying king, to Perfugi. She had recently buried her royal husband, but had refused to wear the expected mourning weeds. Black does not suit her complexion. Could that have been why? She dimly recalls an altercation. One of the sailors had looked at her in a way she did not like. Did she skewer his eyes and then stab the men who came to his aid? Yes, it seems more likely that this was the offence.

How tiresome.

"Offer them more money," Cecilia tells the woman. She refuses to learn her name: she will not be taking her to Elben, so their acquaintance will be brief.

"I will do my best," the woman says, rising but not meeting Cecilia's eyes. Good. Lorena was far too free with her looks. As she leaves, Cecilia says, "Fetch the boy."

Florin is not so attractive now that Lorena is gone, for half the fun lay in watching his sister's reaction to her bedding him. But he still has the virulence and stamina of youth, and his guilt poses a challenge.

She sews as she waits, lounging in her throne, the hem of her silk dress pulled up over her knees for coolness. Her receiving chamber is an airy space made entirely of ancient dragon bone and marble. When she came to Perfugi, a new, wealthy widow, she could not find a palace worthy of her ancestry, but the Gallool dragons that had once lived upon and within the mountain and whose bones alone could provide shelter from the heat of the lava had long since been hunted to extinction. She had Lorena pay the poorer families of the Fisilis quarter, high upon the mountain's slopes, for their old houses' walls and roofs. They could hardly refuse. The Fisilis district is the poorest and oldest of the Perfugian neighbourhoods, built more as a refuge, using the lava as the Elbenese might use water in a moat for protection against attackers. They scrape a living scooping molten rock and harvesting the fire weeds that grow there. With the money Lorena paid them, they could leave Perfugi, if they wished, or find a nicer home in a better district. Cecilia liked to remind Lorena that she could have simply had them killed and their homes ransacked for materials at less expense. She could be merciful. She could even be charitable.

So her receiving chamber was built to her design. A show of opulence and wealth the like of which was not seen elsewhere in the city. Where other nobles and royals masked the walls where they could not afford dragon bone with diamonds or gold, she had no such spaces. All was bone, and all of it was on display.

The boy takes longer than is acceptable. When he arrives, there is none of the flamboyant worship that she enjoys. No eager display of his hardness.

"You summoned me?" he says, hovering just inside the door.

"Why are you so far away?"

There's a hesitation before he approaches. How dare he act as though he is doing her a favour?

"Crawl," she says.

He gets to his hands and knees. That gives her some satisfaction, except that he is still too slow, and . . .

"Are you weeping?" she says, leaning forward.

He mutters something.

"I am your queen," she says. "Speak properly."

"I farewelled her this morning," he says between sobs.

"Who?"

"My sister."

Cecilia does not like the sharp sensation that goes through her chest at the mention of Lorena. She had been informed that her farewell ceremony was today, but she did not see the point in attending. The Perfugians are so maudlin. There are so many events around death. There is the burial, usually performed on the day of passing, before the body starts to bloat in the heat. Then there is a sacrifice to the mountain, where the family gives thanks for keeping their relative safe while they lived. That is followed by a lengthy series of pronouncements at different points in the city, where tales of the dead's life are told by seasoned storytellers and attended by friends and family. And, finally, the farewell ceremony, where dried meat and iced wine are consumed around the grave and the stone is fitted and planted with seeds so that flowers and fragrant grasses cover it as the years pass. Cecilia has never liked passing those cemeteries of coloured hillocks. When a person is gone, they are gone. Why should she honour them when they were weak enough to die?

"It has been a moon or more. Your grief is over," she says. He flinches from his position on the bone floor, as though she has kicked him.

"I'm trying to help," she says, and she really might kick him soon. Such instructions always helped her to get past her girlish emotions when she was younger. *You're not upset any more,* her kingly father would say. *What use are tears to royals?* Or More's gentler: *Do you think you are being hysterical, princess?*

Over time, she learned that they were right. These are weak emotions, and she does not suffer them.

"She was my sister," Florin says, looking up at her. His eyes are bloodshot and he wears an ugly sneer.

"And she was my best friend, but *I* have not been pathetic about it for days and days. I was the one who had to make the decision to sacrifice her. It was very hard for me. If anyone has the right to be upset it is me, not you."

The boy has the nerve to laugh. Cecilia rises, drawing herself to her full height. She was always tall for her age, lauded across the continent as a princess worthy of a divinely blessed family.

"Come here," she says.

Miserably, the boy crawls towards her.

"You are a worm," she says.

He hesitates, then drops to his belly and pulls himself forwards. She will punish him for that pause. She has the perfect needle for the task. When he reaches the lowest of the steps up to her throne, he stops, awaiting her instructions on how to proceed.

"Say you are sorry," she says.

"I am sorry, Your Majesty."

"Tell me you love me."

His lip quivers, but he holds back the tears. Good. "I do love you," he says.

The sight of him like that, as though she is a goddess and he is worshipping her, makes her wet. This is how it's going to be once she returns to Elben and claims a palace (*why* is it taking so long to procure a crew? Oh, her jaw clenches just thinking about it all over again). She will have no need of needles: she will have divine power to wield in sharp points of pain.

She sits back on her throne and spreads her legs. The boy knows what to do. She takes hold of his hair, moving his head to the points that offer most pleasure. This is why she keeps him despite Lorena's death. She was his first, his only lover, and she has trained him to please her body alone. This is how it should be: just as she was mentored in the way of lovemaking before she sailed for Capetia to be married.

"No one else will ever give you what I give you," she says on the whisper of a moan.

His fingers dig into her thighs in reply. "Harder," she says. She wants him to leave bruises. Love notes, like the ones she leaves on his skin.

He gasps for air. She is about to pull him into her again – he should be able to hold his breath for longer by now – when she realises: the worm is crying once more.

"I'm sorry," he says. She puts her foot on his face and pushes him away. Down to the floor, her foot on his cheek. He is weeping openly, the tears wetting the soft fabric of her slipper. How much force would it take to crush the worm? If she put her full weight on it, would the skull give way?

"I love you. I'm sorry," he sobs.

The urge passes. She pushes him off the dais with the same foot.

"I am tired. You may go," she says.

If he tries to grovel, she will choke him. He doesn't. Head down, he leaves drops of salted water on the floor as he crawls backwards out of the chamber. Once out of her sight, she hears him rise and run, footsteps echoing in the bone hallways. Running, running away.

She will reel him back in. It will not take much. When she brings him to Elben, he will know no one and have nothing but her. His goddess. *Damnation, where is her ship?*

CHAPTER FOURTEEN

Cleves

Cleves is dreaming of her again. They are dancing, eyes locked, beneath a dome of bordweal power conjured by their own bodies. The tingling, powerful sensation that she had when she joined with Cnothan on her wedding day courses through her. Courses through her and into Seymour and back again, between their eyes, their hands, Cleves's fingers gloved in Seymour's, music ephemeral and all around them like an embrace.

I think it must be quite something to be loved by you, Cleves had said on their first meeting. In her dreams, it isn't something. It is everything.

As they dance beneath the bordweal dome in the hall at Brynd, Seymour's hand moves up from Cleves's waist and begins to untie the laces of her bodice. Cleves looses Seymour's hair from her hood. Then they are kissing, Cleves's hand pulling Seymour's head to hers, the other hand running along that bone at the base of the neck that has always fascinated Cleves, always been her undoing.

She can never get past that point, always waking before the delicious ritual of the undressing begins. So it is today. She wakes with the dawn, just before the sky lightens but with the birds chittering from their roosts in the castle roof. The promise of Seymour's nakedness is tantalisingly close, if only she could slip back into her dreams and manoeuvre them just so. But once Cleves is awake, she can rarely return to sleep.

Still, it takes her a moment to realise that she has not woken naturally. Someone is loitering outside her door – she can hear the shuffle of their footsteps. She swings out of bed, pulling on a bodice and a pair of breeches, and retrieves a short dagger from one of her practical belts. With the dagger in hand, she tiptoes to the door and pulls it open, hoping to take whoever is beyond by surprise. The loiterer straightens, startled, and Cleves covers the jolt in her stomach with a stiff smile. "Clarice, is it not?" she says.

The Feorwan bows their head. "Your Majesty. My apologies for coming to you like this."

Cleves ushers Clarice into her chamber. "Did any of my people see you?"

"No, I made sure of it."

Seymour's old servant is almost as hunted as Seymour herself, and the people of the Feorwan Isles have born the brunt of Henry's anger over Seymour's betrayal, suffering raid after raid and several punishing taxes that have brought the formerly prosperous isles to famine. There is no shadow of starvation about Clarice, though: their face is round and healthy, their figure as sturdy as Cleves remembers.

"One of your butterflies found me," Clarice says.

It has been a sennight or more since she sent her coded message into the void, care of her most innocuous carrier hawk.

"Where is your mistress?"

"Queen Seymour is in Perfugi. Or she was when I fled."

Cleves goes very still.

"Fled?"

"The dowager queen of Capetia has her."

Cleves swears, a long string of Ezzonidian words that have no direct translation to Elbenese.

"Quite," Clarice says.

"Henry's sister is holding her? You are certain?"

"I saw her taken. Her and the panther."

"And you did not help them? I thought you were supposed to be her protector."

Clarice flushes. "Seymour told me not to. She told me that if anything happened to her, I should inform Queen Howard. I was on my way to do so when your butterfly intercepted my ship."

Cleves closes her eyes and rubs her face. It is too early, and her mind is not working as quickly as it should. She takes deep breaths: Clarice is an ally. Cleves must not lash out at them.

"You must be tired and hungry," she says.

"I am fine."

"Nevertheless."

The servants always leave a jug of purple wine and a bowl of dried fruits in Cleves's chamber so that she can break her fast in solitude. She pours some wine for Clarice, who finishes it in a few gulps.

Cleves swallows. "I am sorry to ask you this but—"

"How do we know she's still alive?" Clarice says.

"Yes."

"Because she must be."

Clarice wipes their eyes on their sleeve, and Cleves turns away, pretending to look at the view from her window. From here she can see a dozen courtyards. The gryphon is dozing, its legs hanging from the tree branch it is balanced upon. The other animals are holed up in their kennels or stables, and the servants are not yet awake. All is still, but for the gentle sway of the trees in a silent wind.

"You should not allow your emotions to cloud your reason," Cleves says.

"If I give in to reason then I will lose my mind entirely."

Better not to have grown so fond in the first place, Cleves thinks. She pours Clarice another goblet of wine and makes them sit.

"If you will not help me, then I will go to Howard as Seymour instructed. And if Howard will not help me, I will return to Perfugi and destroy the city to get her back."

Cleves smiles. "Yes, well, let us not resort to suicide just yet."

Clarice looks at her so fiercely that she almost steps back. "Would you not do anything for the ones you love?"

Cleves laughs. "No one is worth risking your life for, Clarice."

"She is."

Silence falls between them. Cleves feels strangely humbled, even as she pities Clarice for such reckless emotion. She crosses her arms. "Well, before we invade a country, let us sit with reason a while. You saw Cecilia take your mistress and Haltrasc."

Clarice takes another sip of wine. "Yes."

"Did she injure them?"

"No. She had them both shackled and taken back to her palace."

Cleves doesn't ask if Clarice tried to rescue them from the palace. Of course they tried.

"I only know a little of Queen Cecilia, and have never met her. She was in Perfugi already by the time I left Ezzonid to marry Henry. I do know that she is reckless and prideful."

"She's ambitious," Clarice almost spits, as though ambition is a sin.

"So is your mistress, Clarice. She did not become a Queen of Elben by doing nothing. Not if the stories I've heard are to be believed."

It is Clarice's turn to look away, their salt-sun-worn skin flushed.

"She has commissioned a ship," Clarice says after a moment.

Cleves sits on the side of her bed, her elbows resting on her knees. "She is going to return Seymour to Elben."

"To the king."

What little Cleves does know of Cecilia is that she is loyal to nothing but herself and her brother. Such loyalty fascinates Cleves. The way clever people can toss aside their cunning for the sake of something as fragile as love.

"When did the ship leave Perfugi?" She asks.

Clarice smirks. "It had not left by the time I set sail."

"And you had something to do with this?"

"I may have reminded some of the Perfugian sailors of the dowager queen's temper."

Cleves laughs. "Excellent. You have bought us time to think."

"I cannot muster more than my own ship in her defence," Clarice says. "My people . . ."

"They have endured much already for our cause. Yes, I know," Cleves says. It is inconvenient, but she can hardly blame the Feorwans for wishing to protect themselves.

"My ship is fast, but it is not a battleship. And Cecilia was seeking to commission one with cannons. I cannot take it alone."

"Ah, then I must arrange for my fleet of handy warships to storm to the rescue," Cleves says. Clarice scowls: the queens of Elben do not own warships, and they know it.

"If you will not help—"

"When did I say I would not help?"

"You have not said you will."

Cleves cannot help but laugh again. "You are as impetuous as your mistress. I repeat: let me think."

She considers the options as Clarice stomps over to the side table and pours themself yet another cup of wine, downing it while they glower out of the window, as if their gaze could reach across the sea and splinter Cecilia's ship apart. The problem is that no matter which way she turns it, Cleves cannot think of a way to extract Seymour without implicating herself. Without a flotilla at her disposal, the only point to do it would be when they docked or were on the road to High Hall, but that leaves so many variables: for all Cleves knows, Henry is aware that his sister is bringing his errant queen home and plans to be waiting for her on the shore. At that point, Cleves has little hope of retrieving her without being discovered. She has no intention of torching her security before she is ready: she is not Seymour, risking all for a woman who cannot return her love.

Clarice puts her goblet down with a crack, surges forward and kneels in front of Cleves. It is a jarring picture: this Feorwan is not used to supplication.

"If Seymour is going to be on that ship as we believe, then we must intercept it before it docks at Elben. My guess is that I have bought you a matter of weeks only. The winds of the Swegan Sea are in her favour. They will carry her quickly."

Cleves takes Clarice's hand. A pact. Doing as Clarice asks is the only course of action that will protect Cleves as well, but she can make it seem to Clarice that she does it out of affection for Seymour. To have this Feorwan in her debt is no small boon.

"Of course we will rescue her, Clarice."

She stands, bringing Clarice to their feet with her.

"If you will excuse me for a moment, I must send a message to the other queens. They have been concerned for your mistress also," she says. "When I return, we will discuss how to get you back to your ship without being noticed."

As she reaches the door, Clarice says, "I heard something, before she was taken."

Cleves turns, her hand resting on the handle. "What?"

"I was hidden nearby when Cecilia took her. Seymour was going to convince the Perfugian Hleaws to help you. They never opened their sanctuary to her, but there was a voice from inside that said something just before Cecilia's doctrini attacked."

"Do you remember what it said?"

"It was spoken in a strange language. It was not Perfugian."

This makes sense to Cleves, even if it does not to Clarice. The Hleaws in Perfugi are refugees from Elben.

"Likely it was Old Elbenese," she tells the Feorwan. "Can you remember any of the words?"

"I have memorised them as best I could."

Clarice takes a deep breath and closes their eyes, as if summoning a deep spell. "*Lidigarla g restavarla.*"

Cleves wants to write it down, but knows she must not – the parchment might fall into the wrong hands. She summons her own knowledge of Old Elbenese, from her early years on the island, when she sought to understand its traditions. "Let me see. *Garla* means royal, if I understand. Maybe queen? *Resta* is from *retten*, which translates as to go back or return. And *Varla* . . ." Cleves knows she has heard the word before, but she cannot recall its meaning.

"Turret," Clarice says suddenly. "Or – castle? My grandparent used to sing me an Old Elbenese song when I was a child. That was the only word they knew the meaning of. I should have remembered it and connected the two."

"Good," Cleves says. "The queen returns to the castle."

She frowns.

"What is it?" Clarice says.

"There is one word I do not know. *Lidi*. I will consult my books."

They lapse into silence again, both considering the strange voice's instruction. *The queen returns to the castle*. It is so simple. Too simple. Why say it at all?

"Could it be a riddle? The devout are often fond of oblique statements," Cleves says.

Clarice shakes their head. "It was said with urgency. I am sure they were trying to help."

Cleves isn't certain she agrees. For all that she believes in Medren and her divine powers, she refuses to put her whole trust in anyone other than herself. Even the rightly religious can be manipulated. All gods have their schemes. Has Cernunnos's theft of Elben not proven that?

Without another word, she slips out of her chamber. *The queen returns to the castle*. That is a queen's place: their home, their fortress. Cleves is already in hers, and she never intends to leave.

CHAPTER FIFTEEN

Howard

She wakes in Henry's arms. Usually he would be up far earlier than her, leaving her in a mess of sheets to confer with Cromwell or Wolsey, to make plans for foreign expeditions and foreign treaties and political manoeuvres beyond her ken. But this morning her head is still upon his chest. She feels small like this, like a cradled child. But he likes to hold her, and she still wants to please him. She thinks about Voda Kelaverinn's suggestion: *Tell him what you enjoy.*

It is all very easy to say, but to do? She enjoys what her lovers enjoy. Giving them pleasure gives her pleasure. What is wrong with that? Does that not make her the perfect woman?

She shifts in Henry's arms, and the pain that has throbbed gently in her chest ever since his duel with the dragon glances through her like a needle. She has tried not to think on it in the days since the dragon-baiting, for what does dwelling help? She knows what it must mean, of course: he is using her vitality, her youth, her life for his own glory. She knows what Boleyn and Seymour would say to this. Perhaps even Cleves, although she does not know the woman well: how dare he use her so?

They are right. And yet – is this not the pledge she made when she married him? There is a pleasing simplicity in the transaction. If she's honest with herself, the facet of that moment that truly hurts is that he would use her up for sport when he used Boleyn and Aragon and Blount for war. Is her life only worthy of petty conquests?

Goldfoot keens from the adjacent chamber. He never likes to be separated from her but knows well enough now that when the king is at Plythe, he is not permitted to sleep in the same room.

"Your hellfire lapdragon," Henry mumbles, his eyes still closed.

"Mmm," Howard says, nestling deeper into the crook of her husband's arm. Goldfoot keens again, louder this time.

"I'll throttle it," Henry says, turning away from her and drawing the blanket up over his head. She is left, half-naked, half-chilled, on her side of the bed. *I'll throttle it.* Words said by a dozing king are more dangerous than threats shouted by a beggar. She slips from the bed as quietly as she can, sliding her feet into silk slippers. She does not mind the freshness of the morning on her naked body, but she never could abide cold feet.

Her chamber and Henry's are separated by a door concealed within the panelling. It used to creak, which would inevitably lead to Henry calling her back to bed, but she has had it oiled recently. Perhaps it is a small rebellion, but perhaps she is only ever meant for small things: petty conquests, little treasons, sweet ditties sung to a handful of people.

Goldfoot is perched upon the windowsill, snarling at something on the other side of the glass. Sparks hit the lead lattice.

"You must be silent," Howard whispers, closing the partition behind her and holding out her arm for the lapdragon. Goldfoot spreads his wings to their full, not very impressive, width and bares his teeth at the window.

"Are you fighting with your reflection again . . .?" Howard says. Her eyes catch upon the even smaller dragon on the other side of the window . . . and on the paper secured to its leg. She shoos Goldfoot away and lifts the window latch, offering her wrist to the pyttelwyrm. It utters a shrill cry of fear at the prospect of being brought within Goldfoot's range. Such dragons, crossbred long ago with fairies through dark magic, are too flighty to be kept as companions, but they have a fierce sense of direction. She has sometimes wondered whether Goldfoot has a little pyttelwyrm blood in him: his iridescent colouring has something of the fairy about it.

"Hush," she says again, undoing the message as quickly as she can with one hand. As soon as she has it, the pyttelwyrm takes off once more, fleeing the lapdragon. Goldfoot preens his scales, satisfied with his victory.

Howard unfurls the parchment. On it is drawn a complicated cipher. She hates that this was deemed the most effective way of communicating between queens. She struggles with letters when they are separated, never mind when they are intertwined. This one is not so bad: a sun and a moon. No, not a moon: a C. The sun is easy enough to understand: the rays are fully coloured, indicating the sun at its zenith – midday. The C must be: "Cleves," she whispers. Cleves has urgent business with them. Has something happened to her? Or has she had news of Seymour?

Howard must find a way of ensuring privacy from Henry and his household. She has never spoken to the other queens with the king at Plythe. The thought makes her underarms prickle with sweat.

"Howard?" Henry calls from the other room.

"One moment, my king!" Howard says, staring at the paper. How is she going to protect herself? Voda Kelaverinn was the only person in her court who knew of her treachery. He was a safe secret-keeper, his loyalties tied only to her and Boleyn. The others at Plythe? Their ties to Elben run deep. Their fortunes, their families, are owed to the king. Who among them can she ask for help without risking all?

"Howard," Henry calls again, deeper and sharper.

She goes to the little wooden chest that holds the cloths for her monthly courses, prising up the false bottom beneath the fabric. A handful of letters are stowed there – most of them love letters from her childhood, some rare missives from her father. She adds the cipher and replaces the false wood bottom and the cloths, and slips back into Henry's chamber.

The king is sitting up in bed.

"What were you doing?" he says. His injured leg is bent awkwardly. She must be careful.

"Goldfoot was chasing a bee," she says. "I had to let the poor thing out of the window before he caught it."

Henry's eyes crinkle with mirth. "Of course you would wish to save a bee, my dear. You are very soft-hearted. Especially with that badly behaved pet of yours."

Howard does not bother to correct him. When he gave Goldfoot to her as a wedding gift, she tried to show him how much trouble she went to to train the creature, but he did and does prefer to joke about Goldfoot's stupidity. She climbs back into bed and starts to rest her head upon his shoulder, but he manoeuvres her so that she is straddling him.

"Again, Henry?" she says, laughing.

"How can you expect me to keep my hands off of you when you look so delicious?" he says, grinding against her. She laughs again, even as her stomach flutters with panic. She has not been able to conjure the desire, and she is worried that it is starting to show. That his feelings will be hurt. She does not want to make him feel lesser.

She leans down and kisses him, gently, to indicate that she wants to make love slowly. "This is the longest you've ever stayed with me, my king," she says, her lashes fluttering against his cheeks. "Thank you."

He twists to look at her. "Is it truly?"

"I think so."

He strokes her cheek with one hand. The other fondles her breast. "I have not loved you as I should have, Howard. My sweetest of queens. My rose without a thorn."

He kisses her again. A rose without a thorn, she thinks, as she surrenders to him. That is a sweet thing to say. He can be so very kind to her. But then another thought flits through her head: does that not make her incomplete?

Henry does not tire of her until the rest of the court has broken their fast and the golden bells of the palace tower have chimed the tenth hour. He dresses languorously, pausing before he must pull his hose over the bandage on his thigh. Howard is almost out of her mind. She keeps very still in the bed, lest Henry notice how every part of her is desperate to leap from the room. She has two hours. Two hours to fool a friend or confide in them, and she still cannot decide which is safer.

Henry curses under his breath as the hose snags on the bandage. Briefly, the fabric rides up. Howard bites her lip to keep from crying out. The flesh beneath the bandage is grey and seething, a dark reflection of the Kyttle Falls far below. Is it the play of light in this room that makes the wound appear like a tangle of shadowy maggots? Or is Henry's stolen power at war with Boleyn's prophecy?

Henry glances at her, and she quickly closes her eyes. He would not want her to have seen that.

"Do not pretend with me, Howard," he says. "I have had enough of that with my wives."

The little bird in her chest flutters, trying to escape, as she sits up. She is his rose without a thorn. She must be so very soft and smooth. She thinks of her father and her aunt towards the end, when they were in one of their moods. She had to thread honesty through compliments then too, or face their wrath.

"You have not wanted me to ask about it before, my king. I did not know whether you would want me to now," she says. She focuses on the beading of her blanket, pressing copper and amethyst balls into the pads of her thumbs.

"She was a witch," Henry says.

Howard is about to reference Boleyn when she remembers that she is not supposed to know that Boleyn caused the wound. Howard was never there, on that cliff beside the folly at Brynd. As far as Henry knows, no one witnessed Boleyn's bow-work, and the path of her arrow, except Henry and Boleyn herself. No one has publicly acknowledged the injury. Howard almost incriminated herself.

"Who?"

She has never noticed before how small his eyes are. Were they always so, or is this some change in his physique? Or is it that he has never watched her with such suspicion? She is a rose. She opens the petals of her face towards him, as though he is the sun.

"Boleyn, who else?" he spits.

She flutters a hand to her face. "Truly? She did this? So the rumours were true?"

"They usually are."

The bird inside her squeals to be released. She has heard the rumours surrounding her. That she is a whore, loose, a slut, a penny tart, mouth open, legs wide, an easy cunt. She may have no thorns of her own, but she wears those names, pricked under her skin. Mostly she is numb to them, but they will nick her from time to time. In this moment, though, they sear. *They usually are.* It is another test.

She crawls towards him. There is a draught coming from one of the windows, and goosebumps rise on her arms. She wills them warm: Henry must not suspect that they mean fear.

"What are you doing?" he says.

She kneels beside his leg. Delicately, she takes the hose from his hands and pulls it back down.

"Howard—"

The bandage is covering the injury now, and she truly does not want to look at it again. A thick odour of sour milk and iron emanates from beneath the fabric. But she cannot hold her breath, or he will see. Before she doubts herself, she unties the knots and lets the bandage fall away.

It is worse than she could have imagined. There is no blood, no muscle or bone, only a roiling twist of divine power, as if Henry had consumed the bordweal and robbed it of its bruising colour, turning it so purple it is almost ebony.

"It hurts you, my king," she says, trying to breathe through her mouth.

"It's blasted agony."

She frames the opening in her hands, dips her head and licks it. It coats her tongue in bitter rot.

"Howard," Henry says again, half wonder, half repulsion.

She stays there, nose and tongue inside him, for as long as she can bear. It is not so different from when men have held her head over their cocks and pushed them down her throat. At least this time she is the one doing the penetrating. She almost smiles: this is savagery. This is a kind of veiled vengeance.

When she can be sure she will not retch, she pulls back and looks up at her husband. The taste of him is still in her mouth, and she wonders whether her face is coated in the deep purple of his flesh as well.

For a while, it feels as though the two of them are frozen like that. The supplicant and the divine, neither knowing which is which.

"It is your god," Henry says. She hears the true question. It is always the same question. Her father asked it too, with different words. *Do you forgive me? Do you still love me? Does the cruelty of my body not repulse you?*

"Yes," she says. Prickle. Prickle.

CHAPTER SIXTEEN

Howard

She emerges from Henry's chamber like a peacock. Her gown is the colour of the bordweal, her headdress a fan of diamonds, perched atop her curls. Goldfoot balances on her shoulder, his claws digging into the stretch of muscle there. The bird inside her is quiet now. Quiet; not slumbering or cowed as it usually is in such moments, but watchful.

This certainty is a rare and passing gift, and she grasps it tightly.

Her ladies are gathered already. She comes upon them in her receiving chamber, kneeling as if at prayer around the expanse of silk she chose for Mary Boleyn's wedding gift. She pauses in the doorway, watching them. Ursula, quietly stealing pearls from Lady Tylney's pile, waiting for her to notice the prank. Her half-sister Legh, the girl she grew up alongside; both chain and anchor. Lady Tylney, older than the rest of them, yet somehow more fragile than all. And Susanna Horenbolt, the watchful artist, richer in mind and poorer in upbringing.

The distance between her and them feels almost insurmountable, just as it does between her and the other queens. Do they feel it too, with each other? They do nothing but talk all day, and yet Howard realises, in this moment, that she hardly knows them at all.

Goldfoot takes flight. He arches across the room and lands with a mewl beside Susanna. Without looking up from her embroidery, she scoops him into her lap and continues her work. They are an idyll of domesticity. Goldfoot peers at Howard from between Susanna's arms. He has answered the question Howard had been asking herself.

"Susanna, I must talk with you," she says. The women look up in unison.

"Me, Your Majesty?"

"Come."

The silence becomes a living thing as Susanna tidies away her thimble and needle, her thread and her little silver scissors. The other women go back to their work, studiously not looking at each other. There will be whispers as soon as Howard and Susanna are out of earshot. If a king's whisper is a threat, a queen's favourite is a hleope, a piece in a game of oferhlep, to be jumped over or, better yet, eliminated.

Goldfoot, twisting in sunstruck dust, leads Howard and Susanna across the gallery and into a courtyard nestled in a horseshoe of rooms at the centre of the palace. In its middle is an unassuming fountain: a woman in a gown of ancient fashion, standing in the midst of the four famed sounds of Plythe – a whale, a litharbird with its coral feathers and honey song, a selkie and a pyttelwyrm. From each of them spouts a perfect arc of saltwater, pumped up from the river below. If she had not been brought to that very spot on her wedding day, she would not have known that this is, in truth, the heart of Plythe, for the woman's cupped hands are crafted from the spirit stone of the palace. Four years later and she still finds extraordinary peace from remembering that communion of flesh and rock.

Howard bypasses the fountain and goes to a slender stone balcony, its struts decorated with birds and fish. She leans upon it, inhaling the spray from the Kyttle Falls below. Susanna stands, hands folded upon her kirtle, at a distance.

"I need your help," Howard says, quietly so that Susanna is forced to come closer.

"Mine?"

Howard takes one of Susanna's hands in her own. She draws the lady closer, and despite the rage of the falls whispers in her ear, "At midday I am going to be in the music room. I need you to ensure that no one knows that I am there, and that no one disturbs me. Not even the king himself. Do you understand?"

She hardly dares to look at Susanna's expression. Her certainty ebbed away with her words, for it's only now that she truly comprehends what she is asking of her lady.

Susanna's silence is a mirror to Howard's unease.

"May I know why?" Susanna says at last.

Howard is prepared for this question. She does not like to lie – for part of her wants to tell her ladies everything, to trust in their loyalty, and maybe one day she will be at liberty to do so – but nor can she risk the safety of Seymour and the other queens by telling the truth. And while Susanna is the least likely to share a secret, Howard knows only too well the way such morsels of information can be bartered for popularity.

"I wish to study uninterrupted."

Susanna's mouth forms a silent "O". "And you do not want me to tell anyone?" she says.

"If you must, then you must. But I . . . I do not want everyone to pity me, or to think me ridiculous for attempting to teach myself. They all thought me stupid for employing Voda Kelaverrin. They think me beyond hope and I don't want them to laugh if they are proved right."

Goldfoot croons into her ear. She cannot look Susanna in the eye. It is both wrong and a relief, this peeling open of a truth to cover deceit. Susanna's hand jerks, as though she wants to comfort Howard. Howard cannot remember the last time she was held by another woman.

"I will do my best for you, Your Majesty," Susanna says.

"You can pick any of my gowns," Howard says. It is the smallest of thanks for what Susanna is doing, though she does not know it.

Susanna colours and looks away. "I serve you without expectation of gifts."

There is an unspoken end to her words. Howard is certain that she wants to say more.

"Is there something else you would wish for?"

The blush deepens. Below them, a shout goes up from a boat that has missed its mooring.

"I only wonder . . . might you stop the other ladies from teasing me?" Susanna says. "I know that I am awkward compared to all of you. I know that my love of painting is not womanly, but I . . ."

She trails off, her eyes flickering between Howard and the stones upon which they stand. The little bird inside Howard's chest flutters. Susanna seeks a protector, but that has never been Howard's role. How could it be? No one looks at Howard and sees a guardian. They see only the thornless rose, the frightened songbird. She is so small: how could she possibly protect Susanna?

Howard envisions scolding her half-sister Legh, or her elder, Lady Tylney. She cannot imagine either of them accepting a rebuke from their young queen.

But she needs Susanna's help. She is out of time.

"I will try," Howard says, hoping that she does not sound too faltering. She expects a smile, words of gratitude. She does not expect Susanna to burst into tears.

"Hush, Susanna," Howard says, appalled.

"I am sorry," Susanna sobs.

Goldfoot croons from Howard's shoulder. He wants her to comfort the woman, but Howard is utterly unequipped for this display of weakness. When she was a child and sharing a chamber with her aunt's other wards, to cry was to invite cruelty. She is about to say as much, when Susanna presses the heels of her hands into her eyes and says, "I have just been so very lonely."

The bird in Howard's chest emits a single cry, and is still.

Has she not thought the same after every encounter with the other queens? Has she not felt lonely, in a way, her entire life?

Maybe solitude in the midst of company is not simply the way of things, as she had thought.

She embraces Susanna, holding the other woman's head to her shoulder. If the position is awkward for Susanna, who is after all taller than Howard by nearly a head, then she shows no sign of it. She clings to her queen, her hands clawing at her back.

"You are not alone," Howard whispers. The waterfall below them might know whether she speaks to herself or her lady: *she* does not.

In her music room, she lays cushions at the foot of the door and stuffs scraps of fabric inside the keyhole. Susanna may be keeping watch outside, but Howard cannot risk her overhearing talking through the *sunscína*.

The sun is directly opposite this room at midday, so that when the harpsichord is open, the curved glass of the *sunscína* reflects the light onto the walls and ceiling, turning the mahogany to rainbow. On the other side of the window, she can hear the sleep-inducing trickle of water from the fountain in the courtyard.

When she presses the *sunscína*, Cleves, Parr and Aragon are already there, and in the middle of a heated discussion.

"How can we be certain she has not betrayed us?" Aragon is saying. "She has done so before to secure her future."

"And you have never betrayed anyone yourself?" Cleves replies. Usually she clouds her insults in jest and smiles, but not this time. Her hair, usually a little wild, is now positively unkempt. Howard tries to interrupt, to ask what has happened. Only Parr notices.

"Queen Seymour has been taken," she says, and even she is louder than usual – normally Howard has to lean in to hear her. Parr tells Howard what Cleves has already told them, while the other two queens glare at each other.

"We must rescue her," Howard says, as soon as Parr has finished.

"I have an idea—" Cleves begins, but Aragon interrupts her.

"It seems to me that we must first ascertain how much Henry knows," she says. She turns her gaze to Howard. "He has been staying with you for some time, has he not? Is this because he is waiting for his sister's arrival, or for another reason?"

Howard bites her lip. "Cromwell and Wolsey are here as well. He is with them now, but I did not hear them talk of the Dowager Queen Cecilia."

"When did he arrive?" Cleves asks.

"A fortnight ago, shortly after we last spoke," Howard says.

"There has been enough time for her to send a message to Henry telling him of her conquest," Parr says.

Howard says, "I did wonder why he has stayed so long at Plythe. He has never done so before. It would be like him to not confide in me on such matters."

An awkward silence falls upon the group. Eventually Parr says, "Since the Moon Ball, he has only stayed with two women for any length of time. You and Mary Boleyn."

She says this as though it provides an answer, but Howard cannot work it out. Aragon tuts. "The youngest of us and the woman who has already birthed a son to her previous husband. Understand?"

Howard's mouth forms an "O". That explains why he has been more amorous also.

"Of course," she says quietly. "I have been very stupid."

"It helps that you are also very beautiful and very sweet," Cleves says softly. Howard laughs unsteadily. "Yes, I am a rose without a thorn. But we were discussing how to help Queen Seymour."

Aragon shakes her head. "I know Cecilia of old, and my contacts tell me she has changed little. Her most treasured weapon is shock.

Mark me, she will want to arrive in Elben without prior warning and produce Seymour like a magic trick."

"That is good," Parr says, "It will give us time to study the currents of the Swegan Sea, and to pray for Medren's help."

"Could Cecilia's silence be bought?" Cleves says.

Aragon snorts, and the sound is so unqueenly that Howard has to turn away to hide her smirk. "You may buy her for an hour, or a day, but you will have no assurance of her continued loyalty."

"And Henry is her brother," Howard says. She does not want to be silent through this conversation, even though she has little to offer in the way of stratagems.

"That is true, sister," Parr says, although it feels like a pat on the head.

"Then can we exert our influence elsewhere?" Cleves says. "We may not be able to match Cecilia's warship on the ocean, but I could pay someone to intercept them the moment they step foot on the shore."

This seems like a risky plan to Howard, to leave the act until the last possible moment, but she does not like to say so.

"Perhaps I could rescue her," Howard says. "If they are docking at Swegan then . . ."

She peters out.

Parr says, "It is too dangerous. I think we must exhaust our other options first."

Howard looks out to the courtyard, and as the queens continue to argue the best course of action, she listens to the lullaby of the Kyttle Falls through glass. Somewhere beyond that window, beyond the falls, beyond Kywsa Bay, Seymour is caged. How tangled are her feelings, caught between homesickness and the knowledge of her assured death? Howard has never left Elben, though she likes the thought of adventure, loves the idea of bone-built Perfugi and the royal cities of Quisto with their streets of baked terracotta. But she doesn't think it would take long for her to miss the sound of water, or the smell of dew-steeped flowers on a spring morning. She would miss looking up at the night sky and catching the glimmer of the bordweal against the stars.

"There is one course of action we have not considered," Aragon says.

"What is that?" Cleves asks.

Aragon places each word like a stepping stone: heavy, yet somehow inevitable.

"We could do nothing."

At first Howard thinks she must have misheard. But then Cleves laughs scornfully.

"Are you hoping to pick us off one by one, sister?" she says.

"Not at all." Howard might think that Aragon was bored, if it weren't for the reddening of her cheeks. "I am not denying that it would be a great blow to lose Queen Seymour. She has provided us with invaluable information these last several moons. But it is naive to imagine that we can wrest Elben from Henry without some sacrifices. Did not Queen Boleyn teach us as much?"

"Boleyn would still be alive but for you," Howard says impulsively. She is too loud, and looks to the door where Susanna stands guard. Could her voice have carried through the oak?

"Boleyn understood that in a game such as this, sometimes the loss of a queen is the only way to win," Aragon says.

Howard closes her eyes. She sees that moment as fresh as though it just happened. The way Boleyn stepped into nothingness. Her trailing fall beyond the cliff, and then the open sky and the bruise of the bordweal on the horizon.

"Boleyn chose to die," Cleves says. "Seymour has not, as far as we know. I am not suggesting that we put ourselves in direct danger for her sake, but if we do nothing then how can we hope to work together in good faith?"

"I agree, sister," Parr says.

Aragon sneers. "Then offer me a solution that stands a chance of success."

Howard gasps. "I know—" she begins.

"Could one of your nephew's warships be conscripted to take Cecilia?" Cleves says. "Or are you only willing to sacrifice your sisters?"

"I might ask you the same of your royal brother in Ezzonid," Aragon replies.

"I think—" Howard tries again. She dare not speak too loudly for fear of Susanna overhearing. She stamps her foot. Why will they not listen?

"Let us take some time to consult our books and think on a different way," Parr is saying.

"With what time?" Cleves says.

"Please—" Howard says. Then the other three are talking over each other. It is no use. Howard rises from her stool and goes to the far wall. She presses one hand on the tapestry that covers the panelling. It was a wedding gift from her aunt, and once hung in the chamber she shared with Legh and the other wards. The thread has been worn and bleached over many decades, but the girls used to run their hands over the embroidery of the qilin with its graceful body and elegant horn and mournful eyes. When they were children, they would spin tales of how they would break the creature free from the wooden cage that surrounded it. Tales of uncommon bravery and magic that could never work in reality.

"Sister? Howard?" Cleves says.

"I am still here," Howard says. She returns to her seat at the harpsichord.

"You were trying to tell us something and we were babbling," Cleves says.

"It was nothing. A childish idea."

"All the more reason for us to hear it, then," Parr says. "For children can sometimes spy paths that older eyes cannot."

Howard feels as she did the day Boleyn gifted her that book of poetry. The gift of *more*. The gift of *greater*. But she must earn it.

"We could use the bordweal," she says. Then, lest she lose her mettle, she continues without watching the queens' reactions. She works at her gown as she talks, pressing silver silk through trembling fingers.

"I do not know how. Perhaps it is not possible, but the Moon Ball showed us that we *can* use Medren's power, did it not? If we could find a way of communing with the bordweal, then could we not turn it against Cecilia and her ship?"

Outside the door, footsteps thump. Susanna says a few muffled words to someone, and the footsteps recede. In the distance, the bells of Sweillan's sanctuaries toll the half hour. If Howard looks up, she will see the queens' derision.

"Howard," Cleves says softly. She draws her eyes to the *sunscína*. Parr is smiling the way a mother might. Aragon's head is tilted as she watches Howard. And Cleves: Cleves is grinning.

"I do not know how we might make it work either, but it is a good idea, sister," Cleves says.

"I will consult my library," Parr says.

"I also," Aragon says. "To understand how to wield the bordweal would be a powerful move indeed."

Howard tempers her bubbling joy. She does not want them to see how much their approval means to her. "Very well, sisters. I will also study my books," she says.

And like that, they are united in purpose. Aragon looks away, towards a window, bleak sunlight coating her face. "We must consult quickly. With a fair wind behind them, Cecilia and Seymour will reach Elben's bordweal in three days."

"Three days, then," Cleves says. "Three days to riddle Elben's most ancient power and save a queen. How hard can it be?"

CHAPTER SEVENTEEN

Cecilia

The ship is a glorious vessel, a true Perfugian galleon with a hull crafted from dragon bone. No wooden ships can dock in Perfugi's harbour: the lava and the mountain's natural heat would melt the tar and set fire to the wood. The secret to making the old dragon bone vessels is closely guarded by the people of Perfugi; not all the spies in the known world have been able to gain the knowledge, for to do so would be to open the city to foreign invasion, the only other way of entering it being across a slim strip of land, easily defended. Cecilia knows something of the paranoia of small kingdoms. She grew up in one, after all.

As Cecilia's galleon passes the harbour designated for foreign ships – a man-made island a league away from Perfugi itself – she rifles through her letters. More has sent another missive since his one warning of Seymour's arrival. She has not told anyone of her return to Elben. Oh, to see their faces when she steps foot on those shores with their traitor queen shackled and her murderous beast cowed. But there is something odd about More's words this time that she cannot quite fathom.

> I do not always agree with them, but the king surrounds himself with men of impressive mind and spirit. There is a blight, a plague come upon this land, my dear. I am glad you are not here to witness its spread. We may yet prevail, however. Cromwell has

discovered something in my vast library at Pilvreen that may save us all, and the soul of this dear island of ours. It will require courage and strength that I do not know if I possess, but for Elben, for your good brother and for our great God, I am willing to make the attempt.

Cecilia frowns. The plague must refer to Seymour and her notions about the goddess Medren, but what can he mean about the test of strength? There is something portentous about the letter that she does not like. When she looks up from the parchment, the waves are jostling for room between her ship and a lone sail from the Feorwan Isles, which – even as she watches – overtakes them. Those mercenaries of knowledge move swiftly upon the oceans. On the other side of the ship, they pass a trail of smaller bone boats which carry goods between the foreign harbour and the city. Rich silks and velvets, strange spices and jewels with the light of stars within them. Cecilia moves around the deck, wanting to keep the city in view for as long as possible before she faces the unknown of a homeland she has not set foot upon in more than a decade.

The tempestuous mountain upon which Perfugi sits is a flower rusting from the earth, petals of fierce orange breaking through the softer reflection of the sunset on the grey rock that crackles between the lava flows. The city spreads in alabaster tears down its slopes. Cecilia can spy her own palace nestled near the base in the safer, wealthier district. She dashes errant dampness from her cheek.

She recognises Florin's light footsteps, even above the ocean winds. "Her Majesty is weeping," he says. He stands beside her, his eyes downcast. He has been appropriately attentive since the day he ruined her pleasure-taking.

"Do you think me silly?" she says.

"Never, *nes mihohle*," he says. *My ruler-of-the-heart*. She likes the irony that for a country superficially preoccupied with equality, Perfugi's language has so many words denoting authority. She likes, too, these moments of softness between them.

"I will miss its deadly beauty," she says.

"If you were a city," he says, as she knows he will, as he knows he must.

She pats the balustrade next to her, permitting him to lean on it at her side.

"Your palace was the first thing you owned that was entirely yours, was it not?" he says.

"Do not pretend to know me," she says. She is no common lady. She has always owned her own wealth.

"I sometimes think I shall die trying to know you," he says.

She brushes a strand of hair, buffeted by the wind, from her face, and arches her head in a way that she knows shows off her jaw and neck. Florin is watching her worshipfully. She is rather fond of him. She turns her back on Perfugi and pulls him closer, strokes his smooth cheek.

"I am sorry for what happened to Lorena," she says.

His face tightens, but then he nods. Good. She will suffer no more theatrics, and he has learned the lesson. Now that he is more conciliatory, she is beginning to see a way to solve her other problem, for she knows that Seymour is still hiding something from her, and the knowledge itches. "Besides, it was not I who killed her. I gave the Lady Seymour a choice. It was her and her creature who chose to deliver the final blow."

Florin looses a great breath, then nods. His fist is clenched. She almost has him. Perhaps just one more little tip. She kisses him full on the mouth, long and slow as he prefers. When they part, she whispers into his ear, "I miss her also. I wish only that her death will not be in vain."

She walks away. As she goes, she flicks a hand to the nearest servant. "Make sure that our prisoner is fed, do you understand?"

Once out of sight, she trips down the stairs which lead into the ship's bowels. She takes one of the servants' passages, narrow and gloomy, all the way down. The Lady Seymour is being kept in a windowless cabin in the hold. Her room abuts a space reserved for the provisions they will need for the voyage. Cecilia climbs in among the barrels of grain and pushes aside cured meats hanging from the ceiling. She sits on a sack of flour and finds the whorl in the wall that affords her a limited view of the space within; something she had made sure of before requisitioning the ship.

Seymour sits upright on her pallet bed, dressed in the simple green gown in which she was captured. Her eyes are closed, and her hands are holding onto the hem of her gown. Cecilia frowns. It seems as though the hem is solid beneath her fingers.

Before Cecilia can ponder this, heavy footsteps on the main stairs indicate that someone is coming. They pass by Cecilia's hiding place.

Florin is carrying a tray of bread and cheese. The boy is so very obliging. So very predictable.

He enters the room without ceremony, barely looking at Seymour. She opens her eyes as he places the tray in front of her on the rush-covered floor.

"Who was she to you?" she says.

"What?" Florin is taken aback. He steps away from her, as though suspecting witchcraft.

"You have the same forehead as the woman my panther killed. That, and you look as though you would gladly stick that cheese knife in my eye."

Florin's mouth twitches.

"She was my sister."

"I see."

"Are you not going to apologise to me?"

"Why should I? Your sister was trying to kidnap me."

"It was her job."

"Then she should have worked for someone other than Cecilia Tudor. I am sorry for your grief but I will not apologise for something that was not my fault."

Florin snorts, turns away from her. Cecilia thinks he might actually take the knife and stick it in her eye, and the thought makes her heart race.

"You sound exactly like her."

"Your sister?"

"Cecie." There is a strange timbre to his voice, like a creaking oak about to topple. Cecilia doesn't know how to read it, nor does she like him shortening her name. It's entirely inappropriate for royalty. Is that how he and Lorena referred to her when not in her hearing? Like an equal, or a pet?

Seymour begins to laugh. She's such a strange woman – she gives the impression of being a slip of a thing, a waif, until you realise that she is taller than most men. She should be quailing.

"What do you find so amusing?" Florin says.

"I am thinking of my husband, that is all," Seymour replies, wiping tears from one cheek. Her other hand, Cecilia notes, still rests on the peculiarly stiff part of her gown's hem.

"What of him?"

"He has a way of charming brilliant women to fall in love with him despite his many glaring faults. I thought it was a quirk of the divine power he stole, but now I see it is simply a family trait."

Florin and she look at each other for a moment, he standing over her. He breaks the silence. "Are you calling me a brilliant woman, lady?"

"There are worse things to be called, sir," she says.

"I know that. I was raised by one. The one you killed."

Cecilia shifts in her seat, pressing her eye closer to the whorl. This isn't how she expected their confrontation to play out. Her calculations had led her to believe that either it would become heated and violent, or that Seymour's ridiculous morality would lead her to share information with Florin through guilt. This is unanticipated, but not unwelcome. Has she not always known that hate and love are the two most persuasive emotions? And here she has accidentally stumbled upon both. A fascinating concoction.

Florin sits next to Seymour on the pallet and grimaces. "Gods, this is uncomfortable."

"I have slept on worse."

"It is driving Cecie mad that she knows so little about you and where you have been."

Cecilia curses Florin silently. He does not know it, did not even mean it as a question, but it is enough to put Seymour on her guard. She draws away from him. Too direct, imbecile. Florin has not noticed, though, for he continues blithely, "This story of magic and gods and palaces. I don't know what to think."

"What religion do you follow?" Seymour asks.

"I follow my mistress," he says. "She is my god and goddess, my emperor and empress, my king, my home, my heartbeat and breath."

Cecilia draws away from the whorl, winded. It is good, this adoration he shows her. So why does she squirm on her seat? Just because she does not return his feelings does not mean she deprives him.

"It is excruciating to love so fully, is it not?" Seymour says.

"You have a goddess too?"

"I used to."

"Would you have died for her?"

Seymour closes her eyes, then breathes out. "I did, and have done, much else for her. But no, I will never die for her. If I die, it will be for me."

"Then we are not the same."

Cecilia looks through the whorl again. The wall between her and them is not only physical now. She wants to pry these two open, to extract the meaning of this impossibly oblique conversation. They seem to be talking of love, which she understands in a theoretical way, but the weight of their words, the way they do not look at each other and yet sit the same way, suggests there is more to their meaning that she cannot decipher.

"I will never again worship a deity that demands my body and soul," Seymour says. "I do not think any god has that right."

"If you knew Cecie—"

"I know her kind. Grasping for a power that does not belong to them because they lack substance within themselves. How old are you?" Seymour says. Cecilia rolls her eyes and Florin bristles.

"Why ask such a question?"

"You put me in mind of someone I met once or twice; that is all."

"Do they desire your death also?" Florin says. Is he flirting? Cecilia will have his tongue.

"Is she going to kill me on this ship, or let her brother have that pleasure?" Seymour says.

"She wants one of Elben's castles, that is all. And she will use you to get it in whatever way she deems fit. Don't we all desire our very own sanctuary?"

Seymour regards him coolly. "I repeat, sir: is she going to kill me on this voyage?"

Florin takes a deep breath. "Cecie has a reputation. She likes having that reputation. And death does not disturb her the way it may a normal person. But she does not kill unless it serves a purpose."

"So her brother will do it, then," Seymour says. She leans back against the wall of the cell, closes her eyes and smiles.

"You may leave now," she tells Florin.

He stands, looking down at her. "You are strange, lady, to smile at the thought of your own death."

"Yes, I am very strange. Goodbye, my lord."

Cecilia shifts her angle to study Seymour. She remains like that, still and smiling, long after Florin has gone, long after the rats emerge from the shadows to sup on the bread and cheese he brought her. Something about Seymour's questions niggles at Cecilia. She had no regard for what might happen to her once they reach Elben. All her concern was for the voyage. *Why?*

It hits her then. Seymour is not concerned about their arrival, because she knows that someone – either on the ship or beyond – knows where she is and intends to help her escape. Cecilia sits back on the sack. What an excellent, excellent game.

CHAPTER EIGHTEEN

Cleves

Three days

Cleves's library is ill-equipped for telling her of the magic of Elben. Her knowledge is rudimentary. When she came from Ezzonid, she had learned only what was necessary. Her focus was and is ever on the matters she can influence. Divine power had never helped them much in Ezzonid. How could the immortal ever be expected to have compassion for the transient?

By the time she began to wonder if she was wrong, it was too late. She was a finished sculpture, a dry oil painting. Her talents and interests lie in the practical. She was and is and will be this way.

She writes a list to impose some order upon her thoughts:

What exactly is the bordweal?
How might we control it?

These two questions feel insufficient, so she adds one that has nothing to do with the matter at hand, but nevertheless may be significant:

What is the meaning of lidi?

The word that neither she nor Clarice could translate from the ancient Elbenese. The missing meaning spoken from the Medrenkynd's sanctuary in Perfugi: *The queen returns to the castle.*

At least that is easily solved, for she does have a primer of Old Elbenese in her collection. Her library sits in a turret in the third courtyard of Cnothan. She can see it from the window of her study: two towers standing side by side like stern old men conversing.

Lelij trips at her heels with his uneven gait as she passes through the pigs' paddock to reach it. The animals, thinking she is there to feed them, crowd around her, shoving their snouts into her hands and nuzzling at Lelij's scaled body.

"You were fed not an hour ago," she says, slapping their hairy backs to make them move. She has to lift Lelij out of their throng entirely, and the two of them reach the door at the base of the tower ruffled and smelling of shit.

Cnothan's library is not a single room, but a stairway that spirals up and up, every wall lined with books and punctuated with windows. Wealthy Elbenese and Quistoans have a habit of lighting every room with lantern dragons, even libraries where such a tradition is positively dangerous. It seems like an unhealthy obsession, this tendency to cage animals in small spaces for their entire lives. It is one of the many reasons Cleves dislikes staying at High Hall – Henry may hear only pretty ditties from the songbirds he keeps there, but she hears pleas. The particular cruelty of hanging those cages beside the windows, so that the birds can see freedom but never attain it. In any case, Cleves will have none of it at Cnothan. She brought with her from Ezzonid a great number of viggas: blocks of pebbled sap from the vinogl tree, which feeds on starlight. The glowing amber is set in brass struts nailed into the shelves. They cast a pooling light, like sun in a forest.

Cleves selects an armful of books as she climbs, and emerges at the apex of the turret into a round reading room studded with views of the sea, where the amber stones' clouded light gives way to clear, cold daylight.

"Well met, cousin," a voice says from the single reading chair, which faces away from the stairs.

"You become more like my animals every day, Johana, following me around after scraps," she says. She quietly slides the books she was carrying into an alcove, where she hopes he will not see them.

Johana stands and makes a grand gesture of surrendering the chair to her.

"On the contrary, dear cousin. I have no interest in scraps. I enjoy a full belly."

He saunters to the top of the staircase, and bends to examine the pile of books she secreted in the alcove. Her heart stills. He will see the titles engraved upon the spines: all of them examinations of Elben's history and ancient language. Surely he will not know, from those alone, what she seeks?

"Hmm," he says. It is quite remarkable how Johana can imbue a single sound with so much meaning. Pleasantry; a question; an assurance; a hint of a taunt. Then he is gone, whistling an old Ezzonid tune as he wends his way down the stairs. She shivers. The last time she heard that tune, it was used as a lullaby to drown out the sound of battle.

Two days

"Heart," she mutters to herself for the hundredth time. The unknown word – *lidi* – spoken from the Medrenkynd's sanctuary was *heart*. *A queen returns to her castle's heart.* Perhaps it means nothing. Most likely, it means nothing. But if it means nothing, why speak it so urgently through a locked door to an exiled Queen of Elben? Even if Seymour could return to Elben safely, Hyde is lost, broken, its ruins flooded. She is a queen without a castle.

Cleves presses the side of her fist into the surface of her desk. She should be turning her attention to the bordweal, yet she cannot rid her mind of those words. A *queen returns to her castle's heart.* Maybe it is because she cannot conceive of leaving Cnothan, let alone destroying it as Seymour did Hyde. This castle *is* her heart.

She spies movement in the courtyard outside her study's window, and curses.

"If you are seeking to leave, I will gladly provide you with a ship, cousin," she says moments later, staring up at Johana as he clambers up a crumbling series of stones which protrude from the highest wall of Cnothan; a makeshift and dangerous set of steps up to the battlements.

"I would not dream of leaving you, Your Majesty," he calls out, catching his cloak beneath his foot and almost toppling over the edge. "I merely wanted to find the best view of your bordweal."

"You will break your neck, you *droltz*. Come back down and I will show you a safer route."

"Oh, thank the gods," Johana says, returning to the ground with the relief of a sailor reaching land after a tempest.

"Why do you wish to see the bordweal so urgently?" Cleves asks as she leads him away from curious servants to an inconspicuous wooden door at the base of the castle walls.

"It reminds me of home," he says.

"Indeed. Has Ezzonid acquired Cernunnos's protection since my marriage? Do you have your own bordweal now?"

They climb a narrow flight of steps and emerge through a trapdoor onto the battlements.

"No, no, Elben remains its own very special little kingdom," Johana says. Did she dream it or did he place an unnatural emphasis on *king*? "It puts me in mind of your royal mother's obsession, after . . . the *Tilhepf*."

They look together over the battlements, across the sea, where on a sunny day the coasts of Lothair and Capetia can be seen as a grey line on the horizon. Today, clouds obscure that view, but the bordweal remains, an ever-watchful cloak surrounding the island. Was it always the colour of a dying bruise, or did it only become so when Cernunnos wrested control of it from Medren?

She does not want to talk about her mother's frenzy in the aftermath of the *Tilhepf*. It was one of the reasons Cleves was content to accept when her late father told her that Henry was interested in marriage.

"Does she still have that chamber full of relics?" Cleves asks Johana, nudging him and grinning. They can laugh over his foolish aunt together. But he offers her only the ghost of a smile.

"She is quite dedicated to crafting protections for our family. She is a very knowledgeable woman, you know, cousin. She has taught me much these last moons."

Cleves goes still, keenly aware of Johana's probing gaze. Is he trying to tell her that he can help her? That he has the knowledge she requires? She opens her mouth, but the only sound that comes out is a laugh. He may be willing to help her now – her kingly brother, too – but at what price? And what danger would she place Johana in if she were to confide all in him?

Best to attempt it by herself. No confessions.

"And what exactly did my mother teach you?" she says.

Johana shakes his head as he turns back towards the stairs. "No, no, dear cousin. I do not accept scraps, remember?"

One day

Her horse master leans in the doorway of her study, his arms crossed. "A Perfugian ship has been sighted a day's sail from the bordweal, Your Majesty," he says.

"I see. Probably a trade vessel. Any others?"

He shakes his head and she dismisses him. Her people are accustomed to her asking strange questions and making unusual requests. He did not show the slightest curiosity when she asked him ever so casually to let her know what vessels were passing close to her territory. Eccentricity makes for an excellent disguise.

If only it made an excellent teacher, also.

None of them have made headway in their pursuit of knowledge about the bordweal. The lack of cyphers sent by pyttelwyrm confirms it, for even sending the smallest of dragons is risky and they cannot afford to communicate unless they absolutely must.

Her thoughts stray to Johana. He wants to be her confidant. If he truly has the knowledge she needs – if her mother did find more than empty relics and thin superstition – then she has a choice: risk her secrets for a chance to save Seymour, or protect herself and let Seymour die.

She sneered at Aragon for even asking the question. Is she, Cleves, as cold, as selfish as the Queen of Daven?

The thump of blood, of soldiers' armour, throbs through her as she summons a servant and tells them to fetch Johana. He arrives too quickly, as though he has been waiting nearby. It suggests that she is predictable, and predictability when one is plotting treason is a hangman's noose.

They sit opposite each other, and wait for the servant's footsteps to recede.

"Everything?" she says at last.

"A full meal, cousin. A feast."

"And in return?"

He leans back and looks away from her, towards the wall where their family crest is painted in stately fashion: a castle upon a green field rampant.

"You were the first person to know that I would never marry a woman. And I the first person to know that you would never take a man to your bed. Yet now we bargain for each other's secrets."

Her throat is thick. He looks back at her.

"In return you will have everything I can offer, cousin. The loyalty and help of myself, such as it is, and of your mother, and of your sisters, and of your brother."

"The king himself?" Cleves says. Her brother is a wall of a man, in body and mind. They used to jest that she stole his laughter from him when he was a babe in the cradle.

"If you do not believe it is love, cousin, then believe it is strategy."

This makes sense to her. If her brother has heard rumours of the truth of Medren and Elben's castles, then naturally he would prefer his sister to rule the territory of Cnothan outright rather than relying on Henry's favour.

An image of Boleyn, teetering at the edge of that cliff at Brynd, rises to her mind. Cleves cannot understand why she had to jump, yet she admires that she did. She knew, Cleves realises, and Aragon knows, that one cannot spark a revolution with only a single kindling.

So she tells him everything, from Seymour's first visit to that strangest of evenings when Medren's power flowed around her as she danced, to the predicament she and the other queens now find themselves in. Johana listens in silence, his elbows braced upon his knees, his head bowed in thought. He stays that way for a long time after she is finished.

"If you should wish to give me that 'everything' you spoke of, cousin, now would be an excellent time," she says eventually.

"I am *thinking*," he says. He looks up at her, and there is no trace of the jester's spark that usually graces his features. "This is far more dangerous than we had anticipated," he says. "Oh, cousin. What a web you are caught in."

"I was caught in the web, as you call it, when my father married me to Henry," she says. How dare he suggest she has been foolish when all she has done has been so considered, so strategic? "All I do now is attempt to destroy both web and spider."

"And you are set upon this course of action." It isn't a question, yet she feels the need to justify herself.

"The bordweal weakens. If it fails entirely, then Elben's enemies will take it; there is no doubt of that. If we queens reclaim our power, then we can shore it up and Cnothan will remain mine."

Johana is watching her closely. He shakes his head. "I do not think that is why, cousin. Cnothan and Mathmas are the most defensible castles in Elben. With preparation, you could hold it against any army."

She throws her hands up. "What do you want from me, Johana? I have not lied to you."

"I am merely trying to understand why you of all people are setting in motion something that can only lead . . . well. You know where it ends."

She does. The throb of war drums and armour is loud in her ears. She cannot hold her cousin's gaze. So it is worse than they had anticipated: what had they gleaned in Ezzonid? What diluted rumours had reached their spies?

"We used to laugh at the notion that gods would help mankind," Johana says. In times of war, faith either strengthens to steel or dissipates entirely. Her mother and sister had become fanatics. She and Johana: sceptics.

Her heart clenches. Would her mother be disappointed in her if she knew the truth?

In a small voice, she says, "If you had been at the Moon Ball, you would understand. I felt the divine power, Johana. It flowed around me, through me. And it felt like . . ."

What did it feel like? She thinks back to that evening, and how the religious ecstasy and the carnal twisted with each other, knotted together until she could not say where one ended and the other began.

"Do you remember the phoenix?" she says. Johana nods. It had been just before the unrest, when they were still children in mind as well as body. Their parents had taken them to the cloudy peaks of the Rhozche Forest, where the tree trunks are coated in ice and their uppermost leaves are brown from the relentless sun. The hunt that the Ezzonidian royal family takes part in just once in a lifetime.

Johana had climbed one of the trees to look for the bird. When he came back down to the forest floor, his tanned face was crisp with sunburn. As they approached it, they heard its song: a melody like hot glass.

To harm or steal from a phoenix is to be cursed. They had climbed the tree, one by one, to seek the creature's blessing. Her father had gone first and returned humbled. By the time it was Cleves's turn, her limbs were stiff with cold despite the furs she wore. As she moved from branch to branch, her face upturned, pushing through damp leaves, she thawed.

The nest was smaller than she'd expected. The phoenix, too. But oh, though she'd pictured it for months, it was like nothing she could have imagined. Its feathers were long, crisp and in all the shades of sunrise. But it was the bird's face that made her gasp. It looked at her as newborn and ancient at once, with the wonder and wisdom that sees into a soul. She had always been an active child, always climbing, riding, running, but in that moment she felt an immense peace, like climbing into a warm bed after a long day outside.

She was supposed to say words of thanks, a rite the whole family had practised in preparation. But all she could bring herself to say was, "*Bresn*." The Ezzonid word, its true meaning lost to time, to end a prayer.

She was not granted a feather, but her younger sister was. The first to be given a phoenix gift in more than a hundred years. Sybil climbed down from the canopy with the plume tucked into her blouse, her reddened cheeks streaked with tears. They all wept with her, for such a blessing in their lifetime.

"Keep it with you always," their mother had told Sybil. "This is life itself. It is priceless."

They had learned, not five years later, how much life was worth, and how easily it could be spent.

"I remember the phoenix," Johana says. "How could anyone who has seen it forget such a sight?"

"The feeling. You remember that?"

Johana's eyes widen. "The divine power is like that?"

"Yes, Johana, yes."

He does not need to say that he understands. She can see his resolve. If he could feel that way again, she knows he would lay waste to a hundred kingdoms to do so. They all would.

"So," he says, clapping his hands, all jollity once more. The wispy sentimentality in the chamber vanishes. "Tell me more about the Moon Ball. Therein lies the key to your problem, does it not? For when else have you experienced the divine power?"

Cleves surges from her chair, unable to stay still in her frustration. "I have thought on that, cousin, and all I can conclude is that enough queens were in the same place, doing the same thing, that it brought Medren to us."

"Then there you have it."

She clips him around the top of his head as she passes. "*Grolsch*. Even if we could gather the queens in one place without attracting

Henry's attention, how could we possibly do so quickly enough to intercept Cecilia's ship? And besides that, conjuring the divine power is very different from understanding how to wield it."

"Well then, you are all out of time and good fortune," Johana says. He is sitting back in his chair, his fingers steepled together, with that infuriating smile that says *I know something you do not*.

"I am going to throw you out of that window," she tells him.

"Well, it is your window to do with as you wish. But before you do, consider the holy books."

She is no scholar. "Which holy books?"

"The ones that talk of miracles, for what else is your bordweal but a long-lasting miracle?"

He holds up two fingers and a thumb.

"Your mother has studied the scriptures of every faith. There are three ways to beg a miracle from a god. The first: blood sacrifice." He lowers his thumb.

"The second: acts of devotion. Let us assume that this was what brought Medren to you at the dance." He lowers one finger. Cleves stops pacing. There is a flicker of memory: not an image but a feeling, fleeting as an ember. The Moon Ball was not the first time she felt the divine power. Not at all.

"The third—" Johana starts. Cleves holds up a hand. She knows. She remembers.

"Relics."

CHAPTER NINETEEN

Howard

Susanna Horenbolt will not be able to help her. Not if Howard continues to lie to her, nor if she reveals the truth. What Howard and the other queens are about to attempt will either bring about their downfall or herald their rise, and Howard cannot do it alone. Not with Henry still at Plythe.

Susanna is an outsider, little likely to risk displeasing her queen by gossiping to the others, even if she had known the truth. The rest of Howard's ladies are linked by blood or long friendship or ancient familial allies. To tell one of them is to tell all. So tell all she will. Sometimes trust is earned. Sometimes it must be thrown out, like a rope to a drowning man.

Henry spends his mornings hunting in the verdant and richly gamed woods around Plythe, returning for luncheon. While he is gone, Wolsey and Cromwell generally see to the more mundane business of running a country, taking vittles in their rooms as they work. But sometimes they will visit her, and she and her ladies will attempt to entertain these men who smile then roll their eyes when they think she is not looking. If they do visit her receiving chamber, Howard must be plausibly, unsuspiciously absent. She does not have long to take the women into her confidence.

She sets Goldfoot at the door of her receiving chamber, and feeds him a morsel of honeydragon meat from a pouch at her waist. He makes little huffs of excitement as he gobbles it up. "Guard," she whispers.

Her ladies are lounging at the window seat, some of them peering out at the cargo boats making their way towards the machinery at Plythe's base, which will pull them from the water and up into the palace's gut.

"Look, Legh," Ursula says, pointing at a vessel. "That one's from Pkolack. You will have your iced sherbets before long."

Legh is lying upon the floor, as is her habit. She holds a lute loosely upon her chest, and Howard stoops to pluck it from her. The ladies quieten, sensing their queen's mood. Can they too hear the bird's wings beating against her ribcage? And what do they hold in their chests? Loyalty, or betrayal?

Lady Tylney shuffles along the window seat to make room for Howard, and she perches between her women. She looks around them. They are her friends, all of them, and though they are often unkind, she thinks – she hopes – that there is enough love between them to weather what is to come.

Boleyn must have thought so of her sister.

Howard plucks out the first tune that comes to mind: a ditty familiar to all those who grow up in the territory of Plythe. The words follow a fish as it swims along the Kyttle River, tumbles down the Falls and passes whales and so on out to sea.

But she does not sing. She plucks the strings so that anyone lingering outside may only hear the song. She drops her secrets beneath the notes and hopes for mercy.

It is not Legh or even Ursula, the two most vocal of her ladies, who speak first. It is Lady Tylney.

"So you do not love the king?" she says. It is a strange question, given everything that Howard has just divulged. It is not an easy one to answer either.

"I thought so once. But no, I do not think I do."

"Oh, thank the god," Lady Tylney says. She begins to make the sign of Cernunnos – splayed fingers against her chest, like antlers – and then, realising her error, makes a fist of her hand instead.

Legh says, "Is that what you have been doing with all those secret meetings and time by yourself?"

Howard reaches for her. "Yes. I am sorry, sister."

"I thought you no longer liked me," Legh says.

"Why would you think that?"

Legh glances at Ursula. "You spent so much time with Voda Kelaverinn, and you know men – they think that our pursuits are silly and stupid. We thought you must feel the same way."

Howard stops her lute-playing to run one hand down her bodice and gown, which is coated in jewels and embroidered with gold thread. "Do I look as though I think our pursuits are silly?"

Legh laughs. Lady Tylney laughs.

Susanna's smile is a wound. "You lied to me the other day, Your Majesty?"

"A little. Not all." Susanna had asked Howard to protect her from the other women when they turned cruel. And Howard will – she will. But she must be sure of their loyalty first – surely Susanna can understand that?

Ursula is last to speak: "I knew it was the truth. I knew it."

She had been Howard's attendant at the Moon Ball. She had seen Medren's power. She had never commented upon it, so Howard had assumed that she was ignorant to what it signified. She has underestimated them, as she herself has been underestimated.

"You can scold me later for keeping this from you, but in this moment I need your help," she says. She reaches for them all, touching their hands, their cheeks, gathering them towards her.

"You are our queen," Ursula says. And that is that.

Lady Tylney keeps watch at the window of Howard's receiving chamber, which offers a view over the hunting grounds of Plythe. Legh is poised at the palace gates, ready to detain the king and his huntsmen with flirtation. Susanna tarries outside the courtyard where Howard last lied to her. "I will be your last defence," she proclaims, then slopes off to her post with hunched shoulders. And Ursula cleaves to Howard, insisting on joining her at the spirit stone of Plythe, for "I have been reading all kinds of pamphlets about Medren, and I might be able to help if you have difficulties."

Howard feels as though she is fighting to keep her seat on a wild horse, without bridle or saddle. Everything has changed between her and her ladies, and nothing has changed at all. They vie with each other for her favour, move to place themselves in the right way, and all she can think of is Boleyn and her sister who is soon to be queen in her place. What is Legh going to say to the king?

That is a terror for later. She and Ursula pass into the peaceful din of the courtyard, the Kyttle Falls providing comfort and the concealment of noise. Howard steps up to the spirit stone, balancing on a ledge, smooth and slippery with water, provided for such a purpose. The stone woman, her crown almost disappeared, gazes impassively at Howard.

"It is almost midday," Ursula whispers. She is standing to one side, leaning over the fountain but not daring to touch the woman at its centre.

And there are the bells of Sweillan, marking the height of the sun. Across Elben, the bells in other sanctuaries will toll, and those who heave on their ropes will not know that they provide a signal to four queens about to attempt their greatest feat of rebellion yet.

"Do it," Ursula says, bouncing on her toes.

Howard takes the stone woman's hand. The sensation is immediate. She did not understand the strange kinship she experienced that first time, on her wedding day, but she does now. She is communing with the echoes of the queens of Plythe. The fluttering beauty and restless desire of the women who ruled this palace before her.

"Good morrow, friends," she whispers.

The air around her stills, the bubbling water quietens. At the edge of her mind, a voice seems to call to her. It has no words, or is spoken in a language long forgotten and untranslatable, yet Howard understands it. It is the language of the maid walking alone through a darkened wood. The language of a mother thinking with despair upon her daughter's future. It is the language of the woman who makes excuses not to be left alone with her friend, lest his attentions turn romantic. It is the language of danger, both known and unknown. It is a melancholy voice, a nightingale's voice, like wind in starving trees upon a wild mountainside.

Howard does not know what to say or do to make the spirit stone obey her. They are all of them hazarding Seymour's safety on a hunch, on a power whose rules none of them understand. Medren came to them at the Moon Ball – surely she will come to them now?

"Please?" she says.

Nothing changes. The strange language continues, a lilting fall of it, chattering like the fountain.

"I am Queen Howard of Plythe," she tries again. The voice grows louder, more insistent. She thinks of the other queens, who have probably already bent their spirit stones to their will. They will be waiting only for her. If she cannot work out what she must do, will their plan fail entirely? Will Seymour be lost, be taken to Henry and have unimaginable, unforgivable things done to her?

"Is it not working?" Ursula says.

"No," Howard replies. A tear falls, but she does not relinquish her hold on the stone.

"*Make it work*," Ursula says, as though she were the queen and Howard her maid.

"I do not know how. Perhaps if Voda Kelaverinn were here—"

"Oh, fuck your Voda Kelaverinn," Ursula says. She seizes Howard by the upper arms, bracing her from behind. Is Howard a weapon or a shield?

"Try again," she instructs.

"I need your help," Howard says to the spirit stone, her eyes closed, willing every part of her that has ever felt like a queen to rise to the stone.

"You are a queen," Ursula says. "Act like one."

There they are. The words Boleyn said to her on their first meeting. Howard did not say then, and she will not say now: I am a queen in name alone. I never deserved the title like the rest of you. Another tear falls.

"Ursula," she says, half speaking, half sobbing.

Ursula shakes her, her grip tightening. How can such a woman as Ursula, all mischief and flight, suddenly be so fierce?

"I am going to grow angry soon, Your Majesty," Ursula says. "Queen Seymour is depending upon you. The other queens are waiting for you. Are you going to humiliate Plythe?"

Ursula knows she's being cruel. They have all heard the taunts: that Howard won her crown on her back. What else does she have to offer? Not Aragon's mind, Cleves's heritage, Parr's heart. She has only ever had her body.

Her body, and her friends.

Strangely, it is the thought of failing Ursula and her other ladies, not Seymour or Cleves or the other queens, that calms Howard. If they are truly risking their lives for her, how can she not succeed?

"Listen to me," she says, a new steel in her voice.

There is a pause in the chatter, no greater than a breath, before it starts again. This time, though, the language is a little different. Now it is the language of whispered knowledge, of women warning other women. The language of friends walking together through that wood. The language of breath upon embers, blowing and blowing until the flame licks the hearth and the sparks fly. Howard has the strangest vision. A kindly woman – her old nurse – holding her hands and whispering the tongue of the Medrenkind. "*Tavast sigorasus. Solinqui gefoelle*." Together we win. Alone we fall.

"*Tavast sigorasus. Solinqui gefoelle*."

Howard finds herself repeating those words now, over and over again. Behind her, her hands warm and steady on Howard's arms, Ursula takes up the chant. They say the words until they lose all meaning, until they flow through Howard like the River Kyttle's inexorable path. She does not know if they are the right words, but the chatter of the stone falls silent beneath her fingertips. Her eyes are closed, and all she can conjure before her is Seymour's face. In her thoughts, Seymour is shackled. A dark, tilting room, a hard pallet bed.

Something flows through Howard's fingers, through her hair and her chest and her stomach. She knows it. It is the same binding power that she last felt at the Moon Ball. She knows that were she to open her eyes, her hands would be wreathed in the bruised light of the bordweal.

She smiles, and says, "Go to her."

CHAPTER TWENTY

Cecilia

The tenth morning at sea brings the sight of the bordweal. Florin spots it first, and his shout of excitement brings Cecilia up to the deck. Many of the servants on board have never left Perfugi, so they crane over the side of the balustrade, pointing and blabbering.

Cecilia stands apart from them, watching the way the dome that surrounds Elben morphs, flickering from grey to black to silver, as though a permanent thunderstorm blankets the island.

"Will it hurt when we go through it?" one of the ladies asks those nearby.

"Only if you wish to conquer Elben," a sailor replies, grinning at her as he passes. As others who have crossed the bordweal describe the play of bruise-like colours that can be viewed from inside the dome, Cecilia turns to the captain.

"I am going to view it from above."

The captain's eyes widen. "From the scoop, Your Majesty? It's dangerous for someone not used to climbing."

"Then I suggest you don't permit my court to follow me."

She places one boot carefully on the netting that leads to the top of the sails, then another, wiggling her hips to get her gown out of the way of her footing. Once she has climbed into the scoop, far below the captain shakes his head and turns back to the helm. She inhales, enjoying the vertigo. She looks out at the horizon, at the bordweal, and remembers the last time she saw it. The eighteen-year-old Cecilia had climbed up to the scoop back then, too, although she had been more interested in looking back than forward. She had watched the shores of Elben recede, the ugly spires of Cnothan the last things to fade behind the winter fog, and then she had turned to face the barrier that would divide her youthful life as a princess from her adult life as a queen. When they had passed through the barrier, she had closed her eyes and laughed at the sensation – like being bathed in stars. When she had opened them, the blue-green-purple she had known had turned to steel.

It is not as solid as it was all those years ago. It eddies and flows, revealing misty shapes beyond. Cecilia squints, sure she sees movement just behind the barrier. The silhouette of a ship, five-sailed, like the ships of the Feorwa Isles. She may be wrong (she isn't) but the ship does not appear to be moving either across the bordweal and out into the open ocean or towards Elben. It is almost as if . . .

"Someone is waiting for us," she tells the captain as she jumps down from the netting. "Ready the cannons."

"My crew are not soldiers," he says, running his hands through his scraggy hair, following her as she skips across the deck towards the stairs that lead down to the cabins.

"A precaution," she says over her shoulder. "Maybe they merely wish to greet us."

She does not return to her cabin, but takes the narrow stairs down to the hold. A wave tips the ship starboard and Cecilia leers into the wall, scraping her arm. She hopes that her curse will not have alerted Seymour to her presence. Her velvet shoes are soft on the floor, the natural creaking of the ship's bones covering the creaking caused by her step as she finds the whorl that permits her a view of Seymour's cabin.

Seymour is sitting on her pallet bed, still clutching that curiously hard patch of her gown's hem. Cecilia has thought long about how to find out what it is she is holding. Once they are on land, she will send a lady to take the gown by force. If it were the linen shift Seymour was clutching, Cecilia could have a laundrywoman steal it, but gowns, which do not need to be washed, are not so easy.

The ship tips again and Cecilia braces herself. The sound cannot have been so great, but Seymour starts, her hands moving across the object in her gown with increasing energy. The ship tips once more and a shout goes up from the deck. Seymour springs to her feet, looking up as though she can see through the ceiling. When Seymour smiles, Cecilia runs.

Her court are fleeing down the stairs.

"What is happening?" she asks them, but none answer. They push past her, ignoring her outrage. Florin grabs her and hauls her back down with him.

"Release me!" she shouts, kicking at him.

"It's not safe. It's not safe," he keeps saying in her ear. When they reach the nobles' quarters and solid ground, she spins around and pins him to the wall.

"What. Is. Happening?" she growls.

"The bordweal. It does not like us," Florin says.

"That's impossible," Cecilia says. She pushes away from him, dancing out of his reach, and darts back up the stairs, mercifully empty now that her cowardly court has fled below deck. Only the ship's crew remains in the open. They shout instructions to each other, running here and there to the sails, the tiller, the anchor.

"Turn about!" the captain shouts. "Lower the anchor to hard turn!"

Cecilia's gaze is drawn to the great dome of the bordweal. The steel grey has grown white, like the centre of a forge. It roils, with a sound that is part thunder, part predator. As she watches, the white flicks out a great fork of lightning. It hits the scoop where she had, only moments ago, been standing. The wood splinters, sending shards like daggers into the deck. One hits a man in front of Cecilia, stabbing into his back as he runs. He staggers against the balustrade, and does not move again.

Cecilia plucks the splinter from his body. It reminds her of a needle.

"It's the queen!" the captain shouts at her, and it takes her a moment to understand that he does not mean her but Seymour. "She's a traitor to Elben, and the bordweal knows it!"

Cecilia staggers towards him. "It is not her! This is some other power!"

"I'm telling you, it's her! I want her thrown overboard, and that beast with her."

He directs some of his crew to the hold to do just that, and Cecilia brandishes the wooden needle, still dripping with their crewmate's blood. "I am telling you, imbecile, that it is not her. That's not how the bordweal works, or how else would Elben bring political prisoners back to the Tower? How else would foreign diplomats enter?"

The captain pushes her wrist – and the dagger – away from his face. "It's been years since you were here; things might have changed."

His crew makes a run for the hold. Cecilia curses and slashes the captain's face, once, twice, until he falls to the deck clutching bloodied eyes. She runs after the crew, but the captain isn't the first to make the assumption that Seymour is at the root of this. Many in her court are already in the hold, banging on the cabin walls, shouting for her to be thrown out. They're all foreigners. They grew up with the bordweal as a cautionary tale, not a real, practical defence that only acts against armies, not individual traitors.

"Get away from there!" Cecilia says, her voice carrying above the din. Those who understand not to cross her fall silent and back away. The crew, however, do not. They grab axes and rush at the locks on the two doors. Cecilia intercepts the one who is about to loose the panther, stepping in front of him and letting his momentum push him into the wooden stake. He drops his axe, and his body follows it. But Cecilia is too late to prevent the second axe. The metal cleaves with a spark and the door to Seymour's cabin falls open.

Cecilia had half expected the room to be filled with the swirling light of the bordweal, or some such nonsense – the captain's superstitions must have crept inside her head against her will. But no – Lady Seymour stands in the middle of the room, calm as a heifer. Some among Cecilia's court charge forward, forgetting their queen's orders, and lay hands on the woman. They drag her, unprotesting, from her cabin and push-pull her up the stairs to the deck, shouting *witch* and *traitor.*

"You fools!" Cecilia shouts, brandishing the dagger, but her people dart out of her way, their need for immediate survival outweighing their fear of Cecilia. On deck, another lightning bolt shoots from the white centre of the bordweal, rending one of the sails in two and sending the halves crashing to the deck, aflame. In the commotion, Seymour's captors release her. But instead of fleeing, Seymour walks steadily to the prow of the ship, as if communing with the storm. Cecilia follows her, as stealthily as she can manage. She needs Seymour alive, as an offering to Henry, leverage – Seymour and Cecilia's silence in exchange for Brynd.

"I know you are there, Cecilia," Seymour says over the fray. "The bordweal talks to me. It tells me you are come to capture me once more."

"What do you mean, talks to you?" Cecilia says.

"I can barely hear it, but it is there. It has not used its voice for many hundreds of years."

Cecilia is always hungry – hungry for food, for sex, for excitement – but she has never known the hunger that sweeps over her now. It is visceral, this desire to commune with something as ingrained in her identity as the bordweal. How dare this little creep of a girl take what should be Cecilia's by royal birthright? She limps across the deck. There will be some kind of blood rite she can perform to make the woman's power her own: spilling, smearing, drinking. Cernunnos would approve, Cernunnos would help, if she offered him blood.

But as she comes near, Seymour swirls round to face her. She is holding one hand out in front of her, palm up, and in that palm is a ball of bordweal light.

"Come no closer," Seymour says.

"Or what?" Cecilia replies. Her hunger is making her reckless. More than that, Seymour is not wielding whatever power she has been granted with confidence. She holds her hand away from her, as though she is fearful of what it might do. If Cecilia had it, she would be standing tall. She steps closer. Seymour shakes her head, like a mother disappointed in her child.

"Do not mistake my caution for cowardice," she says. She closes her palm over the divine power, squeezing it in her fist. Cecilia readies herself for some blast of pain, but nothing happens. She begins to laugh – at Seymour, but mostly at herself and her crew and court, for being taken in by Seymour's tricks. She has no power. Maybe the bordweal is acting strangely, but this woman has nothing but a fool's bag of japes. Cecilia could almost admire the audacity of it.

Seymour holds Cecilia's gaze, her fist still closed.

Another lighting strike shoots from the bordweal and scatters sparks across the deck. Cecilia ducks to avoid them. At first, she thinks it is the sparks making the deck shake. Then she realises that something else is the source of the vibrations. Something deeper in the bowels of the vessel. Her laughter dies on her lips as she witnesses Seymour's quiet triumph.

A brief silence follows the trembling, in which something clatters up the stairs. The panther, covered in splinters from its wooden cage, bounds into the open with powerful grace. Some fool must have released it, Cecilia tells herself. This cannot be Seymour's doing.

The panther ignores the captain, sprawled on the boards, clutching his face and moaning, and turns its attention to Cecilia. The creature knows the woman who threatened it and its mistress. Cecilia turns her wooden dagger towards it. Another tremble shakes the boat, and the panther splays its paws like a colt, its advance halted. A shout comes up from below, and the cowards who had fled down now erupt upstairs.

"The ship is collapsing!" Florin shouts. He sees the panther and runs towards Cecilia. Perhaps he intends to perform some ridiculously noble sacrifice like placing himself between her and it, as if she would swoon at such a gesture. But he never reaches her. Like the molten mountain of Perfugi itself, the boards of the ship crackle, buckling up and in and out in a wave that flows up the side of the vessel and along the deck.

As though a fist had closed around the ship and were squeezing it tight.

"Impossible," Cecilia whispers.

"Is it?" Seymour says.

The deck disintegrates around Cecilia, and she tumbles into the heaving sea below, bodies and boat tossed around her. The cold is a punishment. She looks for an intact piece of wood and finds one a little way away. Two men are clinging to it. She splashes over to them, clumsy in her drenched gown.

"Let go," she orders them. They ignore her. She curls her legs around one of them. One arm she clamps around his neck. The other she uses to plunge her nails into his eye. The man screams and releases the plank. Cecilia lets go of him and takes hold of the wood, washing the blood and jelly from her fingers. She looks over at the other man. He is staring at her, face pale, mouth a perfect bread roll.

"Let. Go." She repeats. He throws himself back, away from her, and she pulls herself onto the wood, letting it take the weight of her torso.

The hunger has returned. If Seymour truly commanded the bordweal to destroy a warship, then Cecilia must have her power. Nothing else matters.

She searches for the woman and the panther among the wreckage, but she already knows that they are unlikely to be there. Seymour would not have destroyed herself with the ship. Sure enough, Cecilia spies them just beyond the bordweal. The shape of the vessel she had seen before is clearer now, the sigil of the Feorwa Isles on the windblown flag. Someone is throwing a harness down to Seymour. She ties the harness around her panther's belly and the beast is hauled aboard.

Seymour is next, a dozen arms reaching for her. Cecilia watches the scene with a curious emptiness. An emptiness she always feels in the face of the strangeness of commoner families.

She toes off her boots and abandons the wooden plank, swimming towards the ship. They have not yet pulled up the anchor. She grabs hold of the rope, fighting the waves and her sodden gown to heave herself up, hand hold by painful handhold. The fibres scour her palms but still she climbs. There's a small window a little way above her. She levels with it, panting and wincing against the salt in the fresh wounds on her palms, and uses her elbow to smash the glass and then to bend the lead latticework. If she can tear the bottom of her gown off, she should be able to slip inside to safety.

"Oh look, a rat has stowed on board," a voice says from above her head.

A Feorwan sailor with cropped hair and a rounded face looks down at Cecilia. Next to them stands Seymour.

"I am worth more to you alive than dead," she shouts, hoping they can hear her above the sea spray.

"You're worth trouble, is what you are," the sailor says. Cecilia looks to Seymour.

"Remember that I know my brother," she calls.

"Fuck you," the sailor says. "And fuck your brother." They swing an oar towards Cecilia's head, and the last thing she knows is the crush of the plank on her cheek, and the sting of the sea, and then nothing.

PART TWO

CHAPTER TWENTY-ONE

My Lord Cromwell,

I write to you from the town of Swegan, where my enquiries into the nature of the incident at the bordweal continue apace. My news thus far is unfortunate. It seems that it was indeed the king's sister on board the ship in question. I can find no report of any survivors, although my men continue to scour the coast and the waters near here – the tide has already borne some unfortunate victims to these shores. I fear that our only hope rests on the reported sighting of a Feorwan ship, which my sources claim was sailing south – whether to the southern coast of Elben or to Capetia, we have yet to ascertain.

In the absence of more tangible news, I also bring you rumour. I have heard certain peoples in this part of the kingdom discussing the incident as the natural progression of Elben's treacherous queens, leading to a faulty bordweal. This is a supposition that I have encouraged, which I hope will be to Your Grace's approval.

There are some other, less savoury rumours which I have attempted to quash. I fear that these have aligned with the arrival of certain emissaries from the Hleaw tribes. His Majesty has shown leniency in the past to these heretics, but I would urge him to quell his naturally merciful nature in this instance.

I will write again soon with further news,

Your humble servant,

N. Ackworth

My Lord Brandon,

This letter will, I fear, not be welcomed by you. I know and understand your opinion of me, Your Grace, but beg of you to lend this letter your eyes and but a little of your time. We both of us desire the strength and glory of my master – your friend – and our king, and it is in that vein that I write.

As I am sure you have heard through your many connections, I have been engaged for several moons in a quest for knowledge. For no matter what we tell His Majesty's people – no matter what Lord Wolsey and I tell those foreign diplomats stationed at High Hall – we are marching towards a crossroads. I fear that if something is not done, and soon, Elben will turn on itself. Neither you nor I wish to see our beloved country and our more beloved monarch embroiled in the ugliness of civil war.

My access to Bishop More's library and extensive archives has, at last, yielded something of interest. We are about to embark upon an experiment that, if successful, will secure the king's place in the annals of history as one of the world's greatest leaders, a god who walks among us. Yet I cannot do it alone.

I beg of you to meet me, to join with me in my efforts, setting aside old grievances for the sake of our king and kingdom. If you accept, I will be returning to High Hall forthwith, once my affairs at Plythe are settled.

Your humble servant,
Lord Thomas Cromwell

Cromwell,

You make me laugh, sir, at the thought that I would concern myself with petty squabbles with a man such as yourself. Henry has already informed me of your schemes. I will meet with you when I am returned from my estates.

Lord Charles Brandon

Lord Cromwell,

Please find enclosed an account of the correspondences of Their Majesties. As you requested, I have been more thorough of late and as usual, Your Grace is correct – there were several curiosities that may be of significance. Namely:

- *Queen Aragon has invited her nephew's diplomat to stay with her at the Palace of Daven thrice of late, whereas in previous years she has invited him but annually.*

- *Queen Cleves still corresponds with one of her old ladies-in-waiting: a Mistress Paston. This would not, of course, usually be of note except that, as you know, Queen Cleves famously maintains a small household and rarely corresponds with her nobility outside of necessities. However, the correspondence is of little note and largely concerns the Lady Paston's ailing health and their memories of the queen's first year at Cnothan where, it seems, Mistress Paston proved herself a loyal and useful friend.*
- *I have intercepted several brief letters from Queen Parr addressed to minor nobility on the continent. The letters merely invite them to visit. I have looked into the nobility in question and can find no record of anyone of that name. Further enquiries suggest that the letters are being passed on to someone, but I can as yet find no trace of them. With your permission, I will continue my enquiries into this matter.*

Your faithful servant,
N. Ackworth.

Nicholas,

I am particularly interested in Queen Cleves's correspondence with Lady Paston. Look into this further, if you please.

Cromwell

His Majesty King Henry, eighth of his name, Monarch Almighty of the great Empire of Elben, King of the Isles of Feorwa and Protector of the Oracle of Evenesis, issues this PROCLAMATION, to be read in every town square and marketplace in the land.

Let it be known that, in his great care for his people, the king wishes to rid this land of the issue of CRONES which has plagued our kingdom for so long. A REWARD of ten gold coins shall be given to anyone, whomsoever they may be, who can bring a crone, alive and caged, to High Hall. They shall thenceforth be catalogued and destroyed by the king's men.

In his desire for the good health of his people, our kind and bountiful king desires that his people do NOT place themselves in danger by attempting to kill or otherwise harm the crones. This shall be executed by the king's men ALONE.

CHAPTER TWENTY-TWO

Cleves

It is two nights before Cleves hears word of Seymour. She knows that Cecilia's ship was destroyed by the bordweal, and all she can do is hope that this was Seymour's doing. All she can do is drive from her mind the images of Seymour losing control of the bordweal and being destroyed alongside the vessel.

Johana wakes her at midnight. "I have them," is the first thing he says as he slips into her bedchamber and she locks it behind him. "But there is a problem."

"She is alive?" Cleves says, then wonders why this should be the first question upon her lips. Johana pauses. "Yes," he says.

"Where is she?"

"Right here."

Johana goes to a corner of her chamber, knocking on it in a specific pattern, *pum pa pum pum*. An answering knock, and then a panel in the wall slides back. First to step through is the Feorwan servant, Clarice. They bow to Cleves, then hold an arm out to help someone through.

There she is. Seymour's once fine gown is stiff with dried salt, her hair loose and wild. She looks very different from the polite, contained queen Cleves met on a hill not far from here. She looks more worn, and more regal, than the woman Cleves danced with.

The two stare at each other. That dance – the last time they were in the same space – pregnant between them.

"How fare you, my angry queen?" Cleves says at last.

There it is – the flicker of a smile at the corner of Seymour's mouth.

"I knew you would help me," Seymour says. "It was as if my *sunscína* was reassuring me. The bordweal – that was you?"

"It was us."

Seymour's mouth opens, a soft "O". Perhaps Cleves imagines it, but she is sure there is a little disappointment in Seymour's eyes. The next moment, Seymour covers it: "Are you telling me that you and Queen Aragon set aside your squabbling for long enough to work together?"

Cleves laughs. "I am full of surprises, am I not, Queen Seymour?"

"You're not the only one," Clarice says, their jaw clenched. Seymour shoots them a look. Interesting. Cleves has never seen these two at odds before.

"What has happened?" she says.

Seymour cannot look at Cleves. "We . . . I . . . the Dowager Queen is our prisoner."

"I see," Cleves says.

Clarice juts their chin. "I did not agree with this course of action, but Her Majesty believes that Cecilia can be useful."

"She can be," Seymour says. She turns to Cleves. "She wants power, that is all. If we can offer her some, then I truly believe we could wrest her loyalty from her brother."

"And if we have Elbenese royalty behind us, then we stand a chance of bringing the people to our side," Cleves says.

Seymour becomes animated. "Yes, exactly."

"How much does she know?" Cleves says, holding up a hand to stop Seymour from growing too excited.

"She only knows the truth of Medren, and that I am trying to finish what Boleyn started."

Clarice nods. "That's why we kept her on my ship. So she wouldn't know about your involvement, or the other queens'."

Here Clarice's eyes flick to Johana, leaning inconspicuously against the wall next to the secret door. He holds up his hands. "I am merely here to help my cousin and my country's interests. Pay me no mind."

Cleves must think quickly. If Aragon and Seymour are right, then Cecilia thinks she is cleverer than she truly is, and eager for knowledge that she can use to her advantage.

"Can she remain on your ship?" Cleves asks Clarice. The Feorwan shakes their head. "I must return to my country."

"The king is causing your people more trouble than usual, I understand."

Clarice and Seymour dart a glance at each other that Cleves cannot read: is this an ongoing argument between the two of them? Well, it is by the by. Cleves turns to Johana. "I have a little hunting lodge deep in the Gealdrum Forest. It was built since my marriage, so the Dowager Queen will not recognise it, and with enough security – and a good steward – we can house her there for the time being."

Johana shakes his head. "I am no gaoler."

"You are the only one who knows all," she says. She does not say, *The only one I trust*, for she trusts no one wholly but herself.

Johana groans. Clarice shrugs at him. "It is difficult when you are their only friend. You get handed a lot of shit."

Clarice agrees to take Johana back to their ship, and from there Johana will make arrangements to convey Cecilia to Gnottel Lodge under cover of moonlight. Once they are gone, Seymour seems to collapse into herself. Cleves watches her, as disinterestedly as she can.

She might have expected Seymour to be thinner since she became a fugitive. Instead, Seymour looks stronger in every way, even when she is exhausted. Cleves's stomach twists.

"You are tired, I think?" Cleves says.

"I am content."

Seymour's back is straight. Something twists again in Cleves, lower than her stomach now, and she almost laughs at herself. Why does she, the woman who can take a thousand insults and not be angered, have such a weakness for women made of fire?

"Oh, my angry queen has returned," Cleves says.

"No."

Cleves does laugh this time. "She brings a viper to my door and she is the one who is angry."

"At least you still have a door," Seymour says. "I have given all for the cause. Can you blame me for taking risks?"

"Not at all. But then you must not blame me for being cautious."

Seymour looks very much as though she would like to blame Cleves, but Cleves has business to attend to if she is to keep the king's sister under house arrest.

"You are tired," Cleves says again. It is not a question this time. "Sleep in my bed for now, and we will find a better hiding place for you soon."

Seymour looks as though she wants to refuse.

"We can talk later," Cleves says.

"No," Seymour says, but she sways on her feet.

"Come . . ." Cleves begins.

"I must know how we wield the bordweal," Seymour says.

Cleves takes her by the shoulders and steers her towards the bed. She had forgotten how tall Seymour is.

"I swear on my gargoyle's life that I will tell you, once you are rested."

They sink onto the edge of the bed.

"But—"

"Sleep now, my queen."

Seymour shakes her head. "I must know whether you have broken the chains between our husband and us."

Cleves sighs. She is not going to get Seymour to rest until she has answers. "I do not think so. We used the spirit stones to conjure the divine power, much as our combined presence at Brynd conjured it at the Moon Ball. But I have felt no remnant of the power since."

She does not admit that the lack of that power is now a physical ache within her chest. She craves it, as those in perpetual pain crave the ecstasy of the hǣmdran flower.

"But it can be done," Seymour whispers. Her eyes are almost closed. Cleves lays her down upon the bed and draws blankets over her gown. She resists the urge to stroke a stray lock of hair away from Seymour's face. She is neither lover nor mother to Seymour, but a friend and a peer.

"Rest now, my tired queen," Cleves says. She stands, brushing down her gown.

Seymour, eyes already closed, runs her hands over the fur blankets.

"It has been a long time since I have slept on a proper mattress," Seymour says.

"So sleep. You do not always have to be fighting." Cleves moves away, from both the bed and the image of Seymour entangled in her sheets. The thought is very tempting, especially since Cleves's bodice is already loosened. But there will be time enough to try for a tumble later. She likes her women passionate, not exhausted.

"I ask only one favour," Cleves says, as Seymour nestles deeper into the sheets.

"What?" Seymour says. She looks up at Cleves from beneath long lashes.

"Do not drool on my pillows."

Cleves slips from her own bedchamber and leans her back against her door. One breath, two, then she is in control of her senses once more.

CHAPTER TWENTY-THREE

Howard

She says, "Do not go, my love," even as she thinks, "Go, and do not return."

Henry kisses her, but his mind is elsewhere. "I wish I could stay with you for an eternity," he says, but she can see that he is thinking, "I have given you more than a sennight; why must you cling?"

She knows why he leaves hastily, of course. It is because of what she did to the bordweal. And now that she has done it, she can never be the same.

She is used to subjugating her body. It is what a body is for, after all, is it not? To be pressured and pushed and thrown and bruised and used. It is this that made her struggle to understand exactly why Seymour and Boleyn were so outraged by Henry's actions. Why she barely felt any surprise when Seymour told her that their husband was draining them. That is the nature of humanity: to use each other, body and soul, until one or the other is worn out. She saw it with her aunt, with her father. Why should she be any different?

And yet . . .

When the divine power flowed through her yesterday, she felt, for the briefest of moments, what it might be like to have true power. Not the borrowed fineries of her queendom, but real, unassailable control.

It frightens her. She wants it again. She does not know what she would do with it.

In the immediate aftermath of her joining with Plythe's spirit stone, she felt weak, and might have fainted right away if Ursula had not caught her and plied her with sweetbreads and bitter wine. But once the weakness had passed, she could not sit still. She had not needed to, for Master Culpepper came to her not an hour later to inform her that Henry would be leaving within a matter of days.

She did that. She and the other queens. She can still barely believe it.

The king and his closest advisors had been – and are still – like ants without a nest. Their movements are sharper, quicker. Even Henry, who normally has the languor of a man who knows his superiority. But ants without a nest are more prone to biting. She must remember that.

Henry leaps onto his horse's back, athletic still despite the festering leg wound. He holds out his hand, and she kisses it automatically. His mind is on other matters, and so is hers.

The king's train takes hours to trail out of her gatehouse – it is only seeing them in a long line that she realises just how many people follow Henry everywhere. Courtiers and guards and advisors and cooks and comfit-makers and grooms and masters of hound and masters of dragon and masters of falconry and stewards and physicians and cleaners and the boys who clear his shit. It is supposed to be a mark of status, but if one *needs* so many people, then does one have true power, or only the trapperies of it?

She stands there until the king's brilliant white horse can no longer be seen. As she is about to return to the palace, she senses someone approaching.

"His Majesty is concerned about the bordweal." It is Culpepper's voice.

"You are not leaving with the king?" she says. She does not dare look at him. She can feel the warmth from his body on her bare shoulder.

"I thought I could be of more use at Plythe, and His Majesty agreed," he says.

She riddles this. He must be spying for Henry, then, must he not? Yet there is a softness to his voice that does not speak to suspicion.

"Well, I will have my steward find you work, Master Culpepper," she says.

"Anything, my queen."

He is taller than her by some way, with a broad chest and shoulders. Her first thought is that there is something insolent about the way he is standing so close, but that is uncharitable. Her second thought is that he looks as Henry might have once looked, were Henry still twenty or so. An undeniably handsome man, with the wiry vitality of someone who hunts and fights and hawks but does not labour.

"I must go in," she says, darting past him, her eyes on the ground.

She runs into the palace, all the way to the other end of the long gallery to her private rooms. Goldfoot caws from his perch as she slips past him and into her innermost bedchamber. The servants have been here already, cleansing the space of Henry's presence (she had never thought of it that way before, but that's what it is). The remnant of incense hangs in the room – floral sandalwood and comforting sage. The tangled sheets have been replaced with fresh linen and the quilt that is her only heirloom from her much-mourned mother.

She goes to the mirror.

She is feverish.

She unpins her sleeves and frontlet, and pulls the crown from her curls. The strings that secure her gown are trickier to handle by herself, but eventually she manages to loosen them and wriggle from the bodice, before pulling the shift over her head.

There she stands, naked, umber skin turned to deep bronze in the sunlight. She has always known she was beautiful because so many have told her. It has been whispered, moaned, groaned. Sometimes the word has even been used as a weapon. She runs a hand along her collarbone and tries to see what they all see. And she does: she is a trinket of beauty, to be used like a fine instrument or fragile clock. And like an instrument or a clock, she understands her purpose: to delight.

Howard sinks to the floor, sitting upon her discarded finery. She opens her legs, so that she can see her quim.

Tell him what you *enjoy.* That's what Voda Kelaverinn had said before he left. Does a lute feel joy? Does a spoon when it is put in a mouth?

She closes her eyes, thinks of Culpepper and lets her hands roam. She finds a spot along the rim of her ear that makes her sigh; a way of pinching her nipples – more gently than she's used to – that feels exquisite. She touches parts of her body that have only ever been the realm of her lovers, and discovers bliss.

Afterwards, she stares at the ceiling, laughing and raging. Six years of pleasuring men, and not once has she been pleasured in the way she now knows is possible. It calls for revenge, does it not?

The silk chosen for Mary Boleyn's wedding gift is nearly ready. Howard's ladies have been working it for weeks, using the most fragile of threads – the silvery webs of the eadwela spider, which is said to grant happiness. They hunch over the fabric in her receiving chamber, but their conversation is very different from what it was a few days ago.

"I can hardly credit that the king does not suspect us," Legh says.

"He may have his suspicions, but if we acted our parts right then he will have no cause to accuse us," Lady Tylney says.

At the other end of the fabric – at the other end of the chamber – Susanna sighs, picks up her little scissors and starts to unpick some of her work. Howard watches the other women as they take note.

"Have you been clumsy again, Susanna?" Legh says.

Susanna ducks her head as the other women laugh.

"She wishes to do good work. I see nothing shameful about that," Howard says, sweeping into the room. Her women look up, startled.

"Your Majesty, we did not see you," Ursula says. There is something reverently hungry about the way she watches Howard now, ever since she witnessed her wielding the bordweal. Privately, Howard is not sure why: after all, it was Ursula's fortitude that allowed Howard to find the right way.

"I did not mean anything cruel," Legh says.

Howard settles on the floor, halfway between her half-sister and Susanna. "Everyone is cruel from time to time. But perhaps we can save our cruelty for those who deserve it."

Her ladies stare at her. She is shocked at herself, truth be told. She does not know where those words came from: they are like something Queen Cleves or Queen Parr might say. She is not sure they were wise words, though – not to utter at this time, when Legh knows of her betrayal of Henry. Legh has never taken kindly to correction. It is as if Mary Boleyn herself is in the chamber with them, not just her wedding gift.

"I enjoy your wit, Legh," Susanna says. "Only – not when it is directed at me."

"Who should I direct it at then?"

"How about that new lord the king left behind him?" Ursula says.

Howard tries not to react. "Who? Culpepper?"

Legh smirks. "I would rather direct something else entirely at *him*."

The women laugh, and it is as if nothing has changed between them. They accepted the truth of Medren and the bordweal with far more grace and ease than Howard had expected. It unsettles her, until she remembers that she, too, understood it as true so very quickly when Seymour explained it. As if it had merely been veiled beneath taffeta all this time, and they had been willingly playacting.

Howard feels raw and fresh and daring, though, and she does not want them to forget that they are all part of a rebellion now.

"I think Culpepper may be loyal to me actually," she says.

Ursula leans closer. "Do you mean . . .?"

Howard tells them of the part she played in Boleyn's escape from the Tower, and her suspicion that Culpepper knows exactly what she did. "Surely I would be in the Tower myself by now if he was not for our cause?" Howard says.

Lady Tylney breaks the silence. "Do you plan to admit him into your confidence?"

Howard picks up the edge of the swathe of fabric. "Not yet. But I would be grateful if you would all advise me on the matter."

They resume their needlework, and presently servants come to light the candles around the edge of the chamber. Susanna's cheeks are flushed. Legh is unusually silent. And Ursula and Lady Tylney keep darting looks at her. All of them know that something has changed, beyond the storm of Howard's revelation. It is a change that has taken root in the copse of their company, and only time and tender care will dictate whether all saplings will thrive.

Howard was designed to be a sapling. To be buffeted, staked, pruned and fruited.

Can a tree tug itself free from its loamy chains and walk? Can tree turn to gardener?

"I have another idea for the new queen's gift," she announces.

Ursula looks up. "Does this mean I can stop sewing? This thread is giving me a terrible headache."

Howard fingers the silk.

"There will be more sewing," she says to general groans. "But the spider's thread can be set aside for now. And I will sew with you all."

"Are we going to get in terrible trouble?" Legh says, caught between alarm and intrigue.

"Why would we? I am but a silly little queen with not a bad thought in my silly little head," Howard says.

Ursula Askew laughs, full-throated. She crawls across the silk and lays her head upon Howard's lap. "Let us all be very silly, Your Majesty. Let us wreak havoc with our silliness."

CHAPTER TWENTY-FOUR

Cecilia

She has slept in dungeons before, but never against her will. Her kingly Capetian husband had a penchant for sadism, honed over the many decades of his life, and he taught her all he knew in their brief months together. Oh, the fun they had in the depths of the decadent palace of Aviora. This is entirely different. The cell in the hold of the Feorwan ship smells of rotting fish, and although the crew bring her meals, she has to eat them perched on a hard pallet which affords her only a few hours of sleep. She only knows it is night from the timing of the meals, for she sees no sun.

She is running out of escape schemes. She tries attacking the Feorwans when they open the cell door. She tries pleading with them. She tries bribing them and, even though they are at sea, she tries screaming in the hope that a passing ship will hear her. All that gets her is gagged.

She may well lose her mind down here, with no company to entertain her, and no embroidery to keep her mind from unravelling.

"If you keep me here for ever," she tells her captors when they next come with her meal, "then I will be so empty I will be worthless."

She grips their sleeve as she says it, feeling the coarse fabric beneath her fingertips. She rubs a thumb over the thread, and a dozen ways to improve it spring to her mind. Perhaps the way she clings to that sleeve makes her captor understand her sincerity.

"There are plans afoot to take you somewhere where you can see the sunlight," they say, then lock the door behind them, plunging her back into darkness.

"There is nothing I am afraid of," she tells the night, pressing herself against the wall. "There is nothing that can overwhelm me."

Yet despite her fortitude, she rushes to the door when she hears the key in the lock. It is Seymour's friend, the one who knocked her out with an oar the day the bordweal rose against her. They are holding iron manacles.

"Come," they say, and she allows her wrists to be chained, struggling only a little so they do not think she's been cowed. She is Cecilia Tudor. She does not break.

They blindfold her before leading her up to the deck. Cecilia tries not to gulp fresh air. Even through her blindfold she can tell it is night-time. There is a moment where she thinks they are going to throw her overboard, and she cries out.

"Don't be stupid," they say, before steering her into a smaller boat that abuts the ship.

"Where are you taking me?" Cecilia says, permitting herself to be guided onto a hard seat.

No one responds, but she can tell from the splash of oars and the motion of the boat that she is being rowed to shore. She makes an attempt at calculating where in Elben they must be – could they have got as far as Seymour's territory of Hyde while Cecilia was in the ship's hold? – but soon gives it up as hopeless. Geographical calculations were never her strength.

Her backside is aching with a pain that shoots up her spine and into her neck by the time the boat reaches shore, and she is manhandled up a pebbled beach. She hits her legs against the step of a carriage.

"My apologies," the Feorwan says, not sounding very apologetic. "Let me help you in."

"Tell me where I am going first." If she were them, that carriage's destination would be over the edge of a steep cliff. They are fools to allow Cecilia to live, but the soft are often foolish. That was Lorena's weakness, and Florin's.

"Get in and I will remove your blindfold," Seymour says from inside the carriage. The temptation of being able to use her eyes once more is too great. Once Cecilia is settled upon a cushioned seat, and the curtains have been drawn across the windows, Seymour pulls her blindfold down.

Cecilia can see little in the shadows of the carriage: only a single lamp is secured to the wall. There is no crest upon the carriage's innards. She eyes the woman who was once her prisoner and who is now her captor. There is a deeper shadow upon the carriage's floor, at Seymour's feet. The panther, asleep.

"What are you going to do with me?" Cecilia says.

"Whatever I do, it will not involve needles," Seymour replies. "You and I are going to lodge together while I work out how to make use of you."

The carriage rocks as someone climbs into the driver's seat and they begin to move.

"Is there nothing your simpering servant cannot do? I hope at least you fuck them in payment since you have no wealth of your own," she says, loudly enough that she hopes the Feorwan can hear.

"You truly are vile," Seymour says. From the tiny amount of moonlight seeping through the curtain, Cecilia thinks she has closed her eyes.

"At least I am not dull," she says. She leans over and pinches the top of Seymour's hand. Seymour cries out.

"Are you all right, Your Majesty?" the servant calls.

"I am fine," Seymour replies, glaring at Cecilia. Satisfied, Cecilia leans her own head back against the cushioned seat.

"Don't ever treat me as though I'm safe again," she says.

She can feel Seymour's eyes on her for the rest of the journey. She tries to gauge which direction they're going. She thinks they are on the south side of the island, perhaps not too far from Cnothan. The road is jarring, and soon the ache in her lower back cannot be relieved even by moving. When she shifts again, Seymour says, "You are not used to the slightest discomfort, are you?"

"Why should I feel ashamed of that? I dare say neither were you before you ran away from my brother."

That shuts her up. Cecilia decides to have some fun.

"Why *did* you run away from Henry? If you'd been clever enough, you could have kept your dull little palace and worked against him without him realising."

"I would not expect you to understand."

Cecilia laughs, then kicks her shoes off and curls her feet underneath herself. "It is as I thought. You were too stupid to be able to enact a clever plan."

"If you wish to think so," Seymour says. Cecilia leans forward, meaning to pinch her again. Quick as her panther, Seymour slaps Cecilia's hands away and almost topples her from her seat. She manages to catch herself, although it causes the manacles to cut into her wrists unpleasantly.

She laughs. "You are fascinating, Lady Seymour. How can a woman be such a pin poppet one moment and such a needle the next?"

Cecilia has never truly been attracted to women, although she's dallied with a few just to see what it felt like, and she's tempted to try with Seymour. It would certainly pass the time while she works out how to escape.

"I bet my brother had a lot of fun with you," she says.

Seymour stiffens. Ah – so there is a chink in her armour.

"Maybe when he finds you, I can convince him to share you with me before he puts you down."

Cecilia is buoyant once more, trembling with the thrill of the insult.

She has forgotten that the two of them are not alone.

The panther rises like a moving shadow from the floor. It climbs up onto the seat next to her, and then, slowly, climbs into Cecilia's lap, pinning her hands beneath its bulk.

"My apologies," she says, as the panther places its front paws on her chest.

"My apologies, what?" Seymour says.

The panther brings its great face close to Cecilia, golden eyes gleaming with the light of barely contained bloodlust. It licks its lips with a flick of pink tongue.

"My apologies, Lady Seymour."

"No."

The panther bares his teeth. She feels his growl through her gown, a vibration against her skin. She remembers the way he pulled Lorena's oesophagus from her throat.

"My apologies, Queen Seymour."

There is a moment when she thinks it has not been enough. Then the carriage jolts to a stop, and with one swift motion Seymour pulls the curtain back, opens the door and steps down. The panther licks its lips once more, then leaps down after her.

Cecilia waits a moment, forcing her breathing to slow. Then she pushes herself up and peers out of the vehicle.

They are in a clearing in the middle of a manicured wood. Before her stands a house of wooden beams and white plaster that looks like a skeleton in the moonlight.

"Are you going to tell me where we are now?" she asks the Feorwan as they help her down.

"Why would I do that?" they say.

The house is smaller than the lodging she's used to, but infinitely better than the ship's cell. Inside, a large fireplace has been lit and several dogs are spread out on a rug before it, their paws stretched towards the warmth. Above the fireplace, a lighter patch of paint indicates the absence of a portrait; perhaps one that would have given Cecilia a clue as to her whereabouts.

They go through to a small banqueting hall containing a single long table. There isn't even a gallery for musicians, only a rood screen behind which they can play.

"I've seen finer brothels in Perfugi," she says as she is shown to her seat.

"And how we all wish you would have stayed in one," Seymour says, sitting opposite her.

Seymour's panther pads to Cecilia's side of the table and sits upright and watchful just beside her left elbow.

"Would you please call off your beast?" she says.

"No."

A servant enters, bearing a large tray containing a variety of simple dishes: sweet pea soup; hot bread and soft butter scattered with herbs and crisp chicken skin; a cheese encrusted with crushed purple grapes; a dish of aromatic barley scattered with berries and lamb and wine-rich gravy. Even Cecilia must admit that they have been cooked with skill equal to her own palace chefs.

"Maybe once you've been arraigned for treason, I'll hire your cook," she tells Seymour.

"You will be needing a replacement, since I drowned the last one," Seymour replies.

Cecilia laughs.

"I am sorry for my churlishness in the carriage," she says, feeling as though she is growing as a person for this display of largesse. Seymour stiffens.

"Let us not talk of it," she says.

"You're supposed to apologise for nearly getting your panther to kill me."

"Or perhaps I will tell him to finish the job."

"Ugh!" Cecilia bangs her fork on the table, making the rest of the cutlery jump. "I am trying to be friends with you!"

"Why should I desire your friendship?" Seymour snaps, pulling her napkin from her shoulder with a crack and tossing it onto the table.

"Prude," Cecilia says. Seymour's mouth twitches. Cecilia points at her with her fork. "You are. You judge me because I freely do what you cannot."

The panther growls behind Cecilia. She lowers the fork.

"You think I have no hunger?" Seymour says very calmly, reaching for a dish of cucumbers stuffed with bread and cheese. "Believe me, Cecilia, I have appetite enough. Your wantonness is nothing to me. But wantonness paired with cruelty? It is that to which I object."

"That is because you are weak."

"Only in the eyes of those who deem your brother strong."

Cecilia wants to insist that Henry *is* strong: the strongest person she knows beside herself. But she has some notion that this would only prove Seymour's point. The girl has led her down a trapped path. Clever.

"I never understand it when people talk of fucking as some great intimacy," she says, spreading her hands on the table. "To me, it is pleasurable no matter who it is with. It is like eating or sleeping: even if it is not particularly well done, it is necessary to life. Why not find the enjoyment in all of it?"

Seymour is quiet for some time. Eventually she says, "I thought I could feel the same as you about it. But I could not. Perhaps it is because I was not born to royalty."

"What does that have to do with anything?" Cecilia says.

"Even when you married, you were a princess marrying a king. He had to afford you some respect, did he not? Or he risked Henry's wrath."

"Henry would not have cared." But that is not quite true. Henry is a romantic, unlike her or Arthur.

"Your husband did not know that, though," Seymour says. She rises. "I will bid you goodnight. I hope that we will be able to exist together here for a little while, even if I do not trust you."

"You would be a fool to. I will still kill you, even if I do rather like you."

Left alone in the hall, Cecilia thinks of her ship and the way it disintegrated at Seymour's command. Such power, just out of her reach. An image of Florin's face, pale and desperate in the water. Well. He was very fond of her. She hopes his death was quick. She shakes herself and reaches for more food. She must turn her thoughts to the present, and to the future. The past is rarely helpful. She must turn her thoughts to the mystery of the hard shape in Seymour's gown, and the question of where she is – and who this house belongs to. For if they have removed the portraits, then that suggests that this is not one of Seymour's old properties. And if that is the case, then Seymour has accomplices beyond the Feorwan servant. Cecilia is going to find out exactly who they are.

CHAPTER TWENTY-FIVE

Cleves

There is an art to setting a trap. Cleves has laid many in her time. As a child, she became adept at understanding the way creatures moved through a forest or a marsh: boar; the smaller wild dragons of Ezzonid; soldiers; vicious fairies.

The patch of woodland she squats in now reminds her of those days. The air is humid, scented with mud and the tang of bear's garlic. They are only a short ride from the outskirts of Cnothan Town, but no human has willingly come to this wood in many years, despite its rich offerings.

"I do not understand why you did not set your servants this task," Johana says. He passes her another twist of rope, and she secures it to two tree trunks, creating a makeshift fence, a funnel.

"If my husband had sought anything other than living crones, I might have done."

"So you risk my life instead. I am flattered."

"I will remind you again that I did not insist upon your company, Johana. You could always journey to Gnottel Lodge and check on our prisoner."

He has been by her side almost constantly since the moment she admitted her plan to overthrow Henry. She cannot deny that he has been helpful, but she can neither trust nor stomach it. She has been content with her own company for many years. She is too set in her ways to change now.

"From what my servants have told me of Cecilia's behaviour, I think I would rather face the crones."

They move to their next position, tracking a path between ferns and bluebells to a deep trench, freshly dug.

"Why does the king even wish for such vile creatures?" Johana says. He presses a handkerchief over his nose, so his voice is muffled.

"That I do not yet know."

"But you think it wise to help him?"

She casts around for fallen branches, using them to cover the trench in greenery.

"I think it wise to show him that I am willing to do his bidding, no matter how dangerous," she says.

Johana flicks a branch in her direction with his toe. "Do you fear that he suspects you?"

"He would be a fool not to." She throws the branch over the trench, covering the last of it, and stands, out of breath. "Of all his remaining queens, I stand the most to gain from taking back the goddess's power, since I have never been in his favour. And Cecilia's ship was nigh on halfway between Cnothan and Plythe. Of course he will be watching me closely."

"It is perhaps good fortune, then, that your brother has tied our two countries so closely together with this treaty. It offers you some protection, no?"

"Yes, my brother undoubtedly made the deal for *my* benefit."

Johana sighs loudly. The sound clogs the woody air.

She glares at him. "Quiet, cousin; you will alert the crone to my plans."

He pulls a face at her as they used to do when they were children, but when he speaks again he is quieter. "Can you truly blame Wilhelm for treating with Henry? He waited, cousin. *We* waited. When our butterflies told us the rumours, we waited for you. And you never sent us more than niceties."

She stifles a laugh as she kneels, checking from every angle that the trench is concealed.

"What would have been the point? Ezzonid would never have moved against Elben. Even if you were a seafaring nation, you could have sent ship after ship against the bordweal and seen every one destroyed."

"You are no simpleton. You know as well as I that there is more than one way to wage war, and many ways without need of weapons or warships. Is this not the war you wage now?"

He has a point there, but Cleves is not about to admit it.

"Well, I am the way I am, Johana. I have taken you into my confidence now, have I not?"

There is movement in the distance. A crack of branches breaking. They still. Johana swears beneath his breath. "If I die in this godforsaken place, I shall spit upon you, cousin."

It has been a long time since she heard that phrase. It sounds uncouth in translation, but in its original Ezzonidian, it suggests a haunting, the malicious dance of ghosts.

"No one is going to die," she says. Not today, at least, if she has set her trap right. In the days to come? Well. It does no good to dwell on that.

She peers through the undergrowth. "There you are," she breathes.

The crone is statuesque. Even from this distance, she can see it is tall, its spindled front legs almost as long as her body. The tusks that arc from beneath its jaws are russet with stale blood. It has no fur, no scales, only spotted tufts of stiff hair. She is too far away to see its eyes, which are sunken within its skull, but she knows with the knowledge of one who has been both hunter and prey that it watches her as she watches it.

"Stay here and do not move," she whispers to Johana. He stares at her.

"You are using me as bait?"

"No. I am making it think that I am using you as bait."

She does not wait to hear his protestations, slipping away towards the east of the wood where the undergrowth is thicker and the trees change from beech to oak. She finds a particular tree that has obliging roots and low branches, and hefts herself up to a crook. She settles herself there, kneeling so that she can spring up easily, and searches once more for the crone.

To his credit, Johana has done as she directed. He remains beside the covered trench, although his crouch is stiff with terror. The crone continues to watch him, and it is so still that for a moment she wonders if it is a living creature or a statue. Then it turns, just its head, to rest its gaze on her, and she knows that she has calculated correctly.

Since her first year of marriage, she has studied the crones' behaviour, for they have plagued the woodlands of her territories all this time. They are derided as the most abominable of beasts, but she knows something about the power that comes from being labelled unattractive. The way it can be used as a camouflage. The crones, above all else, are intelligent. They can smell a trick, catch a deception. So she has given them one.

Cleves holds her breath as the crone slips closer to Johana. For such an ungainly beast, it can move with impressive stealth, using its long front legs to test a spot, almost as a human would use their hands.

Johana edges back against a tree trunk. He is muttering something that she cannot hear, although she would lay money on it being a string of Ezzonidian curses. Her heart thumps faster, louder. Has she misjudged? If the crone falls into the trench, she will not be able to truss it up for delivery to High Hall. Her plan will come to naught.

"Be clever, but not too clever," she whispers. It is an entreaty, a prayer.

And it works.

As the crone's cloven hoof descends upon the unsupported branch that covers the trench, the creature seems to transform. From stealth, it erupts into movement, so quickly that Cleves almost throws herself backwards and ruins everything. It springs sideways on powerful back legs, charging towards the tree where she crouches.

Cleves bares her teeth in victory.

The crone reaches the bottom of the tree. She can see its eyes now; black pebbles in a rat's head. And in those eyes she realises her miscalculation. She is too high for the crone to reach her with its head, but not with those long forelegs.

She tugs on the rope next to her at the same moment as the beast reaches up and scrapes one of those cloven hooves across her stomach.

A dozen ropes, concealed in the thick undergrowth, spring up around the crone. It is hoisted into the air, legs tangled and tusks tossing furiously. The net holds despite its struggle.

"*Frizun!*" Cleves curses, climbing down gingerly.

"You are hurt?" Johana says, stumbling through ferns towards her.

"Not seriously," she says. Her gown and the many layers of clothing beneath it makes it impossible for her to see the spot where the crone touched her. No blood seeps through, and the fabric is intact, yet her stomach is agony.

They look up at the still-struggling crone. It is only from this vantage point that she sees its teets, shrivelled and milk-dry. Now she thinks on it, it is strange that no one has ever come across a crone with young, or a crone freshly born.

"Will your net hold?" Johana says.

"The rope is made of twisted mægencord," she says. Vines from Alpich used in shipbuilding and the hoisting of rocks.

Johana nods. He looks at her sidelong. "Just out of curiosity, how would you have explained my death to our family?"

"It would not have come to that."

He wants her to apologise. She did not ask for his presence here, and if he is going to hold his help over her head, then she does not want it. She is through with men and their desire for gratitude.

Johana smiles sadly.

"Those soldiers, cousin. That night. You were so open and easy before."

Cleves spreads her arms wide. "Do you not find me convivial, Johana?"

"Convivial, yes. But I miss the earnest girl I once knew. This woman before me is all smiles and smoke. You are like that castle you have holed yourself up inside."

"Come, Johana. You have been at a royal court for as long as I. You know how we must be."

"It is not court that has done this to you."

Cleves turns away from him. She must test the strength of the mægencord before fetching her servants to cage the beast.

"They did not hurt you, *hiwi*," he says, using the Ezzonid endearment for a family member. Cleves does not reply. No, they did not hurt her body. That is true. She was spared that at least.

"People are always hurt in a war," she says quietly. "No one truly escapes unscathed."

Above their heads, the crone sends up a cry; a keening call of fury that sends the woodland birds spiralling into the sky.

CHAPTER TWENTY-SIX

Howard

An idea, perhaps too daring for Howard to execute, flickers on the periphery of her mind. She is scared to look at it directly. As is usual for her, she may be too late, but the thought only came to her when she realised how quiet Plythe is in the absence of Henry's court. It is not the absence of busy noise she notices so much as the absence of whispers. The slight glances and slivering shifts in loyalty; the intrigue conveyed through looks rather than language, every bit as indecipherable as a foreign tongue. They follow Henry everywhere he goes, leaving fruitful information in their wake.

What if she could harness those whispers?

Howard finds herself in the music room, where her harpsichord sits. She raises the lid, heart pounding. Her own *sunscína* is set into the lid of the instrument. It is a beautiful thing, a polished sheet of material that mirrors, when it is not showing her the other queens, the light of the windows and the playful reflection of the Kyttle Falls. If her plan does not work, she will have destroyed an artefact of ancient beauty and power for nothing. But if her plan does work, she may change the course of their endeavour entirely.

She may even make the other queens like her.

Howard tries to prise the *sunscína*'s settings apart, but the wires are too delicate, and her nails make little mark. She casts around the room for a tool. A decanter sits on a low table next to the window. It was a gift from Lord Wolsey, if she recalls, made of finest crystal mined from the mountains below Mathmas. The rock is carved with roosters and waning moons: symbols of fertility. Always, she is a vessel: empty but for the king's thoughts, the king's seed.

She weighs the decanter in one hand, building her courage. Then, with a force she did not know she was capable of, she smashes the decanter against the *sunscína*, shielding her face with her free hand. Glass shards embed themselves in her arm and hair. The keys of her harpsichord are covered in crystal . . . and tiny slivers of polished *sunscína*.

The stone has cracked like a sun, rays reaching from the centre to the very edges. It is not a stone, not really – it is the eye of a goddess, and it has never looked more so than in this broken state, the fractures radiating outwards like flecks from a pupil. Is it not strange, how divinity is so often partnered with the tangible? How immortality can be carved up and plucked out to be shared like a suckling pig on a platter? If she were a goddess, she would make it a point to keep herself whole.

"Oh," she says, a single high note of discovery. Goddesses can afford to be beneficent with their bodies, for they own them outright, and their power is not diminished by disfigurement. Howard has been called a goddess by many men, her husband included. But what they meant was: *you make me feel like a god. You are a goddess by right of belonging to me.*

She wants to own herself. She deserves to own herself.

Howard plucks the silver headdress from her curls and uses one edge of it to prise two shards from the harpsichord – one large, one small. She weighs them in her palms. She knows from Seymour's trick with her broken *sunscína* that whichever piece she keeps with her will still work. The question is, will the other?

A servant knocks on the door. "Your Majesty? We heard a crash."

"You may enter," she replies.

The girl's eyes widen at the sight of the shattered instrument. The servants at Plythe know more about the history of the palace than any of the nobility; they will know that this harpsichord was commissioned by the first queen of this territory, many hundreds of years ago. Elswyth was a famed beauty of Elben, too. Howard wonders whether she would be pleased that this is the only fragment of her life remembered by her country's descendants. Howard does not doubt that there was more to her than a clear complexion and rounded cheek. Would Elswyth be pleased by her shimmering, insubstantial legacy? Or did she, in life, strive to peel back her skin to reveal the woman beneath?

"There was an accident," Howard tells the servant, putting on her best queenly voice. "Clear the crystal. Collect the pieces. I will find some other use for them. We will order a new glass frontage for the instrument's lid."

Once the girl has vanished, Howard flees the room, stowing the *sunscína*'s pieces in the folds of her sleeve. She finds her ladies in the rose gardens, which are verdant at this time of year, an orchestra of petals, from violet to dusky pink to yolk yellow. They are cutting the flowers to dry, wrapping their stems over and over in blue ribbon that has been bathed in the sap of the sereklin tree, which is said to have healing properties. They will give the posies to the almshouses and the leech houses, for the curing of the poor's maladies.

Howard approaches them with the unsteady energy of a foal. She is pleased to see, as she gets nearer, that Susanna is in the midst of them, rather than on the periphery.

"Well met, Your Majesty," Lady Tylney says, the first to spy her.

Ursula Askew studies her with the intensity she always seems to reserve for Howard. "Are you plotting?"

"Hush," Howard says, then flurries the final few steps into their company and pulls them to the ground with her. It is the afternoon and the sun blankets them in warmth, but the grass is still damp, as it always is here with the spray from the Kyttle Falls. The humidity thickens and the women lean in as Howard displays her broken treasure upon her lap.

"Your *sunscína*! Oh, Howard," Legh says. "You always were clumsy."

"It was no accident," she tells her sister. "I wish to see if I can use it for something more than its intended purpose, and I need your help."

There is delighted laughter and the chitter of conspiracy as Howard lays out her plan.

"We ought to test that it works first," Lady Tylney says, ever practical, ever the eldest.

Legh nudges Howard. "You could try it with that handsome new courtier. The one you think might be on your side."

Howard catches a darted look between Susanna and Ursula, and wonders whether they heard the same thing she did. Not *our* side but *your* side. With every fresh day, Howard regrets telling her half-sister all that she has, but it is done now, and she must make the most of it. She is on a heady cliff, as Boleyn was. And like Boleyn, if she is going to fall, she will be the one to step off the ledge. She will not be pushed.

"That is a good thought," she says. Legh was always easily bought with compliments.

Another look between Ursula and Susanna. Then Lady Tylney says, "How do you imagine it will work?"

She takes the two shards in each hand, trying to think clearly. The *sunscína* work only when more than one Queen of Elben touches them. But do they discern between the queens, or do they simply know that a queen holds them? Howard reaches into her hair, finding the spot where her curls are thinning; where clumps of hair have been falling out for the last year, leaving behind itchy, grey skin. She tugs gently and a few strands slide out of her scalp. Swallowing bile and ignoring the way her ladies avert their gazes, Howard winds the strands around the smaller shard.

"One of you must take this, and instigate a conversation with Master Culpepper," she says. "If the *sunscína* works as I think it ought, then I will be able to hear your conversation from here."

"I shall do it," Susanna and Legh say at the same time.

Howard's throat feels tight. "It may be dangerous. If I am wrong about him, then he may find you suspicious."

Legh laughs. "If you fooled him, then I surely can too, sister."

Ursula hisses softly. Legh falters, then laughs again. "Come, Your Majesty, let me do it," she says. Her cheeks are tinged pink, visible despite her russet skin.

"I am also happy to take the risk," Susanna says, watching Howard evenly.

Susanna is the safer choice. Howard knows this. Yet – she *wants* to trust Legh. As children, Legh was ever Howard's protector and advisor, and Howard has seen her manipulate their aunt and dozens of their elders. Howard has no doubt that Susanna would keep her secrets, but she also wonders whether Susanna is bold enough to elicit the kind of information she requires. Would Culpepper not be more suspicious of a formerly timid lady-in-waiting suddenly approaching him? Susanna is the kind of person who can keep a secret, but does not invite them.

"Here," Howard says, offering the smaller shard to Legh. Legh makes a small "O" of surprise before clambering to her feet.

"This will be fun," she says.

"Not fun. Important," Howard says.

Legh huffs. "All right, I know."

She tucks the shard into the bag that hangs from her belt, next to her pomander.

"Good fortune to you," Lady Tylney calls after her.

They all watch as she strides across the lawn, the epitome of confidence. Howard can feel the weight of the others' reservations.

"I know," she says.

Howard shivers, suddenly chilled. Goldfoot, from his midair frolics hunting butterflies, soars across the garden and lands in her lap. He drapes himself across her chest and breathes warm air against her neck. She wraps her arms around him, letting the sizzling heat of his scales comfort her and bring feeling back to her fingers.

"She is not a believer," Ursula says.

"She is a lost soul," Lady Tylney says, her voice unusually soft. "I was once as she is, when I was younger."

Howard remembers then that it took Lady Tylney's family a little while to realise she was a woman.

"She could have damned me to Henry long before now," Howard says. Her family presented her to Henry as a girl of purity, one who had never known the touch of man. Legh could have told him then, or in any of the intervening years, that this introduction was a lie.

The larger *sunscína* shard rests in her lap, beneath Goldfoot's steady weight. No one suggests leaving the rose garden. Were it not for the sun's steady progress across the sky and the shimmering rainbows it makes against the spray of the falls, she might have thought that time stood still.

At last, when Goldfoot's breathing has slowed and his claws flick against her gown as he hunts in his sleep, she senses the *sunscína* stir. She grasps the shard in one hand, keeping Goldfoot pressed against her with the other, and closes her eyes. Could her wild scheme actually work?

All is darkness in her vision, for the other shard remains in Legh's bag, but she hears the click of a door being opened.

"I have been meaning to become better acquainted with you, Master Culpepper," Legh says.

"Oh, sister," Howard whispers.

"Is it working?" Ursula says, placing her hand upon the shard too, as if hoping to channel Howard's queenly connection.

Howard nods.

"And I yours, mistress," Culpepper says. His voice is the slow drip of treacle. "I understand you have the ear of the queen, and are the closest of her companions."

Legh laughs. "Oh, I don't know about that."

Someone plucks an instrument – a lute, perhaps, from the waterfall of strings. She thinks, from the way the sound echoes off wood panelling, that they must be in her receiving chamber.

"You ladies are always with her, always scheming. Such a bond between friends is quite charming, and very intimidating."

Howard can hear Culpepper's smile. She wonders whether there is more to be read from his attitude, and if there is, whether Legh has the skill to do so.

"So we intimidate you? A man such as you, frightened of a group of women. It seems unlikely, sir."

Howard smiles. Susanna has many skills, but she could not have steered the conversation as deftly and as subtly as Legh has done.

"I think we both know that some women have extraordinary power, mistress. Your sister, I think, is one of them," Culpepper says.

"My sister has always had power, sir, even before she got herself a crown. She just does not know it."

It is the kindest thing Legh has ever said. Perhaps the kindest thing she has ever said *about* her. Howard wonders whether this is an apology for her earlier insults, or whether Legh has forgotten that Howard should be able to hear her. Legh is like written scripture to Howard: inconsistent and indecipherable.

There is a scraping along wood, as though someone has thrown themself into a chair. Howard frowns. The only chair in her receiving chamber is her throne.

"I only wish I knew how to assure her of my loyalty," Culpepper says.

"You serve her in her palace – why should she not think you loyal?" Legh replies.

There is a long silence. Howard wishes she could see what is happening. Doubt pools once again in her stomach: are they conveying messages to each other too quietly for the *sunscína* to hear? What exactly are they doing?

"I think you know what I mean, mistress," Culpepper says. Howard can barely hear him, but the words are unmistakable. *Well done, Legh.* She has smoked him out.

"You are becoming tiresome, Master Culpepper. What of your loyalty to me, hm? Are you not going to ask me about my extraordinary power?"

Culpepper laughs, switching from earnest follower to easy courtier.

"Come, mistress," he says. "I have business to attend with the master of dragons. Accompany me for a while?"

Their conversation descends into chattering flirtation as the door opens once more. Howard presses her *sunscína* and sits back on her heels.

"So?" Ursula prompts.

"He knows, and he is for us," Howard says.

The pause that follows echoes her own uncertainties.

"Will you admit him into your confidence?" Susanna says.

Howard shakes her head. She strokes Goldfoot's back; long, gentle strokes. He begins to snore in his sleep. "Perhaps one day, but not imminently."

If she was not carrying this great secret, she would have enjoyed kindling a dalliance with handsome, earnest Master Culpepper. But as it is she is already plagued with doubt over Legh. She will not add to that doubt.

"Not that my opinion matters, but I am glad of your decision," Susanna says.

"Of course your opinion matters," Howard replies.

Ursula seizes Susanna's hand, across their circle of gowns. Lady Tylney places her hand over theirs. They look to Howard. Hers crowns theirs as she says, "We have plenty to be getting on with now, ladies. My scheme works. So let us think how best to use it."

She does have extraordinary power. Culpepper knows it, and so does Legh. With her ladies leaning towards her, drinking up her tasks, she is beginning to know it too.

CHAPTER TWENTY-SEVEN

Cleves

Is there anything more comfortable, and comforting, than a well-kept stable? Cleves does not think so. She has spent many hours in the stables that are housed in the outermost ring of the Castle of Cnothan. Many hours improving the building, with its low, sloping roof of mossed tiles. Inside, the bays progress in rows, each one with its own manger and hay drop. There is something warming about the gentle energy of the horses. She likes to think that they appreciate the calm she has provided, for she has insulated the building against the clang of church bells and the bustle of the square outside. In here, all is peace.

"I resent it," Johana says, following her as she attends to each horse.

"You shock me," she replies. She crouches to examine a canker. The horse nuzzles her head. This is why she only bothers to tame her hair on special occasions.

"I am not a guard, or a gaoler. I am not a trainer of servants, cousin."

"And yet you appear to have done all three perfectly well."

"I am a man of action."

She stands, looks at him over the top of her glasses. He is dressed in a doublet of finest cloth of silver in accordance with Ezzonid's sumptuary laws. His hose is crafted from honeydragon leather, and upon his head is perched the most ridiculous feathered hat she has ever seen.

"I see no sword or dagger, cousin," she says.

"That is beside the point."

The door at the end of the stables opens, revealing Fergus, Cleves's master of horse. He is a stocky man, and his calloused hands speak of a life of labour. Those who attended the Moon Ball would likely not recognise him as her original dance partner before she asked Seymour for her hand and embroiled herself in all this mess.

"Is everything all right in here, Your Majesty?" Fergus says, wandering up the aisle towards them. Cleves pats the horse next to her. "This one seems tender on her left hind."

"Aye. She turned it in a rabbit hole. I'll be wrapping it in warm muslin later today."

Johana snorts. Fergus eyes him mildly. "You don't agree with the treatment, my lord?"

Johana stutters a little, then says, "I can offer no comment on the treatment, sir."

Oh, Cleves is going to enjoy this. She has rarely seen her cousin struggle for a witty retort, but then men who are good with their hands were ever his preference. She turns to Fergus: "I have tasked Lord Johana with the care of a very difficult creature. A fact he likes to complain about."

"*Two* difficult creatures, some might say," Johana mutters.

Fergus sticks his hands in his pockets. "Oh? What kind of animal are we talking about? I'm best with horses but I can usually turn a tricky beast good in the end."

Cleves tilts her head at Johana, smiling benignly, waiting to see how he will reply. Her clear challenge seems to rouse him.

"You might well call them hybrid creatures," he says. "They defy description."

"Mm," Fergus says. "How did you come across them then?"

Cleves shrugs. "I found them in some wreckage, looking very sorry for themselves."

Fergus shakes his head, and turns to Cleves. "Ah, that's bad then, Your Majesty. People meddle, don't they, with nature? It's not right, and it's the beasts that bear the brunt of it, poor things."

"Very true, Fergus," she says. "Very true."

"What would you do, then, to tame such beasts?" Johana asks Fergus.

Fergus eyes Johana's clothes; his unblemished skin and the smooth finish of his nails. "You have grooms, I presume, my lord?"

"I do." Johana instructed his own servants in Cecilia's care. The ones Cleves assigned to him from her own household were severely lacking in the niceties of attending upon an Ezzonidian lord, apparently.

"And they treat the creatures with patience? Kindness? Violence begets violence, you know."

Johana blushes. Though Fergus cannot know it, he has accused him of a sin that Johana, at least, regards as worse than violence upon an animal.

"I am no brute, sir," Johana says. "And nor are my servants."

Fergus shrugs. "Brute or no, there's some brutish practices in this world."

He wanders over to the lame horse and throws one arm around the animal's neck, feeding it a morsel of carrot with the other.

"But with time, and reasoning, and understanding of what brought them to you, you'll find a way," he says. The horse whickers in agreement.

Cleves and Johana say their farewells to Fergus. In the courtyard outside, Cleves leans against the stables and inhales the scent of the gethlewe flowers that drop like lilac stars from branches that embrace the building's white brick. Johana crosses his arms. "Well, I have reasoning, but I do not understand the Dowager Queen and I fear we do not have time. What do you make of my chances?"

Cleves pats his arm. "Were I a gambling woman, I would bet on you all day, cousin."

The truth is, she does not need Johana to *tame* Cecilia, or persuade her to their side. She merely needs him to keep her imprisoned long enough for Cleves to work out how to use her to her advantage. She knows this much about Henry's younger sister: there is no accord that can be made safely with Cecilia Tudor.

"I wish you would ask something else of me, cousin," he says.

"This is what I need from you, Johana. I am sorry it does not involve courting handsome masters of horse."

Johana peers inside the stables, seeing whether Fergus is still there. "He *is* very handsome. I think I might marry him."

"He is already married to a far better man than you."

In fact, Cleves was the one to make the match.

"You leach my visit to Elben of all possible excitement," Johana says. Cleves pushes off the wall and hooks her arm into his as they walk back towards the castle.

"Do not say such things," she says. "With any luck, I will author an uprising, and then you shall have more excitement than you could ever desire."

"*Violence begets violence*, as your man said," Johana says. It is as though he has slapped her. She looks up at him but sees no cruelty in his expression. He squeezes her arm, and sighs. "Sometimes we all have to do things we would rather not, when necessity wills it. For now, I will be your gaoler. I will keep the king's sister so secure that we will have no need of chains."

Cleves stops, gripping Johana's arm.

"That's it," she says.

Johana prises her hand away. "Have you finally gone mad?"

"*Chains*," she says. "What is the one tradition that all queens of Elben must undertake?"

Johana frowns. "Your strange clasping of the castle stone?"

"No!" She bounces on her toes. "That is different for each castle, and the king does not partake. But we *all* are bound to him during our wedding ceremony."

Johana's expression clears. "The silly cloths."

"The silly cloths."

She had almost laughed out loud when Bishop More had bound her and Henry together with the purple velvet. But then the pain had begun; something so visceral and unlike anything she had experienced before. She has never forgotten it. And now she understands why: it was granting her power, the power she was about to receive from the goddess, to another.

"It is so simple, though," Johana says.

"The best tricks always are. And that makes the remedy simple also."

"Destroy the silly cloths?"

She beams at him. "Oh cousin, your mind is as one with mine. It is quite beautiful."

CHAPTER TWENTY-EIGHT

Cecilia

Cecilia and Seymour are largely left alone at the woodland, but for a handful of young servants who assemble and scatter like starlings, their murmuration avoiding her as much as possible. Cecilia does not mind. They all of them look like the kind of dull, ill-educated empties common in provincial manor houses. She has nothing to say to them.

After that first night, Seymour stays out of her way too. Cecilia wouldn't care except she has never been left by herself so much before, and her mind is starting to turn over like tilled soil, revealing all kinds of bugs.

Her bedchamber is small but comfortable, but for a draught that winds its way around the single window. The floorboards creak, no matter how lightly she steps, and the fire sputters. Still, after the cold damp of her ship's cell, she finds herself grateful for the thick blankets and swan-feather mattress.

She roams, circuiting the rooms like clockwork – banqueting hall, drawing room, kitchen scullery, pantry, each time pressing gently against the wooden doors that lead across or into the moat. For all their absence, the servants are diligent about locking any access to the outside world.

She must be smarter than them. She must find another way. She is a wild animal, not meant for any cage.

During her circuits, she pauses whenever she hears the servants talking, pressing her ear to keyholes as she did when she was a child. Most of the time she overhears nothing but banalities: what they are planning for dinner; a complaint about the weather. But she does garner two things. The first is a word she does not understand – *dehanga*. She thinks, from the way it was spoken, spat out upon the stubbing of a toe, that it must be a curse. It is no language she recognises, but that signifies little since she was never an assiduous student. The second is a reference overheard in the kitchens: "Someone will have to be spared. It will take them a full day to get to Dreomere and back." Cecilia may not know her languages, but she once knew Elben well, and with a little time and focus she is certain she can know it again.

She finds a bundle of threads, a needle and a frame in a cupboard in one of the empty bedrooms next to her chamber, and takes them downstairs to untangle the threads, letting the puzzle and the crackle of the fire settle her mind. She lays out the different threads in neat curls: red, green, brown, white, black. So, to Dreomere and back is a full day's journey. The lake, known for its plentiful carp, lies on the border of Hyde and Cnothan's territories. Yet the lodge in which Cecilia is imprisoned is in the depths of a forest. There is no forest in Hyde. *Dehanga*. It does not sound like a Feorwan word – they are all lilts and vowels. But Ezzonid . . . they are fond of inserting many syllables into a short space.

"Oh my, Lady Seymour. You are in league with Cleves," she says under her breath.

Victory pounding in her chest, Cecilia goes hunting for fabric. She can find nothing but some old linen smocks. She roams the other bedchambers, eventually coming to one that is occupied. The fire has been lit, and a chest is open, revealing an assortment of drab, boxy gowns she recognises as belonging to Seymour. She listens carefully, but can hear no floorboards creaking. She checks the hallway again, just in case Seymour's damn irritating panther is skulking, as is his wont. Nothing.

Slipping inside the room and closing the door behind her, Cecilia tiptoes to the chest and rifles through the gowns. She selects the plainest one (they are all plain, but this one is positively drab) and fingers the material, assessing its thickness and whether the threads she has will work with the wool. Satisfied, she stands, when her eye catches on one of the other gowns: the deep green one Seymour wore when she was captured.

Cecilia lifts it out of the chest, being sure not to ruin the folds. She feels her way around the hem until she finds the hard, flat surface that has been sewn inside. She tears the hem apart with practised hands, and removes a sliver of rounded glass. She turns it over, lifting it to the speckled light coming through the window.

"What are you?" she whispers.

She tests a corner against her palm. Sharp, but not sharp enough to be a weapon. The rounded surface puzzles her the most. She feels as though she has seen it before, although she cannot think where.

Reluctantly, Cecilia shoves the shard back inside the dress's hem and takes the needle and some thread from her pocket, deftly re-securing it, making sure no stray ends could betray her meddling. She replaces the gown as she found it and slips out of the room with a different gown, her mind churning.

Seymour comes across her in the drawing room. Cecilia does not bend over her work – doing so makes her neck ache. Instead, she draws her feet up beneath her, curling them inside the chair, and rests the embroidery frame on her raised knees.

"Is that mine?" Seymour says, seizing the gown and almost ruining Cecilia's hold.

"Well, I am unlikely to own such a horrible piece of clothing, so I suppose it must be."

She can see, out of the corner of her eye, that Seymour is thinking of the secrets hidden in her chest, and struggling to phrase her outrage without betraying anything.

"Before you set your panther on me, be assured that when I am finished your gown will be greatly improved."

"That is not the point," Seymour says.

"Merchants used to pay vast sums for my work, you know. I never told anyone that they were embroidered by me, of course. Royalty does not sell their wares like a commoner. But it was gratifying."

Seymour teeters between indignation and curiosity, and then lowers herself into a chair on the other side of the fire, watching Cecilia work through narrowed eyes.

"Why did you choose that gown out of all of my belongings?" she says. Cecilia smiles – Seymour is trying to gauge whether she's found the glass.

"Because it was the first one in your chest?" she lies.

Seymour leans back in her chair.

"This is the strangest peace offering I have ever received," she says.

"You clearly have not lived. My husband, god rest his soul, once gifted me a brooch in the shape of my coney after we had a fight."

"Did you ever wear it in public?"

"What do you think?" Cecilia says.

Seymour sighs. "Of course you did."

"Of course I did."

"I am curious – did you truly think that your brother would give you a castle in exchange for me?" Seymour says.

"Do you doubt your importance to him?" Cecilia says.

"I know that he wishes to have me under his control. But to maintain the pretence that Cernunnos needs him to marry six queens, he would need to marry you. Henry is depraved, but not depraved enough for incest."

Cecilia kicks Seymour on the shin with her stockinged foot. "And yet you think me depraved enough?"

Seymour shrugs. "I witnessed you condemn your friend to death in order to capture me. Who am I to say what lengths you will go to in order to get what you desire?"

Cecilia sticks the needle in more forcefully, and almost ruins the tension in the weave. She does not like to think about Lorena. Or Lorena's brother, Florin. Both dead now. The end of their common little line.

"I would be able to persuade Henry. We would invent a way to explain it to the people."

Seymour shakes her head, amused. Cecilia does not like being laughed at. She considers pricking Seymour with the needle. But then she thinks of another way to wrest back control.

"How do you and your ugly Ezzonidian princess plan on persuading the people of Elben that you should rule instead?"

Seymour makes a valiant attempt to hide her shock.

"What are you talking about now?" she says. It is a weak rejoinder, and they both know it.

"You can drop your pretence. For all your deceit and the pitiful acting of the servants in this house, you cannot hide the truth from me. The Queen of Cnothan is in league with you."

The silence stretches between them, so long that any further attempt by Seymour to deny it would be laughable. Cecilia wants to drive the point in further. She cannot forget the humiliation served upon her by Seymour and her panther.

"I suppose," she says, returning her focus to her embroidery, "that it should come as no surprise that Henry's ugliest queens should turn against him. You, Cleves, Boleyn. You could not gain his attention any other way, so now you seek to overthrow him. He who raised you up."

It is a misstep. She should have remembered that Seymour places no importance on appearance.

"When is the last time you spoke to your brother?" Seymour says.

"We write to each other."

"You think him very noble and just." It is a taunt.

"If he has any fault, it is that he gives his love too freely to those who do not deserve it."

Seymour scoffs. She leans forward, forcing Cecilia to look at her. Such a curious woman – so retiring one moment, on the attack the next.

"What do you know of love? What do any of your family truly understand of the notion?"

"I know that commoners like yourself use my brother's love against him in your grasping quest for power."

Cecilia does not usually put herself out for others, but she will not have this upstart bitch pretend that Henry is ungallant.

"And what does he grasp in return?" Seymour says. The bones in her neck stand out.

"Oh, spare me your outrage."

Seymour opens her mouth to protest, but then thinks better of it. She sits back, looks to the fire as Cecilia returns to her embroidery. To a stranger, it must be the very image of feminine domesticity. As she stitches, Cecilia realises what a mistake she has made in defending Henry so vehemently. For now, Seymour will not believe any attempt she makes at bargaining her way out of this imprisonment. She cannot bring herself to regret it, though. There are but two people in the world she would defend to her detriment, and Henry is one of them.

As if reading her thoughts, Seymour says, very softly, "He saved your life, I think."

He did. Many times over. But Cecilia will be damned before she tells Seymour that.

"He is a good man, and there is no poison you can drip that will persuade me otherwise," is all she says.

"Boleyn thought that way too, once," Seymour says. And that is that.

CHAPTER TWENTY-NINE

Cleves

When Johana comes to her with the simple words, "She knows", Cleves is rather pleased with her reaction. Namely, that she manages to conceal all true emotion.

"I have known of Seymour's rebellion against the king for nearly a year now, and kept the secret to myself for as long. But your servants and Seymour could not keep my involvement a secret for longer than a few days. It is remarkable, cousin."

Johana scowls. "If I did not love you, I would turn you over to the king myself. I have played servant for days. Do you know what that does to a man's self-worth?"

So Cecilia knows that Cleves is allied with Seymour. It follows that Cleves should meet with the Dowager Queen. People like Cecilia and Aragon only make bargains with fellow royalty, and though Cleves does not like it, she knows how to play that game. Such a visit aligns with the other plan that has been forming in her head ever since she and Johana realised that the binding cloths are the key to releasing Medren's power: she must go to the viper's nest. To High Hall. And she must get there before Mary Boleyn's royal wedding.

The benefit of having a small household and a smaller court is that it does not take long for her retinue to be readied, and it is a simple matter to avoid bringing any nobility with her. It is well known that her ways are odd, and that she prefers to travel with animals rather than humans.

It is nearly midnight when she reaches Gnottel Lodge. The new moon lights the clearing in which the house sits, the little drawbridge pulled up across the moat. Gnottel Lodge was built for merriment – weekend parties and the like. Here, Cleves's role is benevolent hostess. Now, though, she feels like a gaoler. There is something deeply uncomfortable about that raised drawbridge. It puts her in mind of another time, when a woodland house intended for banqueting became a fortress besieged. Only that time, she was the one trapped inside.

To her surprise, Cleves finds Seymour and the king's sister sitting in companionable silence beside a fire. The domestic sight – Cecilia at needlework; Seymour dozing over a book – makes her pause. Johana follows her with Lelij, who bleats plaintively when he spies the warm fire. Cecilia looks up, and a predatory smile spreads across her face.

"Has the Queen of Cnothan sent me new fodder?" she says.

Cleves could laugh. She does not know who she is. Cleves wonders whether she should have some fun, but then decides that would be ill-advised with this woman. Seymour was charmed by the trick; Cecilia would not be. Cleves settles for removing her travelling cloak, revealing a gown of royal purple, cut sleeveless in the Ezzonid style. She does enjoy watching first puzzlement then realisation break across Cecilia's face.

"You are Queen Cleves?" she says bluntly.

"For several years, yes," Cleves replies.

Cleves knows what will happen next, and she is not disappointed. It is the same when anyone who has heard tell of the "ugly queen" meets her. Their eyes travel across Cleves's face, and then down her body, searching for proof that she is as repugnant as the rumours say. There are two kinds of people: those who trust their eyes over the rumours, and those who trust the rumours over their eyes. She wonders which Cecilia will be.

"How did you trick him?" Cecilia says at last.

Cleves cannot help but glance to Seymour, who is watching the exchange with studied disinterest.

"Trick who?" Cleves says.

"You are perfectly attractive. Why does my brother say you are not?"

So Cecilia has more wits about her than Cleves had thought. That is interesting. Cleves hands her cloak to a servant and takes one of the spare seats, closest to the fire.

"I am interested that you should think I would be the trickster," she says, patting her lap in invitation to her gargoyle. "Who is to say your brother did not trick me into coming to this island only to humiliate me for his own purposes?"

"Hmm," Cecilia says, sitting back down herself. The two women regard each other, like duellists circling after their first parry. Cleves wonders whether Cecilia is as aware of Seymour watching them as Cleves herself is.

"You must be hungry after your long journey," Cecilia says. She raises a hand, summoning a servant. It is a double test: she is trying to ascertain how far they are from Cnothan, and marking herself as the senior royal. Before Cecilia can order anything, Cleves tells the servant, "The Dowager Queen is hungry, and I would welcome some wine."

She smiles at Cecilia. Cecilia smiles back.

Johana ruins the moment by snorting. He pulls a chair across the room and places it beside Seymour. "May I join you in watching the tournament?" he asks.

Seymour smiles up at him. "Should we take bets, my lord?"

"It is bold of you to assume that I have money with which to bet. I am, after all, merely a third cousin of the King of Ezzonid."

Bread, cakes and fruit are brought, along with a jug of fine white wine from Gkontai, one of Cleves's favourites.

"Rather than spectating, would you care to join us, perhaps?" Cleves says to Seymour and Johana. Tempted by the smell of food, Lelij climbs off Cleves's lap, stretches and turns his attention to Seymour. Haltrasc watches him nuzzle his mistress and growls half-heartedly – territorial, but not so much that he can be bothered to rise from his snug place by the fire.

"First you take my panther's affections; now you make a play for my gargoyle," Cleves says.

"I believe the panther was a gift," Seymour says, scratching Lelij's muzzle. "And besides, I do not believe that anything with a soul can truly be stolen: it merely gives its heart elsewhere."

There is much that Cleves could say to that, much that she wants to say. Where do you give your heart these days, Queen of Hyde? Or: I am a thief and should like to test your claim. But Cecilia and Johana are here, so she merely says, "I know little of hearts or souls, so I will bow to your expertise, my angry queen."

She slices a piece of hard cheese, ignoring the way Cecilia is looking between her and Seymour, as though she has stumbled upon a great secret and cannot wait to share it. Cleves returns her attention to her. "So, Your Majesty. Now we have caught you – or stolen you, whichever way you would have it – what are we going to do with you?"

"I am shocked that you do not already know," Cecilia says.

"If anyone were to ask me, I would say get rid of her," Johana remarks, taking a bite of an apple. He chews, then looks at the fruit appraisingly. "Truly, these are the only delicious thing to come out of this country."

"That is one option," Cleves agrees.

"Cecilia believes in her brother's great love," Seymour says. "Perhaps we could bargain with him for her safe release."

Something passes between Seymour and Cecilia then – Cleves realises that this was a barb on Seymour's part. She does not believe that Henry will save his sister. But Cecilia does. Cleves wonders how she can use that.

"I assume you desire a throne of your own," Cleves says. "Perhaps your brother would be willing to give up his grasp upon Elben in exchange for his sister taking . . . shall we say Brynd?"

Cecilia scoffs. "You think to exchange a kingdom for a castle?"

"A stolen kingdom for a freely given castle," Cleves says.

Cecilia appears to consider this. "He will not like it," she says at last.

"No, I don't imagine he will."

Johana takes another bite of his apple. The crunch echoes around the room.

Cecilia flicks her hair behind her shoulder. "Shall I write to him to begin the negotiations?" she says.

Cleves is almost disappointed. Cecilia has capitulated far too easily to be sincere. She is in some respects extremely clever, and in others hopelessly transparent. But Cleves plays along; she may as well allow Cecilia to think she has the advantage. "Why don't you take a few nights to think it over? It is no small negotiation we are asking you to undertake."

Cecilia stands, smooths her gown. "Good night, ladies," she says, and sweeps from the room. Johana spreads his hands. "I am confused. Am I a lady or am I invisible?"

Seymour leans towards Cleves. "She is lying, of course."

"Of course," Cleves says, leaning in too.

Johana looks between them. "I think I must be invisible. I shall take myself outside, ensuring any little butterflies that may be lurking nearby are safely tucked away." There is a stifled sound from just beyond the door, and Johana raises his eyebrows at them as he leaves. Alone with Seymour, Cleves finds herself emboldened and terrified all at once. It is strange: attractive women do not usually frighten her. Usually, she knows precisely what to say and do once she is alone with them.

But then Seymour has always held a different space in Cleves's mind. Cleves still remembers reading the letter from her informant, and learning of the lady-in-waiting who had been sent to kill her mistress, and who had instead fallen in love with said mistress and seduced a king. Did Seymour realise, Cleves wondered even then, just how remarkable she was?

"I have brought trouble to your door," Seymour says. They are still leaning towards each other. It is imperative that no eavesdroppers hear them.

"It is your way, is it not?" Cleves says.

"I thought you might be angry with me for saving Cecilia. But you do not seem to be angry, or sad, or pleased . . . All I ever seem to do is amuse you."

Good, Cleves thinks. *It is working then.*

"The world, life – these things always amuse me."

"And what we are doing – plotting against a king, leading our country towards civil war – is that also amusing to you?"

Seymour is looking at Cleves in a way she does not like. As if Seymour knows something of Cleves. As if she knows something of soldiers and the cries of battle in the night.

"Well, if our little princess is to be believed, her brother's love for her will circumvent all need for civil war, will it not?" Cleves says. She laughs at her own joke.

Seymour's expression clouds, and Cleves sees that she has been too opaque. She pulls gently at one of the stray locks of brown hair peeking from beneath Seymour's hood. "I am committed to this cause, if that is what concerns you," she says. "But we cannot all be so serious all of the time, my angry queen."

Seymour goes still then, like the eye of a storm. She touches Cleves's face. A brief touch, like a lapdragon's kiss. "You speak of my anger as though it is a rare beast, Queen Cleves, but to me you are the strange one. I cannot understand how you are not angry. How do you remain in such good cheer through everything that has happened to you?"

"What has happened to me?" Cleves laughs. "Born to a royal throne. Married to a king. Queen of my own castle, with wealth and lands aplenty. What do I have to be angry about?"

There is a pressure upon her chest. She has never told anyone of that time in her life, and she never, ever will. It is hers to remember; hers and her family's. No one else shall ever hold that power over her.

Seymour frowns, her hand dropping into her lap. "Ezzonid was a troubled country when you were a child, no?"

"That was a matter for my father and his people. It did not touch me." Her voice must be colder than she intended. Seymour lets out a little sigh of frustration.

"In any case, I am not always so serious," Seymour says. She is so charmingly earnest. Cleves takes her hands and pulls her to her feet.

"Prove it then," she says. "Dance with me."

"But there is no music," Seymour says.

"Is there not?"

Cleves likes issuing challenges like this: daring people to play the fool as Cleves has played the fool during her marriage. The reaction she receives shows her the measure of a person more than any conversation. For an instant, she thinks Seymour will fail the test. Then Seymour straightens her shoulders, offers her hand to Cleves and bows.

"May I, my lady?"

Cleves takes the proffered hand, and they draw closer. Cleves leads Seymour slowly across the room, their steps light upon the flagstones. As they move, Cleves tells Seymour of her theory about the binding cloths, and that destroying them might be the key to ending Henry's theft. Seymour makes little answer. She pulls away and takes the lead, lifting her arm so that Cleves may spin beneath it. They come together once more, palm against palm, chest to chest, and Cleves no longer knows who leads and who follows. There is no flautist, no fiddle, no harpsichord, but – oh yes – there is music.

Seymour brushes her thumb across Cleves's knuckle. The sensation, gentle though it is, sends shivers across Cleves's entire body. "I think you are angry too, in your own way," Seymour says. "I only hope that you do not keep it so bottled up that it eats away at you from the inside."

Cleves looks up at her. "You are mistaken. There is no anger in me. You have enough for the both of us."

Seymour hesitates, then bends down to whisper in Cleves's ear, "Well, if you ever wish to scream, I will willingly listen to you."

Cleves is on a precipice, the wind all around her. The ocean looks so very inviting. Seymour's hand strokes little circles on her back that she can feel through her bodice. Her breath on Cleves's earlobe conjures long nights and warm skin.

She steps back from the edge. "I must go," she says. She cannot quite bring laughter to her voice. Seymour drops her hands. "Now?" she says. "I thought you . . . I thought you might stay the night. That is – is it not dangerous to travel in the darkness?"

"Not in my territory," Cleves says. She is on more certain ground now. "Besides, I wish to reach High Hall in plenty of time. We would not wish Mary Boleyn to receive an unsettled wedding gift now, would we?"

Seymour does not return Cleves's smile, but turns towards the fire.

"Go well," she says, her back to Cleves.

"I will return with news of the binding cloths," Cleves says, the words a plea. Seymour does not reply.

As Cleves mounts her horse, Johana silent on his beside her, she does not look back at Gnottel Lodge. Safer by far to look ahead. Only ever ahead.

CHAPTER THIRTY

Howard

Susanna knows a jeweller in Sweillan, a young man keener to curry favour with her than with his queen. Howard has never before employed craftsmen in her territory, usually commissioning the fashionable jewellers of Capetia and Perfugi, or some of the royal craftsmen at High Hall, but she is pleasantly surprised by the quality of the Sweillan boy's work. Within a few days, he has fashioned a dozen brooches and chains, each one artfully concealing a piece of Plythe's *sunscína*, wrapped in a lock of Howard's hair. She only hopes that the other queens will not use their *sunscína* before Howard has a chance to tell them what she has done, or they will wonder at being able to hear the recipients of Howard's gifts.

One goes to Lord Cromwell and one to Wolsey. She thinks of sending one to Henry himself, but baulks at the last moment. She cannot shake the thought that he understands her better than anyone and that he will see through her ruse. In any case, she worries that he would not like her choice of setting for the brooch.

The success of her plan relies on Cromwell and Wolsey wearing the jewellery as much as possible, or having intimate conversations in the same room as the pieces. For several days after her gifts are delivered, she hears nothing through her *sunscína* and almost gives up hope. Perhaps her chosen design is too gaudy for the lords? Or perhaps she is simply listening at the wrong times. But then, almost by chance, she presses her *sunscína* on a whim and hears a voice.

"Does Wolsey know?"

Howard starts, swinging round to see who else is in her bedchamber with her. It is empty.

"Not from me, my lord, but others saw the survivor being pulled from the water. It is beyond doubt that he is from the Dowager Queen's ship. Undoubtedly one of Wolsey's spies will have been among the crowd."

Slowly, Howard turns back to the *sunscína.* She presses her ear against it.

Now that she knows what she is listening to, she places the voice as belonging to Cromwell. The same deliberate intonation, every word an arrow. It worked. She grins, pounds her fists and feet on the bed. She wishes she could tell the other queens to go to their *sunscínas* immediately, but she has no way of reaching them quickly enough.

Cromwell speaks again. "Lord Hunsdown did well to secure him at his home. Take this, and see that the survivor is kept away from anyone but my people."

There's the clink of a purse of coins being handed over, and then a door opens and closes as the messenger rushes out.

Howard puts the *sunscína* down. Lord Hunsdown is one of her nobles. He has a house in Sweillan; she dined there once. If there is a survivor on the ship that brought Seymour to Elben, then should she not attempt to reach him first? Should she be trying to gain her own information from him? Should she . . . Howard draws her knees in to her body . . . Should she kill him to protect information about Seymour and the power that sunk the ship?

She wishes she had Boleyn, or Seymour, or even Cleves to tell her what to do, but she could not arrange to speak to them before the morrow. She is on her own.

Goldfoot caws sleepily from his curled position on her bed. Howard bites her lip. What would Boleyn do?

Goldfoot snuffles again. Howard studies him. She goes to the bed, sits next to him and strokes his silken scales.

"My dear," she whispers. "Do you want to play a game?"

Goldfoot wraps himself around her shoulders as she trips down to the gatehouse, her cloak heavy upon her shoulders. "I wish to take a ride," she tells one of the guards, and a groom is dispatched immediately to bring a jennet for her and a gelding for Ursula, who is the only passable horsewoman among her ladies.

"Are you certain you know what to do?" she whispers to Ursula.

"Do not doubt me, Your Majesty," Ursula says, fevered light in her eyes.

Howard's mare is delicate and fast – Henry likes to send them to her as gifts, and in truth they are usually too quick for her liking, but today that works in her favour. She does not complain when a guard mounts a sturdier cob behind them; to do so would look suspicious.

She urges her horse out of the palace and sets off at a canter down the road that leads west towards Kywsa Bay. The mare pulls at the bit and bucks, sensing Howard's nerves.

"Soon," she says softly. Goldfoot is crouched upon her shoulders still. The lapdragon never strays far from Howard unless she instructs him. She gathers the reins and her courage. She lifts her free hand before her and flicks her wrist, rotating it away from herself. It is a subtler movement than Goldfoot is used to, but he sees it nevertheless.

With a long, loud caw, the lapdragon launches himself into the air and speeds away towards the sea.

"My dragon!" she cries, as loud as she can so that the guard will hear her over the wind. Then she takes the reins in both hands and pushes them forwards, giving the jennet her head at last. The mare is taken by surprise for an instant, then her stride lengthens from canter to gallop.

"Your Majesty, wait!" the guard shouts, but she could not rein in the horse now even if she wanted to. There is a doubled shout and Ursula screams. Howard dares a single glance back: Ursula has thrown herself from her horse into the guard's path. As Howard watches, Ursula crawls stiffly to her knees, the guard leaping from his own horse to check on her. Gallantry can be so very useful.

Howard returns her attention to the road ahead, clinging to her mare's neck as they hurtle after Goldfoot.

Once or twice Howard is certain she is going to fall, or that the mare is going to trip on a stone and take them both down, but the creature is sure-footed and the worst injury Howard suffers is a cut along her collarbone from an errant branch. The River Kyttle runs on Howard's left, widening into a bay and a shoreline that stretches with sun-blessed sand along the coast as far north as the eye can see. Above them, emitting the occasional caw, Goldfoot hovers.

When the town of Sweillan comes into view, its docks reaching fingers out into the ocean, Howard sits back, calming the mare with her voice. This time the jennet readily falls into a trot, tired from the long gallop. Howard turns her from the road and climbs off, leading the horse into a thick and unkempt woodland before letting her loose. It is not ideal – the creature is clearly an expensive animal – but Howard must be able to claim that she was thrown from her back. That done, Howard removes her fine cloak and gathers it into a bundle, stuffing it up underneath her loose bodice to give the impression that she is pregnant. Beneath the cloak, she wears the simplest of her dresses: a plain ochre cotton gown that she likes to wear when she has her monthly course, for it is light enough to keep her cool and eminently comfortable. She pulls another length of cotton from her sleeve and winds it around her hair, binding the wild curls that are one of her most recognisable traits. As she works, Goldfoot lands on a branch above her and sways his long neck from side to side, as if in question.

"You must stay hidden, little fire," she tells him. He caws mournfully. She tucks the last of her curls beneath the cotton.

She has no mirror, but she feels different. She must trust that the disguise is enough.

"Do you recognise me?" she asks Goldfoot. He tilts his head to one side.

"I'll take that as a yes."

She thinks of Cleves and Parr and Aragon, and how they might look at her if she manages to find this survivor. She imagines Aragon's raised eyebrow, Parr's rueful, admiring smile. Cleves's laugh, and the comment on how Howard will lead them all before long. Howard straightens her back, leaves her doubt in the woodland with the jennet and strikes out for Sweillan.

As she nears the town, the road fills with people: traders hawking sweet pastries and trinkets; stalls lining the road with spices and exotic fruits and fish brought straight from the docks. On every street corner stands a sanctuary, Cernunnos' golden antlers protruding above doorways or from the top of bell towers. The town smells of woodsmoke and faeces, and more than once Howard nearly trips over a rat. She cannot cover her mouth and nose, for to do so would betray the fact that she is unused to the smell. Instead, she can only try not to gag.

It has been some time since she dined with Lord Hunsdown, but she trusts her memory of the route to his home. It lies on the north side of Sweillan, as far away from the smells and sounds of the docks as possible while still offering the lord easy access to the town. Howard winds her way up to higher ground, and before long she sees it – a fine, timber house, surrounded by walls of red brick.

A guard loafs at the gate. Howard does not approach him but skirts the walls, looking for the servants' entrance. She wonders whether any of the other queens even have knowledge of where their servants' entrances are. She and Legh often snuck out of their great-aunt's at night-time. She knows how they work.

There – an unremarkable wooden door to the side of the property.

She knocks, keeping her head down. A woman peers out.

"What is it?" the woman says.

"Laundry, good mistress?" she says, spreading her hands in the attitude of one desperate for work.

The woman eyes her rounded belly and her expression softens.

"I might have something. Come in and take the weight off your feet."

"Thank you," Howard says, following the woman into a kitchen hot with steam and the smell of sage. Howard sits as directed on a stool in the centre of the room, and an urchin scampers over her feet in pursuit of a slug, its prickles catching on her kirtle.

The housekeeper disappears into the depths of the house, leaving Howard with only a young boy for company. He eyes her from his place by the fire, where he rotates a pig carcass, sweat dripping from his forehead. Howard does not have long to find the survivor before her continued absence would raise suspicion.

Her plan is flimsy. It could go wrong at every turn, but she has to try. She is no Boleyn, nor can she see three moves ahead in a game of *beaduläc* as Voda Kelaverinn can. But this is the best she can do. Her hand goes automatically to the antler pendant resting on her breast, an outward sign of her fealty to Cernunnos. She drops her hand to her heart, and silently sends a prayer to the goddess.

If you can hear me, my lady, please look kindly on my efforts, and send me a little of that bordweal luck.

"I can do that for a bit, if you'd like a break?" she says to the boy. His eyes dart to the passage down which the housekeeper has disappeared.

"If you're quick, she'll never know," Howard says. The boy's eyes narrow and her breath hitches. She's been too eager to labour. She shrugs and leans back, forgetting that she's on a stool, not a chair, and almost topples off, catching herself just in time. "Suit yourself," she says, and stretches out her legs the way Boleyn once did when she was pregnant, when she thought no one was watching.

The boy leans forward, looking at the passage again.

"All right. Just quickly, mind."

Before Howard can get up, he darts to the door, welcoming the cool air outside, even if it does smell of shit.

Howard jumps to her feet and, rather than take over at the spit, slips into the passage. Ahead lie the public rooms – offices and a small banqueting hall lined with flaking murals. She turns right and takes a narrow staircase up to the bedrooms, counting on the survivor being confined in one of them.

This part of the house is alien to her, for she never stayed overnight, choosing to travel back to the comfort of Plythe instead, much to the chagrin of her court and servants, who were tired and feared the night-time journey. Oh, how she regrets her arrogance now.

She ducks into an empty room to avoid a servant, then passes from door to door, listening with increasing frustration for a hint that someone might be inside. She can hear nothing through the oak.

Howard takes a deep breath, closes her eyes and then begins to open each door. If she sees someone who isn't the survivor, she will simply have to make up some excuse.

The goddess must have heard her prayer, though, for the third door she opens contains a simple bed and a boy with skin almost as dark as hers. He looks very young in sleep, and with a jolt, Howard realises that he must be of an age with her. Voda Kelaverinn's words come back to her: *I think myself old*. Which is as much to say: *I think you young*. Yet Voda is not much older than Henry.

Howard slips into the room and closes the door behind her. The boy lies peacefully on top of the bedcovers. He is dressed in the light colours of a Perfugian, though his clothes are little more than rags now, and his bare arms are covered in blisters and bruises. There is no doubt in her mind that this is the survivor.

Howard pulls a chest of drawers across the door to bar anyone else from entering.

"The women in my life have done many strange things, but never that," a gravelly voice says. Howard whirls around. The boy is watching her through barely open eyes. His accent is Perfugian, but his Elbenese is otherwise perfect. Howard wishes she knew a few words of his language – it might make him more likely to trust her.

It is very odd to be addressing a stranger who is lying abed. She does not know whether she has the power, standing over him as she is, or he, since in a way this is his room. Her heart is hammering so fast she can barely hear the words that trip from her tongue.

"I am here to rescue you, sir," she says.

The boy looks at his bed, around the room, in feigned confusion. "How strange. I thought I had already been rescued. Perhaps it was a dream."

"You were rescued from the sea. The person who wishes to interrogate you is worse than the ocean's depths, believe me."

She does not know if that is true. Lord Cromwell has never seemed perverted, but he is not above using torture. She must stretch the truth in order to gain this boy's trust.

"Who is this person who is so terrifying?"

"Lord Cromwell."

"Is he not the king's advisor?"

"Neither he nor the king are your friends, sir."

"But you are." The boy's eyes dance, despite his weariness.

"I work for someone who will treat you fairly. They can offer you freedom. Or passage back to your homeland if that is what you desire."

"What I desire . . ." The boy's mouth twists. Howard has the strangest feeling that she is looking into a mirror; not that the two of them look alike, but that they *are* alike. Like her, this boy is untethered. Like her, he can no longer see the path ahead.

Howard kneels beside him. Beneath her sleeves, she fingers the golden bangles concealed there. The boy watches her. He is still lying down, but he is attentive. Relaxed but respectful. Then his eye catches upon the cut on her collarbone. He sits up, mindless of his own extensive injuries.

"You are hurt," he says. He scrambles along the table beside his bed. "The physician left some bandages . . ."

He finds a stray piece of cloth and some rubbing alcohol, and turns back to her. He hesitates. "Would you prefer to tend to yourself?"

Howard feels as though she has been struck. It is akin to the moment at the Moon Ball when Cleves spoke to her in the midst of her panic. Sometimes only a few words can make one realise a falsehood that one has carried for so long it is part of your skin.

With one question, this stranger has exposed the lie of Henry's love. For he has never sought permission to touch her. She takes the cloth and bottle of alcohol and mutely cleans her wound. Then, impulsively, she slips one of her bracelets from her wrist and hands it to him. The boy's eyes widen at the sight of the gold. He presses it gently in a way that tells her he understands precious metals. His fingers leave a faint print on the jewellery.

"I am Queen Howard of Plythe, sir. I am working with Queen Seymour against my husband. He is not a good man. I ask for your help."

She is surprised that her voice is more certain than she feels, as though simply taking action has lent her confidence.

The boy begins to laugh. Howard stands. She doesn't know why it matters so much to her that he believes her.

"I don't care that you don't believe me," she says.

"Oh, I do," he replies, wiping tears from his eyes and leaving bloody streaks on his cheeks. "I do believe you, Your Majesty."

"Then why are you laughing?"

"You would not get a queen in my country who would break a prisoner out of their gaol. But I should have known. You Elbenese royals are a different breed altogether."

Of course. He was on board the Dowager Queen's ship. The way he says it, full of admiration, makes Howard's stomach twist uncomfortably.

The boy hesitates only a moment longer before nodding.

"*Fescesta*, I will help you," he mutters, in a way that makes Howard think it is some Perfugian curse. He swings his legs painfully slowly to the floor.

"I am not going to be as fast to make an escape as you may like, though." She wedges her shoulder beneath his arm and helps him to his feet.

The sound of voices echoes down the gallery. A moment later, someone attempts to open the door and finds it jammed.

The goddess's favour has run out. Their easiest exit is blocked.

"The window is big enough, I think," the boy says.

Howard peers through it. He's right: it is big enough and she should be able to smash it, but it opens onto the road below – cobbles and stones.

"The drop would kill us," she says.

"Then – can you fight? Because otherwise I think we may both be about to be tortured."

They cast around the room for possible weapons and both seize upon a candlestick. The boy relinquishes his grip at the same time as Howard relinquishes hers, and the stick clatters to the floorboards.

"Please, you," he says.

"No, you should . . ." she says.

They smile uncertainly at each other.

"You look like you need a weapon more than I do," Howard says. The boy laughs.

"That is true. You seem very capable. I definitely am not."

Howard feels a little drop in her stomach. It occurs to her that this is the nicest thing anyone has ever said to her, and then it occurs to her that that's a rather sad state of affairs.

The door rattles again. They will need to move quickly or more will arrive, and then they will stand even less of a chance than they do at present. The boy hefts the candlestick. Howard notices a pile of wood next to the fireplace. She takes the longest lump she can find and thrusts it into the flame. Common firewood would take far too long to light properly without kindling, but this is ambawood, treated with oils from Pkolack, and it catches immediately.

"Ready?" Howard says.

"One question," the boy says. "It is a strange question."

"Is now truly the time for strange questions?"

"When I inevitably shout your name as we rush through this house, or as I am stabbed to death, what would you like me to call you, since I assume I cannot call you Queen Howard?"

Howard hesitates. "Katheryn," she says. It's the name she'd always have wanted to be called, if she hadn't been the oldest daughter of her absent father.

"Thank you, Katheryn. And I am Florin."

They smile at each other, and then, as if reading each other's minds, shove the chest aside, pull the door open and charge forth, candlestick forward, flame bright.

CHAPTER THIRTY-ONE

Cecilia

Her bargain with Seymour and Cleves does not grant Cecilia the freedom she had hoped it might. She supposes she ought not to be shocked: a treaty does not mean trust, no matter how pretty the contract is or how swirling the sovereigns' signatures. Besides, her lie is only one kind of trap. She must make more.

She gets rid of the panther first – she will never be able to gain the beast's loyalty, and he is too quick and silent. She cannot move freely around the lodge without him coming upon her at inopportune moments. She lays in wait for him one morning, clutching a knife from the supper table. Cleves's people pounce on her before she can harm him, of course, but harming him was never her intention. The next day, Seymour sends him away to keep him safe.

Next, she must discover exactly where she is.

"If you keep me inside for ever," she tells Seymour one morning, "then I will be so empty you will not be able to bargain for me. I will lose my mind, you know."

She grasps Seymour's sleeve as she speaks. It is the same ruse she used upon Seymour's servant, and as with the servant, it works. These weak people and their weak hearts.

That afternoon, Seymour comes to her with manacles, and once they are secured around Cecilia's wrists, they leave the house.

"We will not walk far," Seymour tells her. Cecilia does not care. She casts her face to the traces of sun which make their way through the tree canopy. She does not need to speak, only to feel the rays upon her skin, to hear the birdsong unimpeded by glass and lead, to smell the bluebells crushed beneath her feet.

Seymour chooses their route well. Once Cecilia begins to take note of her surroundings, she can garner little from them that she does not already know. They are somewhere in Cnothan, but there is no sound of running water that might tell her which way is inland and which way the sea. No roads. Not even a rocky outcrop that might speak of the soil's fabric.

Cecilia is almost ready to turn back, her feet beginning to tire, when she spies smoke curling from above the trees. She bends their path towards it, hoping that they might stumble across some hamlet or farmstead. Seymour and Cleves cannot have many loyal to their cause, or they would not keep her so isolated.

The trees open into a little glade. Cecilia halts at the sight in its centre. A pit has been dug, and from the embers within comes a stench so vile that bile rises in her throat. She knows that smell. Sometimes the people of Perfugi fall; sometimes they are pushed into the lava which serves for rivers in that city. She recognises the scent of burning flesh.

Covering her nose, she notices the dregs of a tent, abandoned at one side of the glade. A tent, not a homestead . . .

"They were Hleaws," Seymour says, behind her.

Cecilia swirls round. Seymour is standing at the very edge of the glade, unwilling to approach the horror.

"You knew this was here, and you led me to it anyway?" she says.

"I knew it was here. But you led us, Cecilia."

Cecilia looks back towards the pit. She knows what she is going to see, but she cannot stop herself. She never could. Arrow-shot pheasants; aged hounds that never woke up; even her own wounds. She must always peer at death, or its companion, pain, and marvel at their rotten stillness.

It is a family. Their features are indistinguishable, but their sizes are not. Remnants of cloth remain. One of the children clutches a doll in its charred hands.

"This was done on your brother's orders," Seymour says. She has crept closer, but she looks only at the tent – the circular, moveable home favoured by the people of that faith.

"You cannot know that," Cecilia says.

"It is happening across the island, because he knows that your family's great deception is coming into the light at last. While the Hleaws were dismissed, he could allow them to survive. But not now."

"Then it is you and your allies who are to blame," Cecilia says. Her brother would never order this unless it were necessary. Henry is not like *him*. Henry despises gratuitous violence. He, of all of them, was always the gentle one.

Seymour laughs.

"Do not dare to mock me or I will strangle you with these manacles," Cecilia says. She is roiling inside, like the lava of Perfugi.

Head tilted, Seymour says, "It is simply astounding to me how someone as ruthless as you can be so wilfully blind."

"You knew my brother for a year, girl," Cecilia says. "I have known him my whole life."

"You have not known your brother for twenty years," Seymour says.

"He wrote to me."

Seymour laughs again.

"And you can know a person only through their writing. You must be an oracle."

The lava inside her moves slower. She looks back at the charred bodies. There must be some clue, in that pit, to their crime. They must have been plotting treason with Seymour and Cleves, and her clever brother learned of it. He would have wept over their deaths, just as he used to weep over the death of a favourite horse, or the prisoners in the Tower when they were brought to the block.

"Did he ever speak to you of our brother?" she asks Seymour.

"No."

It is easier to continue staring at the body of that child. What she is about to tell Seymour, she has never told a soul; not even Lorena.

"Our half-brother, really. Well, we are all half-siblings. My mother was the Queen of Plythe, of course, and Henry and our older sister's mother was the Queen of Mathmas. Arthur's mother was the Queen of Hyde. A nasty, hidden place for nasty, hidden secrets."

She risks a glance at Seymour, but the other woman is too interested in her story to be insulted.

"The rest of us visited High Hall often, but Arthur was raised there."

"Because he was the heir," Seymour says.

Cecilia closes her eyes. She could never decide whether she despised or enjoyed visiting High Hall. She adored playing with Henry and flirting with his friends. But Arthur would always, always be there.

"I was eight. That means that Henry would have been thirteen, and Arthur fifteen," she continues. "He came into my room one morning – Arthur, I mean. He was in one of his rages. It was not the first time it had happened, but it was the most violent."

Seymour steps closer, raises a hand as if about to grasp Cecilia's arm. Cecilia moves away. She does not wish for pity. For some unthinkable reason that Cecilia hates herself for, she needs Seymour to understand that she, Seymour, is mistaken. That Henry is a good man, no matter what mistakes passed between them as husband and wife. That is the only purpose of her story.

She tries to explain, to make Seymour understand, but the words will not come. It is as if his arm is against her neck, as it was that day, pressing, pressing until her life narrows to his vicious eyes and a blooming pulse through her skull.

"You need not speak," Seymour says. She presses her hands against Cecilia's back. They are gentle at first – a question. But when Cecilia doesn't move away, Seymour presses harder, and Cecilia leans back against those hands, putting as much of her weight on them as she can. Her chest, opened, loosens. Arthur's spectre falls away.

"Henry pulled him off you, didn't he?" Seymour says.

Cecilia nods. When she can speak again, her voice is thin and childlike. "He stayed close to me whenever we were at High Hall together. He always took the brunt of Arthur's anger. Always stepped in front of me. *Always*."

There is a long silence, but it no longer feels like victory. She is too raw for celebration.

"I can see why you would think him a good man, when he showed such bravery as a boy," Seymour says at last.

"You are despicable," Cecilia says. How can Seymour still talk as though Cecilia is in the wrong, after that confession?

Seymour ducks into the Hleaws' wrecked tent and emerges a moment later. She presses something cold into Cecilia's hand.

"I do not claim you lie. I merely ask you to think on who Henry might have become, after Arthur's death."

Cecilia remembers that day, too. And the day afterwards, when she visited Henry in his chambers and found him withdrawn, not equal to celebrating with her. She opens her fist. It is a chain, broken next to the clasp, and upon it hang six orbs. A mark of faith, like Cernunnos's antlers, or the guirnalda favoured by the Quistoans.

She looks back at the bodies. When they were alive, the chain must have belonged to them. Something is growing in the pit, beside the remains. Cecilia crouches, trying to understand what she is seeing.

In the crook of the dead child's arm, something fungal unfurls before her very eyes. It is the pink of flayed flesh and its frills, though delicate, inspire a visceral repugnance. It spreads even as they watch, an unnatural growth reaching over the Hleaws' bodies and through the dying smoke, climbing the sides of the pit.

They start back, away from the horror. Cecilia realises that she is clutching Seymour, and Seymour is clutching her.

"Let us leave this cursed place," Seymour says.

They return in silence, their eyes on the path, their minds darting from the malice of that glade to the malice of a long-dead prince. It is only when they enter the grounds of the estate that she realises she is still clutching the Hleaws' chain with its six orbs. Clutching it so tightly it has left angry marks on her palm.

Cecilia should cast it away. To even be touching it is a show of disloyalty towards Henry. She pushes it into a pocket. She will show it to him when she sees him. He will have an explanation. He must. He must, or what is her lineage but screams and smoke?

CHAPTER THIRTY-TWO

Howard

Howard can barely control her excitement as she presses her *sunscína* and waits for the other queens to appear. They will be so pleased, tell her that she is brilliant, the best of them, how could they have doubted her. She has secured the only survivor who might be able to tell Henry that Seymour was aboard that wrecked ship. She has bought them safety, for a little longer.

But Cleves is the only one who appears.

"I think it is just you and I, sister," she tells Howard. "I am told that Aragon and Parr are playing host to some of Henry's closest advisors. Wolsey and Cromwell and the like. Perhaps they are not as resourceful as you when it comes to avoiding detection."

Howard appreciates the compliment, but cannot help but be disappointed. She had hoped to reveal her rescue of Florin to all of them. Even Aragon, surely, must be impressed by her daring. Still, Cleves will make a most gratifying audience.

"I have done something that I think you will like," she says. Cleves smiles when she tells her of her experiment with the *sunscína*. She bites her lip when she relays what she heard of the survivor from Cecilia's ship. But when Howard talks of her rescue of Florin, Cleves's expression darkens.

"In any case, I have him in my holding now," Howard says, her voice smaller than she had intended. She rocks in her seat, unsure why Cleves is silent.

Eventually Cleves speaks: "Did you not consider the danger, Howard?"

"Well, yes, but—"

"Did you not think that it might have been better to send word to the rest of us? I have people in Sweillan who could have conspired to rescue this boy without any suspicion falling upon you."

"There was no time – Cromwell's men were at the door. We fought our way past them when we left."

Cleves's eyes widen. "Did they survive?"

"Well . . ." She is no murderer. She only wished to escape.

Cleves rubs her face. "I will see to it that no suspicion falls upon you. I will employ my resources to talk of another young woman seen heading north with the prisoner. That should allay any misgivings about you."

Howard swallows. "I thought you would be pleased with me."

Only a few moments ago Cleves had praised her, called her clever, but if she truly believed that why does she dismiss her now?

"I can protect myself," Howard says.

"Yes, clearly."

Howard flinches. Cleves sighs. "There is just so much to be done, sister. I did not expect this surprise."

"What more can we do?" Howard says. "Tell me and I will help."

"I have it in hand."

Howard grows hot. She is still bruised and aching from her adventure, and yet she is here and the others are not. *She* has done something, at least. Yes, it may have been rash, but at least it was *something*.

"Are you not lonely?" she whispers. "Are you not so terribly lonely, sister? Because I am."

Cleves stares at her.

"I know what you all think of me," Howard says. "I know that none of you enjoy my company. But you said something to me at the Moon Ball. Do you remember?"

Cleves nods. "I remember."

"Your words – they altered my life's path. Without your words, I would not be here. I would not have joined the dance that night, and I would not have joined Boleyn. But ever since that night, you have disappointed me, sister."

The smile that is never far from Cleves's lips falters. Any jest she had been about to make falls away. Her walls are built and are crumbled in the same moment. Then it is back, that dancing smirk.

"I disappoint many people," Cleves says. "And yet somehow I have learned to live with myself."

"Do you? Or do you stagnate?"

Howard should not be talking in this way.

"A fiery queen," Cleves says, and whistles.

"Stop that," Howard says, and the frustration is so great that she stamps her foot. "Stop throwing me crumbs of appreciation that mean nothing!"

The two queens stare at each other, an impasse reached. Howard realises that she is crying. Of course she is, child that she is. But the tears keep coming.

Into the silence, Cleves presses a hand to the *sunscína*. "We must find the binding cloths," she says. She is gentle, but firm, ignoring the fact that Howard is openly weeping.

"Why?"

"I believe they hold the key to freeing us from Cernunnos's control."

Of course. Now that Cleves has said it, it seems obvious. It is the one ritual that tied the queens to their king. If the cloths are destroyed, then perhaps the bond will be also.

"They are kept at High Hall, are they not?" Howard says.

"They are, sister. But we have little hope of finding where unless . . ."

They smile at each other. Cleves has left the sentence unfinished for Howard: "Unless the king intends to marry again."

She and Ursula follow the path into the woods near Plythe that afternoon, telling the guards that they are hunting for fresh blackberries. A girlish hunt.

But they do not find blackberries. Instead, they find a woodsman's ruined hut, and a boy upon a truckle bed. The hut is little more than four cragged walls, the thatch roof and its timbers having succumbed to rain and rot long ago. Florin is shivering inside it, but he is alert, and he makes an attempt at a bow when he sees them.

"I will leave you alone," Ursula says, raising her basket to indicate that she will look for fruit by herself.

Howard looks towards Florin, feeling suddenly uncertain. Cleves thinks she has been stupid.

She knows it is a risk, of course she does. But something beyond her ability to put into words tells her it was a risk worth taking. That it is a risk Boleyn would have taken.

And look where that led Boleyn.

"I think you're a good person," she says, more to herself.

He frown-smiles. "Is that a compliment or a question?"

Howard approaches. "The brilliance of Elbenese humour is that you will never know."

"Well, that sounds like a recipe for anxiety."

Florin's expression turns thoughtful a moment later.

"I think you are a good person too," he says.

"I try to be."

"Do you believe in true love?"

The question is so unexpected that Howard stutters, worried she has given him the wrong impression. He would not be the first man to declare himself when she had not meant for him to develop feelings. Usually she would take pride in such unintended seduction, but this – this would be awkward and counterproductive. The other queens would talk about her as some harlot. Florin holds out his hands, placatingly.

"Not you, Your Majesty. We barely know each other."

"Oh," she says. Then, "Oh," with more relief.

"I speak of another. An Elbenese lady whom I loved. Love. She always spoke in such a way, so I never knew if she was teasing me or praising me."

Howard thinks of Henry, and her stomach twists painfully. "That sounds . . . intoxicating."

His face lights up. "Yes. That is the word for it. But intoxicating is not always a good thing, is it?"

"No."

Howard does not want to have this conversation, but Florin is lost in his own rumination, and she is not sure that it would be right to break him out of it. For trust is born of familiarity, is it not? And she needs him to trust her.

"This lady – will you find her again?" she asks.

Florin shrugs, his eyes downcast. "I do not think she is alive."

"The ship," she guesses.

"The ship, yes."

She thinks of the way he laughed when she told him she was a queen, and she makes another guess.

"Henry's sister. Cecilia."

He looks up at her, eyes wide. "How did you know?"

"She is alive, Florin," Howard says, grasping his hand. "My friends have her in their custody. But she is alive, and unharmed."

His reaction is fascinating. It reminds her, in a strange way, of Boleyn in her final moments – the way she had stood on the edge of that cliff, poised between victory and hope and the dregs of adoration, and then resigned herself to what must come next.

"You wish to go to her," Howard ventures.

Florin laughs. "No," he says. "And yes."

"Please do not betray me." Howard removes her hand from his and wraps her arms around herself. Her chest is tight. Cleves was right. She has been so foolish.

Florin reaches for her. "Oh, Katheryn. We both of us have trusted the wrong people in the past, I think."

"Yes."

"I have been thinking a lot about love, since before I even stepped foot on that cursed ship. I thought for the longest time that the kind of love that can survive deep, deep hurt must be the truest kind of love."

Howard thinks of Henry, and then she thinks of her father.

"But now you are not so sure?"

"Now I think . . . is that not the definition of intoxicating? To crave something even as you know it is poisoning you?"

They are both silent for a long while. The birds whistle above them, communing in their own simple way. The earth feels cold and reassuring beneath Howard's knees, as though it is the only solid thing about her.

"I think . . ." Howard begins, her thoughts fractured, her heart hammering, as though she is cocooned within a sanctuary's confessional. "I think you are right, but I do not think you are alone. I think it is the most human thing about us."

"You think we crave the poison?" Florin says. There is no judgement or laughter in his question. If she had not met the same curiosity in Voda Kelaverinn, she would not have trusted it.

"If it is the poison of love, then yes. I do." Howard says.

"Is that not the saddest thing you have heard?"

She laughs. "I think it is the saddest thing I have said. Maybe the cleverest, too."

Florin tilts his head. "I doubt that."

Howard shrugs, stands, stretches. She accepted Boleyn telling her she had some intelligence. A man telling her the same thing is different. It makes her feel as though they are offering her a concessionary prize. And while she is relieved that Florin does not harbour hopes in that area, she does not need him to lie to her.

"I have placed my life, and the lives of my sisters, in your trust. I did not have to tell you the truth, Florin, and I did not seek any assurances from you. But if you betray us, I will see to it that the woman you love has her throat slit and I will have her head presented to you on a jewelled platter. Do you understand?"

"My word, you are a queen," he says, staring up at her.

"Do you understand, sir?"

Ursula's voice breaks through the silence. "Is all well, Your Majesty?"

Howard spins round. Her lady teeters in what remains of the doorway, her basket piled high with purple fruit.

"All is well, Ursula. Let us go." She passes her friend, ignoring the thumping in her head. She has never spoken in such a way before, and already the anger that drove those words is ebbing from her. He may despise her now, but she does not mind that as much as she once would have.

Intoxicating.

CHAPTER THIRTY-THREE

Cleves

The journey to High Hall takes longer than Cleves had expected, even travelling the scrind road with its strange, ancient magic that never fails to make her heart race. The mismatch of her horse's steady gait with the speed of the trees and fields whipping past them is vertiginous. Yet, the journey is more full than usual. Minor nobility, keen to gain favour as much as money, pack the road with their entourages. Nearly all of them drag cages and crates. Crones, skin loose from long hunger, bare their teeth through iron bars. The sound of tusks scraping along the inside of crates underlines the keening cries of the captive beasts.

"These people took no issue with endangering their servants," Johana says, as they watch a nobleman wearing the marsh-ready boots of Hyde shout at his entourage to quieten their crone.

"And their servants will remember that, Johana. As ours did."

When they finally reach High Hall, the palace is rife with activity. At the centre of Elben, the island's beating heart, High Hall stands unmoving as people from across the known world, and from all ranks, flurry through the passages and courtyards and sanctuaries and kitchens, the gardens and greenhouses, the courts and banqueting halls. It is, and always has been, too much for Cleves. It is not the busyness that she dislikes so much as the secrets. Intrigue rests in High Hall's shadows like fog. And that is precisely why she has come here now: because intrigue and secrets are what she requires.

Her wing of High Hall is the oldest part of the palace, the rest having been demolished and rebuilt over the years. Where the other wings are rounded or hexagonal, hers is angular and made of the hard, grey stone favoured by the ancient rulers of Elben. She imagines the queens of old, supreme in their rule, not subservient to any man, striding across the flagstones. She wonders whether they were the ones who instructed the design of the cupboards hidden within the walls, for the keeping of useful cutlery and linen; whether they thought of the lowered daises around the fireplaces to create cosy seating areas. She wonders whether the rest of the palace used to be like this, or whether it was only ever Cnothan's wing that was, and remains, so practical.

Johana follows her through her chambers, and behind them trail her animals, Lelij strutting at the head of the procession.

"Does your household not mind you bringing so many animals into the palace?" Johana says.

"Perhaps they did at first. Until they realised that my animals smell no worse than many of the courtiers, and are housetrained a good deal better."

Johana laughs as he follows Cleves deeper into her rooms. She must freshen herself after the long journey. Even though it was several days ago, she cannot shake the thought that Seymour's peppery scent is still upon her after their dance.

A copy of Holbein's portrait of her has been hung on the wall of her antechamber, though she has no memory of ordering it. A gift from Henry, she supposes, intended as a further humiliation. She glances at it as she splashes her face in fragranced water. She and Holbein are cut from the same cloth: able to tread their own winding path while giving the impression of following the more direct route. He truly is a remarkable artist.

"I must show my face briefly in the public spaces, or questions will be asked as to why I have come here," she tells Johana. "But I need to get to the gardens before dusk."

"Am I to be your guard?" Johana asks.

"It is more likely that I could protect you, cousin. No, you are here to distract anyone who might wish to speak to me while I run my little errand."

"And am I permitted to know the nature of this errand?"

She dries her face on padded linen. "That rather depends: are you willing to keep a secret in the face of torture, should you be found out?"

Johana considers this. "Since I have no phoenix feather to protect me from such horrors, I shall not be greedy. You may keep your treasures in different chests."

"Now you begin to understand why I was reluctant to tell you everything, cousin," she says. "It was for your protection as much as my own. Come, Lelij."

The gargoyle lollops over, and she picks him up. He is really too large to be carried much, but she knows that where she is taking him, he will be ridiculed. If he is in her arms, courtiers will be less likely to laugh openly, for to do so would be to openly laugh at a queen.

With Lelij chirruping happily in her grasp, Cleves leads Johana through the double doors which mark the boundary between her rooms and the public galleries of High Hall. On the surface, everything is the same as it ever has been. The songbirds in their cages hang from every windowsill, singing in a way that has always, to Cleves, sounded like a plea. The courtiers dart between groups in a complicated dance of superiority that only those practised in the art of politics can interpret.

The changes since her last visit are less obvious, but profound. Usually each courtier would wear a favour – a handkerchief, a doublet – the colour of their chosen queen. When Cleves had last been here, a few had worn orange to show their loyalty to her; many more had worn white or copper for Parr and Howard. Now, no one bears any queenly colour on their chest. This is not a matter of one queen being out of favour. After Boleyn and Seymour's betrayals, after Henry's public humiliation at the Moon Ball, the only fealty that can be exhibited is to the king himself.

They take the wide staircase which leads to the upper floors of the palace, closer to Henry's quarters. It is busier here. Courtiers begin to take notice of her – it is unusual for Cleves to come to the public chambers of High Hall, after all. They bow, but few approach, and her smile becomes more affable, her body language more approachable. No one would possibly think boring, ugly Queen Cleves capable of treason; the only thing she cares about is her animals. Cleves has traded on her eccentricity for so many years, using it as a disguise. But when people look for a threat, sometimes it is the eccentric ones they turn on first.

The sun is beginning to set. Shadows elongate across the floorboards and rugs, making sundials of people. She is on the northern side of the palace now, and nearly at the right entrance to reach her mark. She has been seen and noted. Perhaps she did not need Johana after all.

"Your Majesty. What an unexpected pleasure to see you at High Hall."

A shiver runs up her spine. She turns to face a broad-shouldered man whose skin is darker than hers. He has a strong brow and an easy, laconic smile.

"Lord Brandon," she says, shifting Lelij's weight into one arm and offering her hand for him to kiss. "You are looking as tall as ever."

There is mirth in his eyes. "I hardly recognised you without your entourage."

He twirls around the room theatrically. "Only one gargoyle? No cows? No cats or pigs to accompany you this time?" Then his eyes rest on Johana. "Ah, my mistake. You have brought a foreign dog after all."

Johana bristles at her side, but smiles at Brandon pleasantly. "And yet you are doing all the barking, my lord."

As Brandon laughs merrily, Cleves remembers why she has always avoided him. He is cruelly charming, the cruelty mellowed by the fact that he is just as content to receive an insult as to deliver one. Still, if he weren't so lazily handsome, he wouldn't get away with half of the japes he pulls. She makes a formal introduction between Brandon and Johana, and the two men bow to each other.

"Lord Brandon is my husband's favourite person in the entire world," Cleves tells her cousin.

"After his beloved queens, of course," Brandon says. "Present company excepted."

Cleves puts a placating hand on Johana's arm. If he tries to protect her, she will not be able to escape this unwelcome interaction. Thankfully, Johana understands her. "Actually, my sources tell me that cousin Cleves ranks at least fourth now," he says.

Cleves considers this. "My, my. That is quite a promotion."

Brandon laughs again. "You are a good sport, Your Majesty. A very good sport."

"It's one of my many talents," she says. "Another is knowing when to leave before the insults become too much for even me to bear. Excuse me, my lords."

Cleves slips away. She has other matters to attend to, out in the gardens of High Hall. Cromwell and Wolsey may lead Henry's spy network, but theirs has nothing on hers.

"Good morrow, Edith," she says, as she approaches the woman labouring in a flower bed on the north side of High Hall's gardens. The woman stands from where she's been kneeling over some pots, adding soil to them before planting them up. She has a bairn tied to her chest with a swaddling cloth. Cleves stumbles for an instant, wondering, and then realises that the babe is too young to be who she thought it might be.

"Your Majesty," Edith says, bobbing a curtsey.

"How are you finding my fertiliser?"

"Very well indeed. It is making our plants prosper," Edith replies. Neither woman looks the other in the eye. Perhaps they both fear that if they do, someone will realise that they are communicating more than they appear to be.

"And your family? They are well?"

"They are. My mother-in-law is kept busy with my niece."

"She is nearly one now."

"Just turned. And already running my mother-in-law in circles."

"Very good."

Cleves has only had sight of the Princess Elizabeth once, briefly, in the days before the Moon Ball, so she does not know why she is so relieved at this news. She cannot, of course, talk freely of the princess or the old stewardess of Brynd, Mistress Syndony, in this place, but Syndony's secret network of family agents was in place long before Boleyn's fall, and has remained strong even with Syndony in hiding with her young charge.

Cleves peers at the plants Edith is potting up. "Roses. Are these for the royal wedding then?"

"The new queen favours them, so His Majesty has ordered the sanctuary full of them."

"Quite an undertaking."

Edith casually looks around to be sure they are not being overheard. She returns to her work, and Cleves makes a show of smelling some jasmine climbing up a nearby wall.

"To the king's face, Mary Boleyn is shown all due deference," Edith says.

"And in his absence?"

"Despite the general dislike of Queen Boleyn, no one favours the match. Those who despised Boleyn fear that the whole family is tainted with treachery. Those who loved her despise Mary for her betrayal."

"And yet he is set upon it," Cleves says.

"Perhaps he truly loves her."

"Or perhaps if she has no friends, she will be easier for him to control," Cleves says, raising an eyebrow.

"There is more." Edith draws closer to Cleves under the pretence of inspecting the petals of the nearest rose bush. "Bishop More has come to stay at High Hall. He spends much of his time in his rooms. When he does come out, he is not himself. Some say he is dying."

"And what do you say?" Cleves asks.

Edith shakes her head. "There's something strange going on here. I cannot put my finger on it, nor find out anything more. Only a few servants are permitted into the bishop's rooms and they are all loyal to Cromwell. I can get nothing from them."

"Cromwell?" Cleves says. She had not been particularly interested in this news before – what is an ailing Bishop to her? – but now she is. Cromwell and More have never been allies. Has that changed? The thought makes her uneasy. When a wolf like Cromwell takes an interest in someone like More, it can only be for one reason: he is hungry for a kill and senses weakness. But what is the manner of More's weakness? she wonders. Captive crones and a dying bishop. What is Cromwell brewing in the secret parts of this palace?

CHAPTER THIRTY-FOUR

Howard

Howard knows something of desperation. The festoons and garlands that adorn every rafter and door at High Hall reek of it. She has never attended any wedding at High Hall but her own, but she has heard about plenty. This kind of decoration is not normal. Usually it is only the sanctuary and the new queen's rooms that are so festooned. This is excessive. The palace drips with wealth and opulence, all of it cold and empty.

Howard is not brave, like Boleyn. She has no intention of attending Mary's wedding as Boleyn attended Seymour's. She does not wish to incur Henry's wrath. She is at High Hall for something far more important than a chance to see the traitor sister. What a triumph it would be for her to find them. An end to their secret war against Henry without a sword drawn.

But not attending the wedding publicly does not mean she cannot attend it in secret. With Tylney in charge of bringing Florin into Plythe's household, Howard made her way with a small retinue to High Hall, arriving on the morning of the royal wedding. She dispatches Ursula as her ambassador as soon as they arrive, then changes into a gown of dark damask that moves like shadows.

There is a cove just above the sanctuary, hewn from ancient rock and covered in irregular carvings – the result of centuries of lovers wishing to mark their presence, Howard assumes. Henry once told her that the cove was intended for certain members of the royal family to attend service, but given what Howard knows now of the history of the palace – that it was originally a place for the six Queens of Elben to convene – she wonders whether it had a different purpose.

Howard settles into her hiding place, waiting for the ceremony to start, watching as the guests assemble in the pews below her. She wonders whether her wedding gift will work as intended.

The choir, a group of younglings with exquisite voices, begins to sing. Howard was among them once, when she was but a girl. It was how she caught Henry's eye. It has been a long time since she sang with the same abandon she once did.

The pews are emptier than they were at Howard's wedding, although that is perhaps simply because the many girls with whom Howard shared a bedchamber insisted upon attending. Howard recognises few of these guests – Mary's two children, a girl and a boy, sit quietly in matching black outfits. But Howard cannot see Mary's charming brother George or his spouses. Where are her parents? Howard heard that they moved to the family home of Hever in the wake of Boleyn's arrest, but she assumed they would be in attendance. Is their absence a sign of Henry's displeasure, or theirs?

Henry arrives next, the light from the stained-glass windows making the play of the divine power across his skin look even more dramatic. And then there is Mary, walking slowly up the aisle. She has seen Mary Boleyn a few times, at the Moon Ball, but has never spoken to her. It is interesting, Howard realises, that she remembers each instance of seeing the woman, despite their lack of formal introduction.

She is undoubtedly beautiful, and even more so today in her wedding dress. Her sister's was red and indulgent, from what Howard heard. Mary's is black. The colour of mourning. The colour of grace. Both attributes suit the woman, for she looks, as she has her hair dressed in a glorious crown of plaited curls and iridescent black ribbon, every inch the woman who knows she has sold her soul, and who is already feeling the cost.

Mary is wearing Howard's wedding gift, as Howard had hoped she would – an inconceivably long cloak that ties around the neck. The ivory silk has been hand-stitched with beads that shimmer under light and shadow. Howard's fingers still remember the ache of the needlework. Some of her ladies grew blisters from the long days working on it. Howard leans forward, waiting, waiting.

The sanctuary is the only place in High Hall with stained-glass windows. What few remember, though Howard does, ever since Henry made a passing remark about it, is that the glass has been treated with a particular oil in order to make the colours more vivid. That oil, brewed from the sap of the dreorum tree, does strange things to light. And when it lands upon the beads sewn across Mary's cloak, they turn from white to deepest scarlet. The cloak becomes a trail of blood that stretches out behind her. All fifty feet of it.

The guests murmur in alarm. Henry blanches. Ursula's expression, from her place in the pews beside the other ambassadors, is fascinating: it reminds her of Bishop More when he is at his most fanatical. It is Ursula who has understood Howard's intent better than anyone else. She has invoked Mary's dead sister, and her wedding dress, like a curse.

"Get it off," Mary says, her voice high, her fingers fumbling on the fastenings.

The cloak is whisked away, tied back up in its sheaths of taffeta and hidden from view and memory, as if it had never existed. Howard smiles. Mary may never look at the cloak again, but she will remember it. She will know the ache of uncertainty over Howard's gift: was it a generous but misguided present? For surely Howard is far too eager to please to have intended it as a slight. She is, after all, the rose without a thorn.

Henry murmurs something to Mary, and gradually her shoulders relax. He leads her to the front of the sanctuary, where Bishop More stands before the altar and the great horns of Cernunnos. He has always been a stiff, gentle figure, and on the sickly side of thin on account of his rigorous worship. But now his face is devoid of colour, the skin sagging. He stands oddly, as though one of his legs cannot bear weight. When he speaks, his voice lacks vigour.

As Henry and Mary face each other, there is an air of inevitability about their mannerisms. Not devoid of affection but certainly devoid of joy.

Howard's eyes stray from the couple to the true object of her interest. At the front of the sanctuary, on the altar, should sit six boxes of different materials: the boxes containing the queens' binding cloths, long wefts of purple fabric through which each queen unknowingly gave her bordweal power to the King of Elben, permitting him to syphon her very life force. It is these, if they have interpreted the customs right, that the queens must destroy if they are to break Henry's hold upon them.

Yet as More raises his hands in greeting, Howard realises that only one box is set upon the altar. It is as they feared: of course Henry will not make the binding cloths readily available, not any more. Yet she finds this fact strangely comforting. It proves that she and Cleves are correct in their reasoning, for if the binding clothes weren't significant, Henry would not have changed the tradition of displaying all of them.

Howard leans back, out of sight, as More binds Mary and Henry, their pledges of loyalty and love barely registering. She hears the clanking of the ceremonial dragon as it is slaughtered, its inner flame undoubtedly golden, just as hers had been, just as all the other queens' had been. All pomp and nothingness.

Well, it is time to find her fellow thief.

When Mary's binding cloth is placed inside its box of beaten copper, Howard rises silently and descends from the cove into the passageways that lead away from the sanctuary.

As she rounds a corner, slipping from shadow to shadow, a hand shoots out from an alcove and grabs her wrist. She almost cries out, until she spies Cleves's heart-shaped face peeking out from beneath a servant's cap.

"Well met, sister," Cleves whispers, holding a finger to her lips. They both look back towards the altar, waiting for the box containing Mary's cloth to be returned to its hiding place. Cromwell now steps forward. At first, Howard thinks he must be congratulating the new Queen of Brynd, but he barely acknowledges Mary. He bows to Henry, and the king embraces his advisor.

The divine power that always glistens across Henry's skin seems to spark. And for an instant, Howard thinks that some of that power is transferred to Cromwell.

Howard and Cleves stir.

"There is something new," Cleves whispers. So she did not imagine it.

Cromwell is the one to collect the box containing the binding cloth. He is the one who conveys it out of the sanctuary. He is the one they must follow.

Without speaking, the women slip along the passageway, giving Cromwell plenty of space, always keeping a corner between him and them. He leads them round and down, round and down, and more than once Howard thinks they have lost him. They are deep in the bowels of High Hall, beneath the ancient dungeons and cellars filled with prisoners and fine wines imported from sunnier climes. Cromwell's footsteps echo strangely, each one punctuated with dripping water. Howard begins to worry that even she will not be able to remember the route out of this maze, when Cromwell turns a final corner.

Cleves and Howard peer round. Their throats are stripped by the heat emanating from the room beyond. It is almost impossible to see the details of the room clearly through a miasma of smoke. A low growl shakes the stone above and around them. Howard braces herself against the wall, fearing that the tunnel will collapse.

"We must be beneath the Tower," Cleves whispers.

That would make sense, for the Tower is surrounded by a moat of fire, kept alight by ancient dragons imprisoned beneath.

The queens tuck themselves into a darkened crevice and watch as Cromwell approaches the wall at the far end of the room. He presses his hand against one of the stones. Smoke rises from the point, and something else too: a spark of divine power. Their eyes did not deceive them: somehow, Henry gave part of his own power to Cromwell. Howard is almost breathless, not just from the heat, but from the *trust*. For all his talk of love for his queens, he never entrusted even Aragon, his most humble, loyal and true wife, with even the smallest spark of his (*their*) power.

A deep groan, as if from some tortured giant, emanates from the wall. Its echoes mix with the roars of the Tower dragons, filling Howard's skull.

A cavity has opened where he touched the wall. In it sit five boxes, and a space for a sixth. Howard knows her own immediately – made of iced silver, it is to her mind the most beautiful of the binding boxes. Cromwell slots Brynd's neatly between the golden box of Daven and the steel box of Hyde. He makes the sign of Cernunnos before the cavity, and it closes once more.

Howard grips Cleves's hand, pressing herself back into the crevice, as Cromwell passes from the room and returns to his business on the upper levels. When he is out of hearing, Cleves shakes her head, smiling.

"What amuses you?" Howard says.

"The arrogance of that man," Cleves says. "If I were him, I would be far more cautious. We are well hidden, certainly, but hardly invisible."

"Maybe the luck of the goddess is on our side," Howard says. Surely this only serves to prove that her rescue of Florin, daring though it was, was not overly foolhardy. Certainly not worthy of the scorn Cleves had heaped upon her.

Cleves sighs. "Let us hope that we have not used it all up, then."

She listens carefully. “I believe we are safe. Come.”

They dart into the room, coughing through the heat, and approach the wall. Now that she knows where to look, Howard can see the faintest outline where the cavity must be. Cleves produces a knife from her pocket and attempts to prise open the stone. They take turns, their sweat hissing as it falls.

“It’s no good,” Cleves says, wiping her forehead.

Howard will not give up. She was going to be the one to free them all. She cannot fail them now. She digs the knife between stone, pushing and pushing.

“Howard, stop,” Cleves says.

“No,” she cries. She does not know what is sweat and what is tears.

The knife breaks beneath her grip. She and Cleves look at the broken blade on the flagstone floor, then Howard turns and hurls the useless handle into the passage.

Cleves picks up the blade, and then the handle, and returns. “I will not tell you to be calm, because I fear you will stab me,” she says.

Howard closes her eyes and laughs.

“I don’t understand how you can be so calm,” she says. “I feel as though I am always about to trip myself up. I just want all of this to be done with.”

“I know.”

Howard leans back against the wall, letting its scorching heat burn her. Cleves fiddles with the knife’s pieces, not looking at Howard as she says, “In my experience, wars that are begun quickly are rarely ended so.”

Howard frowns. “In your experience?” Thanks to the bordweal, Elben has not seen a war since Queen Isabet. She grows, if possible, even warmer as she realises she does not know anything of the history of Cleves’s country.

“When I was eleven, a distant cousin of my father took a fancy to the throne of Ezzonid. It took five years for the matter to be settled and peace to be restored.”

Five years of civil war. Howard examines Cleves: the sturdiness of her figure, the way she always holds herself so upright despite her apparent cheer. Five years, and she was eleven when it began. That would make her the age Howard is now when it ended. At least the uncertainty of Howard’s own childhood was never marred by violence.

“I am sorry,” she says. She wishes she knew the words to convey the depth of how she feels, which is so much more than *sorry*.

"Yes, well, I am still smiling, am I not? I still have all my limbs and all my wits," Cleves says.

Howard would like to ask more, but doesn't want to upset Cleves. She rests her head against the wall. "What are we going to do about these binding cloths, then?" she says.

Cleves examines the place where the cavity appeared. "We need the divine power, I assume. It is clear that is what Cromwell used to open it."

Howard looks at her hands. "I have not been able to conjure it since the Moon Ball without my spirit stone."

"Nor I," Cleves says.

Howard closes her eyes, thinks of that moment when Ursula took her by the waist and made her believe that she *could* be a vessel for divinity, instead of simply a vessel for Henry's desires. It seems impossible that she, of all the queens, might be able to conjure the power without the spirit stone, without the might of the others bolstering her.

She recalls that moment, out in the courtyard, with the sound of the Kyttle Falls drowning out the tumult of her thoughts. She recalls Ursula's solid heft behind her, and the belief in her voice as she commanded Howard. The sense of her ladies, scattered throughout Plythe and yet all connected to her through a single, invisible purpose.

"*Hilareth*," Cleves says. Howard does not know what it means, but the exhale of the word makes her open her eyes. Cleves is staring at Howard's hands.

Barely visible through the steam of the chamber, barely there at all, is a flicker of bordweal light. It is not only the blue-green-purple of a bruise: it is the orange-red-grey-gold of sunrise too.

"Oh my lord," Howard says. Something flutters in her chest. She has the sudden urge to dowse her hands in water.

"Quickly," Cleves says, forcing Howard to stand. Before the power fades, she presses both hands to the place where the cavity opened for Cromwell.

Sharp pain shoots through her fingers and into her bones. She thinks she screams, but perhaps it is only in her head. For there, clear as though he were in the chamber, looming between her and Cleves, is Cernunnos.

She has only ever seen paintings and sculptures of him: the great, antlered god. They have always been stylised. Lashings of gold plating. Swooping strokes to suggest form without being explicit.

The Cernunnos – the real Cernunnos – is both alluring and grotesque. His antlers are honed to cruelty. His body is human but his nails are brutish. His legs are bloated with muscle, and his skin is pale beneath a bruise that covers his whole body; a joyless imitation of the bordweal's colours.

She thinks her hand may be fused to the wall, fused to this apparition, but then she is pulled away, the skin on her palm tearing, leaving a crisp layer of darkness on the wall, like a water print, that is soon burned away.

Cleves holds Howard's face between her hands.

"Howard, can you see me?" she says.

"I can see you," Howard says hoarsely.

"What happened?"

Howard begins to tremble. Cernunnos's presence is still within her, a scornful rebuke.

"It was not the divine power we needed to retrieve the binding cloths. It was *his* power."

Cleves seems to sink. "Of course it would be," she says. "Of course it would be. That is why Cromwell did not take more care."

The brilliance of the hiding place reveals itself. Neither they nor any of their followers will be able to access the cloths here, for they can never, will never, wield Cernunnos's specific power – the power that is his alone, not Medren's, weaker though it is.

Henry is always cleverer than her, always ahead, even when he thinks her harmless. Howard had thought that, because Seymour triumphed on account of Henry underestimating her, that Howard might be able to triumph the same way. But Henry does not make the same mistake twice.

"What do we do now?" Howard says.

Cleves pats Howard's arm. "We find another way. We grow cleverer still."

She cradles Howard's head as Legh once did. "And we try to learn how you just wielded Medren's power, you brilliant child."

CHAPTER THIRTY-FIVE

Cleves

Cleves is never uncertain. She knows her mind. But Howard has unsettled her. She does not like that she is so shocked by the young queen being able to conjure a power that none of the rest of them can. She does not like what it says about her – *her*, the queen who should know just as well as Howard what it is to be underestimated and scorned. It niggles as she travels back from High Hall, Johana at her side.

"Did you enjoy your time spent with the noblemen of High Hall?" she asks him, keen for distraction.

"As a pig enjoys the slaughter," he replies airily.

"Do not tell me you prefer spending time with men who have integrity, Johana, or I shall not recognise you."

"I do not care a damn for integrity. I should merely like a man with a sense of humour that doesn't revolve solely around breasts and cocks. Is that too much to ask?"

"Strange, I thought you enjoyed cock."

"*Some* cock. I do have standards."

"Maybe if it was served to you alongside a good Elbenese apple."

They do not look at each other, but she can tell that he is smiling as broadly as she. She glances over at him.

"Did you truly not enjoy it?"

He shrugs. "I came to Elben to be of service to my favourite cousin. I was of service. Thus – I am content."

His words are so devoid of his usual scalding wit, so free of the manipulations she has navigated at High Hall, that her heart twists. She reaches out to him, across the gap between their horses, and he catches her hand. They stay like that, their hands rising and falling with the horses' gait.

"This is nice," he says, so softly she almost does not hear him.

The sun is high in a clear sky, and the trees are puffy with buds and blossom. It must have rained overnight, though, because the welcome chill of a dewy morning is still in the air and the horses' hooves pat the ground rather than knocking it.

He's right. She has always been adept at making easy conversation, but it has not been safe for her to form attachments without some level of guile. She had almost forgotten what a comfort such friendship can be: a sheltered cove in a stormy sea.

"Are we returning to Gnottel Lodge, cousin?" he asks her.

"Why?"

He looks ostentatiously at their surroundings. "Perhaps because we took the turning to the Gealdrum Forest instead of the road to Cnothan a full half-hour ago?"

Cleves looks around sharply and realises that he is right. Idiot.

"Why did you not say at the turning?" she says.

He shrugs. "I assumed you were thinking on a certain queen and were eager to reach her."

She pulls her hand from his and taps him on the knee. "I like you at present, cousin. Don't become presumptuous again."

He laughs and holds up his hands in surrender.

"I simply think that you should do what is necessary to remove her from your head. Kiss her, sleep with her, be done with her. That was ever your way, was it not?"

"It was," she says. Then again, softer: "It was."

She has not played fair with her lovers. She, who has always considered herself a person of integrity. Has she been selfish to treat them so, even if she was always honest about what she had to offer?

She shakes her head.

"What thought has turned you so serious?" Johana asks.

"I am wondering whether a castle can ever change its foundations," she replies.

Johana throws his head back, staring at the sky as he considers this. "Yes, I think so," he says.

"Truly?" She licks her lips. She does not like the way her body feels – like it is floating, untethered.

"Certainly. If one is willing to pull down the rest of the castle and rebuild it stone by stone."

Her breath hitches. "But then it would be a different castle entirely."

"Would it?" He does not look at her, only at the road ahead. "If it was the same stone, the same design. Would it be a different castle, or simply one built on surer foundations?"

He nudges his horse closer, so that his boot touches hers.

"Are you thinking of redesigning Cnothan alongside your plan to overthrow your husband?" he says. "Or do we talk of a different castle?"

She is about to respond with a witty deflection, but the softness of his enquiry merits the softness of honesty, inasmuch as she is able to give it.

"The phoenix," she says.

"Yes?"

"I think that was the happiest, most extraordinary moment of my life."

"Mine too."

She can see Gealdrum Forest in the distance now. Its dense canopy – ash, sweet chestnut, poison yew and needle holly – is a line of soldiers on the horizon.

"In some ways I think I have spent my whole life seeking that same happiness," she says.

"And in others?"

"Running from it." She gulps. She had never realised before. She has pursued small, immediate pleasures – reading in solitude, a tumble with a pretty woman, the soft nuzzle of a loving dog – and thought that she could build them, brick by brick, stone by stone, into a greater happiness. A phoenix happiness. But she is starting to see that there is a greater happiness to be found, not in the strong walls of a castle, but in the silent rage of the tidal wave. Who would not run from such a wave? Only those who do not fear to drown.

"Stop," Johana says, taking hold of her reins and tugging her horse to halt. He dismounts his own steed, and waits for her to do the same. Their horses wander to the side of the road to graze as Johana takes both her hands in his. She looks up at him and sees a rare sadness in his brown eyes.

"Iklehafor hi lada ganasz, perigord," he says. It is a line from an old Ezzonidian lullaby, one she has not heard in many years. *The gods owe you nothing but happiness, heart child.*

"What if the ecstasy is not as I remember it?" she whispers.

He pulls her into his chest, holding her tightly.

"What if it is better?" he asks.

She cannot think of anything she wants more. She cannot think of anything more frightening, or more impossible.

They reach Gnottel Lodge long after luncheon.

"Cousin," she says, as she and Johana dismount their horses once more. "Would you be so kind as to keep our visitor out of the way? There is a private matter I must attend to with Queen Seymour, and not in the way you previously suggested."

Johana's mouth twitches, but he nods and enters the lodge without another word.

She meets Seymour in a bower on the east side of the lodge's gardens, secluded enough that they will not be overheard, and open enough that they will see anyone approaching. Cleves cannot meet Seymour's eyes; she is still raw from her conversation with Johana. Besides, there is more urgent business to attend to. She pulls her *sunscína* from its place upon her bodice.

"I left mine in my chamber," Seymour says. "I fear Cecilia spying it."

"Very wise," Cleves says. Seymour looks sideways at her. "No jest? Are you feeling well, Queen Cleves?"

"Last time we met you complained that I find everything too amusing. I am merely trying to make you happy," Cleves says. Her twisting stomach settles. This dance of wit and flirtation is safe, known.

Together they press Cleves's *sunscína*, waiting for the birdsong around them to fade as the other queens appear. It does not take long for Cleves to explain what she and Howard discovered about the binding cloths.

"So they are beyond our reach," Parr says.

"I could have told you that Henry would be far too clever to allow you to simply take the cloths," Aragon says.

"Then what would you have us do, beyond waiting and praying?" Cleves says.

"That is not—" Aragon begins.

But Cleves can only see Howard, and the way she shakes her head slightly, as if she could foretell Cleves's reaction. Cleves has never cared about disappointing anyone before; not since her little sister Sybil would chide her for being too boisterous, or too merry.

"My apologies, Queen Aragon," Cleves says.

The women stare. Aragon pauses, mid-aggrandisement. Cleves takes a deep breath. "My apologies," she says again. "I recognise that you are gathering all the knowledge you can from your extensive connections abroad and in Elben. My frustration stems from the fact that all the knowledge in the known world will not help us if we cannot seize those binding cloths and rid ourselves of this tie to our husband. And I cannot see a way through by myself, much though I have tried."

Somewhere during her speech, Seymour has taken her hand. Cleves wonders that she did not notice; that her heart did not leap at the contact. She looks down at Seymour's fingers, cocooning her own, and Seymour withdraws them quickly, as if she herself did not realise what she was doing.

"It seems to me that if we cannot get to the cloths, we must make Henry bring them to us," Seymour says.

"But he will recognise a trick," Howard says, her voice timid. "Boleyn tricked him. Have the last few days not proven that he will not stand to be tricked again?"

They lapse into silence. Cleves watches their pensive faces, and something unfurls in her chest. She can still feel the warmth from Seymour's hand.

"We do have one advantage," Cleves says. "We know him. Truly know him. He has shown each of us shards of himself. We have never before been able to comprehend him because we have never spoken honestly to each other. It is surely one of the reasons the Kings of Elben have fostered our dislike of each other."

"But he knows us," Aragon says. Cleves wants to say, *does he?* But Howard speaks first.

"He knows my body, but he does not know me," she says, quiet but fierce.

Parr nods and addresses Aragon. "It is true, sister. Henry sees your dedication, he sees your stateliness and your maternal instinct, but he does not perceive all of you, I think?"

Aragon's expression twists then, almost imperceptibly. Cleves's interest is piqued: which part of Parr's speech did she take issue with, and why not contradict her if she disagrees?

"Well, I imagine I know him best since I have been wed to him the longest," Aragon says. "I can tell you that he believes in marrying for love. That is, I suppose, why he has always been so cold to you, Queen Cleves. He courted me, romanced me, after Arthur's death. While ours was a marriage of state, it was also a love match, no matter what some may think."

It is Aragon's peace offering. Cleves wonders whether she can risk some humour.

"I believe he does love you, sister, but do not pity me. I have witnessed how he treats the wives he loves. I rather think I have had the better marriage."

"Hmm," Aragon says.

They trade more thoughts, and gradually a picture builds of the man they all married. Cleves wonders at it, for while she has heard much of Henry's generous and uxorious nature, she has rarely witnessed his wives talk of it with such warmth. Of his particular ability to make them feel like the only woman he truly loves. It is Seymour's words that help Cleves see a way forward, though:

"He wants to be seen as a good man. Is that not what connects all of our experiences? I believe that he struggled – perhaps struggles still – with the deceit that forms the foundation of his power. Cecilia has told me a little of their childhood. He once spoke to me of his heartache over Queen Blount's death. I did not understand it fully then, but I do now. He knew that her untimely death was his fault, and it tortured him."

"She was devoted to him," Parr says. She has spoken little thus far, so when she does the other queens fall silent. "Perhaps that is why it plagued him so – because he knew that she was the very embodiment of humble, loyal and true."

"That is what we can use," Cleves says, suddenly full of fire. "He may know enough not to produce the binding cloths, but he believes, despite everything, that he is a good ruler, that all he does to us is in the service of his country. If that is the image he wishes to foster, then we use his own hypocrisy against him."

"How do you suggest we do that?" Aragon says.

Cleves closes her eyes, letting the plans and the plots take hold of her. "We suspect that Cromwell is searching for some ancient magic, some ritual, that will permit Henry to take Medren's power for himself without needing us. What if we could hand him such a ritual? One that would feed into his need to be viewed as a good king making noble sacrifices?"

"And to show that we are good wives," Aragon says. "Do not forget that it is that which he seeks above all. That is what all of us, yourself excepted, Queen Cleves, have in common. We have adored him, either truly or through performance."

There is an ache in the older woman's voice. Poor fool that Aragon is, she loved the man, perhaps as much as Boleyn loved him. Perhaps more.

"Humble, loyal and true," Howard says. They each of them pledged to be that wife.

"Sacrifice," Aragon says suddenly. "We sacrifice our bodies to his glory, his power, every day. And yet he continues to use us up. What if we simply offer him a way to bring the slow sacrifice of his wives to a speedy conclusion?"

Cleves nods, working it all through in her head. "So we feed him a believable lie: that if we die – *with* the binding cloths – then our power will be entirely his. It places us in great danger—"

"And that is why he is likely to believe it," Parr says. "That is why he might be willing to bring the binding cloths to us."

Aragon coughs. "We can use my network. And Queen Cleves's also. But nothing must be traced back to us, or Cromwell will grow suspicious."

"Some of the Feorwans are willing to help us," Seymour says.

Parr smiles, a mischievous glint in her eyes. "Let us sow our seeds, then."

They plot through the afternoon, honing their lies, going back again and again to the kind of story that Henry is telling of his life, his legacy. For is there anything more powerful than feeding a narrative already underway? Is that not how Cleves has survived her marriage? Because she has fed the story of her unattractiveness with morsels of quirkiness, with sweetmeats of ridicule?

When the sun is low in the sky and the birdsong has quieted, they say their farewells. The *sunscína* blank at last, Cleves turns to Seymour beside her.

"I think this could work," Seymour says. Her smile is radiant, like the brightest star at midnight.

"I think so too," Cleves replies. Her chest is full of flowers, their petals bursting forth with the scent of victory, heady with her own cleverness. She takes Seymour's face between her hands, leans forward and kisses her.

CHAPTER THIRTY-SIX

Cleves

She tastes of marchpane and autumn. Of rain upon an ocean.

Seymour's hands tangle in Cleves's hair as their tongues meet.

When they part for breath, Seymour says, "I have been waiting for you to do that for so long."

"If I could have reached through the *sunscína* to do so, I would have," Cleves replies.

She is about to push Seymour back upon the bench so that she can better explore her body when someone coughs nearby. She and Seymour spring apart. It is Johana, his expression caught between mortification and glee.

"You took my advice for once, cousin," he says.

"What do you want?" Cleves growls.

"Supper is laid. Should I partake with the Dowager Queen alone?"

Cleves looks to Seymour. They should eat. They will need their bellies full for what Cleves has planned. But she does not want to wait. Her desire is hot and Seymour's eyes are dark. Then Seymour's stomach rumbles, and the spell is broken.

"We will join you," Cleves says.

They follow Johana as he bounces across the gardens. Cecilia is already seated when they enter the hall. Cleves schools her expression: it would be deadly for Cecilia to understand what is between her and

Seymour. Such knowledge is power, and Cleves will never allow anyone to hold that kind of leverage over her.

But as the dishes are brought out, Cleves's gaze is drawn back to Seymour no matter how hard she tries. Their dinner is less lavish than those at High Hall and Cnothan, but delicious and warm nonetheless. Stews of lamb, sprinkled with crisp fairy wings from the territory of Hyde. Tench from the nearby Fietherford, roasted upon beds of roots and river leaves, salty and flaking and pungent with herbs. And a cake in the centre of the table, one of Cleves's favourites – Johana must have requested it from the kitchen for her, for it is a specialty of Ezzonid. A tower of pancakes, layered between melting cheese and honey, drizzled with thick cream and salt.

"Shall I open the negotiations with my brother, then?" Cecilia asks as Cleves tries not to watch the way Seymour licks her lips after a sip of wine. The truth is, they should not need Cecilia's help if their plan works, but it would make things easier if Cecilia believes she is still going to get her palace.

"Yes, write your letter," Cleves says. "We will send it to him, after we have read it, of course."

"Naturally," Cecilia says, dipping her head. The submissiveness is out of character. Seymour wipes her chin with her napkin, ever so delicately.

"What will you do to my brother, if he concedes to your demands?" Cecilia says.

She takes a whole fish onto her trencher and digs a fork into its skull, extracting the eye and biting it like a cherry. Cleves can hear the little globe pop.

"In my country, we keep noble prisoners in fine style. He could live out his life in great comfort somewhere in Elben. Maybe you would like him to be in your territory of Brynd?"

"So you would not seek to hurt him?" Cecilia says. She takes a bite of flaky flesh, then pulls a fish bone from her mouth, laying it out upon her plate.

"I think losing his kingdom and seeing the downfall of his family's legacy would be punishment enough."

Seymour speaks from the other end of the table: "You do choose the strangest people to care about, Cecilia."

"I might say the same about you," Cecilia says sweetly. Cleves stills. Does Cecilia know about them? But then Cecilia adds, "Your love for that upstart Boleyn is well-known. Even my washerwoman back in Perfugi knows you wanted to fuck her."

Seymour's gaze darts to Cleves. Cleves shakes her head: the taunt does not affect her. How dare anyone shame Seymour for her heart?

"Does that not reflect more poorly upon your brother's judgement than upon Queen Seymour?" Cleves says. Cecilia purses her mouth. She excuses herself soon afterwards, and Johana follows her, humming his way out of the room in a manner that makes it clear he knows what is about to happen as much as Cleves and Seymour know it.

Their coupling is inevitable, and Cleves savours that certainty, letting the stirring in her belly thread through the rest of her body. She and Seymour continue to eat in silence, the only sound the scrape of forks upon plate and the crackle of the fire.

Seymour is the one to break it. "It does not trouble you that I harboured feelings for Boleyn?"

"Why should it? I too have harboured feelings for others."

The truth is, her thoughts around Boleyn and Seymour are complicated and myriad. She is not by nature a jealous person, but she also knows that Boleyn marked a crossroads in Seymour's life; a hinge around which her destiny rotated. The Seymour Cleves is attracted to is one who would not have existed without Boleyn. How can she be jealous of such a person? And yet . . . it is hard to seduce in the company of a ghost.

"Ah," Seymour says, pulling a cake filled with cherries towards her and taking her fork to the whole cake instead of merely taking a slice onto her plate. "And did you flirt shamelessly with my predecessors too?"

"You believe I have flirted shamelessly with you?"

"Well," Seymour says, pouring cream over the cake. "The way you behaved with me at our first meeting was hardly a little flirtation."

"Ha!" Cleves says. "You have clearly never been properly seduced if you believe that to have been shameless."

Seymour sits back in her chair and observes Cleves in a way that makes her want to leap over the table and retreat all at once. It is a bold look, a challenging look. "I think it must be quite something to be loved by you, angry, angry queen," she says, in playful mockery of Cleves's voice. "And you tell me that is not seduction?"

Something sparks inside Cleves. This is the moment: her chance to satisfy her infatuation with the Queen of Hyde. How could she have been so frightened of it? How could she have thought of it as a tidal wave? If they bed each other, then they will know each other, and there is nothing like knowing to cure an infatuation. It is not as if she is in love with Seymour. It is not as if she will never want to let go.

"No, my Lady Seymour, that is not seduction," she says.

"What would you do if you were truly seducing me then?"

Cleves does not care that it is a ploy to force her into showing her cards. She knows exactly what she wants to do to this woman.

She rises from the table and strolls towards the fire to stoke it up.

"First, I'd make sure the only shivering you'd be doing is because of me," she says.

"Then?" Seymour says. Her voice is different. Cleves turns to see Seymour crawling across the table towards her on her hands and knees. Her bodice isn't cut low, but at this angle Cleves has a clear view of the delicious crevice between her breasts.

"Then," Cleves says, climbing onto the table herself. "Then I would draw upon your skin with my fingers, tracing the edge of your gown."

They meet in the centre of the table, platters of half-eaten food all around them. Seymour nuzzles her nose against Cleves's, her lips so very close, her breath a blessing upon Cleves's cheek. Cleves unclips Seymour's hood, drawing it gently back, revealing her hair. "Then I would strip you bare and touch every single part of your body, feeling for the places that make you gasp. And those places? I would worship them."

"Fine words, Queen Cleves," Seymour says. "But you know I place more stock in action."

Cleves tangles her hand in Seymour's hair. Their mouths meet in a kiss that is at first crushingly brutal, but quickly softens into something far more glorious. Cleves cannot help but moan. Seymour's lips are soft, and she tastes of honey and salt.

Cleves needs every part of her body to be touching every part of Seymour's. She breaks away from the kiss, breathless, and lifts Seymour to a kneel, wrapping an arm around her waist to pull her even closer.

"Is this enough action for you?"

She trails her tongue across Seymour's ear and down her neck, inhaling her scent – heart smoke, cloves and a hot, metallic hint of dragon's blood.

Seymour drags Cleves's face up to her own and kisses her long and deeply. "I want to undress you," she says against her mouth.

This has always been one of Cleves's favourite parts of a seduction. Women have so many clothes. The anticipation, as each piece is removed, revealing a little more skin, is deliciously painful.

She reaches around Seymour to undo her gown, not needing to look to know where to find each dress pin holding the gown in place. Seymour moves her attentions to Cleves's ear, nipping gently at her lobe.

"Do you want this gown off or not?" Cleves says.

"Treat it as a test," Seymour whispers.

"You are a test, my lady," Cleves says, trying to ignore the deep shiver running through her body as Seymour scrapes her nails through her hair with one hand, the other pattering fingers down her chest bone, towards the place where her smock dives beneath her gown.

At last, the gown is loose enough for Cleves to tug the piece over Seymour's head. She pulls the sleeves off next, letting her hands run down the bare skin of Seymour's shoulders as the fabric comes away from the rest of her outfit. Then the frontlet and the kirtle, abandoned on the table, and Seymour is left in only her linen smock and her stockings.

Cleves runs a hand up Seymour's leg, but Seymour stops her.

"You still have far too many clothes on, Queen of Cnothan," she says. She pushes Cleves around with surprising strength, cradling her back with her body. Cleves watches the fire hazily as Seymour takes control. She isn't used to this – she is usually the one leading the seduction. She is the one who delivers pleasure, who does the worshipping. And she has always been at peace with that – it is altogether safer.

Soon Cleves is only in her linen shirt and her breeches. Seymour cups her buttocks and squeezes.

"Do you know the parts of you I have longed for the most?" Seymour says. Cleves flushes.

"Your arms," Seymour continues, her hands running up to Cleves's shoulders. "Goddess, those arms, Cleves. They were my undoing from the moment we first met."

Cleves leans back and kisses Seymour again and again, so Seymour will not see the tears that have sprung to her eyes. It is one thing to know that you are not unattractive. It is quite another to feel it after seven years of being told by everyone that you are – even if you were the one who engineered the slight.

Seymour pulls away, perhaps sensing her turmoil.

"Did you ever truly doubt it?" Seymour says.

"Never," Cleves lies.

Seymour sees the lie. Of course she does, with that sight that is so quiet and so sharp. She climbs off the table, pulling Cleves with her, and moves them to the chair by the fireside.

"What are you doing?" Cleves says as Seymour pushes her into the seat.

"This is my seduction," Seymour replies. She pulls Cleves's breeches off and parts her legs, kissing her way up each one. The fire hisses. The warmth Cleves feels as Seymour's tongue finds the centre of her pleasure is nothing to do with the flames from the hearth.

All reason flies from her mind. All regret at waiting so long to do this, all fear of doing it too soon, or at all, is banished by the rightness of Seymour's mouth hot against her most intimate part.

They worship each other through the night, sometimes playful, sometimes serious, only ever stopping to stoke the fire. Fingers on and inside each other, tasting each other and themselves. They both understand how to pleasure women, and their experience makes their time all the sweeter. Cleves has never understood men's obsession for virgins. The notion of being the only one to possess a body is alien to her – why should it matter? Seymour's experience is one of the greatest joys of their coupling. She knows how to speak to Cleves. She knows where to touch, how to explore, and she knows what pleases her and how to communicate it. It is liberating, joyful, sensuous, and Cleves has never been more satisfied.

As Cleves lies back in the chair by the dying fire, a slumbering Seymour draped around her and the sun promising dawn through the windows, Cleves knows that the tidal wave is upon her. She is drowning, and it is exquisite.

"This was nice," she murmurs against Seymour's hair.

"It was more than nice, you fool."

Cleves strains to surface, reaches for the shore, "We simply needed to do this, didn't we? Now we can be allies once more."

Seymour is nearly asleep, but Cleves thinks she hears her reply through the drowsiness. "If you say so, Queen of Cnothan."

CHAPTER THIRTY-SEVEN

Cecilia

They think her an idiot. They think she does not know that they are lying to her. They think she does not see that they have been fucking each other with their eyes throughout the meal. As if Cecilia of all people cannot see desire when it is before her.

She makes sure Johana sees her enter her chamber, and waits until his footsteps recede. Then, kicking off her shoes, she slips out once more and tiptoes on stockinged feet to Seymour's room. Usually Seymour keeps it locked, but with Cleves here she has been distracted. Cecilia turns the door handle, holding her breath. Miraculously, the door opens.

Cecilia goes immediately to the trunk, throwing it open and tossing piles of gowns onto the floor in her haste to find that simple one with the hard hem. It is still at the bottom of the trunk – how predictable. Cecilia tears the stitches, pulling the shard out and moving it in the light this way and that. It is hardly a knife, but with enough force it could be used as a weapon.

Now for the second part of her plan.

Johana's chamber is at the end of the hallway, in the wing furthest from the banqueting hall. That will work in her favour. His door is locked from the inside. He does not, after all, have the temptation of a haughty queen to distract him. She knocks softly.

"Who is it?" Johana says.

"Your cousin is making all manner of irritating moans in the hall beneath my chamber," she says.

"And? I did not think you a prude," he replies.

"I wish to sleep."

"So put a pillow over your head. I am not going to interrupt my cousin when she is having a good time."

Cecilia sighs, frustrated. "Let me be clear, sir," she says. "If you do not tell her to be quieter, I shall set up such a racket that it will be impossible for her to have any pleasure at all."

Johana curses. There is the sound of a key in the lock, and then the door is opened. Johana is in his nightshirt, and if Cecilia did not suspect that her gender was not his preference, she might have been tempted to try a little pleasure of her own. But now is not the time. Before he can say anything more, she steps towards him and punches the shard into his stomach.

She has never stabbed anyone before – not like this, anyway. The wet slip of blood and organs, the breathy gasp, is not to her taste. He staggers back, crumpling to the floor as she pulls the shard free. Cecilia looks around. There are only a few places where the keys to her freedom could be. She searches the trunks first, ignoring Johana's laboured breaths.

"Where are they?" she mutters, as one after another of the trunks yield nothing but clothes. She peers beneath the bed, pulls apart the pillows and cushions. Nothing. She is running out of time: who knows how long the queens' coupling will last.

She kneels before Johana. His face is unusually pale. A pool of blood gathers around him.

"Tell me where the keys are or I will drive this shard into your cock next," she says.

He struggles to focus on her, but when they come the words are clear: "Fuck you."

Despicable heroism. He knows he is dying; she cannot touch him now. She leans in once again. "You have not the strength to scream. I think I could use this on your treacherous cousin before she realises I'm even in that hall, don't you?"

The gathering night makes him slow to comprehend her. She presses home the point: "The choice is very simple, sir. My freedom, or your cousin's life."

Cleves will die soon either way, of course, but he's not in any state to realise that. He moans, wracked with guilt in his final moments, but eventually he makes the right choice. He reaches for one of the floorboards. Cecilia finds a crack in it and prises it up, tearing her fingernails in the process. Beneath the floorboard: the keys to the lodge.

"My thanks," she says, stepping over him and tripping down the stairs. Before long she is embracing the chill night air. The stables are on the other side of the courtyard, and it only takes a few lashes with a spare piece of rope to force Cleves's stallion to accept her.

Then she is away, galloping through the forest along the road that brought her carriage here. She may not know where she is now, but if she keeps to the road, she will surely come upon some landmark, either a scrind road or else the coast, from where she will find a village or town.

She laughs as the breeze tousles her hair and the tree branches whip her face. What a glorious, glorious escape.

CHAPTER THIRTY-EIGHT

Howard

When Howard was a child, her aunt used to tell her that she was far too confident for her own good. Her father, when he visited, which was rarely, used to tell her it suited her. The two voices warred throughout her childhood, one claiming sovereignty due to presence, the other sovereignty due to blood. They have continued their war in her mind ever since she left her aunt's house and gained the Palace of Plythe. She is, in some ways, aware that it is those two voices who keep her ladies and household on their toes: one moment she is all give, the next all punishment; father and aunt. And Henry. Oh, Henry is both at once, and his voice in her head is the loudest of all.

Plythe, too, is full of questions. They whisper to her as she paces from bedchamber to receiving chamber: will the plan work? What use are you? Did they not give you a role because you have nothing to offer?

The other queens were kind when they spoke in the *sunscína*. She thought, until the very end, that they were finally forging the kind of alliance she had dreamed of. And then they had said their farewells and Howard had realised that she alone of the queens had been given so little to do. Cleves and Aragon are to use their spy networks and foreign connections to sow the rumours of an answer to Henry's problem: that if he spills his queens' lifeblood upon the binding cloths,

Medren's power will be unassailably his. Seymour will ensure that all the components of the plan come together. Parr is the gatherer, using Mathmas's remote location as a secret store. And Howard? *Ensure your lapdragon is well-trained – keep listening for Cromwell and Wolsey in your* sunscína. Small, conciliatory tasks. Scraps of usefulness.

"There is only one way forward," Lady Tylney says when Howard expresses her sorrow.

"What is that?"

They are in Howard's receiving chamber, and there is lively chatter from the rest of her ladies and groomsmen on the other side of the room. Musicians play a merry tune to drown out her conversation.

"You must forge your own role, regardless of the other queens."

"I do not wish to interfere with what we have planned."

"What they have planned. And you would not be interfering. You would be helping."

Howard looks up, and inadvertently catches Thomas Culpepper's eye. She thinks often of the conversation she overheard through her *sunscína*. She wants to trust him, but she fears that too many people already know her truth. Too many people with loyalty to others.

As if her thoughts have conjured him, Florin enters. He wears the garb of the servants of Plythe, although his manner is quite different to that of the rest of the household. There is something about the way he moves, like a swordsman, nimble, that is inescapably foreign. He carries a copper jug, scented with the sweetness of elderflower wine.

"Are you certain about this plan, Your Majesty?" Ursula says, allowing Florin to fill her bone cup.

"Why do you ask?"

Her mouth twists, and she shifts in her seat. "Are you certain that it *is* a lie, this idea of spilling your blood upon the binding cloths?"

Howard laughs. "None of us are witches, Ursula. None of us truly understand how the goddess's power works."

"Sometimes divine power *does* work like that, though, Your Majesty. The spilling of blood upon divinity *can* wring change. Think of the origin of the Pilvreen garnets."

Howard labours to understand. The Pilvreen garnets were created when the blood of innocents was spilled upon the burial site of Elben's first queens. Is Ursula saying that the lie they fabricated might work?

Legh nudges Ursula with her shoulder. "When did you become a religious scholar, Miss Askew?"

Ursula scowls. Howard pats her hand. "Even if you are right, Ursula, I have no intention of spilling any of my blood. None of us do. It is simply a ruse to reunite us with our binding cloths."

"Then all rests on you surviving to the Moon Ball," Ursula says. "You must make him believe you remain humble, loyal and true."

Howard thinks of Mary Boleyn's train turning scarlet. She was foolish there. She placed petty vengeance above her own security, and although she cannot bring herself to regret it, she knows it has made her vulnerable.

Goldfoot wakes from his nap on Howard's lap, stretches, yawns and crawls the short distance to Lady Tylney's lap, where he curls up and falls asleep once more.

"I must put on a show to prove I am still Henry's," she says.

Ursula looks at Florin. "If you were our queen here, what would you do to prove your loyalty?"

Florin considers this. "I would travel to High Hall and sparkle there, as only Queen Howard can sparkle."

The suggestion is not as terrifying to Howard as it might once have been – she does love to be seen to be beautiful, after all. But something does not feel right about it.

"What troubles you?" Lady Tylney says.

"I think that is what I might do now," Howard says slowly.

"Now?" Florin says.

"The wife that Henry believes me to be would not act like that. I fear that in travelling to High Hall, I would only prove that I am not that woman."

That is when it strikes her: Florin has never known her as the girl she was only a year ago. *As only Queen Howard can sparkle.* That is his image of her: the queen who breaks into great houses to save a stranger. The queen who tricks her guards and binds her ladies to her.

That is who Howard has become. But it is not who she must be for Henry.

"I know what we must do," she says. "And it must be all of us. You are going to find me very tiresome."

"Excellent: I shall not have to lie," Legh says.

Florin fetches parchment and quills, and Howard and her ladies labour over their correspondence. This group of strays will bark and mewl as they are expected to. The recipients, and those who intercept their letters, will read what they want to read: that Howard is mortified that the rare fabric she bought for Mary's train turned scarlet; that she is terrified of being suspected of disliking Mary; that she is irritating her household with her worries. They paint a picture of a fluttering songbird without a voice.

Howard summons the jeweller from Sweillan who made her *sunscína* chains, and commissions one final gift. Two roses, one soft gold and one red and white, intertwined. The red and white rose is studded with diamonds to signify thorns, and the petals of the yellow rose open to reveal a tiny replica of Holbein's portrait of Howard. It is gaudy, but clearly expensive. The Tudor rose, and the rose with no thorns, cleaved together. The jeweller affixes the piece to a pin, and once she can be certain that her ladies' letters will have been read by Cromwell and Wolsey's spies, Howard sends it to High Hall with a letter in her own laboured hand.

> *My deerest King,*
> *I am so hapy that you are well. You are my sun. Will you visit me at Plythe the soonest? For I am so desiros of you.*
> *Here is a gift for you, my lord. Will you ware it always?*
> *Your own rose,*
> *Howard*

Florin reads it, his lip curled. "But this is not you," he says.

"It was once," she replies, and she feels a great rush of pity for the old Howard.

Legh reads it next, and nods. "It is exactly as you speak to him when he is here."

Her ladies leave her alone, and she reads the letter over and over. Does she show the right amount of improvement in her letter writing? Are these the most perfect words to charm a clever, suspicious king? She is so caught up in her study that she does not realise Florin is still there until he places a hand upon the parchment, covering her writing.

"I have never seen you so doubtful before," he says.

"You have never seen me around the king."

Florin nudges her hand. "He is not a king, though, is he? He is an interloper. You are the true monarch."

Pretty words, but he cannot know that they wound. She scratches the itchy skin on her scalp, pulls at the hair there. A curl feathers to the floor. Without that same interloper, she would have never been queen.

"Have I ever told you about my time in Cecilia's household?" he says.

"Never."

He sits on the floor beside her, crossing his legs. "She used to discuss great matters with my sister, then order me to come to her. Every time, I used to think – she is going to trust me with her confidence. This time she will ask my advice. And every time she would greet me with her gown already on the floor."

Howard traces her handwriting.

"It is so difficult not to feel grateful, when someone like Henry notices you," she says.

"All my friends told me I was lucky to have captured her interest."

"My father and great-aunt said the same thing. It is the only matter they ever agreed upon."

As they look at each other, Howard's shoulders relax, though she had not known they were tense.

"If you were to see Cecilia again, what do you think you would do?" she asks.

Florin laughs bitterly. "I wish I knew. All I know is that I would not betray you, Katheryn. Beyond that, I can make no sense of my feelings."

"We are a fine pair, are we not?" Howard smiles. "A pair of cracked vases."

"Broken vases," he says. Goldfoot lands neatly on Florin's shoulder, nibbling his ear.

"Broken things can be improved upon if they are mended by the right hands," Howard says. She thinks, unaccountably, of Cleves.

"I would not have believed that before I met you," Florin replies. "But this palace: it gives me hope."

CHAPTER THIRTY-NINE

Cleves

Knocking wakes Cleves from her slumber. Seymour stirs in her arms, and shivers. The fire has gone out.

"I have not kept my promise," she murmurs, reaching for the nearest piece of fabric – Cleves's own gown – and wrapping it around her lover's shoulders.

The knocking comes again, more urgent this time.

"A few moments!" she shouts.

"I'm sorry, Your Majesty, but it's your cousin. He has been . . . and the lady . . ." It must be one of the servants. There is real terror in their voice, a terror that seeps through the door, across the hall and into Cleves's bones. Cleves sees that Seymour is blearily awake.

"Something has happened," she tells her.

Silently, Seymour rises and the women hurry to pull on their apparel, lacing each other into their bodices with a haste they did not have last night.

When they open the door, the servant is pulling at his doublet in distress.

"Show me," Cleves says.

The servant's words make no sense. Johana has been . . . what? Restrained, perhaps, or injured? He is not clumsy but perhaps he took a fall. The other words – *and the lady* – hover on the edge of her mind, but she will not entertain their meaning. If something truly dreadful had happened, she would have heard it. She would have sensed it, even through the delirium of last night.

The stairs are steep, the gallery long, and all she can hear as she follows the servant is the beat of her hurrying shoes in time with her heart.

They reach his room and the servant steps aside, unwilling to enter. There is a lump on the floor. *Discarded clothing*, she thinks. *Thoughtless.*

She stops in the doorway. The servant, next to her, looks away.

Someone's hand rests upon her shoulder.

"Cleves, I'm so . . ." Seymour says.

Cleves shakes her away and stumbles into the room, her knees landing hard on the coagulating ooze seeping from Johana's body.

She bends over him, putting her cheek very close to his mouth. She closes her eyes so that she does not have to look at the gore spilling from his stomach.

Was that? The faintest warmth, there and then not, there and then cold.

"He lives," she says.

"Fetch a physician," Seymour tells the servant.

"Is that . . .?" the servant says. Though her eyes are still closed, Cleves can hear the unfinished question – is that safe? Is that allowed, given we are all of us traitors in your presence, Queen Seymour?

"Here," Cleves says roughly, reaching into her gown's pocket and pulling out a purse of coins. The servant takes it. It is enough to buy the physician's silence, and the servant's risk, too.

"Hurry," Seymour says.

Two sets of footsteps then – one hurrying away, one towards. She smells Seymour's scent: heart smoke and cloves.

"I am here," Seymour says.

No. Cleves cannot admit joy, not now.

"Johana?"

It takes him an age to muster the strength to answer. His speech is more breath than words. "I'm sorry."

"She is gone," Cleves says.

"Mmm."

Seymour rises again, and instructs another servant to ride out after Cecilia. Maybe they can intercept her before she finds civilisation.

"Can you hear them?" Johana says. His hand finds Cleves's.

"Hear who?"

"Them."

He could not have conjured that night better with a thousand words. The intonation could be nothing but the nightmare of their childhood, one that pursues them from country to country, castle to castle.

The soldiers.

She does not want them to be the last thing he hears. "No, I do not hear them," she lies. "This is what I hear."

She hums the lullaby of their childhood, one that she has not heard since before the unrest. It is a lilting tune that winds like the courtyards of Cnothan in circles and steps, climbing to a sweet point.

How weak he looks. Her cousin, who can match her barb for barb. He smiles. His teeth are blotted with crimson.

He mouths something.

"I cannot hear you, cousin," she says.

His hand edges from the wound on his stomach.

"Cousin, no," she says. "Save your strength."

She presses her own hands to the injury. Blood pulses slowly through her fingers. Surely she is strong enough to hold him together? Surely she could scoop the gore up and push it back inside him? Build him again, plaster over the cracks of his wound?

His hand comes to rest next to one of the legs of his bed. He taps the wood.

"I cannot reach," Cleves says.

Seymour is there in an instant, stepping over the raised floorboard from which Cecilia must have taken the key to the lodge. She peers underneath the mattress, then turns her attention to the frame of the bed. Johana watches her, his breathing light and laboured.

Cleves has never minded silence before, but this is intolerable.

"Where is the physician?" she roars.

"I think I have found something," Seymour says, feeling with one hand inside the bed frame. "There is a hollow in the wood."

She pulls out a velvet pouch, the vivid orange of Ezzonid. She brings it to Cleves, and without another word presses her own hands to Johana's wound so that Cleves can look inside.

The velvet's sunset umber turns scarlet in her hands. The parcel is light and strangely warm. From it, under Johana's glassy gaze, she pulls a cushion containing a dozen golden dress pins.

To the unknowing eye they are no different from any royal dress pin used to secure a frontlet or a veil, a ruff or a collar. But Johana would not have hidden them if they were not important. She holds the cushion up to the light, and understanding washes over her like dawn.

The head of each pin is adorned with a molten sliver of phoenix feather.

She never knew what became of Sybil's gift. She assumed it was secreted in a vault, like the binding cloths beneath the Tower of High Hall. But she knows, the way she knew when she laid eyes on the bird as a child, the way she knew when she communed with the bordweal, that she holds the deepest, most precious magic.

Johana tries to speak. She bends over him.

"You were always very good at staying alive, dear cousin," he breathes. "Promise me you will never stop being good at it."

"I promise," she says. Her throat is tight.

He closes his eyes.

"Keep running," he whispers, though she can hardly hear the words.

She and Seymour stay there, hunched over him, as his chest rises fainter and fainter, and the pump of blood through Seymour's fingers ebbs. How can one so sharp die so quietly? How can her cousin, who has survived so much, be felled by a petty princess? It is not right. It is not just.

At some point, Seymour rises. Cleves is aware of her talking to the servants and, presumably, to the damned late physician. In one hand she cups Johana's cooling cheek. In the other she holds the cushion. The feathery pinheads make dots of warmth on her palm.

"Cleves," Seymour says, kneeling beside her once more. "Cleves, we must flee. Cecilia has still not been discovered."

"Yes," Cleves says, but does not move.

"She has my *sunscína* too," Seymour says.

Of course she does. Cecilia has played them both for fools. At least they had enough foresight to conceal the other queens' part in their treachery.

Strangely, it is the thought of those other queens – of Howard, really, and her determination to place herself in the greatest possible danger in order to benefit them all – that brings Cleves to her feet. She turns to the servants. "Wrap his body. In Ezzonid it is customary to bury our dead in the Desa Savalis, but we will not be able to ship him back to my homeland."

She cannot bury him in the Lake of Souls, but she can find another body of water for him to rest in. "Take him to the Dreomere," she tells them. The mere is the largest of Elben's lakes, and bridges the territories of Cnothan and Hyde. It does not hold the religious significance of the Desa Savalis, but perhaps it will be enough for his spirit to find peace.

Next she must think to the future. Always ahead, for insanity lies behind. Perhaps, on some level, she has been preparing for this ever since she committed to toppling the King of Elben. She can see the events that will undoubtedly follow.

"If Henry is at High Hall, then we have a day at least before he could bring an army to Cnothan," she says. She runs a hand through hair still tangled from her night with Seymour. That night feels like moons ago, and also so very close – her body still bears the marks and heat of their lovemaking.

There seems only one thing to do. "I must return to Cnothan and raise the drawbridge," she says. Seymour's head snaps up. "Why?"

"It is one of the most defendable of the castles. It is my home."

"But you won't be able to leave. We have only just committed to our plan for the binding cloths," Seymour says, crossing her arms.

"You would have me simply hand over my castle?"

"It is only a castle." Seymour surges forward and takes Cleves's hands. She kisses the knuckles. "You could keep Cnothan and never defeat him, or leave Cnothan and stand a chance of overthrowing him."

"You underestimate my cunning, my Lady Seymour."

"Why are you so afraid?" Seymour says.

"Just because you decided to destroy your safety for the sake of a grand statement does not mean I am a coward for not doing the same." She wishes Seymour could understand that she must consider her position as a royal not only of Elben but of Ezzonid. She may be considered eccentric, but she must uphold her royal duty. An eccentric with a castle has power. An eccentric without a castle has nothing.

Seymour's eyes glisten. "I do not understand what you can hope to gain from your course of action. It is short-sighted."

Cleves turns away.

"I must make arrangements," she says. She must get out of that cursed room.

She never spent any time in her own bedchamber, so her belongings remain packed in their trunks, ready to be returned to the carriage. It will be a blessedly quick escape.

Seymour trails behind her. "Let us discuss this a little longer, Cleves," she says.

"You can come with me back to Cnothan, and I will protect you, or I will give you a horse and the means to get you to Mathmas, or wherever you choose to go."

Seymour grabs her arm, forcing her to stop. "I do not require your help," she says. She shakes Cleves's arm, her grip unforgiving. "If it comes to it, Clarice can take me to Mathmas. I am telling you that you have a choice to make. A choice between your old way of life, safe and lonely, and the promise of a new life, dangerous but full of possibility."

"No, I have a choice between my home and belongings and status, or being homeless and alone and in danger."

Seymour's face goes blank. "It is a shame, given what has passed between us, that you think you would be alone."

How dare Seymour attempt to make last night more significant than it really was. They were both lustful. Cleves has been wanting Seymour since their first meeting, and Seymour was probably lonely and in need of satiation.

She says, "Well, at some point I will stop making you angry, and then what will we have, my angry queen?"

She has set it up nicely for Seymour to quip back, *You will never stop making me angry.*

"You are grieving. You are not thinking clearly," Seymour says.

"Come with me, at least as far as Cnothan," Cleves replies. "We can argue all the way, I promise. When we arrive, you can decide whether you are going to stay with me, or whether I am going to deliver you to your Clarice and their ship."

Eventually, Seymour nods. Cleves leads her down to the waiting carriage, hands her in and climbs in beside her. She pulls the curtains across. "Go!" she commands the driver, and the carriage springs away.

Inside, Cleves turns her attentions to Seymour. It is so much easier to lose herself in a fine woman's mouth and breasts and neck and stomach than to think on that blood-drenched lump on the floor of Johana's room. But Seymour stops her.

"I will hold you, and no more," Seymour says. She kisses Cleves on the mouth, then folds her in her arms. It is not what Cleves would have chosen to do, but there, with her head resting beneath Seymour's chin, all of her frantic purpose rushes from her. They sit like that in silence as the carriage bumps along the scrind road, and all the while the cushion and its beautiful cargo warms her thigh, where it rests in her pocket.

Well, Cleves had one night with Seymour. One night, before she walls herself off from the world and Seymour makes her escape. She must be satisfied.

One particularly big jolt throws them from their seat. They land on the floor of the carriage, arms and legs tangled.

"What is it?" she calls, as Seymour struggles to extricate herself.

The voice that answers her is not the driver's. It is a voice she has not heard since the Moon Ball.

"Well met, wife."

CHAPTER FORTY

Cleves

Many people assume that Cleves enjoys chaos. She does, after all, keep a menagerie of animals and likes to surprise others. What they often miss is that her animals are meticulously well-trained, and when she is the one enacting the surprise, she is in control. There are few people who have given Cleves a pleasurable surprise. One of them is Seymour, with the way she sawed through her dress with that crone's tooth, a simple act of rebellion that made Cleves's heart leap.

No, she does not like surprises in the least, and she has taken every measure possible to ensure that they do not occur.

The carriage's curtains are still closed. The driver is talking loudly to the king. Cleves hurries to make herself presentable, her heart hammering in her throat and her chest and her stomach all at once. Seymour curls herself in the furthest corner of the carriage.

Cleves pauses, her hand on the carriage door. She reaches for her lover.

"I will protect you," she mouths.

Seymour is trembling, her eyes wide. Cleves knows this feeling. She had many such experiences in the years since the soldiers came. She knows that Seymour needs peace, needs her to hold her as she gains control of her body.

The fact that she cannot give Seymour what she needs makes her fists clench.

"Queen Cleves? Are you stuck in there?" Henry calls.

Cleves opens the carriage door and steps out.

Henry is riding a fine grey stallion that seems, like his master, to look down upon her. Cleves drops a curtsey.

"Your Majesty, what an unexpected and pleasant meeting."

Henry grins, all his teeth showing. "Forgive me for not warning you of my arrival. I took it into my head to surprise you, but it turned out better than I could have devised, meeting you on the road like this. I hear you have come from one of your hunting lodges?"

There's an edge to his voice she knows well. Her mother used to use the same voice when she wanted her to guess the source of her displeasure.

Cleves surveys Henry's train. She spies only a few armed men. This is a guard, not an army. He cannot know yet. He and Cecilia must have missed each other on their dual journeys. She recalculates how much time she has: Cecilia may be reaching High Hall by now, and that means that a messenger, riding swiftly on the scrind road, may reach Cnothan by dawn. There is time. There is time.

She has been silent for a little too long. Henry and his court are staring at her. She realises that her fingernails are still crusted with Johana's blood, and clasps them behind her back.

"I am honoured to receive you at our shared home," she says, allowing her Ezzonidian accent to become more pronounced. It is a reminder that she is royalty even without her Elbenese title. She has the backing of a royal house.

Henry smiles genially. "Forgive me, my queen. I have been lax in paying my attentions to you lately. I felt it only right that I should rectify that error."

She calls for her horse and swings into the saddle. As she settles there and gathers her reins, Henry joins her side. "Don't make me the cause of your discomfort," he says. "If you wish to travel in your carriage, please continue."

She thinks of Seymour.

"And miss a rare opportunity for my husband's company?" she says. Better that he think her desperate for his affection than that there is anything in that carriage to warrant her attention.

"I would not mind," he says. "A carriage is sometimes more appropriate for a woman, I think. Too much horse riding changes the physique."

He glances at her arms, visible through the thin silk of her blouse. She wants to laugh, because she loves her arms, and their strength. If he wished to needle an insecurity, he could not have chosen a poorer area.

"I am fond of an active physique," she says blithely. He shifts uncomfortably in his saddle, and she notes the bandage around his leg. So the injury that Boleyn had caused him does not seem to be healing. "Perhaps it is you who requires a carriage?"

She is banking on his pride preventing him from acquiescing. It is undoubtedly a risk, but easier for her to take him and his men out by surprise should he see Seymour before they reach Cnothan. She wants to bait him, but she does not want to initiate violence unless she must.

Henry forces a laugh. "Quite right. You are far more able than I at present. My other queens are too demanding for my current state. I rather hoped you would provide me with your excellent company and formidable advice while I recover."

Cleves has to admire the manoeuvre. In a single sentence he has been outwardly gallant to her, while making it clear to their company that he finds her repulsive and is desired by his other queens. She has spent so long cocooned in her own cleverness in tricking him into never having lain with her, that she must not forget that he is still a dangerous opponent.

They ride into Cnothan, the people of the town pointing in wonder at the sight of their king in their very own territory, in the company of their poor, strange, abandoned queen. Before long, shouts of joy ripple through the town. Her subjects rush from their houses to see their monarch, doffing their hats, kneeling, offering babies for him to bless with his divine power. He is magnanimous. Cleves, at his side, thinks her smile will dry there and become a fixed expression.

Once they reach the castle, it is a scramble to find suitable rooms for her guests. Unlike the other queens, she has never cared to keep any ready for the king and his people. After all, he has so rarely visited her, there did not seem to be any point.

Her servants hurry like fine horses, all upright and prancing, to prepare everything in a manner that does not appear panicked. They must be wondering what has caused this visit. The people of Elben may not know all that passed at the Moon Ball, but any fissures in the brittle authority of royalty have a way of trickling down the ranks in any country. It is like a stone thrown into a pool. The effects are being felt most fully in High Hall, but that does not mean that even the lowliest worker in the furthest reaches of the Heahmore mountains does not feel some of the anxiety of a country on the brink of turmoil. It exhibits in strange ways: great shows of patriotism, or more willingness to risk all for the silliest of perceived riches. In her people, who are used to balancing the warring attitudes of loyalty to their absent king and loyalty to their strange but present queen, it mostly exhibits as an overwrought yet surly deference to Henry. Her maidservants curtsey deeply and offer cakes warm from the kitchen with the impatience of a dog doing a trick under duress. The grooms remain in a permanent bow in Henry's presence, yet they reserve their warmest smiles for Cleves.

She thinks of Seymour, the woman who travelled through half a dozen foreign countries as a hunted exile. The woman who broke a condemned queen from the most feared building in all of Elben. The woman who has been spy, assassin, lover, leader – cowering in Henry's mere presence.

Then she thinks of the bloodied shell of her cousin.

The whole family is a canker.

She visits the kitchens to inspect the food preparations. A dozen cooks sweat over wide metal pans that rest in a long stone counter, beneath which are lit a dozen fires. From the pans rise the aromas of spiced chickpeas, bread soaking in sugared milk, and pottage. Children barely out of their weeds take turns to rotate spits laden with capons, pigs and one of Cleves's prized honeydragons, slaughtered as soon as news of the king's arrival reached the kitchens. Cleves's eyes skate over all as she nods along to the head cook's hurried list of dishes. The king's taster walks slowly behind every cook, lifting lids and dipping a finger into every sauce and oil before transferring the finger into his mouth and sucking it clean with a pop.

"Is it good, Your Majesty?" the cook says, wiping their brow on their apron.

Pop. No poison, then.

"It is more than I deserve," Cleves says.

She can delay no longer. She returns to her banqueting hall, where Henry is already seated at the high table, in the seat that Cleves usually claims for herself. When he spies her, he rises and bows, all gallant in that way she has learned means he is at his most dangerous – it is the gallantry he showed to Boleyn the day before he sentenced her to death.

She takes the seat on his right. The air is thick with expectancy. It blooms throughout the hall from the whispers of her nobles, the not-glances of her household. She and Henry barely speak to each other as the servants fill the tables with dishes: dressed piglet and roasted swan accompanied by breads as white and fluffy as snow for the humans, and grain and offal for the animals lined up at long troughs at the sides of the hall.

"You have certainly made Cnothan your own," Henry says, helping himself to a trencher. He pulls the swan closer, plucks out a few feathers and digs a spoon into the pie beneath, piling chunks of meat and gravy onto the bread.

"I am well contented here," she replies. She makes herself dig into her own selection as heartily as she usually would. No fear of a man, king or otherwise, is going to keep her from good food and a full stomach.

"My people tell me you do not stay much in contact with your family back in Ezzonid."

And there it is: the opening gambit. She grins. "I am flattered. I did not think your people would bother themselves about me."

Henry grins back. They are two wolves, baring their teeth at each other. "It is my duty as king to be informed of all that happens in my country, is it not?"

"I merely wonder at your care over my letter-writing when you have so many other concerns to occupy you."

"What concerns might those be?" he asks.

He observes her as he chews. A challenge: will she admit to knowing that his rule is the weakest it has ever been? Oh, she can play that game.

"Well, I imagine you must be concerned about the crones. I know that I am. They have killed several dozen of my prized sheep these last moons."

There – the shield of her eccentricity is raised. All she has to concern herself with are her animals. Henry laughs. The sound rolls around the hall.

"Yes, wife, I am very concerned with crones."

He darts her a nasty little glance that sends prickles up her arms.

"Is that why you decided to visit me now, so soon after your wedding, husband? I would have thought you would have wanted to be near to your new bride."

Henry makes a noise in the back of his throat. "I come on your account, wife. There is some news that I wished to share with you. I wished to be here to grieve with you."

Ice settles in Cleves's stomach, but all she says is, "Oh? And what is that?"

"One of your old ladies-in-waiting passed away recently. She left me a letter in her will."

"Hardly a meet inheritance for a King of Elben, I would think, but I am sorry to hear it. Which lady died, for I have heard nothing of the matter?"

Medren's power sparks across Henry's jaw, lending his words an extra sting. "Why, your closest lady, from what I have heard. The Lady Paston."

And suddenly, Cleves knows just what the letter contained, and why Henry is here. She recalls another letter, sitting in a locked drawer in her study, waiting, waiting for a reply.

Your Majesty,

I have something of a cough at present, and have been forced to take to my bed. I find my mind wandering to the past as I lie here . . .

Lady Paston was the mistress who bedded Henry on their wedding night, without his knowledge, and the letter, she is in no doubt, contains the truth of her lie. She had meant to respond to the woman weeks ago, but in the midst of Johana's arrival and Seymour's rescue, she neglected her correspondence. She has barely had time to keep Cnothan running. She can imagine what happened: Paston, receiving no word of reassurance from Cleves that their deceit did not affect the bordweal's strength, confessed all to Henry from her deathbed.

Fruisch. Idiot.

Six years ago, she staked her wits on being able to become a Queen of Elben without ever knowing a man carnally, and now both of those things are in jeopardy. For if Henry has realised that he has never topped her – more than that, if he has realised that she never intended him to do so and that she is, in fact, desirable – well, that is a humiliation which only one kind of control can remedy.

"Truly, you look very ill at this news," Henry says, taking another bite of his swan.

Cleves could easily continue the conversation in this manner, batting insults disguised as compliments. But what would be the point? He has laid out his hand, and all she can do is play her best cards in return. The trick will lie in wording it in such a way that she can deny all knowledge if she needs to in the future, just as she did when discussing rebellion with Seymour at their first meeting. She bites the head off an asparagus and crunches on it as she considers her next play. Now the true dance must begin. She must get every footstep right, or forfeit her crown, her castle, her body.

"I grieve for her, of course, sir. And I understand the purpose of your visit. Now that you know the truth, you have come to show your gratitude, no?"

One side of his mouth curls. "Gratitude? At a deceit?"

She stares at him, wide-eyed. "But I believed I was acting on your own wishes," she says.

"What do you mean?"

"Master Cromwell told me that you could not bring yourself to desire me. So I thought to make our wedding night pleasurable for you. Lady Paston was only too happy to oblige, as you can imagine."

She makes herself look him up and down, and tries to picture in his place the kind of woman she finds irresistible. Tall, darker-skinned, quiet and fierce. She feels a blush creep up her neck, as Seymour, naked, head thrown back in ecstasy just the night before, springs to mind. It seems to work, because Henry looks suitably pacified. These kings, going through life never being refused and assuming it is because their charm is an irrepressible force.

"You have endangered my country's defences, my lady. Did you not think on that? I was prepared to do anything to protect Elben—"

"Let us not continue to lie, my lord," Cleves says. Her heart pounds. This is the most audacious part of her play. He goes very still.

"You dare accuse me of lying?"

"It is an open secret in Ezzonid, the truth of Cernunnos and the woman god. What was her name?"

"Med—" he stops himself, too late. His fist clenches on the table, a spark of divine power lifting from the knuckles and dissipating into the air.

"Medren, that is right. We have always known, my lord. All of the fuss of the binding and the bedding. I knew it did not matter to the bordweal."

"You knew . . ." he repeats slowly. "You knew and married me anyway?"

She shrugs. "I am a Queen of Elben. I have my castle. What does it matter if you possess some divine strength? What use have I for such things at Cnothan? It is not as if it affects me."

She watches some colour return to his face. These white-as-bone people are amusingly transparent, showing their embarrassment and fear so clearly on their skin. With any luck, he believes her ignorant of the fact that his leaching of the divine power also leaches his queens of their lives. If she made it apparent that she knew all, he would not believe that she would not care. A little lie can sometimes be concealed if one covers it with enough truth.

"You danced with the traitor Seymour at the Moon Ball," Henry says.

She leans her head on her hand, her elbow on the table, quizzical.

"Yes, that was a strange night, was it not? It was rather amusing, watching those two women lose their minds."

"You thought them insane?"

"I can think of no other reason why they did what they did."

"Seymour visited you before the ball. She did not mention her and Boleyn's plans to you then?"

Cleves laughs. "Now you mention it, I think she may have tried. I must admit, my mind was on other matters. There was a crone in the woods, and it was destroying my flocks. I have been breeding a new type of sheep. Would you care to see it while you are staying at Cnothan?"

Henry's frown deepens, and Cleves wonders whether she has pushed the personality she has carefully cultivated beyond its limit.

She sips her wine, desperate to moisten her mouth.

He is still watching her.

"They make very soft wool," she adds, as if waving an alluring gem just out of his reach.

"I think I have treated you unfairly, my lady wife," he says. "You have qualities beyond what most people understand."

"Thank you," she says.

He stands. "Shall we have some music?" He claps his hands for the fiddlers in the gallery above to play something more lively than a madrigal. He turns to the man standing behind them. "There will be no need to stay in my chamber tonight. Find yourself somewhere else to sleep."

The man bows, and Henry flicks a glance towards Cleves. It is an invitation. A test. And she knows just what to do with it.

They drink more wine and exchange pleasantries, and clap as members of Cleves's household dance for them. Henry laughs when one of Cleves's pet goats decides to join the frivolity and ends up tangled in the legs of a couple. When she deems it safe to do so, Cleves excuses herself and hurries to the stables, making sure she is not being followed. A storeroom spans the loft space above the stalls, reached by a narrow wooden staircase tucked into one corner of the harness room. Up here, the warm, heavy smell of animal is replaced by the scent of the sky buckthorn garlanded across the beams.

Cleves picks her way between crates and discarded saddles. But she is not stealthy enough, for as she reaches the far end of the room a hand slips around her waist, and another covers her mouth. She recognises the scent of cloves.

"Now I have you," Seymour says, her breath tickling Cleves's ear in a most distracting manner. Cleves pulls Seymour's hand away and twists in her arms. She had intended to kiss her with all the pent-up fear and anger of the day. But now that they are face to face, she cannot. It is not from lack of desire, but because she wants something more – confession. And that realisation frightens her more than anything else that has happened.

"What did Henry do?" Seymour says. "Are you safe?"

A laugh bubbles up in Cleves's throat. "Yes, my angry queen. I have set things in motion. Tonight, I want you to join me."

"To do what exactly, my cautious queen?"

"How would you like to kill the king?"

CHAPTER FORTY-ONE

Cecilia

Cecilia bears her captors no ill will for their deception. They did exactly as she would have done: lied in order to get what she wanted. She rather likes them for it. She rides fast through the forest at first, until she is sure she has left the grounds of the lodge. Then she slows, wary of the moon leading her astray. Shadows can play tricks on a mind, even one as strong as hers.

She finds a river and follows its stream down, down towards the sea. She reaches a town by dawn. The houses are as crooked and ramshackle as the Castle of Cnothan along the coast, but it is only when she sees the bridge in the centre of the settlement that she knows where she is.

The legend says that spirits gather at the Fietherford crossing at every full moon. So it follows that the townspeople would build two bridges, one on top of the other. An ancient one of obsidian and pearl, sitting in crumbling beauty, provides a way across for the spirits. Directly above it, in common stone, is an arched bridge meant for the living.

She has never seen it before: much of her childhood was spent in her mother's Palace of Plythe, or at High Hall, and she never had cause to venture this far into Cnothan's territory. She never had the curiosity either, for Cnothan is famously an old and ugly part of the country. It is too rainy to be enjoyable, and its exports of meat and wool and grain never held any interest for her finer tastes. Still, she takes some joy in watching the sun rise over the Fietherford, reaching between the bridges to point up the river, towards the centre of Elben.

She does not venture into the town itself. She is still in Cleves's territory, and she does not know how many of the people are loyal to their queen. She now knows how to reach High Hall. She rides for the scrind road, stopping only to exchange Cleves's fine, tired stallion for a rested gelding of lesser quality.

As she canters, she thinks of her childhood. Were Elben's roads always so ill-maintained? She swears they were smoother when she was younger. But then is it any wonder that Cleves has allowed her roads to fall to ruin?

They do not improve by the time she passes out of Cnothan and into the outer reaches of High Hall's estates. She breathes more freely now. She has outrun Cleves and Seymour. She has outwitted them both. She laughs, long and loudly, daring her voice to reach them in their love-blind stupor.

The guards at the gates of High Hall do not recognise her, and while there's no reason they should – she was a girl when she was last here, after all – she gives them short shrift until they let her through. Lord Cromwell, an upstart of a man whom she has heard of in letters but never met, comes to greet her.

"Your Majesty," he says, bowing deeply over her hand. "We feared you lost at sea. What an unexpected honour to have you here."

"Where is my brother?" she says, cutting off whatever overblown compliment he was about to deliver.

"He is gone to Cnothan, Your Majesty. There are matters on the south coast he must attend to."

She laughs again. What a merry dance she and Henry are doing around Elben, while two of his queens are leading a merry dance of their own.

"You will want to call him back. Immediately."

She has never thought much of Cromwell – More has never been complimentary about him in his correspondence – but to his credit he does not question her. He merely nods briskly, and sends for a scout and a fast horse. When they are brought, he turns to Cecilia expectantly.

"What should my man tell His Majesty when he finds him?" he says.

Cecilia leans in. Henry will not thank her for broadcasting what she must say to the entire courtyard. "Tell him that unless he kills Cleves immediately, he has not one but two traitor queens to conquer. She is with Seymour now, and once they know I have escaped their clutches, they will have nothing to lose beyond attempting Henry's life."

The messenger trembles as he mounts his horse and gallops for the south. Cromwell is watching her, assessing her. Her news does not appear to have surprised him as much as she would like.

"Stare at me much longer and I will have your eyes out, sir."

He drops his gaze. "Forgive me, Your Majesty. I had heard many tales of your beauty, but fewer of your cleverness. I was merely wondering at the fact."

She sweeps past him, ignoring the compliment even as she glows from it. Here is family. Here are people who truly understand all that she has to offer. At last, she is home.

CHAPTER FORTY-TWO

Cleves

Cnothan at night is usually a comforting place for Cleves. It lacks the lantern dragons that keep some palaces lit gently through the darkest hours, but because of the castle's position on the south coast of Elben, exposed to the ocean on three sides, moonlight usually streams through the windows, stretching like a cat along the thick carpets.

Tonight, though, even with Seymour at her side, Cleves does not feel as though her castle is her own. Henry's household occupies rooms which should lie empty. His guards lounge in inconvenient places, and while they are not plenteous enough to guard every single route to the king's chamber, they make it difficult. Suddenly, her home is a forbidding maze, every dead end a death sentence.

Seymour and Cleves tread in slippers through winding galleries. The cries of the animals in the courtyards outside lend a mournful quality to their journey. Cleves has never been superstitious, but it is difficult not to take the noises as a portent. She shakes her head to clear it of such thoughts. She is cautious. She has planned this out thoroughly.

"We must be certain it isn't a trap," she had told Seymour again and again.

"I know," Seymour had said. "I know you think of me as impulsive but I do actually have a brain and a sense of self-preservation."

Cleves had put her hand over Seymour's. "Do not think I underestimate you. But nor should you underestimate how this is going to feel.

All that anger bottled up inside you may come brimming forth when you are close to him. Do not allow it to cloud your judgement."

"No angry queen?"

Cleves had slipped a hand around Seymour's waist then pulled her close for a kiss. "Save the anger for later, when you and I can unbottle it together."

Every so often, they come across a guard, or one of Cleves's servants, doing last-minute preparations for the morning. Little do they know that if all goes well, their king will never see the dawn. At these moments, they retrace their steps, Seymour following Cleves as she finds an alternative route. The journey from stables to king's chambers would normally only take a matter of minutes, a quick line west and up through the castle, but tonight it is an hour before they come close, and the moon is high.

She removes a hand mirror from her pocket and angles it around the corner to the passage at the end of which Henry's door lies. A man, tall and muscular, one of Henry's strongest and most loyal bodyguards, stands straight and wide awake, sword sheathed at his belt. The sight should inspire fear, but Cleves can only feel relief.

Henry has the kind of pride that permits him to believe he is impervious to trickery, but he has had some knocks of late. Boleyn's betrayal, even if he did not understand her intent to unite the queens, must have made him doubt everything. There is a reason he is visiting all his remaining queens, even her: he is trying to gauge their true loyalties, trying to sniff out their lies. Yet he has brought the same number of guards as normal. If he did not have a guard at the door of his chamber, she would have known that *he* was trying to trick *her*.

She nods to Seymour and they retrace their steps for the last time until they come to an aged stone pillar bearing the bust and head of a former Queen of Cnothan – Swynford, if she recalls correctly. The woman had a delicate face but, from what Cleves has fathomed from her study of the castle's history, an iron grasp of Cnothan's finances and an unorthodox insistency on maintaining her lover in her rooms, with the king's full knowledge, despite public condemnation. Cleves thinks she might have rather liked Swynford.

She heaves on the bust, and a mechanism concealed in the base of the statue clicks into place. Behind the pillar, a wooden panel slides open to reveal a narrow passageway. The women slip into it sideways, edging their way along until the outline of a doorway, similarly narrow and etched in moonlight, reveals itself.

They are very close now. Cleves takes Seymour's hand and squeezes, once, and Seymour squeezes back. Ready. Calm. Focused.

Cleves flicks up the catch that keeps the door to the king's chamber locked from the passageway, opens it silently and slips into the darkness of the room. She emerges behind a tapestry. Seymour waits in the passageway, ensuring that they are not taken by surprise that way. Cleves uses her mirror to make sure that Henry is, as he'd implied, alone in his chamber. The space is round and sparse, and the king is visible in the bed – his auburn hair, so like Cecilia's, splayed out upon the pillow and lit up in the moonlight like an effigy. Cleves examines every shadow. All is still. All is as it should be. She fingers the knife in her belt.

With a cat's grace, she ducks out from behind the tapestry and darts to the door, behind which Henry's guard is keeping watch. She produces a wooden wedge from her pocket and slips it beneath the door. It will not stop the guard entirely, but it will buy her a few moments, and a few moments is all she needs. If all goes to plan, the guard will not even realise the door has been wedged shut until the sun rises and the king does not.

That done, Cleves turns to the bed. She draws the knife from her belt, feeling the heft of the stone hilt.

One step, two. Henry stirs, and Cleves freezes, but his eyes remain closed. She inches closer to the bed, calculating which angle she should approach from. She cannot get close enough to him to give herself enough thrust to be sure of killing him without getting on the mattress itself, and that means waking him.

Seymour, crouched so as to not be seen, makes her way to the other side of the bed.

When Cleves is certain that Seymour is in place, she hides the knife behind her back, and sits. Henry does not open his eyes, but says, "Is that you, my Queen of Cnothan?" His voice is low, purring. It reminds her in a strange way of Queen Boleyn. Cleves only met her once, but was immediately struck by her sensuality.

She inches closer to him, across the mattress, until she is kneeling next to him. She has the advantage now. His eyes are still closed. She produces the knife and holds it above his chest.

"Yes, my lord. It is I."

She wants to add something like *The last person you will ever see*, but that would be foolish. With all her strength, she brings the knife down over his heart.

It should be enough. And yet she is prevented. For a moment, she thinks that whatever prophetic magic prevented Boleyn from killing him on that clifftop at Brynd is at work again now; that they do not have five queens after all, that one of them is secretly working against them. Then she realises that it is the divine power – *her power* – working against her. And that means . . .

"Thank you, my lady," Henry says, his eyes open now, that calm smile playing upon his lips. "I did not know how I would justify executing a Princess of Ezzonid, but I think this will give me reason enough."

He sits up, and the knife meets his chest. Cleves steels her wrist. She is strong enough, both in will and muscle, to drive the blade home, yet Henry's stolen power is stronger still. As he rises, Cleves's wrist is pushed back, back, back.

"You are clever, my Lady Cleves, but I am cleverer still. Did you truly think I would not have guessed your ploy? Did you think I would underestimate you as you have done me?"

Cleves cannot bring herself to drop her hand, even though she knows it is futile. All she can do now is hope to distract him for long enough to allow Seymour to make an attempt. So she shrugs. "I did wonder, but you had so many guards, I thought it was worth a try."

Only now does Henry grip her wrist with such inhuman strength that she is forced to open her hand. Her bones crack, a jolt of pain so excruciating she cannot help but make a little, plaintive cry. The knife drops, and Henry swipes it off the bed.

"I do not make the same mistake twice, my lady," he says, his voice low and pleasant. "But I am not a monster. I wished to believe all my remaining queens loyal, but I knew as soon as I saw you this morning that you are no true Queen of Elben."

"On the contrary, sir, I am a truer monarch of this island than you and your family of usurpers have ever been," she spits through the agony.

Henry's grin widens. "You have been talking with my Lady Seymour. You had better show yourself, Mistress Bitch. I know you are behind me."

Seymour rises like an avenging shadow. She has her own knife, and she uses it now, plunging it deep into Henry's back. His breath puffs upon Cleves's face. It smells of the cloved swan he ate at supper. He coughs, blood spraying across her. She should be glorying in this moment. It is done. She – they all – are free. Cnothan is hers.

Yet something doesn't feel right.

"Move away from him," she says on instinct.

Seymour straightens. "You do not need to fear him any longer. I do not."

"Move away," Cleves says, this time reaching past Henry and pulling Seymour towards her with her one good wrist, scrambling back over the bed.

Henry's cough turns into a laugh.

The guard on the other side of the door knocks. "Your Majesty?" he says.

"Everything is all right," Henry replies, not a trace of pain in his voice. He looks at his wives, his eyes glinting with malice. "I am well," he says.

The divine power floods his skin, as if someone has lit a flame upon his body. If Cleves thought the pain in her wrist was bad, the full-bodied agony that follows eclipses it. Beside her, Seymour curls over, collapsing on the floor, her arms clutched to her stomach. Cleves manages to stay on her feet by clinging to one of the bedposts.

The light around Henry is blindingly beautiful: blue-green-purple, it ripples across him, drawn to the place where Seymour stabbed him. It floods the wound, healing it from the inside out, knotting sinews back together, regrowing flesh and skin. And Cleves feels every movement because the power is coming from her, drawn out of her like hair tugged from its roots, like nails pulled from their beds.

She feels blindly for Seymour's hand as she says, "You cannot take us both."

Henry snarls. "I have no desire for either of you. I am no rapist."

From her position on the floor, Seymour laughs wildly. Henry's gaze snaps to her. "Is that the tale you tell yourself, Lady Bitch, to justify what you have done?" He kneels next to her, and his voice is low and ferocious. For a moment, Cleves thinks he might bite Seymour's ear off. "I truly loved you. If you had ever said no, I would have stopped. But you didn't. Because it suited you to use me, to make me think you loved me too."

He believes it, too. There is little more dangerous than a righteous tyrant.

From her angle, leaning on the bed, she sees something, though. Despite the pain he is inflicting on them, he is not totally healed. She thinks of the festering wound on his leg, the one Boleyn left there before she tumbled to her death. Then she thinks of his power that is truly hers, and the way the queens wielded it together to bring down Cecilia's ship.

She wonders if they can do so again, just the two of them.

Cleves drops to her knees as Henry continues to whisper vicious nothings into Seymour's ear. The pain is lessened now, but Henry does not seem to have noticed that he is no longer draining her – perhaps he is too focused on Seymour, for she remains curled, like an urchin. Cleves drags herself towards her lover, until she is within reach of Seymour's leg.

"I'm going to make an example of you," Henry is whispering to Seymour. "I'm going to tie every one of your limbs to a different horse and whip them until they froth. You will feel them pop out of their sockets, one by one, and then the flesh and sinew will tear too, until the horses finally pull you apart."

Cleves grasps Seymour's ankle and tries to drown out his voice, reaching instead for that small, quiet part of herself that was waiting for her to call upon it when she used the spirit stone. She does not know if it will work without the stone, but she hopes that the Moon Ball, and the divine power that danced through the queens then, will come to her once more in Seymour's presence. She thinks of their lovemaking the previous night, not of the act itself but of the feeling of communion, oneness, rightness that filled her.

"And the delicious part is that I will make sure you live through it all. No easy death for you, my little lying queen."

Seymour's ankle twitches in Cleves's grasp. Does she understand what Cleves is trying to do? Has she felt some spark that Cleves has not?

"You think it's your power, do you? Well, let's see how much it feels like yours when I use it to keep you alive while your limbs are ripped from your fat body."

It starts as rage – for how dare anyone speak to her angry queen like that? – but then it blossoms into something new, something dangerous. It is the kind of anger she saw in Seymour when they first met. The kind of awe she felt when she danced with the other queens beneath dragons at Brynd. It is the kind of emotion she has always tried to mask behind jollity, because anything else in a woman as contrary as her would be threatening. Too much, they would say. She is too much.

Well, tonight she will be overflowing with her muchness. She will crack the walls and let the flood in.

The feeling, fulsome and hot, fills her body. A flame of blue-rose-green flickers across her hand and up Seymour's ankle. Seymour goes still. The flame flickers back up Cleves's arm and grips her by the throat, where it seems to scream, *Release me.*

"No," Henry says, watching the light. There is alarm in his eyes. He focuses his own power and she feels hers begin to wane. She does not know how to hold on to it yet. She must act quickly.

"You cannot take it from me," Henry says, and there is something pitiful in his voice.

"Not yet, perhaps," Cleves says. "But soon."

Before the power ebbs from her entirely, she uses one final burst of anger to fling herself upon him. She aims not for his eyes or his heart, but for his leg. She feels along the limb until he gasps in pain, and then she digs her finger into the wound, sending the bordweal down her arm not to heal, but to poison.

Henry roars. The door bursts open, Henry's bodyguard taking in the scene – two queens, one a traitor, somehow in his king's chamber.

"Run!" she shouts to Seymour, and Seymour pushes to her feet. Cleves gives Henry's wound one final dig, wedging her finger in until it meets something ungiving and Henry makes an incoherent gasp, like he had forgotten what pain was until that moment. Then Cleves is taking Seymour's hand and the two women are running, running, pushing past the bodyguard and streaking down the passage, out of the castle and into the bleak night of homelessness.

They run across the courtyard to the stables, shoving past servants who do not know whether to aid or hinder them. Seymour fumbles with the bridle, and in the torrent of her emotions Cleves almost shouts at her, until her stewardess appears. There is a moment of suspense, where Cleves and her servant look at each other, unsure how this is going to play out, and then the stewardess is slipping the bit into the horse's mouth, and Seymour is tightening the girth, and they are mounted within moments.

To this point they have been almost silent. Cleves is grateful that she has never seen fit to shoe her horses, preferring to ride them with care instead. It will make their escape all the quieter.

But then a cry of an altogether different kind rips the air, somewhere between a cat's mewl and a bird's call of danger.

"Lelij!" she says.

The gargoyle had been slumbering in her chamber, on the other side of the castle. The commotion should have been too far away to wake him, and yet that gentle creature knew, even in sleep, that his mistress was distressed.

He erupts through the castle's doors now, a scattered, unwieldy beast with legs and neck too long for his body. Henry's guards are not far behind him. Some appear on the ramparts and take aim at him with crossbows. He pauses, confused, as arrows skitter across the cobbles around him. The dear, silly creature will be killed if he does not move.

"Cleves!" Seymour shouts, urging her horse towards the drawbridge.

"I will follow!" Cleves shouts. She steers her horse towards Lelij. She throws herself sideways, gripping her mount's body with her thighs and calves, steering it with one hand as the other reaches for her gargoyle. And then he is in her arms, scooped into her chest and still cawing.

"Quiet," she hisses, labouring to right herself in the saddle while turning her horse. Lelij muffles his calls of fear in her chest, and she covers him, bending low over her steed's neck to avoid the arrows.

Another cry goes up from inside the castle, as if the very stones of her home have turned against her.

CHAPTER FORTY-THREE

Cecilia

The news arrives at High Hall in such a flurry that even Cecilia cannot properly delight in the chaos it causes. By the time the messenger Cromwell sent to inform Henry of Cleves's betrayal arrives at Cnothan, the news of Seymour and Cleves's attempt on the king's life has made its way like wildfire through the villages and towns of that territory and all the way to Cromwell's spies. For a few hours, it seems as though Seymour and Cleves have been apprehended as they fled the castle. Then another messenger appears to say that they have, in fact, escaped to god knows where.

The territory around High Hall rings with church bells, all of them raising a hue and cry. Some sanctuaries toll funeral bells, having heard wrongly that Henry has been assassinated. Wolsey, cursing loudly at all who dare approach him, sends his men out on horseback to set the priests right. It would never do for the people of Elben to believe their king dead when there is no prince to succeed him.

Cecilia swirls through it all, barely talking to anyone but listening to everyone. Most fascinating are the varied reactions of the courtiers, and the way those reactions change when they notice her loitering nearby. Incredulity that their great monarch might be brought low; intrigue; gossip. She likes to wave at those who seem excited to let them know she's heard them. They're the ones who bow lowest of all as she trips out of the room. The air smells of the musk of change.

But even Cecilia tires of it eventually, and makes her way, floor by floor, up to the Royal Sanctuary, where she finds More on his knees, his hands clasped before him in prayer. She pauses in the doorway. When she last saw him, his hair was darker, not shot through with grey. He was softer, too – he used to enjoy his meals, but she thinks, looking at the way his robes hang from him and the bones jutting from his wrists, that it has been some time since he allowed himself to truly taste food. His eyes are closed in devotion as she kneels quietly beside him. She feels like a girl again.

"Hello, my lord," she says quietly. More startles, his eyes opening, and the move is so exaggerated that she might have thought it an act if she didn't know him better. He was truly communing with Cernunnos.

More smiles, his wrinkles deepening. The whites of his eyes are shot with red.

"My Lady Cecilia, come home at last."

She throws her arms around his shoulders, and he stiffens for a moment before returning her embrace.

"I never thought I should see you again, child. I prayed for your soul, lost at sea."

"Well, I always did like to surprise you."

They retire to a little antechamber set aside for the clergy to entertain guests and take refreshments. Here, in the light through the windows, Cecilia sees even more starkly how More has aged.

"You are not well," she says. She wants to kneel at his feet, as she used to, but she is keenly aware of the difference between the girl she was and the queen she is. She doesn't know how to reconcile the two, how to thread them together for him. More's grip on his cup of wine tightens. "I am well enough, my dear. Do not concern yourself with me. But tell me, by what miracle do you come to be here? Did the great god pluck you from the debris of the ocean and set you safely down in High Hall?"

She pauses. Guilt is not her way, but this is one heartbreak she does not relish delivering. Not to him.

She tells him everything: what truly happened at the bordweal; how powerless she felt and how jealous; she tells him about Medren and of Cleves and Seymour's treachery, and then of her plan to ask Henry to give her Cnothan once Cleves has been removed. Through it all, she searches his face for the surprise he must be feeling. But she can find nothing in his reaction to indicate that he is shocked.

"You knew," she says, letting the hurt seep into her voice.

"Some of it," he admits, sighing heavily and taking another long gulp of his wine. "You have heard about what happened at the Moon Ball."

"The impression I received was that no one gave it credence," she says, realising how naive she must sound.

"Most did not want to give it credence, myself among them. But . . ." Here he sighs shakily. "Something happened in that hall, Cecilia. Something irrefutable."

She finds herself leaning forwards, desperate to understand what has shaken the man she thought unshakeable.

"What was it?"

"It was . . . faith."

Something shivers up Cecilia's back. She would usually reply with a cutting rebuttal, but More looks so frail that she cannot.

"And yet you are still here. Still with my brother."

She is not one to judge. After all, she bends and switches her loyalties according to convenience. But More was never thus.

"I have wrestled with my conscience, believe me. And yes, I have chosen to surrender myself to the mighty Cernunnos. His may not be the oldest faith, but I feel certain that his is the true one."

"He is stealing another god's power."

"Religions rise and fall, my dear. I have taught you this. Just because the heathen gods and goddesses of old exist does not mean we must blindly worship them. We know better. We know the right of kings is absolute. And has your brother not ruled this kingdom well? Kept it safe? Elben's continued success surely tells us that Cernunnos is the promised Haehfader, no matter that he vanquished another to rise."

Cecilia stands, towering over the old man. "Who are you trying to persuade?"

More's wrinkled hand shakes as it lifts the cup of wine to his lips once more. "I never thought to be lectured on principles by you, my dear princess."

"Dowager Queen," Cecilia says.

"Old habits, Your Majesty," he replies, not meeting her eyes.

His hand shakes more violently, and the sleeve of his robe rides up. Cecilia catches sight of an ugly welt that wraps around his wrist.

"That is from no sack cloth," she says, seizing his hand to look more closely.

"A fall," he says, withdrawing his arm with surprising strength and pulling down the sleeve. "I am very pleased to have you back at High Hall, my dear. Very pleased."

But he turns away, setting down his cup and moving back into the sanctuary, back to his kneeling place at the pews. Cecilia knows better than to attempt to continue their conversation.

She thought that speaking to her old tutor would give her some clarity on how to secure Cnothan for herself. But she finds herself in greater turmoil. She has never truly understood religion, or why so many choose to kill and sacrifice themselves for its sake. The notion of an all-seeing god is too intangible for her to take seriously. For her, life is to be consumed, and what may or may not happen in the afterlife is something to be tackled then and not before. She is a queen, after all, and she reckons that gods, like humans, do not mind a bargain.

"What should I do?" she says, to the room rather than More, but it is More who answers.

"Trust in me and your brother, as you always have. Enjoy your time at High Hall."

He has never dismissed her before, but this – this is a dismissal.

CHAPTER FORTY-FOUR

Cleves

The race from Cnothan is a blur. They ride through the night, hardly knowing their direction, hardly speaking, but always they keep the coast in sight. Seymour glances that way often, until Cleves realises that she is looking for Clarice's ship, or any vessel bearing the mark of the Feorwa Isles – the crescent moon emblazoned on its sails.

"They cannot come to shore," she says, more harshly than she intended. When they were only suspected of aiding Seymour, Henry authorised raids upon the isles. If they were seen taking both traitor queens on deck, he would slaughter their entire people.

Seymour nods and does not look that way again.

When the sun is up fully and they risk being seen on the road, they slow to a trot and steer their horses into the cover of the fields and copses of western Elben. Cleves's mind frays, snippets of long nights and longer days crouching and running and fleeing through Ezzonid mixing with the journey through Elben. She starts to think as she did then.

"We should lay false trails," she says. Her throat is scratchy from disuse.

"How?" Seymour says. She leads Seymour towards the sea, dismounting as the soil gives way to sand dunes.

"Careful," Seymour says, nodding towards a party of cockle pickers who are scouring the beach a little distance away. Both queens are dressed in men's weeds, which in itself is not too unusual for the working women of Elben, but Cleves's cropped red hair is conspicuous. She rips one of the sleeves of her blouse and wraps it around her head like a turban.

They wander together down the beach, away from the cockle pickers. Seymour picks some seaweed that has washed up in the shallows. They chew on it, trying to ignore the grit stuck in the fronds.

"There," Cleves says, pointing to a small boat anchored just offshore.

Seymour baulks. "That is someone's livelihood."

"It could throw them off our trail," Cleves says.

Seymour shakes her head, and Cleves falls back on her usual levity. "You did not seem to mind about your household's livelihoods when you consigned Hyde to the ocean."

Seymour looks as though she's been slapped.

"That was . . ." She peters out before she can finish her empty statement. *Different*.

"Very well, show me what to do," Seymour says. They wrench a hole in the wooden boards and push the boat out towards the ocean.

"If all goes well, it will sink a few miles out," Cleves says. "The owner will think it was stolen and if Henry's people come to hear of it, they will wonder if we left Elben entirely. It would fit with your past behaviour. With any luck, they will look for us in Ezzonid or Perfugi."

They return to the horses in silence and continue their journey, but that small act has given Cleves back some of her mind. For now, at least.

They come to the outskirts of Gemǣres, straddling Cnothan and Plythe, at dusk of the third day. So much has occurred since Cleves was last here that she can scarcely credit it. Then, she feared that Howard would be the queen to reveal their treachery to Henry. She chuckles to herself: she thought so much of her own cleverness that she could never have foreseen that she would be the one to be discovered first.

"Should one of us enter the town to buy bread?" Seymour says.

"It would be too dangerous," Cleves replies. "Gemǣres is well-connected. They will have heard the news already. Better for us to find vittles in one of the hamlets to the east, where travellers rarely venture."

Just as they start to look for somewhere to bed for the night, the peals of the town's church bells reach their ears. Usually, such sounds make

Cleves smile, for they are normally signals of celebration, but this is a warning. She looks at Seymour and sees her own tightness mirrored there.

"Do you think that's for us?" Seymour says.

"It would be too much to hope that Elben has been invaded, so yes, I think it must be for us."

"Two traitor queens on the run."

"Not even Queen Isabet could do as much," Cleves says. They smile at each other – it is the first time they've done so since their night together. The memory rears between them, and Seymour shifts. Cleves looks away. "We should keep moving. Travelling through the night is difficult, but it will help us evade notice. We can sleep during the day."

Seymour looks at her quizzically. "You know a lot about evading capture for a queen born of royalty, my lady. I thought this was supposed to be my area of expertise."

"Have you not heard? I am the strange queen. I know all manner of things I should not."

They stray further from the road, trusting the guidance of the moon and the constancy of the lyssa star, shining low in the sky. When their horses are dragging their hooves and Lelij is mewling softly in complaint from his saddle bag, they come to a long row of liftathen flowers. Even in moonlight, they are all bright reds and oranges, like dragonflame.

"This is the border of my territory," Cleves says.

Other territories are more nebulous in their boundaries, but the romantics of Plythe have for many hundreds of years marked their first loves by planting these flowers at the border of the territory as a declaration of affection. The flowers live for several decades, but do not seed by themselves, the particular fairy that once spread them having been hunted to extinction many years ago, so it is possible to know exactly which flower belongs to which couple. Stones, carved with the couple's initials, litter the ground, each one set beside a flower when its seed was planted.

"How lovely," Seymour says when Cleves explains the tradition to her.

"For something as fleeting as youth and love, we do spend a lot of time attempting to make both eternal, don't we?" Cleves says.

"You do not believe love can be eternal?"

"Death does rather get in the way, does it not?"

They find an accommodating oak, the trunk large enough to cradle them both, and huddle together in a crook between its exposed roots. Seymour throws her cloak across them both, and looks up at the spidery outlines of the tree's barren branches.

"Sometimes I like to imagine what trees like this have seen," she says. "How old do you think this oak is – one hundred, two hundred years?"

"Three at least," Cleves replies. Her throat is tight again.

"Just think of all the kings and queens it has survived. All the wars. Can you imagine, it would have lived through the Hydden Uprising, and the Battle of Kywsa. It might even have lived through Queen Isabet and the Massacre of Pilvreen. Imagine how vast these roots stretch out beneath us, probably so much further than the branches we can see. Probably down to that stream over there in the distance."

Cleves closes her eyes, leans her forehead on her knees. Seymour's words worm their way into her mind as she strains to open her throat, as if her body is inhaling thoughts instead of air.

"Sometimes, when I was abroad and alone, I would wonder whether what Boleyn and I did had all been for nothing. I couldn't see how to bring everyone together. And I got to thinking about those roots. The way that the first queens were buried in that cave where others could find them and learn the truth. Then how Queen Isabet acted upon that truth, like a sapling sprouting from the roots of those buried queens. She was cut down, but the roots remained for us to find. So even if we are cut down before our tree flourishes, I have hope that our roots will remain, unseen but strong, and the sapling of our rebellion will sprout again one day."

It is only when Cleves feels water on her cheek that she realises she is weeping. Seymour shifts beside her.

"Cleves?" she says gently, then, more urgently: "Cleves? Speak to me."

Cleves cannot talk. Her throat is utterly closed, her body like a rock, her arms locked around her knees. Seymour places the back of her hand on Cleves's cheek, feeling for fever.

"You are safe," she says. "Cleves? You are safe. This will pass."

She does not attempt to prise Cleves's hands apart, as others have done in the long distant past. She settles in front of her and rubs Cleves's arms in long, slow strokes, up and down, up and down. Gradually, Cleves's sparrow-like breaths slow to match the movement. Her throat opens, and all Cleves is left with is a bone-deep weariness.

"What do you need?" Seymour says.

What Cleves truly needs is to taste Seymour, and to know that she can still arouse her. But to ask that would be to use Seymour. She shutters herself. "Nothing. I am tired."

She closes her eyes and curls up inside the cloak. A moment later, Seymour settles with her back against Cleves's.

"Thank you," Cleves whispers, half hoping that Seymour will not hear it, will not understand that Cleves is now in her debt.

"I am not the only angry queen here tonight," Seymour says. "I wish you realised that."

Cleves thinks then of Johana. He never looked for love in his lifetime either. Death was far too near. It feels near tonight, too.

CHAPTER FORTY-FIVE

Howard

It is Culpepper who brings the news. He appears in the entrance of her receiving chamber like a ghost. That's when she knows for certain that *he knows*. They must look a strange sight: Howard sitting on the floor with her ladies, Goldfoot curled up on her throne. The lacquered walnut is strewn with velvet cushions, the detritus of Susanna's fine paintwork and, stowed beneath the cushions, religious pamphlets sent to Ursula from across the Swegan Sea.

"There is a reward laid out for the capture of Queens Seymour and Cleves," he tells them. "A thousand gold coins."

Susanna whistles. Lady Tylney looks at Howard, eyes wide. How can Seymour and Cleves hope to remain free with such a sum upon their heads? Such wealth would be enough to rival many nobles of the realm.

Culpepper hovers.

"Trot away then, pretty pony," Legh says, flicking a hand in dismissal. He flinches, looking to Howard, but she focuses on collecting Susanna's fine brushes, scattered across the floor. By the time she looks up again, he has gone.

"Close the door," she says, and Lady Tylney hurries to do so.

They drop all pretence of disinterestedness as soon as the lock clicks. Legh sits up; Susanna sets aside her miniature.

"Should you send a message to the other queens?" Ursula asks.

Howard shakes her head. "I dare not risk it. We will all of us be under greater scrutiny now."

Goldfoot yawns. His teeth are two rows of the thorns she does not have.

"We must help them, though," she says, more to herself than to her ladies.

The rush of the Kyttle Falls fills the room, as it always does when no one is speaking. It is one of the things she loves about Plythe: the torrent is always a companion.

Perhaps sensing that something is amiss, Goldfoot slithers from the cushioned throne and climbs into Howard's lap.

"Shall they come to Plythe, do you think?" Legh says, sounding rather thrilled at the prospect.

Howard tries to imagine that she is Cleves or Seymour. "No," she says. "They will not look to the closest safe place. They will look to the safest."

"That is Mathmas, then," Lady Tylney says.

Yes. Mathmas and Parr. There was a time when Howard might have felt such a choice as a slight. Perhaps there is still a pinch of melancholy, but she can recognise that it would be the wisest place for them to go.

"They will pass through Plythe's territory then," Ursula says. "I could go searching for them."

"I think that would be foolish," Susanna says, echoing Howard's thoughts. "If Her Majesty is being watched, then we are likely being watched too."

Howard holds up a hand, and the women fall silent. Goldfoot nibbles the trim of her dress. Howard wishes she could work out a plan thoroughly, then lay it all before her ladies like a feast, but her mind does not work that way. She must speak her thoughts to understand them.

"What will they need to get to Mathmas safely?" she says.

"Food and water, without needing to venture into any village where they might be recognised," Lady Tylney says.

"Cloths for their courses, too," Legh adds.

"Weapons," Ursula says.

"Good." She stands, holding Goldfoot against her chest, and goes to the door, where she calls for Florin to join them.

"I need you to put together several packages," she tells him. "You must make sure they are both small and light."

Once he is gone, Howard turns back to her ladies. "Now we must work out how to convey such items to the queens without raising suspicion."

"The easiest part of the whole plan, then," Legh says.

The women exchange ideas, each one as unworkable as the last. Howard hears them all as she walks the length of the chamber, wishing for some strike of knowledge from Boleyn's spirit. Goldfoot nips at her ear.

"Oh!" Howard says, stopping suddenly.

"You have an idea?" Lady Tylney says.

"I don't know." Their expectant expressions almost cow her. "I was only thinking: would it not be wonderful if we could send Goldfoot out to drop the packages upon the queens. But he is far too recognisable. It would not work."

"But we can disguise Goldfoot," Susanna says. "Nothing so easy." She goes to the little chest where she keeps her paints. Howard clutches Goldfoot tighter. She knows it is a foolish worry, but she loves her dragon's iridescent colouring, born of coal and pearls.

"Will it not hurt him?" she says.

Legh huffs. "Do you want to help your friends or not?"

"I would never harm him," Susanna says. She selects a small glass jar filled with brown powder, and then another filled with deep green. Howard brings the lapdragon to Susanna and he sniffs curiously at both jars. Susanna croons over him, explaining, as if he could understand, how she will mix the powders with gesso and water to create a paste. How she will transform him from one of the most precious pets in Elben to a common, wild hatchling.

Howard leaves Goldfoot with Susanna and goes to her bedchamber, and the nondescript box where the cloths for her monthly courses are kept. She empties the box and unpicks the hidden bottom, revealing beneath the slim pack of correspondence. Among them: the cipher Cleves sent all those moons ago, when she summoned the queens to their *sunscínas*.

By the time she returns to her receiving chamber, Goldfoot is barely recognisable. The usual sheen of his scales is muted in browns and greens. Susanna even traces puckered scars across his body. He is no longer a pampered lapdragon but a war-weary wild dragon, a victor even in his youth.

"My, you look very brave, my dear," Howard tells him. He caws, stretching his neck up to her, delighted with all the attention. She holds Cleves's cipher to his snout.

"Can you smell her?" she says. He snuffles at the parchment, and for a moment she's worried he may set it alight. He caws again.

Lady Tylney joins them. "I have sewn a handful of bags," she tells Howard. "It is not my best work, but they are strong and small and made of a light enough fabric that Goldfoot should be able to carry them."

"And we have traced their likely journey," Ursula says, hurrying over with Legh, a map of Plythe's territory held open between them. She points to several charcoal crosses marked hastily across the parchment.

"They will avoid the scrind roads and the main thoroughfares if they have any sense," Ursula explains.

"There are dozens of coppices and the like not far from the coast," Legh says. "They make for excellent hiding places."

"And we can all guess how you know this," Howard says, raising an eyebrow at her half-sister.

Legh shrugs. "Well, ever since Boleyn turned you into a proper queen you told me to stop having my assignations in the palace. What was I supposed to do?"

There's a knock on the door, and Florin enters to their silence. Howard had imagined him pouring necessities into a sack for them, but he has been far cleverer. He holds a tray, the kind that any servant might bring to their queen. Upon it are several silver domes which, when uncovered, reveal plates of dried meat and fruits, hard biscuits, clean cloth and healing herbs.

They set about dividing everything between Lady Tylney's bags.

"Should you leave a cipher inside them, so that they know they're from you?" Susanna says.

"It doesn't matter if they know that we sent them," Howard replies. "Better to do without and be safe."

Legh pauses, watching her, frowning.

"What?" Howard says.

"Nothing."

When all the bags are ready, they open the windows and let the sound of the falls join their excitement. Howard feeds Goldfoot a strip of dried meat from her pocket and sets her nose to his snout. She dare not coddle him for fear of ruining Susanna's painted disguise.

"Fly swift and strong, my dear," she tells him. "And come back to me safely."

At first, she worries that they have loaded him too heavily. He tumbles out of the window, the bags he clutches pulling him down. The next moment, he rises, his little wings beating powerfully. He emits a final *caw*, then rises above them, above Plythe, heading west towards the coast.

Hand pressed to her chest, Howard runs out of her receiving chamber and across the gallery to the windows on the other side, searching the skies for a glimpse of her companion. Her friends follow her.

"There he is," Florin says, pointing to a distant flicker.

"There he is," she whispers.

Florin takes one of her hands. Ursula takes the other.

"He is a brave boy," Susanna says, placing a hand on Howard's shoulder.

"He'll find them if they're to be found," Legh agrees.

Warmth spreads through Howard. She is surrounded, cocooned. She thinks, *This is what it is to be a queen.* She has never felt her royalty so strongly as she does now, when she has worked as one with her friends, and they as one with her.

A whisper of jasmine floats through the gallery, though no jasmine grows in the grounds of Plythe. Her heart quickens.

"*Your Majesty*," Ursula says.

Howard follows Ursula's gaze. Across her hands, entwined in her fingers like ribbon, is the bordweal light.

Howard starts back, as though she might be able to throw off the power tingling across her hands and up her arms. Then she begins to laugh.

"You are a goddess," Ursula says.

Her friends crowd around her. All but Legh, who stands apart from them. Howard doesn't care. She revels in their wonder. She is so thrilled that she almost does not hear the applause. Low and strong as a church bell.

Gradually, the group falls silent. They turn, searching for the source. And there, from around the corner, steps Culpepper. His face is bright and open and gleeful. He pushes through her companions, kneels before her, takes her glimmering hands in his and kisses them.

CHAPTER FORTY-SIX

Howard

Howard has been caught out many times in her short life. She remembers being caught by one of her aunt's servants with her music teacher. She had frozen, a hand over her mouth, wishing his body was big enough to shield her. It is the same now, as Culpepper looks up at her. She needs to hide.

"You *are* a goddess," he says, cradling her hands in his own. It is as if she has been coated in the gimrodor oil that coats the dragons guarding the Tower, turning them to stone.

"No, but I worship one," Howard manages to say. She dare not look at the others; if she looks away from Culpepper, she may miss a hint of any deception.

"And I worship one also," Culpepper says. He is as earnest as he was when he brought her that wine on the day of the dragon-baiting.

"How long have you known?" Howard asks. There is no point in pretending any more. All that she can do is to work out whether he is truly loyal to her.

"Guess," he says, cocking his head.

She thinks back to the moment in the courtyard outside her wing at High Hall, when she sought to help Boleyn escape. He certainly did not know then. He was even churlish at her demands. But he knew by the time Henry brought him to Plythe. She decides to flatter him: "Not long after our first meeting."

He beams. "So you do remember me."

"Of course I do."

He stands, evidently deciding that it is safe to do so. For an instant, he is a little too close to her, and he seems to realise it because he steps back, out of her space. He still has not looked at any of her companions.

"I heard rumours about the Moon Ball a few days after the trouble at Brynd, and could not rest until I had unearthed the truth," he says.

"Who else knows?"

He shrugs. "I dared not ask for the very same reasons I assume you dared not ask me." He swallows, as if he doesn't want her to see how hurt he is over her distrust.

She tries to see the situation through the eyes of her fellow queens, to understand what she should do next, but she cannot think herself into their heads. She cannot imagine any of them finding themselves here: for the only one of them brave enough to help Boleyn the way she did, all those moons ago, is Seymour. Yet Seymour would never have surrounded herself as Howard has surrounded herself. If Howard is to see a way forward, she must do it through her own eyes, with her own wit.

"Do you pledge yourself to me?" she asks Culpepper.

"You have my whole life," he says. He gives the promise lightly. She tries not to judge him for it: who but she can know the struggle of finding the right words?

"Charge me with any task," he says.

He is asking for a test, not a task. Such a request is unlikely to comfort her: she knows all about tests and passing them with a disloyal heart. The air is oppressive. Too many are watching her.

"You have the king's ear?" she says.

"I have his favour, and that is the same thing."

It is not. She should know.

"I want you to find out where the Moon Ball is going to be held," she says. It is the only information she can think of that will help them without giving away more to Culpepper than she is comfortable doing.

He bows. "Consider it done."

He leaves without a single glance at any of the others. Not even Legh, who he previously treated as an intimate.

They all of them wait until they can no longer hear his boots.

"Do you trust him?" Lady Tylney says.

"I do not know," Howard replies. She looks down at her hands. The glimmer of the bordweal light has vanished. She cannot help but feel as though something has been stolen from her: she should be elated, but all she can feel is doubt. A reckoning is coming, and she must know who is truly on her side.

That night, Howard climbs into bed beside Legh. It is as if they are children again, girls of ten and eight, inseparable in their shared loneliness. Legh stirs and turns, still half asleep, to face Howard.

"Wake up, sister," Howard whispers. She squeezes Legh's arm.

"Howard?" Legh mumbles.

"I wish to talk to you."

At first, she thinks Legh has fallen asleep again, but then she sits upright with a start, almost toppling Howard out of the bed.

"Good lord, what are you doing?" she says, a hand pressed to her heart.

Howard struggles to disentangle herself from the sheets.

"I did not mean to frighten you."

"You never *mean* to do anything," Legh says. The conversation is slipping away from Howard before it has even begun. She grasps at it.

"Sister. May we talk? Just you and I? Without any of the others?"

Legh remains hard, her hand still on her chest like a shield.

"What do you wish to talk about?"

"*Us*."

Legh smirks. "Coming into my bed. Talking about *us*. You act as though we are married."

"Please stop," Howard says.

"I am only jesting."

Howard spins off the bed and paces to the other end of the chamber. The strangeness of the room makes her realise she has never been here before. Four years since she married Henry and Legh entered her household, and she has never been inside her bedchamber. She who used to share a mattress and all her secrets with her half-sister.

"We used to be so close," Howard starts.

"Ask me what you really want to ask me," Legh says. She is on her feet beside the bed, bare feet planted solidly.

Howard wavers for a moment, her own determination faltering in the face of Legh's challenge.

"Are you working against me?" The question lands like lead between them.

"Well," Legh says. She laughs, a fluttery sound soon dampened. "Well. Have you asked anyone else that? The quiet little artist who watches more than she speaks? Did you ask her? Or the boy who's in love with the king's sister – did you ask him?"

"No," Howard says. She feels as though she is eight again, standing in front of her aunt after a misdemeanour.

"No." Legh smiles bitterly. "No. You have only asked the half-sister who has protected you and taught you and stood by you since you were barely out of the cradle."

"You have been so cruel of late," Howard says. "Am I not entitled to ask why you act so?"

"I have only been to one Moon Ball, Howard."

Howard blinks at this sudden diversion. "What?" she says.

"You took me in your retinue in your first year of marriage, and never again since," Legh says, slicing the air with her hand.

"And that is why you dislike me?"

Legh utters a loud, crumpled noise and balls fists into the blankets. She will wake the rest of the household. "I do not dislike you, Howard. I am saying that you were cruel to me long before I was cruel to you."

Howard stifles a laugh. "It's only a ball, Legh. This is so small."

The laughter dies in her throat as Legh fixes her with tear-brimmed eyes.

"Not to me."

Outside the window, an owl hoots.

"Not to me," Legh says again.

Howard casts about her. She lands upon a trinket box displayed upon a chest. She brandishes it at her half-sister.

"I gave you this. I gave you half the gowns you wear." She throws up her arms and gestures to the chamber, with its walls of shimmering silverbirch and golden lanterns. "You live in a palace because of me. Would you rather be back at our great-aunt's, sharing a chamber with a dozen other abandoned girls?"

"I know," Legh says. She dashes a tear away from her cheek. Howard feels her own tears crawling up her throat.

"I have tried so hard to please you, Legh."

"I know."

"So what more do you want from me?" A sob escapes. A great, wrenching cry. "I do not know what more I can give. I have tried so hard. So, so hard."

And Legh is there, wrapping her arms around Howard as they, girls of ten and eight once more, cling to each other and sink to the floor in their nightgowns. Theirs is not a language of words; it never was. To find the right way of saying something was pointless, for it would not be heard, and so language itself became worthless.

"I am not Mary Boleyn, Howard."

"I know."

"I can see you all thinking it."

Howard *has* been cruel. If Legh had turned against her, it would have been on Howard's head as much as on Legh's.

"I am sorry, my dear."

They pull apart, facing each other on the floor. Legh kneads her nightgown.

"Sometimes," she says. "Sometimes I have this notion that you are on a boat, travelling down the Kyttle River. And the falls are just there, and no one can tell you to bring your boat to shore. And I don't know if you are going to survive the drop and make it out to sea, or whether you are going to be dashed on the rocks and drowned. And I can't bear it, Howard. I can't bear it."

Howard cups Legh's chin in her hands. She presses her forehead to her half-sister's. "It is so strange to me that you should describe me so, because I do not feel that I have moved, ever, my whole life. I have been passed from cage to cage to cage, and I might beat my wings against the bars, but they are always too strong, and the lock too tight."

Legh wipes first Howard's tears, then her own, with shaking fingers. "Well then," she says. "We had better find the key, little sister."

CHAPTER FORTY-SEVEN

Cecilia

Cecilia had thought that Henry might hurry back to High Hall to see her, his adored sister, as quickly as possible. After all, she has secrets that she wishes to divulge to him. But he spends several days fruitlessly hunting his errant queens across Elben.

The shard of not-glass she stole from Seymour's dress hasn't left her person since she escaped captivity. Its strange warmth has been a constant reminder of its mystery. It is no weapon, and it does not seem to be a tool, but it was precious to Seymour – why?

She feels sure that Henry or More would know what it is, but Henry is absent and More . . . Since their conversation, she cannot bring herself to confide in him further. To do so would be to grow the heaviness in her chest that blooms whenever she thinks about the bishop.

By the third day, her impatience outweighs the fact that she is superior to almost everyone in this palace. Sometimes one must tussle with a groom to get the best horse.

"Take me to Master Cromwell's chambers," she tells a passing servant. He is carrying a tray stacked with goblets and jugs of wine, but he knows better than to delay her. She wonders whether the servants are learning quickly, or whether her reputation precedes her.

She had assumed that Cromwell's rooms would be on one of the lower levels of High Hall – the fifth or sixth, perhaps, with Henry's other low-born advisors. But the servant leads her almost to the top of the palace, to the second level. They are above even the sanctuary and the rooms of religion here. Only Henry's private chambers surmount them. Cecilia thinks of her own rooms on the fourth floor, and flushes at the insult. When Henry returns, he will move her up to the second level. Perhaps he will make Cromwell switch.

When she is admitted, her irritation only grows. Cromwell has wasted the space. The walls are bare but for a portrait of Henry and a set of antlers for faith; the furniture is sparse and practical, used primarily for teetering piles of books, letters and rolls of parchment. There is no beauty, no eye for a handsome painting or a comfortable cushion. And these are some of the grandest rooms at High Hall, with their towering windows admitting views across the northern gardens and Aragon's greenhouses. It is criminal.

Cromwell is little better. She must have met the man when he was beneath her notice – some secretary to Wolsey, one of dozens – and he has made little effort to look the part of a chief advisor. He wears a simple black jacket over his shirt, shapeless and strange next to the tailored doublets currently in fashion.

"Princess Cecilia," he says, looking up from the letter he's been reading next to the light of the window. She would have liked him to show more surprise at her visit, but she has heard that this man never displays emotion if he can help it.

"Queen Cecilia, if you please," she says. Why does he keep forgetting?

Cromwell's smile thins. "Of course, we must be precise. Dowager Queen Cecilia, it has been a delight to have you back at court."

There is a little snigger from behind her, and she whirls around. She had thought Cromwell alone, but another man lurks in the darkened part of the chamber. He lounges in a chair, his long legs splayed in a V.

"Charles Brandon," she says, replacing the flutter in her chest with rock.

"Princess," he replies, hauling himself up as though it is far too much effort to show her respect. She rolls her eyes. "If you will insist on calling me by that unimaginative, youthful nickname, you can at least bow to me."

He does so, bowing so low over her outstretched hand that it becomes insulting once more. When he rises, he takes his time examining her body. She is suddenly keenly aware that the last time he saw her, she was a girl. No matter that she still attracts attention wherever she goes. No matter that she bathes in phoenix blood to maintain her youthful complexion. She is still a woman of thirty-five, standing before a man who fucked her last when she was eighteen. She cannot hold back the ageing tide entirely.

She raises her chin and makes sure that he sees *her* examining *him* as well. He must be in his forties now, and it shows. His waist is thicker than she remembers, and those who look closely may see that his ash-brown hair is streaked with grey. He still has the same insouciant manner that renders him handsome at whatever age: an untamed stallion. One that dares the rider to mount.

"Well, well, well, Cecilia Tudor, I never thought to see you in these halls again," he says. The mockery is familiar. When she was younger, he had teased her for being so young, for being his friend's little sister, for trying to play on his level. But today she is equal to it.

"Charles Brandon. I really thought you would have found yourself a house of your own by now, instead of clinging to my brother's doublet still."

Charles laughs, showing all his teeth.

"Why would I want my own house, where I have to pay for my own food and my own servants and take responsibility for things? The horror of it."

Cromwell coughs. "Was it me you wished to see, Your Majesty, or my learned Lord Brandon?"

Cecilia bites her lip. Cromwell is right – she has been sidetracked, and in doing so she has given Brandon power. Briefly, she wonders at the two of them being in the same space. As far as she remembers, Charles was just as clear on the proper tiers of nobility as she was, yet he seems to be waiting on the inferior man. Why?

She pulls the shard of glass from the length of blue velvet she wrapped it in, and holds it up to the light.

"I took this from Seymour before I escaped. She attempted to hide it from me. I would like you to tell me why it was so precious to her."

For the first time since her entrance, Cromwell looks genuinely interested. He places the letter he was reading on a nearby table and approaches.

"May I?" he asks. She hands it over reluctantly.

"It is *mine* now," she says as he carries it closer to the window. Brandon follows him, and the two men examine the glass.

"Fascinating," Cromwell mutters.

"Broken glass," Brandon says, and turns back to Cecilia. "So, my lady, what did you learn in Perfugi?"

Usually, she would entertain the man. But Cromwell is turning the shard over and over, and the more he does so, the more she feels on the precipice of something wonderful. There is something obscene about the way he is examining the piece, as though he is peering beneath a woman's shift.

"You know what it is," she says, side-stepping Brandon and taking the glass from Cromwell.

"I have a suspicion. You see the patina, and the curve of the surface?"

"I have noted it, yes."

He touches it again. "And you only found the one piece?"

How dare he avoid telling her what he knows when it was *she* who did the hard work of finding it? She snatches it from his grasp. "What. Is. It?"

"I think you have found part of a *sunscína,* Your Majesty," he says.

Brandon snorts. "That was a tale for children, surely?"

If Cromwell responds, Cecilia doesn't hear his words. A *sunscína.* She is holding ancient power. Power that is part of her very being, the way that stories told to children form the core of the adult they become. She can barely breathe.

"How can you know?" she whispers.

"The thought of them interested me for a while, so I found out all I could about them," Cromwell says.

Brandon huffs a laugh. "You are such a little gargoyle, Cromwell, with all your books. Go hunting, man. Go fuck a woman. Or a man. Or neither. Or both."

"*Quiet,*" Cecilia says.

She is not a woman of books herself, but she knows the value of those who are. Brandon may not appreciate what she has found, but Cromwell does.

"Do you think every queen has them?" she says.

Cromwell is staring out of the window, hands clasped behind his back. Brandon throws himself back into his chair with a loud sigh.

"If one exists, then it would follow that six do, or did, if they have not been broken and lost to time. I think it safe to assume that at least one other queen has knowledge of the *sunscína,* or the traitor Seymour would not have kept this so close to her person."

"So Cleves had one as well," Cecilia says.

"It answers the question that has been pecking at me: how did Boleyn and Seymour plan their betrayals? I think you have brought me my answer."

She does not like the way he says that, as though she is one of his secretaries.

"Are you going to try to get the whole set then?" Brandon asks. She understands Cromwell's flinch: the question is too petty for an item such as the *sunscína*.

"I might have done once," Cromwell says. "But the truth is it matters little now."

"What do you mean?" Cecilia says.

Cromwell and Brandon have a silent conversation that Cecilia cannot interpret. It is too shadowed with scorn and long disagreement and envy.

"Tell me immediately. What could possibly be more important than ensuring the other queens do not have use of their *sunscínas*?" she says, moving between them so they cannot continue their silent argument.

Brandon is the one who answers: "There are things in motion now, my lady. Things that make some childhood story irrelevant."

"How?"

"We are not the ones who have the authority to tell you," Cromwell says. His voice is once more as calm as satin.

So she must wait until Henry returns. She thinks about pressing them, but something tells her that a threat will not move either man when it comes to this secret.

"Shall I accompany you back to your rooms?" Brandon says.

It is a tempting offer, even if he is a little old for her now. When she was younger, and decided to make him her first lover, he was an excellent teacher. Part of her wishes to show him that she is now in a position to make him the pupil. But the *sunscína* is warm, and the knowledge of it is still bursting inside her.

"I need no guide in my own home," she says. She does not look back as she leaves.

It is only later, as she sits in the window seat of her bedchamber and turns the shard over and over as Cromwell had done, that the tightness in her chest starts. For if such an item is no longer important to Cromwell, then that means that the queens are no longer important. And if the queens are no longer important . . . why are they still alive?

CHAPTER FORTY-EIGHT

Cleves

Cleves's plan to throw Henry's hunters off their trail seems to work. Their disguises – old, wretched garments and road dirt – hold well enough for the common folk of Plythe's territory, most of whom have never seen them in person.

It is on their sixth day of trekking through woods, skirting villages and scavenging from scrapheaps and the forest floors that they spot the Heahmore mountains, the border between the territories of Plythe and Mathmas. The hills of Plythe, soft as a woman's body, covered in heather and grass, will turn harsh and unloved.

"The Palace of Plythe is perhaps a day's walk behind us," Seymour says softly, as they stare up at those forbidding mountains. It is a shame that they had been forced to leave their horses behind when they left the roads.

"We would be fools," Cleves says.

"I know."

The thought of all the comforts that would be afforded them there is tempting all the same. Cleves smiles to herself. There had been a time when none of them would willingly have visited Plythe for longer than a few days. Howard was too much for all of them. Her bright little song in the cage of her brief life was too high and too loud. None of them saw that it was her way of reconciling herself to her marriage. None of them even believed her capable of such bargaining. That is Cleves's shame to bear. Which of them have not made such pacts with their souls? Does it follow that their own, quieter, more brutal bargains were more admirable?

Seymour touches her hand. "Are you all right?"

"I am always all right," Cleves says, taking Seymour's hand and pulling her along, starting to run.

"Cleves, stop!" Seymour laughs.

"Why? With the breeze in our faces and the sun on our cheeks, what could be more wonderful than this?" Cleves raises her voice above the birdsong.

Lelij joins the romp, cawing as he leaps after them, deer-like.

The muscles in her thighs ache as she pulls Seymour up the hill. They come to a panting stop at the top and look out over Howard's territory. Hills glide like raindrops down towards the distant sea, where the last of the sun trails a finger across the ocean.

"It is beautiful, though," she says. Seymour rests her head on Cleves's shoulder. "If I had to be on the run with anyone, I am glad it is you," she says.

"Did your Clarice not offer the same scintillating humour?" Cleves asks.

"My Clarice and I spent much of our journey trying to unwind half a lifetime of resentment and inequality," Seymour says. "It was full of love but not of humour."

"But you tried to change for those you love," Cleves says. She massages her breastbone absently.

"Of course. We are not set in stone, any of us, are we? It makes me laugh to think that my brother Thomas probably still thinks of me as a mouse. I cannot imagine how he received the news of what happened at Hyde. He must have wondered whether a changeling took me."

We are not set in stone. But she is. She has served herself well all her adult life, just as she is. There is nothing wrong with steadiness.

"Thomas, he is not in Elben?" she says, keen to change the subject. Her eyes are drawn to a fleck swooping and soaring across the fields.

"I think he is in Avahuc now. He was sent there as an ambassador several years ago, just after Henry married Parr."

"Ah," Cleves says. She shades her eyes, the better to see that fleck.

"Yes. Ah."

"You did not seek him out after you left Elben?"

"I thought it best not to. He can be hot-headed, and I never could tell which direction his temper would take."

"And Henry would undoubtedly have people watching him," Cleves says.

"What is that?" Seymour says, spotting the same shape Cleves is following.

They draw into the safety of the trees. It could be a wild eagle or young dragon on an evening hunt. Those would be the better options. She heard that Wolsey used to employ trained gryphons for the purpose of spying. Could this be one of them?

"Should we run?" Seymour whispers.

There is something about the way the fleck flies that nudges Cleves's memory. She understands animals and can usually read their movements as she would a letter. This fleck is not moving like a wild animal. It is moving with the purpose of a hunter, but not the guile.

"Get behind me," she says, pushing Seymour deeper into the cover of the trees. She pulls a little knife from her pocket and, crouching, makes her way down the slope towards the shape.

If it is an animal sent to spy, she must not let it return to High Hall. And if she fails at killing it, perhaps she can at least lead it away from Seymour.

As the shape nears, she sees, even in the dim light of dusk, that it is a dragon. Despite the murky green-brown of its colouring, it flies with an elegance she has rarely seen in the most expensive of pets. Its movement is like her favourite dance, the Almain. It is such a shame to have to kill so beautiful a creature. She holds the blade between her thumb and index finger, and prepares to heft it towards the dragon.

The creature calls out, a soft, cautious sound that reaches her like crickets on a breeze.

She curses, drops her knife, heart pounding. And something thuds onto the ground in front of her.

In the deepening evening, she cannot see it, but a moment later the lapdragon lands in front of her. It tilts its head, as if asking her a question.

"Cleves?" Seymour says.

"I thought I told you to stay in the trees?" Cleves says, not taking her eyes from the lapdragon's.

"I grew worried."

Seymour reaches Cleves and stops.

"Is that . . .? What has she covered him in?"

Cleves holds out her palm. The dragon sniffs it, then huffs warm air: she is allowed to touch him. She runs a single finger across a few of his scales, and it comes away with green.

"Paint," Cleves says.

Seymour laughs, crouching to lavish praise on Howard's pet. Lelij, hearing adoration for something else, lollops to join them and rolls on his back in front of Seymour so that she can scratch his stomach with one hand and pet Goldfoot with the other. Watching Seymour so simply happy makes Cleves's stomach twist.

"Howard has sent us something, I think," Cleves says.

The lapdragon hops off the parcel he dropped, and they open it.

"Oh, she is wonderful," Seymour says, snatching one of the hard biscuits and crunching into it like it's a sweet pear.

"She has thought of everything," Cleves says, noting not just the thought behind the gifts – sustenance, healing herbs and clean cloths – but also the caution Howard displayed in camouflaging Goldfoot and not including anything identifying in the parcel. Something inside her relaxes. "You will outwit us all in the end, little songbird," she whispers.

Reluctantly, they send Goldfoot on his way, back towards Plythe, and stumble back to the cover of the wood and a bed of soft ferns.

It is only later, as Seymour slumbers, head on Cleves's chest, leg thrown over her own, that Cleves remembers how unthinkingly she pushed Seymour out of potential danger. Johana told her to keep running, and she did not. If she carries on in this manner, she will not survive. She cradles Seymour's head, kisses her hair. She had better start running again, but tonight she allows herself to dream.

CHAPTER FORTY-NINE

Howard

It takes only a matter of days for Culpepper to find the information she asked for, though she cannot fathom *when* he did so, for he seems to shadow her. Applauding her when she plays the harpsichord in her music room. Watching from the tower tops if she takes a walk with her ladies. Nudging Florin aside if he leans in too close as they discuss Perfugian customs.

When he comes with the news, though, she is alone, in her own private chambers. The servant looks pointedly away when they tell her he is waiting.

It would have been more proper for him to find her in her study, even though she so rarely goes there now that Voda Kelaverinn is gone. But despite his protestations of loyalty, she is wary of angering Culpepper. Until she *knows*, the way she knows her ladies, the way she knows Florin, she cannot risk alienating him. Still, she slips out of her bedroom and finds him in her antechamber, examining the veneer on one of her jewellery boxes.

When the servant has gone, he bows low over her hand.

"Have you been busy, Master Culpepper?" she says.

He runs a hand over the veneer, where a rose is picked out in cherry and sandalwood.

"This is fine craftsmanship."

"It was a gift from my husband. Florin tells me it was likely made in Perfugi."

He looks puzzled, then remembers. "Oh, the Dowager Queen's young toy? You know, if I had realised who he was, I could have helped disguise him a little better than as a servant. He'd have been less conspicuous if he'd come into my service."

"Well, no one has found him yet," Howard says, moving away from the jewellery box. "Did you find out what I asked?"

He follows her across the room. She doesn't know why his touching the box grates so – it is hardly as though the item means much to her. "It is very irregular. I don't think you will be able to guess where the Moon Ball is being held."

It is a challenge wrapped in charm. It reminds her of her first lover, who was so adept at delivering insults wrapped in compliments, then weeping when she expressed hurt.

"Is it High Hall, perchance?" she says.

A tight flicker crosses his handsome features. "How did you know?" Then, more shrewdly: "Did you engineer it so? How? How did you trick the king?"

She tilts her head. "You seem angry, Master Culpepper."

He bites his lip, then smiles and comes closer. So close she can smell him – bergamot and peppercorn. "Forgive me. I only wish you would trust me. I could be so useful to you if you only told me all." He sighs. "But I understand. You must be careful, and you have seen me close to your husband."

"If I trust the wrong person, I and all who follow me die," she says.

"I would die for you," he replies.

"For me? Or for the goddess Medren?"

He laughs. "It is the same to me."

There is little more than a breath between their bodies. The topmost buttons of his doublet are undone, so that she can spy his chest beneath. An old scar runs across the skin. She traces it, and his smile widens.

"What happened?" she asks.

He shrugs. "That dragon we used for sport."

She remembers, then, the way he lashed the creature to bend it to his will, and the care he took over her when Henry injured her. She knows, better than anyone, that a person can hold many facets within them. A hall of many mirrors. What she does not know is which facet is the true Culpepper.

Tentatively, he places his hands on her waist. She could almost feel safe with him. She should feel safe with him. He wants to help. He pulls her closer. The hardness beneath his hose ignites something she had thought dormant.

"I've seen the way you look at me," he murmurs, before pressing his mouth against hers.

Her mouth opens automatically. His tongue meets hers, and he sighs very softly, as if he has imagined this moment for so long. He backs her up against a chest, his hands stroking her arms, twining in her hair.

He is a very, very good kisser. His touch speaks of attentiveness and respect. Yet she is frozen still. She suddenly imagines herself a doll being played with. But dolls do not have voices. They do not move themselves or say yes or no.

All this time, she has thought this his test. A test she set for him. But it never was. It was a test she set for herself.

She presses a hand to his chest, stopping the kiss.

"Kneel," she says, her voice husky.

His mouth goes thin, but then he drops to his knees before her.

She thinks of the way she has explored her own body of late, and leans back against the chest, pulling up her skirts.

"Here," she says, guiding his touch to the point of exquisite pleasure. As soon as she moves her hand from his, he goes faster, harder. Too hard.

"Gently," she says, closing her eyes, trying to lose herself.

"I know," he says, easing only a little. It is still too much.

The freeze is seeping up her body once more, like mould. She shifts, moving his hand away, and drops her gown.

"What's wrong?" he says.

"Kiss me," she says.

He does so, then grabs for her again. "Let me bring you to a finish," he murmurs against her lips. She stops his roving hand. "Not now. Tonight," she says. That satisfies him.

Suddenly, he is all upright, all command, all gloating smile.

"I have never seen your bedchamber." And he makes for the door to her most private room, as if it belongs to him.

"What do you gain?" she blurts out.

He turns, his hand resting on the door to her room.

"What do you mean?"

"Why are you really helping me? Why are you so quick to commit treason?"

He shrugs, that smile still there. "Because yours is the true cause. It's just the right thing to do."

"But why is it the right thing to do?" she asks.

He laughs. "If you cannot tell me, then why are *you* so willing to commit treason?"

"I . . ." She flounders in the face of his laughter, in the face of her own tumbling thoughts. For she has asked herself, time and time again, why she is doing what she is doing. She has no real wish for the power that comes with being a true ruler. She is not certain that she is a good queen; she does not have the attention span or the education for it. So why has she risked everything for these queens who barely tolerate her?

Some rageful creature lets out a shrill note inside her, and is still, and her thoughts settle.

"Because I have been told that I am lesser when I am not."

Culpepper nods, like a teacher. "Exactly," he says. "Exactly."

He holds out a hand, inviting her to join him. She does not take it.

"What will happen next?" she asks. If he will not answer philosophical questions, perhaps he will answer practical ones. He returns to her, cupping her face in his hands.

"We will destroy the king. There will be some fighting, I'm sure, but with your power and Queen Cleves's and Seymour's power against him, the king will fall. You will be Queen of Plythe in your own right. You and I can marry, and I will be your devoted helper in managing your new kingdom."

He kisses her again.

In another life, she would have missed the implication of that word: *kingdom*. But she has known Boleyn, and Cleves, and Voda Kelaverinn, and all the other queens. In another life, before Boleyn, she might even have convinced herself that this was love.

But not this life, not now.

"What if I do not want that?" she asks.

Culpepper makes a noise in the back of his throat.

"I mean it. What if I do not want to marry you?"

He sighs and looks to the ceiling, as if all her questioning is growing tiresome. "We would make a handsome pair, would we not?"

Something flicks in her mind. He turns for the door, but before he can reach it, Howard seizes the nearest heavy object – a bust of some long-ago queen – and hefts it with all her might at the back of his head.

CHAPTER FIFTY

Howard

Culpepper teeters, touches the back of his head. His fingers come away bloody. She does not wait for him to counter her attack. She is Goldfoot, descending upon her prey. She throws herself at him before he can recover, and they fall in a tangle of limbs and gown to the floor.

"You're insane," he pants, grappling with her as she, straddling him, reaches for the bust. He pulls at her hair, and a clump comes away in his hand, grey and rotting skin entangled in its roots. He gags and flicks it away. She almost laughs that in such a moment he is so preoccupied with her body. It gives Howard the space she needs to seize the bust once more.

He wrests her off him, rolling her over so that she is beneath him. All the feigned adoration that he tried to charm her with is vanished. All that remains is his truth: flared nostrils and a hand upon her throat, squeezing, squeezing.

"Stupid bitch," he says.

Through the desperate thump of blood in her ears, Howard thinks she hears a shout. Perhaps it is her own. This is not her end: she will not be brought low by this grasping boy. Never again will someone call her *stupid* and live.

Though the arm clutching the bust feels so, so heavy, she brings it up as hard as she can against his jaw. He falls off her with a curse. She does not think on her burning chest, nor the pain in her throat.

She brings the bust down, again and again, upon his head. Warmth sprays across her face like kisses.

"Your Majesty, stop!"

Arms wrap around her, drawing her away from the bloodied lump. It is her ladies and Florin, brought to her side by the noise of the fight.

"What did you do?" Lady Tylney whispers.

"He was not worth risking my life for," Howard says. She lets the bust drop to the floor and heaves, needing to fill her bruised body with fresh air.

Florin sways. Legh cannot look at Culpepper's prone body, or the blood that is pooling on the floor beside the mess that was once his head.

Susanna is even paler than normal, her lips a thin line. "What do you need us to do?"

Florin, Susanna and Legh roll Culpepper's body up in one of the throws from Howard's bed; Lady Tylney fetches water and vinegar; Howard and Ursula set to scrubbing at the blood. As they work in silence, Howard begins to shake. Dreadful, body-wracking tremors that make her drop her brush. Lady Tylney folds her in her arms. This time, Howard does not resent the maternal gesture.

"I should not have . . ." Howard stutters. "He was going to . . ."

She wants to say *trap me*, but that is not quite right. He wasn't bad. He wasn't evil. He did not deserve to be killed. And yet she had to kill him. Because he was going to own her, as Henry has owned her.

"Do you despise me?" she says. There is a lull in the room, as every one of them pauses.

Legh breaks the silence. "I dislike you much of the time, sister. But this is not one of those times."

"You are our queen," Ursula says fiercely, continuing her scrubbing. "We will do whatever you ask of us."

Lady Tylney tuts. "Well, *I* most certainly shall not do *anything* you ask of me, but you have not yet asked something that I would not give."

Howard wipes her eyes. "I have no wish to own your souls. I am not Henry."

"No, you are not," Florin says. "You have shown me, in the brief time I have lived in your palace, what true royalty looks like."

She does not know how to answer such a statement.

"What a time to grow sentimental," Legh says. She is right.

"We must get him out of the palace," Howard tells them.

"The river would take him out to sea," Susanna says.

Florin shudders. That would have been his fate, if he had not washed ashore.

"There are too many boats. Someone would see him," Howard says.

"We could bury him in the woods," Florin suggests.

"No," she says. "Poachers frequent those woods."

She goes to the window and looks out over her grounds. If not the woods, then where? Do they have the means to leave the grounds of the palace? For nowhere else is sheltered. It is all lawns and herb gardens and jousting arenas . . .

She thumps the windowsill.

"The dragon that was used for the baiting – is it still kept on the estate?"

Lady Tylney's eyes widen as she nods.

Howard doesn't know how she is so clear-headed. Is this how Seymour felt, that night she rescued Boleyn from the Tower? She will collapse later, but for now her mind must work the hardest it has ever worked.

They roll the blanket, with its body inside, to the window. Below them is a little rose garden with a low hedge. With much effort and a little swearing, they heave Culpepper over the balcony. He drops onto a hedge below, one side of the throw unrolling to reveal his bloodied arm. Howard and her friends look at each other. It is awful and it is ridiculous. A chuckle bubbles up Howard's throat, and soon they are all hunched over with mirthless laughter.

"It is too much," Howard says. She feels feverish. "It is not even supper and I have killed a man."

Ursula doubles over. Florin shakes his head and mutters something in Perfugian.

They collect themselves and make their way down to the rose garden, attempting a ladylike stroll with Florin following behind, as a servant should. When they reach the rose garden, they hunch over the body, debating how to move him without anyone spying them.

She directs some of them to ensuring that the rest of the household does not approach the east side of the palace, while the rest of them manhandle Culpepper's body towards the trees, past the stables, to the stone cave where the poor scarred dragon is tethered, the bones of goats and sheep and unwanted puppy litters scattered around it like a hoard.

The dragon rears its head when it sees them, its cracked lips peeling back to reveal rows of teeth. The others pause, unwilling to come within the creature's reach.

Howard holds out one hand, panting with the effort of dragging the body.

"You recognise him, don't you?" she says. Goldfoot is clever enough to understand a gift when he sees it. She knows – oh, she knows now, all too well – that those creatures people believe to be dumb are often merely misunderstood. "I thought you might like to have your revenge."

The dragon snorts.

"Take it closer," she tells the others.

"Are you mad?" Florin asks.

"It will not hurt us," she says, although she's not certain of that at all. "It cannot reach him this far away. We must get closer."

"Do as the queen says," Ursula says, her brow dripping with sweat. Four of them pick up Culpepper again, and heave him towards the dragon, dropping him within the circle of bones. The skeletons rattle and crackle, protesting at his weight.

"Now get back," Florin says, pushing Howard and Ursula behind him. But the dragon sniffs the air in two long, growling inhales. It uncurls from around its tether and drags itself, pockmarked with branding and spears, creased with claw marks, over to Culpepper. It nudges him with its muzzle, sniffs him and bares its teeth once more.

It is at that moment, as if the goddess herself wished to witness Culpepper's final humiliation, that the man wakes. He was not dead at all. It takes him a moment, through the wound in his head, to realise where he is. His eyes widen on the dragon's open maw. He screams as the dragon begins to feed, from the bottom up. Her ladies-in-waiting turn away, but Howard watches it all, for she is a queen, and queens take responsibility for the lives they snuff out.

CHAPTER FIFTY-ONE

Cleves

Coldfoot finds them more easily over the coming days, and his packages keep them from needing to venture into the realms of man. They remain in the forests of Plythe and flee from any sign of humans. In doing so, they forget that other more dangerous creatures exist in the land of Elben.

"With a full stomach and some luck, we should reach the Heahmores by nightfall," Cleves tells Seymour one morning. They have just woken and Seymour's hair is escaping its braid. Lelij yawns loudly, then ambles over to lick their faces. Seymour cossets him, her expression sober.

"You are missing Haltrasc," Cleves guesses.

"It was for the best – he would be too noticeable on this journey. At least your Lelij is small and easily hidden." Her voice is bright like glass.

Cleves lifts Seymour's chin, forcing her to look at her. "You miss him," she says again.

"Like I'd miss a limb, were I to lose one."

Cleves pulls Seymour to her feet. "Come, I have a plan to make you smile, my angry queen."

She thought she had heard it the night before, and she was right. She follows the faint bubble of running water and at last emerges into a clearing through which runs a merry stream.

"Excellent," Seymour says. "Henry's dogs will not be able to trace our scent if we travel through the water."

That had not occurred to Cleves. "Indeed, but I had thought we could use it for the more pressing matter of washing the gargoyle spit from our faces."

To demonstrate, she pulls her mud-stiffened shirt over her head and then wiggles out of her breeches. Seymour is not so bold. She takes off her boots and stockings, then wades into the stream after Cleves. They squeal as the cold water bites their feet, but it is a welcome pinch. The stream is shallow and the water clear, running over large rocks rather than mud or pebbles.

Seymour splashes Lelij, who gambols on the bank. Cleves wades out, naked, into a deeper part of the stream, relishing the numbness across her skin. She watches them in their joy, the woman and the gargoyle. She did that to Seymour. She put the laughter in her throat. When Cleves first met Seymour, the other queen never smiled, never laughed. She has never seen her so happy as when they have been homeless together.

Cleves's heart tightens and her stomach twists, and she can no longer work out whether it is with love or fear. She is a fixed point. She is a runner. She is a solitary castle. She is unencumbered and content to be so.

Seymour turns to her. Cleves cannot let her see the turmoil within her. She grins, holds out her arms, displaying her naked body, and falls backwards into the deeper water. Seymour's laughter echoes around the clearing.

"You fool!" Seymour crows. "You will die of cold before we reach Mathmas!"

Cleves flails over to her lover, keeping her body in the water as she skates across the shallower rocks.

"No, my bright star, I shall make you keep me warm," she says, and with a deft swipe she takes hold of Seymour's bare ankle and makes a show of trying to pull her into the water with her.

"I am clothed! I am clothed!" Seymour laughs.

"Well, we should do something about that, shouldn't we?"

In short order, Seymour's clothes and undergarments are thrown to the bank, where Lelij proceeds to curl up upon them, and Seymour is in the water alongside Cleves.

"Are you shivering?" Cleves says.

"Of course I am shivering – it is freezing and you are mad."

"Come here."

Cleves pulls Seymour back to the deeper water and aligns her naked body with her lover's. They are neck-deep, and where their skin touches Cleves can feel nothing but warmth, and where their skin does not she can feel nothing at all. She tangles her hands in Seymour's hair, kisses her.

"It should not be allowed, you know."

"What shouldn't be allowed?" Seymour says.

"You are beautiful when you smile, when you are sad, when you are angry, when you are joyful. No one should be beautiful all the time."

"It is not all the time," Seymour says. She pulls Cleves even closer, and whispers in her ear: "I am beautiful when I am in love."

They kiss as though they have eternity, as though they have seconds. This is the impossibility of them: that the two of them can fit so perfectly even though it cannot be for ever.

She is so lost in the ecstasy of Seymour's body against hers that it takes her some time to realise that Lelij is growling. He is facing away from them, no longer curled up on Seymour's clothes, but front legs and head close to the ground, back legs up, tail whipping from side to side.

"What has he seen?" Seymour whispers.

Cleves swims, as quietly as she can, to the bank and peers over the edge. The light in the clearing almost makes it impossible to see anything beyond the treeline. Almost.

"*Gherzst*," she swears under her breath.

Cleves points to the shape moving in the shadows beneath the branches. A shape with tusks, and abnormally long front legs.

A crone.

They could not be more vulnerable. She is a fool to think that Seymour's smile could be more important than their safety. And now they are both naked, their clothes and belongings strewn on the bank. The only way to retrieve them is to get closer to the crone.

"Why has it not attacked us already?" Seymour whispers.

Cleves cannot answer that. She contemplates their options – they cannot leave without their clothes, or they will not survive the freezing nights in this part of the island. They will certainly not survive the climb into the Heahmores.

She must retrieve their belongings. She tries to think of a plan, one that will account for the crone's natural behaviour, but her head is too full of the *thump* of soldiers' boots. In any case, the crone is not behaving naturally, or it would have killed them both as soon as it spied them so defenceless in the stream.

That fact gives her hope. Perhaps the crone is not hungry. That has never stopped them before – they are renowned for killing all in their path even when sated – but maybe this one is different.

"Stay there. If it comes for me, swim upstream with Lelij," she says.

"No—" Seymour starts, but Cleves does not have time to argue.

She slips out of the water and crawls towards the still-growling gargoyle. She tosses Seymour's clothes behind her, hoping that they will land close enough to the stream for Seymour to grab them. Her own clothes are nearer the trees.

Her existence narrows to the crone and her, just the two of them staring at each other. She is reminded of another forest, another time, when she had risked Johana to please a false king. Then, there was a clear reason why the crone did not attack immediately. Now, there is none. *Why?*

As she reaches her clothes and gathers them up, she understands why. The crone's head and front legs are clear to see, but not its hind body. That – the impossibility of it again, so many impossibilities today – is *in the ground*.

She inches closer. The crone struggles, thrusting its head forward, attempting to impale her on its tusks. But it cannot reach her. Her eyes did not deceive her: the crone's body is embedded within a circle of fleshy mould. As she watches, a waft of decay unfurls from the monster, and as it does so, the mould sprouts. The crone's body pulls, agonisingly, up from the ground. It takes Cleves a moment to understand further: the crone is not embedded in the ground. It is being grown from that mould.

She starts back, pulling on her clothes, cramming the parcel containing Howard's supplies into her pocket. Seymour is out of the water and dressed, clutching Lelij to her chest.

"Run," is all Cleves says.

They run for what seems like hours, always north, always seeking the end of the wood. Cleves would welcome even a soldier, for that would be a monstrosity she understood. But a beast that is not born, or hatched, but that sprouts from the ground? She has never in all her long studies of animals heard of such a creature.

They reach the base of the Heahmore mountains long before nightfall. The freshness of their swim is a childhood memory. They are scratched and bruised, and their feet are all blister. Better this pain, though, than waiting to allow the crone to finish its strange birth and catch up to them.

"I think we must stop," Seymour says, clutching her ribs.

They are on the ascent already, and the path ahead grows rocky. A chill wind blows from the west, up the incline from the sea, and buffets the mountains' feet. Cleves wants to keep going, to put as much space between them and that crone as possible. She looks back. The wood and its stream are barely visible on the horizon. She tries to reason with her panic: crones are territorial. Even with their scent in its nose, it will not leave the trees.

"Very well," she says.

They find a divot in the rocks – not quite a cave, but not exposed either – and nestle down there. There at last Cleves tells Seymour what she saw, and what it must signify. Seymour covers her mouth in horror.

"I must have seen this too, near Gnottel Lodge," she whispers. She tells Cleves of the strange pink mould that she and Cecilia found in the burnt remains of the Hleaw camp.

They stare at each other.

She had always thought the crones were unnatural, but now she knows it. They must be a sickness, a plague. She edges towards knowledge, pondering everything she knows and does not know about the beasts. Why else would the murder of Medren's worshippers spawn that mould? Why else would crones spread so rampantly during Henry's reign alone, when Henry alone has used Medren's power so much more voraciously than any of his forebears.

The truth creeps over her like that unfurling mould. Cleves might not believe it if she did not know something of the strange workings of this island, where slaughter can turn crystal to garnets, and a goddess can break her eye into stones of power. Elben is Medren's, and it is corrupted. The crones are that corruption, blooming into rotten existence again and again, until it can be cleansed.

CHAPTER FIFTY-TWO

Cecilia

She hears news of her brother's return to High Hall from listening in to the servants' gossip. They whisper of his anger, trade favours to avoid serving him. She remains in her rooms, waiting for him to visit her. Surely – *surely* – he will come to her with a tired smile, fold her in his arms and welcome her home? She is not merely his beloved little sister, after all. She is the one who, of all his clever spies and their clever masters, found out that Cleves is in league with Seymour. She is the one who captured that same traitor queen and brought her back to Elben. It is not Cecilia's fault that Seymour bested her. No one knew that Seymour and Cleves had the ability to wield the bordweal.

But Henry does not visit her. He barely leaves his rooms, if what she overhears is correct. Brother and sister, once inseparable, now separated by three floors, eighteen years and many centuries of secrets.

Eventually, she goes to him. Of course, she has forgotten the protocols of Elben, having lived so long in Perfugi. High Hall is his: it would not be appropriate for him to come to her. He has been waiting for her, probably. Probably desperate to see her, but unable to be the one to descend to her rooms. She imagines him starting out on the journey through the passageways and grand staircases of the palace, only to have Cromwell intercede and remind him of the proper way of things.

She must not keep him waiting any longer.

Henry's rooms, at the apex of High Hall, are empty. A guard hovers in the doorway, too cowed by her to keep her out but not so cowed that they will leave her alone in there without the king.

"Where is he?" she asks, wandering around the space.

"I believe His Majesty is in the sanctuary," the guard says.

She shivers at the thought of that solemn space just below them.

"I will wait for him to return then," she says.

The tapestries on the walls here are all religious, featuring the heroic deeds of Cernunnos or Aethelred – she doesn't know how Henry fucks surrounded by them. It is very different to when she last visited these rooms, the night before she began her voyage to Capetia, for her marriage to the ageing king. Back then, Henry was still a young king, and the rooms were still in large part their father's. Plain walls and draughty windows. They have been made more comfortable now, but there is still something indefinably familiar about the space.

She cannot put her finger on it until she comes upon a prayer book, very old, left closed on a chest all by itself. She starts back and almost trips over her gown in her haste to get away from it.

"Are you all right, Your Majesty?" the guard says from the door.

She ignores him and, with some effort, makes herself approach the book once more.

With a single outstretched finger, she flips the cover open. Inside there are no pages, or no intact ones at least. Instead of prayers, beautifully illustrated, a little chamber is cut into the parchment. The strength leaches from her body. It is empty.

"I threw them away." Henry's voice.

Cecilia keeps her eyes on the book.

"Good," she says.

As he approaches, she can hear the limp in his gait. Shuffle thud, shuffle thud.

"Did a lioness take a mouthful, brother?"

"Two alley cats, more like," Henry says. She turns around then. His face is still youthful, but the way he carries himself is so much older than when she last saw him. His doublet makes his shoulders seem broader than they truly are, and his beard is wirier than it once was, even though it holds no flecks of grey.

She waits for him to open his arms to her, but he does not.

"You grow old, brother," she says.

"Is it any wonder, with a sister like you?"

She prods him. "I shall remind you that I am not the sister waging war on you."

His features cloud further. She feels a familiar tightening in her shoulders. He must catch her expression, for he holds up a hand.

"I am weary, not angry, Cecilia. I am glad to find you alive. It was not what we had thought these last few moons."

He lowers himself onto a long chair, and she joins him, eyeing his left leg, which is extended stiffly. She despises maladies, the sick, the diseased. It is a distaste she always shared with Henry.

"You are wounded, not weary. What did they do?"

"Prised open an old injury."

She cannot help but smile. She can admire courage and cunning, even in those she detests. She looks back towards the prayer book. "When did you throw it away?"

He laughs joylessly. "That is what she wants to know. That is what she wants to discuss, after all this time."

"I know why he was the way he was," she tells Henry.

"You've been talking to Seymour. Of course you know."

He closes his eyes and leans back. Cecilia has never been the type to comfort. Touch, when it is not accompanied by pleasure or pain, is useless to her. But she feels an urge to comfort her brother now. She grips his shoulder.

"I want Cnothan for my own," she says. "And in return I will give you all you need to crush your errant queens."

Henry shakes his head. "I cannot give you Cnothan without my people growing suspicious that I do not fill it with a new queen of my own. They will say the bordweal won't be strong enough."

"Then get More and the other bishops to spread a new lie. Say that Cernunnos came to you in a vision and permitted anyone of your blood to take one of the palaces."

She stands and paces to the window. Why is he not more excited at her offer? His queens have just injured him – him, who should be untouchable – and he seems unbothered.

"Cromwell thinks there is another way," Henry says. "A way that will allow us to keep things as they are."

"What other way?" she says. She is only half listening to him. After all, if he is denying her her palace, then what use does she have for him or his religion? She may as well have stayed in Perfugi. She may as well have made her bargain with Cleves and Seymour, self-righteous though they are. Henry drones on about something in Bishop More's books and a strain of Cernunnos's religion adopted in certain spheres on the continent. At any other time, Henry would have considered it blasphemy, but now it suits him, he seems to be listening.

"You tell me of theory but not of practice," she says. "What exactly is Cromwell brewing?"

Henry shakes his head. "You will see when it is done."

Cecilia has a notion of starting her own form of religion. After all, everyone seems to be doing it. The nobility of Elben may be more likely to follow a woman of Tudor blood than the foreigners and commoners that are the current queens of Elben. She could do it, only it seems like such a lot of hard work. Why should she have to be the one to do the labouring? Just as she is on the verge of getting very angry indeed, and throwing something at Henry's head, he says, "But tell me what you know, and if it's helpful I will give you something better than Cnothan. Better than any of the six castles."

She scoffs. "Are you going to abdicate and hand me your throne, brother?"

He stands, flexing his hands. The divine power prickles on his knuckles, and her eyes dart once more to the empty book of horrors. Henry approaches her, and she half expects him to throttle her. Instead, he takes her hands in his and smiles properly for the first time. He smiles as she had wanted him to when they first saw each other.

"When Cromwell succeeds, I will be more powerful than ever before. I intend to do more than any of my forbears, Cecilia. Elben is the chosen land of Cernunnos. Yet we are small amidst the empires of Quisto and Capetia. Why should we not equal them, or even take them for our own?"

She raises an eyebrow. "Unless you imagine me picking up a sword, which I guarantee I shall not do, I do not see how this could possibly benefit me."

Henry's smile is almost a sneer. "Then you lack imagination, sister. I will need loyal lords and ladies, dukes and duchesses to keep the empire under Elbenese control. Why should not you take an entire country for your own dominion?"

The thought takes root in her heart, a little thorn that bleeds victory. She throws her arms around Henry's neck and holds him there, rocking back and forth in her excitement. "Oh, brother, I knew you would not disappoint me. I'm going to be a queen again!"

CHAPTER FIFTY-THREE

Cleves

The mountains of Heahmore are like daggers and swords, each one a battle, together a war. Cleves has no energy for anything beyond the journey. She has blisters inside and out – on her feet, her hands, her heart. It is a quiet misery.

As they climb and dip, climb and dip, taking paths that they are never certain are true paths, the wind rakes at their faces until their skin is peeling and raw. They barely speak. At night, frozen and hungry, they satiate themselves on each other in the absence of food, and it is never enough, for Cleves knows that when they reach Mathmas, she must extricate herself from Seymour. It will be for the best for both of them.

As the sun sets on their third day in the mountains, they reach an isolated town. The buildings loom over the street, as if they are about to topple onto the vendors who sell their wares from makeshift stalls. Cleves notes the lack of beggars, the way that while there is poverty here, there is little evidence of famine. She nods to herself: that is no easy feat to manage in a territory such as Mathmas, where little grows. Mindful of how recognisable Lelij is, she gathers the gargoyle into her arms and hides him beneath her cloak. His trembling warmth steadies her.

They pass a shelter, which must once have been a cowshed or some such, where a group of children crowd around a fire, sipping at warm milk and examining a pamphlet under the tutelage of a young Feorwan.

"They are teaching them to read," Seymour whispers. "Is that permitted?"

"It is not," Cleves says. The women smile at each other. Only the nobility, religious men and certain professions are allowed an education of this nature. Certainly these people would not qualify. This is undoubtedly Queen Parr's doing. Cleves has barely spoken to her; she is usually so reserved. Now, though, she could almost look forward to spending more time with her.

At the end of the town, the road leads towards the cliffs, and the distant towers of the Castle of Mathmas can be glimpsed through the fog that hangs constantly this high up. They may as well be in the clouds.

"Should we go directly there?" Seymour says.

"Not without warning," Cleves says, and leads Seymour over to a young woman selling good brown bread which makes Cleves's stomach growl.

"Can you tell me where the blacksmith might be found?" she asks. The woman eyes her curiously. "You have no horses," she says.

"It is not his services we seek. His mother was an old friend of mine."

This seems to satisfy her, and she directs them to an alleyway off the high street. They hear the sound of metal on metal and see the sparks flying long before they reach the blacksmith. The man is bent over a short knife, the blade black and sharp, and Cleves remembers something her master of horse once told her about black heat: it is the most deceptive moment of forging, when the metal looks cool but is hot enough to kill with a touch. They wait at a distance, feeling the heat seep into their warmth-starved limbs. Eventually, the blacksmith straightens. He examines them both, then nods to the door behind him, which must lead into his home.

"She's been expecting you," is all he says.

Seymour looks at Cleves uncertainly. Cleves leads the way, ducking beneath the low doorway into a simple, single-roomed hovel. She hates that she cannot stop herself from being constantly aware of Seymour's presence, as if she is one of her organs.

A doll lies on a wooden table, which is covered in the marks and stains of hard use. There is a ladder at one side of the space, which leads up to a loft, and it is here that she spies movement. A young, pale face peers down at her. The girl is not yet two, but already has a shock of red hair and a pretty scattering of freckles across her cheeks, which is tight and curious. Seymour follows Cleves's gaze and gasps.

"Is that—?"

"You have come then," another voice says from their left. An older woman, her skin a few shades lighter than Seymour's, stands upright in the doorway. One of her hands is holding a crop of purple carrots. The other rests on the head of a rather magnificent silver dragon.

"Good morrow, Mistress Syndony," Cleves says. Lelij pops his head out from beneath her cloak and chirrups at the dragon.

Seymour is clutching her chest, looking between the two women and the Princess Elizabeth. Cleves smiles tightly at her. "Did you think I would employ anything less than the best for my spy network?"

Syndony closes the door firmly behind her. She looks up at Elizabeth. "You can come down, Bess; they are friends," she says. With a steadiness belying her young age, the girl climbs carefully down the ladder and toddles over to them, looking up at Cleves and Seymour as if she were a judge and they accused of some crime. Cleves kneels and holds out her hand in greeting. It has been some time since she conversed with someone so young, but something about this child makes her think she is equal to it. Elizabeth examines her hand, then takes it in her own and shakes it firmly.

"In my country we say '*Gretal*', when we greet a stranger," Cleves says.

"Gret-al," Elizabeth repeats haltingly.

"Very good. *Hichoprac bool, missat crene*," Cleves says. "That means, 'Well met, little princess'."

Elizabeth stares at her. Syndony coughs. "Yes, well, she is not yet two, and I have not had the means to teach her all the languages yet."

"How long have you been in contact with each other?" Seymour says. Syndony and Cleves do not look at each other. How can Cleves admit that Syndony has been in her employ for many years, since the year she became Queen of Cnothan, in fact? Seeing that she will not get a straight answer, Seymour asks Cleves another question: "Why did you not tell any of us when we were concerned for the princess?"

"I had to place Mistress Syndony's safety above all else. I was not certain that the other queens could be trusted."

"And what of the last few weeks, when it has just been us?" Seymour says, her voice rising. Cleves looks at the floor, her stomach writhing. Syndony picks Elizabeth up, jostling her in her arms. "I take it you'd like me to get word to Queen Parr of your arrival?" she asks, ignoring the tension.

"Yes, mistress," Cleves says.

"Give me a few hours. You may wait here. I'll have my nephew fetch you some food."

Cleves and Seymour sink into the chairs beside the table as Syndony leaves with Elizabeth. The dragon, Urial, nuzzles Cleves's hand, perhaps remembering that it was she who bred him, perhaps simply recognising a lover of animals. Lelij chirrups again from Cleves's lap, warning the dragon off from his mistress.

The silence stretches out between them until the blacksmith appears with cheese, a pot of honey still on its comb and some hard wafers studded with seeds and herbs. Their hunger overcoming all else, the women smother the wafers with soft goat's cheese and drizzle honey on top.

Cleves takes a bite and leans back in her chair.

"Well," she says, trying to lighten the mood, "I had to give you something to be angry at me about, or what would happen to us?"

"Why do you do that?" Seymour says.

"Do what?"

"Turn everything into a jape? Act as if nothing matters?"

Cleves does not have an answer.

"Not everything has to be serious," she says.

Seymour throws her hands up in frustration, wafer seeds spilling to the table. "There is so much that is going on in your head and you will not tell me even half of it."

"You may have my body and my desire, but to lay claim to my thoughts is too much, my lady," Cleves says. How dare Seymour try to prise her open, to lay bare the innermost workings of her mind, when she has revealed nothing of her own heart?

"Why is it too much?" Seymour says. "Do you not love me?"

Cleves loses her breath. She flounders and Seymour, seeing this, presses her point. "Well? Do you, or not?"

Cleves will not lie to her, but she cannot admit the truth either. So she says the worst thing she could say: "Well, you do not love me, so . . ."

She does not know what point she is trying to make, only that she absolutely must divert the conversation. Damn her obsession, damn that moment Seymour tore her skirt with the crone's tooth and tore through Cleves's defences at the same time. Seymour has gone very still, and very soft, as though someone has punctured her.

"If that is what you believe, then I do not know why I am here," she says. She stands, gathering one final wafer and a large slice of cheese.

"Where are you going?" Cleves says.

"To find Syndony," is the terse reply. Seymour pauses at the door. "For all that you claim to despise her, you and Cecilia Tudor are very alike. She too will do anything rather than admit the truth of her heart."

"Just because I am wise enough not to declare my weaknesses for all to see does not make me like that woman," Cleves says.

Seymour smiles sadly. "It is a weakness, is it?"

If Cleves thought she could not feel smaller, she was wrong. She wants to kiss Seymour, she wants to press her against that doorway and make her never leave. But most of all, Cleves wants to run. The *thud thud* of the soldier's steps is thumping through her head so hard that she barely hears Seymour's parting words: "I think I am cursed to love women who can never love me back."

The next moment, she is gone, the door closing gently behind her.

Cleves closes her eyes, tightening and loosening her hands until the thumping recedes. When she has control of herself again, she shrugs, smiles ruefully, though no one can witness it. Well, it had to end when they reached Mathmas anyway. They will be friends by and by. It is for the best. She deposits Lelij on the floor beside her, stretches her legs out, pulls a blanket over her lap, and takes another wafer. Syndony will be back soon, and they will visit Parr and finalise their plan. This is what is important. They will defeat Henry, kill him, and she will go back to Cnothan and continue her life as she always has. Perfectly content.

She does not notice that she is crying until she tastes salt in the honey.

CHAPTER FIFTY-FOUR

Cecilia

Cecilia never ventures into sanctuaries unless she cannot help it. They have always made her uneasy, even when she was a young girl when her only god was her father and the law of his word. They are too full of judgement; they make her want to shout merely to hear something. They are empty, and they make her worry that there is an emptiness inside her.

But once Henry has promised her a throne of her own, she finds she must know precisely how he is planning on securing it for her. And that means spending time with the man who has her heart, and who she no longer seems to know at all.

"Your knees will be ground to dust," she says, as she strides into the sanctuary and finds More, predictably, praying before Cernunnos's altar. She holds her chin high, daring the god to strike her down. *You hold no fear for me any longer, upstart and interloper.* She thrills at even thinking the blasphemy.

More tilts his head so she can see him smiling. "We all return to dust eventually."

"That is cheery," she says, sitting beside him, her back to the altar. She sees the disapproval flickering in More's eyes and grins.

"You do not have to always be so contrary, my dear," he says. "We will admire your spirit even if you occasionally behave properly."

"But then how shall I needle you all?"

More allows Cecilia to lift him to his feet. If he were not so stoic, he would be groaning in discomfort.

"What is wrong with you?" she asks.

"Do not worry about me."

"I'm not worried about you; I'm impatient," she lies. "What is going on in this palace? Henry says Cromwell has found something in your library, something that will win him an empire, but everyone is keeping tight-lipped about what that entails."

"They say nothing because it does not concern you," More says, leaning on Cecilia as he lowers himself into a pew.

Cecilia prods him. "If it concerns my family, it concerns me. What are all of you boring old men doing?"

More raises an eyebrow. "I thought I was not such an old man."

"Answer me."

More squeezes her hand. "Lord Highfather, Mistress Boleyn did not cause me so much trouble."

Cecilia lets that statement hang in the air, not because she is shocked or offended, but because both of them know that it is dangerous to utter such words. Boleyn, though Cecilia barely remembers her from her court in Capetia, can never be spoken of unless it is to condemn her as a traitor and witch.

"You liked her," Cecilia says.

"No," More replies quickly.

"Admired her, then."

"She was difficult."

"You like difficult women."

"I most certainly do not."

"You like me."

"You are different."

Cecilia feels a sudden rush of affection for this old man. She grasps his hand, the skin paper-thin and flaking like dandruff. Normally, she would never deign to touch such skin, but More is right – she and he have always held special places in each other's regard.

"You were always very patient with me," she says.

"Well, you had plenty of impatience from other areas."

They do not speak of her father. They do not speak of Arthur.

"What is happening here?" Cecilia says. Her voice is quiet but she uses the words like little needles, each one a stab, telling More that she is not going to give up until she has answers.

"My dear . . ." he says, his eyes closing. She is going to press her point further until she realises he is shaking. The movement is so slight at first that she barely notices it, assuming it is some part of his ageing condition.

"My lord?" she says, her hand tightening around his.

The shaking intensifies, until his entire arm is shuddering and the only fixed point is her grip. His eyes are closed, his mouth stretched open in a grimace of pain.

"What is happening?" she says, louder.

"Leave me, Cecilia," he manages to whisper through clenched teeth.

With anyone else, she would have been out of the door already, but she feels a foreign flare of panic for someone other than herself.

"Help!" she shouts. "Someone fetch help!"

More's grip on her hand is now so strong that her bones crack beneath the pressure, but she does not cry out for herself. His free hand claws at the back of his neck, and at the exposed skin on his arm which is already red-raw and covered in scars, barely healed. She tries to block him with her body. "No, no, stop that, you imbecile," she says. Inside she is a drowning child in a frothing sea. "Help!" she shouts again.

There is a commotion beyond the narrow world of her existence, which features only her and the agony of this dear man. Then strong arms are pulling her away. Someone else – Cromwell and one of his men – work to prise More's hand from her grip, and she shrieks, unsure if she is shrieking because of the pain from her broken hand or from the fury of being manhandled.

"Leave him be," a voice says close to her ear. "My lady, leave him be. Cromwell will take care of him."

"Cromwell hates him. Cromwell will kill him!" she shouts, not caring that the man can hear her. Brandon's arms are still pulling her away, gripped around her waist as she struggles against them like a feral cat. Cromwell does not look up from his ministrations of More when he says, "I can assure Your Majesty that I mean your tutor no harm. I will ensure he receives the help he needs."

"What is wrong with him? You will tell me, sir," she says, as Brandon drags her out of the sanctuary and into the quiet chamber beyond. Usually this space is filled with supplicants, waiting their turn to make confession, but now it is empty but for Cecilia and her captor. She finally breaks free and whirls round to face him. Charles Brandon looks, for the first time in her memory, earnest.

"What is wrong with the bishop?" she says again, battling to control her panic.

"You need not worry about him," he tells her, hands splayed.

"Does my brother know he is ill?" she says.

"Of course he does. As I said, it is all in hand. Please, Cecilia. He is not ill. He is on . . . a journey."

Brandon guides her to a seat at the corner of the room. She would not usually follow him, except her legs are unaccountably unstable. She sinks onto the bench and gathers herself, the muscles and bones in her neck tightening and straining. Brandon sits beside her.

"What kind of journey?" she says.

"Ah, princess . . ."

"Stop calling me that."

"Are you not a princess, princess?"

"I am a dowager queen, and I will hurt you."

"I would enjoy that."

She springs from the seat, pinching herself to stop the tears. She will never allow anyone to see her weep. Brandon places a gentle hand upon her shoulder.

"I am sorry you witnessed one of Bishop More's episodes. They can be alarming at first, but I assure you that they have been occurring for some time, and we have them under control."

"It is something divine, is it not?" she says. She cannot comprehend any other reason More would allow his body to change thus. When it comes to Cernunnos, he has never known anything but martyrdom.

"You always were sharp as a pin."

"I am right, then."

"Your brother cannot know I've told you."

"You've told me nothing. I guessed."

He squeezes her shoulder. "You understand the divine power better than most, don't you? Strange, given you're a rather heathen woman. Well, you know that it always costs mortals to meddle with divinity. The bishop is willing to pay that cost."

She must return to her rooms then, although she does not remember the journey, only that she is staring out of the window at the hunting grounds and, beyond that, the Tower. *It always costs mortals to meddle with divinity. More is willing to pay that price.* She knows from her conversations with Seymour that the queens, too, are paying the price, willingly or otherwise.

What cost did it extract from her cold-eyed father?

And what cost does it extract from the brother who once saved her? Would he save her still?

CHAPTER FIFTY-FIVE

Cleves

Syndony escorts them into the Palace of Mathmas under the cover of a full moon. They take the narrow alleyways that run parallel to the main street of the town, where only stray dogs, stray wild dragons and rats move at this time of night, foraging through the detritus of the day. Cleves is thankful for the need for silence. Seymour has barely spoken to her since returning with Syndony, arms full of fennel and a pigeon carcass. Cleves had attempted to lighten the thickness in the room as they plucked the bird, but Seymour had not smiled, and Syndony, head bowed over a needle as she mended some of Elizabeth's clothes, had raised her eyebrows but not her head. Cleves wonders whether they spoke about her at all, or whether Syndony was merely reacting to the mood. She does not mind. If Seymour is going to play childish games, then Cleves has no time for her. It only reinforces Cleves's knowledge that their relationship was never tenable.

The alleyway dwindles into a dirt track which runs up the mountainside, the kind of steep, uneven ground that goats take, their hooves more suited to navigating the sheer drop on one side than Cleves's boots. If she had been as starved as she was when she arrived in the town that morning, she might have been tempted to sink to the dirt and refuse to go on, but with smoked pigeon in her stomach, she is almost equal to the trudge.

At the base of Mathmas's outer walls, the path climbs up over a series of rocky steps, ending at the gatehouse and two forbidding, studded oak doors. A smaller door is set into them, and on this Syndony knocks four times. Immediately a bolt is drawn back from the other side and the door is opened. Cleves follows Syndony into a square, cobbled courtyard.

Lanterns line the walls. The moonlight already gives the courtyard an ethereal quality, and the soft light from the lanterns adds to it. Honeysuckle climbs the stone, reaching into every nook, its winding branches swelling to a thick trunk on the far side of the space. Despite the season, it is already flowering, and Cleves spies the occasional fairy darting in and out of the blossoms, selecting the finest petals for their nests. Lelij gambols after them, already at home here.

Everywhere else she looks, Cleves sees practicality and function. The centre of the courtyard houses not a fountain or a statue, but a covered well. Great wooden tubs are filled with fruiting trees and herbs rather than roses, and the alcoves house not statues but painted calculations. Cleves examines the closest one: it details the amount of grain the castle holds in storage.

Cleves and Seymour follow Syndony into one of the halls that leads off the courtyard. Queen Parr waits inside, dressed in a simple, deep blue velvet gown with an embroidered hem of silver flowers. She comes towards them, her smile slight, her hands crossed over her stomacher.

Before she addresses the two queens, she turns to Syndony, and bows her head in respect. "Thank you, my lady," she says. Syndony bobs a curtsey and, with a nod to Cleves and Seymour, takes her leave. As she passes Cleves, Cleves is sure she hears Syndony mutter, "Foolish." Then she is gone.

Cleves turns to Parr, keen to take control of the situation. This may be Parr's castle, and she has no intention of superseding her authority within Mathmas's walls, but Parr needs to understand that just because Cleves is homeless for now, she still deserves respect. She cannot quite articulate why it is so important for her to do this. She has a sense that she has lost Seymour's goodwill, as well as her home, and she needs to find a sure footing.

"There is much for us to discuss," she says. "You must have heard news from High Hall? Do they have an inkling of where we are?"

Parr's smile is a riddle. "You both must be exhausted after your long journey. The Heahmore mountains are unforgiving for those on foot. Permit me to show you to your bedrooms, and we can talk more in the morning. You need not fear my household. I keep few and they are all in my confidence."

Another queen who has trusted people around her. Cleves only had Johana, for the briefest time.

"I would rather speak now, in the privacy afforded by night," Cleves says.

"I will be happy to take some rest," Seymour says, stepping forward. "If you would please show me to my room, sister?"

"Of course." Parr leads Seymour out. Cleves waits, determined not to follow them. She walks the circumference of the hall, examining the huge paintings whose paint is flaking, injured by the salt of the sea air. She sometimes has the same issues at Cnothan; all the coastal castles do.

Parr returns before long, just as Cleves is examining a portrait of one of the former queens of Mathmas. The most famous one, if Cleves is not mistaken – she knew of her even before her engagement to Henry caused her to study the history of Elben. In her studies, the woman was described as a fierce force, but to Cleves's eyes this woman looks entirely submissive. The portrait shows her sitting, a small dog in her lap and her hand placed on a pile of religious texts. *I am humble, loyal and true to the faith*, the portrait is saying. There is nothing fierce about that.

Parr stops just behind her.

"She was a widow, like you, I think," Cleves says, nodding at the painting.

"She already had three sons from her union with her first husband. I suppose that made her more appealing to the king."

The unspoken lands between them: unlike Parr, who was widowed twice before becoming queen, and remains childless. Not even a rumour of pregnancy to sustain her reputation. Cleves dares to ask the question she probably should not; if they are to work together, they must understand each other, and Cleves finds it difficult to understand one such as Parr.

"Do you wonder why our husband chose you, then?"

Parr shifts.

"I look the very part of humble, loyal and true, do I not?"

"Yet here you are, plotting rebellion with his least favoured of wives." Cleves finds the thought amusing. Parr evidently does so too, for she moves forward to stand beside her, still looking up at the portrait.

"Oh, I don't know. I suspect my other queenly guest could challenge you."

Cleves barks a laugh.

"I wonder where we rank alongside Boleyn."

They turn away from the portrait and walk to the long table in the centre of the hall, sitting at one end. Cleves finds herself at once charmed by this woman, and also angry with her. She is so stoic in her sadness, and it is making Cleves want to bend in the opposite direction. She doesn't understand where this anger of hers is coming from: she never used to be angry, even when she was being humiliated. She has not been this angry since . . . well, since she was a child. And now all of this. Seymour, damn the woman, has turned her into a fishwife.

As if hearing her thoughts, Queen Parr extends a hand across the oak, stopping short of touching her. "Queen Seymour seems out of sorts tonight," she says. Cleves wants to make a joke about *my angry queen*, but that would imply a familiarity that is no longer present.

"I think it is hard not to be out of sorts when one has fled by foot across half of Elben with no clean clothes and even less food," she says.

"Is that the reason?"

"Is it not a good reason?" Cleves leans back in her chair and crosses her legs.

"You barely looked at each other tonight," Parr observes. She is staring at Cleves with those direct eyes, so light a brown they are almost glassy. Cleves crosses her arms too.

"Despite Queen Boleyn's best efforts, I do not think any of us are truly united, no?"

Parr nods slowly, accepting that Cleves will not be drawn into discussing her feelings for Seymour. "No, and that is our failing, although I have turned our plan over and over in my head. It is sound."

"The most important thing is to gain the binding cloths," Cleves says.

"All is in hand," Parr says. "Now that you and Seymour are here, we should work through the final details."

Cleves shakes her head. "Not now Cecilia has Seymour's *sunscína.* We cannot be certain that the king has not worked out a way of using it."

"We must all meet in person, then," Parr says.

They lapse into silence. Cleves thinks of Seymour, so close and yet an ocean away. Then her thoughts stray to Johana, and the way he held her hand at the end. She coughs, adjusting her seat. The portraits of the former queens of Mathmas seem to judge her.

"Did you ever consider returning to Ezzonid?" Parr says.

"No, of course not." But even as she says it, Cleves does wonder why she never seriously considered this option. She could just as easily have boarded a ship at Cnothan. Instead she rode unthinkingly into greater danger, greater hardship, with Seymour.

"Hmm," Parr says, casting her eyes up to the patterned ceiling.

Cleves laughs. "All you Elbenese women are so reticent. You do so enjoy making sounds instead of using your words."

Parr's smile is arch. "You have words enough for all of us when it comes to Queen Aragon."

"Well, Quisto and Ezzonid are enemies of old; you cannot expect us to be too civil."

"Then we come back to my previous question: if Ezzonid is your country, why did you not return to it?"

"You did not strike me as one of those who would be unwelcoming to foreigners, sister," Cleves says. She is on surer footing now, jousting with barbed jests.

"Not unwelcoming. You simply puzzle me, Queen Cleves. I cannot make out your motivations for joining Boleyn's cause."

Cleves shrugs. The tale of the phoenix was for Johana alone, for he alone understood it. "I might ask the same of you and Aragon."

"You might. But I asked first."

Cleves stretches her arms in a mockery of exhaustion, and rises. "Forgive me, sister, but I do find myself tired after all. May I trouble you to show me to a bed?"

Parr leads her to a chamber in the west wing of the castle, a building built into the promontory of the cliff face which looks out across the ocean to Quisto's eastern empire and the great tundra of Pkolack. It isn't lost on Cleves that she has been placed in one of the most remote rooms – for all that Parr has apparently told her household of their aims, she perhaps does not trust them as much as she has made out. Still, the room is comfortable enough: the bed is covered with a precious dragon hide that should do more to keep out the northern chill than any wool or fur. Parr shows her a secret latch above the mantelpiece, which opens a chute at one side of the fireplace.

"This is an old escape route," she tells Cleves. "If Mathmas should be taken, you can flee through here and out onto the cliff face. It is not an easy journey, and the fall is perilous, but it may be better than the alternative."

Cleves nods. Parr leaves her to sleep, even though the sun is stretching purple fingers over the horizon. At the door, Parr pauses, looking at the floor.

"Queen Seymour is in the room next door," she says, casually.

"I see," Cleves says, her defences rising at the implication. Parr sighs, then turns fully to face Cleves. "There was a man I knew when I was younger. I loved him deeply. So deeply it drove me to distraction. And it drove me to terror too. He was, is . . . not a wise choice. So I ran – into three different marriages."

Parr runs a hand down the side of the doorway, as if wishing she could reach through time to counsel her younger self. When she looks back at Cleves, that small, sad smile has returned. "It did not bring me happiness or comfort to run away, Queen Cleves. And I have been running for so very long, certain that duty would heal this pit in my soul where he should be. You ask my reason for joining Boleyn's cause? That is my reason, meagre though it may be. I join for my twenty-year-old self, and the hope she voluntarily extinguished. If I could speak to her, I would say . . ." She stops, throat clogged.

Cleves finishes the sentence: "That sometimes it is better to fall off a cliff edge than to remain inside the castle?"

They stare at each other, the threads between them forming knots of understanding.

"Exactly," Parr breathes. Then she is gone, and Cleves is all alone.

PART THREE

CHAPTER FIFTY-SIX

My Lord Cromwell,

As you directed, I have been paying close attention to the correspondence between our queens. I am happy to say that there has been nothing to report of late. Queen Howard seems isolated. Her letters are all to her degenerate father stationed abroad and the great-aunt who was her guardian, as well as some missives to old friends. She mentions a fear that the traitor of Cnothan will make an attempt upon her, and asks her relatives for advice on how to comfort our king, but that is all.

The Queens Aragon and Parr appear to have had some disagreement, the cause of which I cannot fathom, but their usual manner of writing to each other regularly has become more stilted. I trust that this will be welcome news to Your Grace.

Your faithful servant,
Nicholas of Mearreth

Nicholas,

Provide me with a comprehensive overview of the letters and items sent to the queens from other parties, if you please. And continue to monitor any letters containing mention of the heretical religion.

Cromwell

My Lord Cromwell,

The number of gifts sent to the remaining queens of Elben is negligible, having been in decline for the past several moons. Undoubtedly, all wish to demonstrate their loyalty to our beloved king. Queen Aragon continues to receive small trinkets from her nephew in Quisto: an assortment of spices, very beautifully packaged in gilt silver pots; a guirnalda made with fairy pearls; a roll of fine blue damask set about with bright sapphires.

The only other gifts of note were three embroidered cushions sent to Queens Aragon, Parr and Howard from a lesser noble in Gkontai. The cushions bear the same motif: a songbird picked out entirely in silver silk in the centre, with a border of alternating pomegranates and roses. My men examined these gifts at the dock in Brinhafn but I can find no record of a ship from Gkontai that arrived that day. I have enclosed a faithful rendition of the motif, but my men could see nothing else untoward and therefore no reason not to permit them to be delivered.

You faithful servant,
Nicholas of Mearreth

Nicholas,

I see no need to trouble me with intelligence of crafted items featuring birds and flowers. Exercise better judgement in the future.

Cromwell

His Majesty Henry, eighth of his name, Ruler of the Eternal and Divine Kingdom of Elben and Defender of Cernunnos, hereby invites you to the five-hundredth

MOON BALL

To be held at the great palace of High Hall

A celebration of our great god and our queens, humble, loyal and true, who wield the bordweal by the grace of His Majesty and god.

CHAPTER FIFTY-SEVEN

Howard

When a songbird first flies, it is stuttering. Howard has watched the fledglings perched on the edge of the nest they were born in, their mother nearby, tweeting impatiently for them to fall. Howard once spent a full morning watching those nesting on the windowsill outside her room pluck up the courage to take their first flights. There were six of them in total, the shells from which they hatched long since eaten, their nest filled with white faeces. First one, then another, took flight, their little wings unused to catching the currents. The third took longer, and when it jumped, for a brief moment Howard thought it wasn't going to survive, as it plummeted out of view. But there, a second later, she spied it fluttering up to the branch where its siblings and mother sat. She thought, by the time the sixth leapt, that they would all make it. That there was something in a bird's memory, perhaps from its ancestors, that told it exactly how to make that first leap.

The little body lay at the base of the house for days as rats and wasps made a feast of its bones.

Howard is not sure whether she is still perched on the edge of the nest, whether she is plummeting without an idea of how to beat her wings or whether she is flying, uncertain, towards the branch that means safety.

Her ladies are all a flutter too. Gone are the conversations about who is courting whom, of which gown is the most beautiful (it is always Howard's), of which music they are to dance to before supper. Ursula now openly reads her book of Hleaw prayer, a horseshoe of rapt ladies kneeling around her.

That is how Florin finds them, when he comes with the gift.

"This was sent to you from a duke of Gkontai," he says, handing her a parcel wrapped in silk.

"Why?" Legh says. Lady Tylney tuts at her, but Legh shrugs. "I do not mean it like *that*, only that Howard has never received anything from anyone there before."

"Maybe they wish to form an alliance," Ursula says, setting aside her prayer book.

Howard opens the letter that accompanies the gift. Voda Kelaverinn would be proud at how she sounds out the characters.

To Her Majesty Queen Howard of Plythe, of the great Kingdom of Elben,

Hearing of your great beauty and your preference for the finest of fabrics, His Excellency the Duke Vinoft of the twelfth district of Gkontai sends you this cushion from his most perfect craftsmen. He begs Your Majesty to recommend him to your great and kingly husband, and remains,

Yours faithfully.

"He merely wants me to broker some favour with Henry," Howard says, feeling a little bereft as she turns to the present itself.

"Oh, how horrible," Legh says. For once, no one contradicts her.

The embroidery is poorly done; anyone with the smallest knowledge of the craft can see that. The songbird is uneven and the fabric bunches at the corners.

"Does this duke from Gkontai despise you?" Legh says, as she and the ladies pass the cushion round. It is an appalling misuse of such expensive thread. Florin peers over Lady Tylney's shoulder. "I do not understand. What is wrong with it? It is obviously a bird."

Ursula shoots him a withering look. "If you had practised embroidery for even a year, you would recognise how bad this is."

Howard looks up, her worries that she had inadvertently displeased Gkontai dissipating.

"Someone bring me a knife."

"Are you planning on killing someone else, Your Majesty?" Susanna teases, but Howard only grabs the cushion from her, running her hand over the bird, seeing if she can prise it apart with her nails. Ursula hands her a penknife, and she drives the point beneath the thread.

"It is not *that* bad," Lady Tylney says.

Howard saws at the motif until the threads break. Florin whistles quietly. For sewn tightly between image and the velvet base is a further piece of embroidery on simple linen. This embroidery is far finer, the work of a practised hand:

Five remain. Sanctuary of the Blessed Litavis on the fifth day of the seventh moon.

Howard laughs. *Five remain.* That must mean that Cleves and Seymour have reached Mathmas safely: five queens are still loyal to Medren.

Florin is staring at her with his mouth open.

"Do women do such things often?" he asks.

She is about to say, *No, but we ought to,* and then she remembers what Cleves said to her at the last Moon Ball. "Perhaps not exactly like this, but in a hundred other ways, yes."

Florin nods and turns away thoughtfully.

"The fifth day of the seventh moon is only a few nights before the Moon Ball," Lady Tylney says.

"Where is this sanctuary anyway?" Legh asks.

"It is in Mathmas," Ursula says. "Well, it is near the intersection of Mathmas, Daven and Plythe."

Howard smiles at her. She had been about to call for a map of Elben. "Do you have family near it?" she asks.

Ursula shakes her head. "It is a ruin. It was once a holy place for the Hleaws, before it was razed by King Ricard in one of his holy purges. I read about it."

Howard reaches for Ursula's hand, looking round as her ladies begin to plan how they might be able to transport her in secret to the sanctuary and then on to High Hall for the ball without Cromwell's agents getting wind of it. Yes, sometimes trust is earned, and sometimes it is gifted, and sometimes it is both.

CHAPTER FIFTY-EIGHT

Cecilia

The palace is transformed into a place of jubilation. Garlands of spun gold are strung from beam to beam. The doorways are decorated with flowers from the wild meadows of the Nameless Lands, conveyed at great cost of life and coin from the unknown reaches of the world. Wine spouts from every fountain. Musicians prepare their performances in every public chamber.

Nowhere is quiet, and yet nowhere is louder than Cecilia's mind. She trips from room to room, admiring the craftsmanship, taunting the servants, and yet there is a listlessness to her that she cannot shake.

So when, one night, she is woken from her slumber by an uproar, she thinks it must have been a dream. When the sound comes again through the darkness, her second assumption is that a lantern dragon has escaped its cage. They did so often when she was a child, and she always loved to see if she could capture the creatures before the servants did. It was amusing to pull their wings to make their light turn from gold to shimmering blue, a natural consequence of their pain.

The child within her awakening, she reaches for a robe and pulls it around her nightshift to ward off the miserable Elben chill which permeates even the most well-insulated palaces at night. As she pads to the door and presses her ear to it, someone in a far-off passage says, "Wake the king immediately!" It might be Cromwell, although she has never heard panic in his voice before.

The spark of intrigue is truly alight within her now. She slips out of her rooms and follows the sound of servants, delighting in the strangeness of High Hall at night and thanking any god who might hear that her rooms are so close to the centre of the palace, for if she had been lodged in one of the queens' wings, she would not have heard the commotion.

It is only as she gets closer to the noise that a hint of unease seeps in. That cry, halfway between groan and roar, like oak toppling.

It is the sound of a crone, she swears it. The creatures may move almost silently, but when they have the bloodlust upon them, they can be loud.

The sound comes again from just above her, from the sanctuary itself. Cecilia pauses, wondering whether she should return to her rooms and barricade herself in, when she hears human voices. Her brother's voice. More's voice.

No one could convince her to place herself in the way of a crone but those two men. Footstep by footstep, she forces herself onwards. They do not seem to be alarmed.

The sanctuary door is ajar. She peers inside, but can see no monster. More is draped across the altar. His back is bare, great welts striping it. They seem to move across his skin, but it must be a trick of the shadows. Henry and Cromwell are hunched over him, muttering words of comfort. To one side stands Charles Brandon, watching impassively.

Cromwell looks over his shoulder. "Close the door, if you please, my lord."

Brandon scowls at being given an order by an upstart like Cromwell, but does as he's told. Cecilia ducks back, but not quickly enough. She freezes before Brandon's stare.

Brandon hesitates, then presses a finger to his lips and closes the door a little, leaving the thinnest of cracks for her to listen through. She has a sudden, vertiginous memory of twenty years ago, of listening at this exact same door to the sound of their father being informed of his eldest son's death. Cecilia was not yet ten. The catch in their father's throat as he turned to Henry and said, "You are my heir now, my son. There is much you must learn. Much you must accept if you are to rule Elben peaceably."

And Henry, in a small, high voice, had replied, "I will make you proud, Father. You and Arthur."

She digs her fingernails into her palms and concentrates on the present.

"It is not working," Henry says.

"I just need a little longer—" Cromwell begins.

Before he can finish, Henry flies at him, taking Cromwell by the neck and pinning him against the sanctuary wall. Cromwell does not claw at his hold as most would. His feet dangle from the floor: he is being choked, and he does nothing to prevent it. Cecilia covers her mouth. There's a burst of divine power, running all the way from Henry's chest, down his arm and into his hand, and a spurt of blood erupts from Cromwell's neck.

Cecilia throws herself away from the sight, pressing herself against a wall for support. She has never minded blood. She has extracted enough in her time. But the expression upon Henry's face – that she cannot shake.

Cecilia wills herself to simply listen. She does not need to look as well.

There's a thud as something heavy crumples to the floor, and then laboured movements.

"Do you need a physician, my lord?" Henry says. His voice is gentle, as it was when they were children. When he came to her and proposed marrying her to the ageing king of Capetia. How can her sweet brother hold such gentleness and such violence so close to each other?

"No, Your Majesty, I will be quite well," Cromwell says, though his voice is hoarse.

"The ball is approaching. I must have them by then."

"My tests are proving fruitful," Cromwell says. "If you will only permit me to accelerate them, then I believe we can bring the matter to a head."

Cecilia gets the sense that the others are uneasy about Cromwell's assertion.

"I have witnessed the process," Brandon says. "It is extreme."

There's the sound of uneven footsteps: Henry's, Cecilia assumes, since he is the only one with a limp.

"My friend, are you strong enough?" he asks someone.

"If the Highfather wills it, my body will withstand," More replies eventually.

Brandon makes a strangled noise in the back of his throat, as Cromwell says, "Very well. Shall we begin tonight?"

"No," Henry says, his voice thick. "Let the bishop rest. You can begin at first light."

"You will not watch?" Cromwell says.

"No," Henry says. "You understand, dear friend?"

"Perfectly, Your Majesty," More replies. Cecilia stifles a sob, though she does not know why.

She presses into the shadows as Henry strides out of the sanctuary. She will wait until More is alone and then plead with him not to go through with whatever terrible experiment Cromwell is inflicting upon him. No one is worth such pain, not even the king of Elben. Not even a god. But Cromwell, that crow of foresight, says, "I will accompany you to your rooms, my lord, and have my men stand guard to ensure you sleep well. We must see that you have strength enough for what is to come. I would hate to see you brought low in the pursuit of such good work for our king and country."

"That is unnecessary, I assure you."

"Nevertheless, we cannot be too cautious. I know you have many supplicants, and I would not want them to wake you before it is time."

It's a lie. More does have supplicants, but none who would plead with him so early. Cecilia edges closer to the open door, debating whether to simply erupt into the room and drag More to safety herself. If she had been in Perfugi still, in her own place of power, she would have done. But High Hall is different. Something about this place has made Cecilia Tudor uncertain. By the time she has convinced herself to do it, Cromwell and More have left out of the other entrance, taking the quickest route to More's rooms.

Brandon comes to her.

"Do you have your answers now?"

"You piece of shit," she hisses, pushing him because she cannot punish herself. He catches her arms and pins them to her sides. "What if he dies?" she says.

"Then he ascends."

She spits at him. Still, he holds her arms. She stands on tiptoes and bites his cheek, leaving deep crescents in the flesh around his beard. Brandon growls. She wants him to backhand her, so she will have an excuse to push her nails into his eyes. But when he speaks, his whisper is gentle.

"What is more important to you? That queendom your brother promised you, or the well-being of an old man who does not value his mortal body? Think, Cecilia. Put these ridiculous emotions aside and think."

She still struggles in his grasp, but the weight of his words is heavy and dangerous and calming.

She stifles a sob against his chest.

"He is the only one I truly care about," she whispers into the fabric.

"I know. That is why I wanted you to hear him. He's doing this for you as well. He wants you to have your queendom."

She looks up at him and swallows the lie, relishing its sweetness even though she knows it is rotten. What would she even do anyway? She could never persuade More to anything, just as he could never persuade her.

"Take me to my rooms," she says. He picks her up, cradling her against his chest as he marches down to the fourth level. Perhaps there is something to be said for the strength and confidence of older men.

Inside her chamber, he lays her on her bed. Her robe falls open, revealing her shift, and before he can move away she grabs his hair and pushes his head between her legs. He makes a sound of surprise but attends to her obediently. She maintains her grip on his hair, as she used to do with Florin, and squeezes whenever the thought of what might happen to More intrudes upon her pleasure.

She has him attend to her until she falls asleep, sated. She never sees More alive again.

CHAPTER FIFTY-NINE

Cleves

It takes three days, avoiding the scrind road, to reach the borders of Mathmas and the island's central estates. Parr's household rests at one of her noble's estates to make the final preparations for their entrance to the Moon Ball. Parr, Cleves and Seymour, however, ride at dawn on the fifth day of the seventh moon for the Sanctuary of the Blessed Litavis.

"The stories say that it was built by the Medrenkynd who came before the Hleaws," Parr tells Cleves as they ride. "The site is at the confluence of three of the most bountiful parts of Elben. People would bring their harvests to share with those from the more destitute regions on the night of the divine moon."

"The night we now hold the Moon Ball," Cleves says.

Parr purses her lips. "They did not just steal our power. They could not even trouble themselves to create their own celebrations."

They emerge from heather and gorse into a peaceful, flat and flowered glade. In the centre of the open space is a ramshackle tower with several narrow wings branching out from its base, and so many windows Cleves feels as though she is being watched by a great spider. The old plaster is crumbling and the stone is blackened from the fire that was meant to destroy it, but for a place that is so rarely used and with such history, it is in remarkable condition.

A scattering of horses and servants already populates the space, and one comes forward to take their horses as they dismount. Cleves glances over at Seymour, who has been silent their whole journey. She is speaking in a low voice to Parr. Cleves is not insecure, but she cannot help but wonder whether they are discussing her.

"Shall we go in then?" she says, striding ahead of them.

The doors of the sanctuary open into a wide hall from which several passageways lead off. What must have once been a grand spiral staircase leading up into the tower crumbles into charcoal not five steps up. The place is devoid of furniture or decoration, yet it still feels oddly occupied, as if the spirits of long-ago communes still roam the stone floors.

"Through here," a voice says from a doorway at the far side. Cleves follows it into the central place of worship. A dozen people turn to face them. At the head of the room is Queen Aragon, on a wheeled throne, her daughter, the Princess Tudor, standing on her right. Howard is dressed regally in a gown of gold silk, more structured than the flowing gowns she used to favour. Behind her stand two of her ladies. There are a handful of others: trusted servants, and a few representatives of the Feorwa Isles, here at Seymour's invitation.

Howard's smile when she sees Cleves is bright. At least one queen is still pleased to see her.

She takes a seat opposite Queen Aragon, twitching her rather bedraggled riding skirt into its proper place. Seymour and Parr take their places, and finally Syndony leads Princess Elizabeth to the last chair. Cleves notes the way Aragon and the Princess Tudor watch the little girl, with a hunger Cleves does not like.

"Now we are all finally here, perhaps we can begin," Queen Aragon says, dragging her eyes away from the child.

"Won't your king be suspicious? All his queens disappeared from their households?" one of the Feorwans says.

"One of my ladies-in-waiting is a passable mimic of me. She has taken my place in my absence," Aragon says.

"My mother receives few visitors these days," Princess Tudor adds, "so it is really only about having a presence . . ."

"Hush," Aragon says, and the princess falls silent. The girl looks to the floor. Admitting her mother is no longer in favour with the nobility of Elben, or is too much an invalid to receive guests, will not be something Aragon would want this company to know. Cleves almost feels sorry for her.

"I am visiting my Lady Tylney's family estate. She is in my confidence," Howard says.

Parr raises an eyebrow. "And I live at Mathmas." There is general laughter at this: there is a reason Cleves and Seymour fled there. It is the most unreachable and easily defendable of the queens' castles.

"Very well," Aragon says. "Let us—"

Cleves holds up a hand. She is teetering on the edge of a precipice. "May I speak a few words before we begin, sister?" she says.

Aragon looks as though she might object, but then she bows her head. "Of course, Queen Cleves. The floor is yours for as long as you need it."

It is the most gracious thing Aragon has ever said to her.

She stands. What she is about to say is too important for a throne.

"I have been accused of being reticent," she begins. She looks at each of the queens in turn, ensuring that she has their attention. She comes, last of all, to Seymour, and from her she does not look away.

"Perhaps I have been wary. I have wanted us to examine our plans before acting hastily. Many of you have been frustrated with me. I can understand that. But I hope that once I am finished speaking, you will understand me better too.

"Some of you may have heard of the *Tilhepf* – the Unrest?" she continues. "I was seven. My father had just inherited the throne from his uncle, who was not a popular ruler. There was another noble, a very charismatic duke, who had an old claim to the throne through his maternal line, and he saw a chance to take the crown of Ezzonid."

"The civil war," Howard says softly.

"Yes, well, these things happen sometimes, as we know," Cleves says, shrugging. Inwardly, she chides herself. She should not make light of this, even if sincerity makes the memories more painful.

"It was . . ." Cleves closes her eyes, but that only makes the images more vivid. Maybe that's what she needs. She has spent so long packing them away, burying them deep inside herself, and now they are rising, rising, like bloated bodies in a lake. "We moved a lot. From place to place. The tide between the two forces – my father's and the duke's – kept switching. The battle-lines kept being redrawn, sometimes so suddenly that we would be woken from our sleep in order to flee to safety, because the lodge we were staying in was about to be overrun. Our allies changed constantly, so I never knew whether the lord who was hosting us would attempt to turn us over to the duke after supper.

"Sometimes my parents would leave us with one noble or other, so that we stood a chance of escaping should they be captured. But for the most part, my sister and cousins and I went where they went. My brother insisted upon fighting. I suppose it was his own inheritance he was fighting for."

She breathes out. There is more that she could tell them about the soldiers' boots and their laughter, but that is a story to be whispered, not declaimed.

"My point is that though our claim is sound, though Henry is the interloper, we are about to plunge Elben into civil war. Deposing a king is never clean, and it is never without bloodshed. Songs are sung of the Massacre of Pilvreen. Think of the songs they will sing about what is to come, and tell me I am wrong to be reticent."

Silence falls across the space. A glittering silence that fills the building with dread. Cleves tips her head back and stares up at the rafters. In that moment, she can sense the history of the building. It was indeed a holy place, for what is a holy place but a space where grief and joy can exist together in the presence of awe?

Parr stands. She takes Cleves's hands, squeezes them, then turns to the others. She addresses not their fellow monarchs, but those standing behind them. "What Queen Cleves has so bravely said affects all of us, but we queens have the most to gain from victory. I believe that our way forward can only be accomplished with the blessing of those who will not win a throne. It is not too late for us to change course: we could all of us flee Elben, and leave it to Henry and Cernunnos."

Aragon stirs. "You may flee, but I shall not. My daughter is owed her inheritance."

Cleves wonders whether she knows that those are the words Boleyn might well have spoken were she still alive.

One of the Feorwans – taller and broader than Clarice next to them – steps forward. "We will throw in our lot with you, in the hope of a kinder future for our lands. You talk of bloodshed, Queen Cleves: Elben may have been free of it under the king's rule, but Feorwa has seen plenty."

Cleves suspects that less bloodshed is not all they hope for. A weakened Elben in the wake of a civil war will, after all, be less able to keep hold of their colonies. This is a play for independence. While the royal in her may baulk, the part of her that has sought for so long to build her own little fortress understands only too well.

Syndony raises a hand next, commanding attention with that simple gesture as though she too were a queen. "My childhood was spent in the worst kind of penury. I have no parents, for they left me on the steps of a sanctuary when I was a babe. I learned at a tender age that Cernunnos is not merciful. I learned that nobility is not either, unless it can wring something from you. I found work as a washerwoman at Brynd, and I listened and I learned. I bore children and I raised them and I taught them to listen and to learn also. Forty years later, I became stewardess of Brynd, and not once did I hold any loyalty in my heart to anyone but my own family."

Princess Elizabeth looks up at her. "Then mother."

"That is right, little princess," Syndony says, her voice softening. "Then I met your mother. My point is, you have asked." Cleves cannot ever imagine Syndony weeping, but the woman is blazing with unshed emotion now. "You have asked, Queen Parr, Queen Cleves, as Queen Boleyn chose to ride to her death rather than force her people to fight for her. *That* secures my loyalty, and the loyalty of my people."

The glittering stillness is with them, around them once more. Cleves can almost taste it – the feeling of the phoenix and its majesty, the sunlit glory of that memory.

"Well," she says, her throat thick. "If we are agreed, then I have one final suggestion to make."

"Go on," Syndony says.

Cleves swallows. "We must let Henry find out that Seymour and I will be at High Hall."

She raises her hands to quell the inevitable protests. "Listen to me, I beg of you. When Seymour and I almost killed Henry, he was triumphant at having found us out. I think it has become an obsession of his to prove that he will not be hoodwinked again by any of his wives."

Aragon nods. "I can see that being true."

Cleves continues: "We have fed him a believable lie about the binding cloths. He believes that spilling our lifeblood upon the cloths will secure his theft of Medren's power. He has believed it because it appears to place us in great danger."

"It does place us in great danger," Aragon says. "If all does not go to plan, we all of us will have our throats cut before the nobility of Elben."

"But he also knows that we need the binding cloths in order to separate ourselves from him. He will be at his most insecure that night," Cleves says. "The weakest part of our plan is that Seymour and I have no clear way of getting to our own cloths. We merely hoped that we would be able to reach them once the others are brought to the banqueting hall. But what if we were standing beside all of you? What if Mistress Syndony found a way of letting Cromwell know that Seymour and I are planning to infiltrate the ball in order to steal them?"

Parr seems to trace the plan with her fingers. "We make Henry think that he has triumphed. He thinks that the divine power will be entirely his with each queenly throat he cuts. He is already desperate to capture you both for your treachery. That desperation will blind him to our deceit."

Howard leans forward. "I do not know if it is a double deception or a triple deception, but either way, I think it will work."

Everyone turns towards Seymour. "If you say no, then it shall be a no," Cleves says.

She cannot riddle Seymour's expression. It is pregnant with . . . what? Praise? Desire? Whatever it is, she finds no doubt in it.

"It is a good plan," Seymour says eventually.

Aragon taps the armrest of her throne. "Very well. We should all be returning to our households. We have already tarried too long."

"Wait," Howard says. She trips into the centre of the circle. "I do not care if you think it silly. I want us all to take hands before we leave this place. The next time we see each other will be at High Hall and on the brink of victory or despair. But in this place of all places we ought to recognise our sisterhood."

Cleves readily takes her hand. When did their little songbird grow so bold as to command her fellow queens? One by one, the others follow. Parr, and then Seymour, facing Cleves in the circle. And finally, her chair pushed by the Princess Tudor, Aragon. She grips Cleves's remaining hand with iron strength.

"Five united," Cleves says, echoing the oracle's words that brought Boleyn to their doors. She thinks of Mary, to the east of the island, in her lonely castle at Brynd. Poor, deluded woman, to set herself apart in such a way by betraying her own sister and denying the goddess who could give her so much more than a castle and a mere consort's crown.

"Goddess. Medren," Howard says, her eyes closed. "If you can hear me, shine your favour upon us. Know that we work to free you, and to return your land to you."

The answer is almost instant. Aragon flinches, utters a little, "Oh". To the rest of them, who have felt the divine power before, it is surprising but not shocking.

Cleves laughs to see the light – its purple-green-blue joined by oranges and pinks – dancing across her skin. Whenever she has witnessed Henry using his divine power, it has always seemed too raw, too *childish*. This feeling flowing through her is neither gentle nor aggressive.

To Cleves, it is the inevitability of the seasons – snowfall and the unfurling of spring. To Howard, it is the tumble of Goldfoot through the air. For Seymour, it is the muted roar of the ocean, or a waterfall. Parr feels it in her core, a burst of ecstasy the like of which she has only experienced once in her girlhood with a man of charming danger. And Aragon? For Aragon it is a silent predator, like the *gealgena* dragon housed inside the great tree at Daven, feeding and sustaining, feasting and sustaining.

CHAPTER SIXTY

Cecilia

She is not so frightening, and yet there is something about being a *woman* who is considered frightening that makes her doubly so. Not so much to other women – Seymour and Cleves showed that – but to men. They make so much of her intimidations. It fascinates them.

"You will let me through," she says to the men who guard her brother's rooms on the utmost floor of High Hall. She bares her teeth at them like a feral dog. Their eyes widen even as they smirk and bow and withdraw their crossed spears to permit her entry. Such simple creatures.

Henry is elsewhere in the palace. She tries not to wonder whether he is with Bishop More, or whatever is left of him. Wherever he is, it suits her well, for she has other business in his rooms. She does not go rifling through his belongings as she might have done. No – she knows exactly where the object of her desire lies.

The book is where it was the last time she was here, at the far end of the room. Her father used to tell them that it took a dozen monks' lifetimes to copy out the holy text and illustrate it with mother-of-pearl paint and gold leaf.

Its stiff leather shell bears no title. Its only decoration is a stylised pair of Cernunnos's horns etched into the front cover. She almost loses her nerve as the memories crowd upon her. If she was a weaker woman, she might turn around and run back to her own chambers and crawl beneath her covers, trembling. But she is not weak. She is the strongest of women, forged in Capetia and Perfugi and the royal lore of Elben.

With one finger, she flicks open the cover. The pages have been hollowed out – all those lifetimes' work, excised. There is nothing inside the hollow.

Before she left her rooms, she secreted her strongest, fiercest needle in her gown pocket. She produces it now and holds it up to the little dragon furled in its glass cage on the wall above the book. The needle's point is too sharp to be seen clearly, but the thicker end is carved into a snake's head. It is an ancient artefact once belonging to the royalty of a long-forgotten country somewhere in the region of Lothair, smuggled out and bought at great cost. A fitting weapon to destroy the treasured possession of a long-dead brother, he who might have been king.

She brings the needle down upon the book, seeking to rend the leather, to destroy it utterly. A hand blocks hers, grabbing her wrist.

"You should not be in here, sister," Henry says.

He looks tired. His whole body is angled to one side, as though it pains him to put weight on one of his legs.

"Why have you kept it, Henry?" she says. She puts as much weight as she can into the hand holding the needle, so that if he slackens even a little, she will have her victory.

"You cannot go around destroying anything you fancy," he says.

"Why is it here, in your room?" she says. If she had been in Henry's position, even if she could not have destroyed the book entirely, she'd have locked it up in some chest in the furthest reaches of High Hall.

Henry pulls her arm away from the book and, with his free hand, manhandles the needle from her grasp. The force he uses is not quite painful, but it is inevitable.

"These are my rooms. This is my palace. I can keep what I like and I don't answer to anyone, least of all you, Cecilia."

"What does that mean, *least of all me*?" Why is he acting as though she is a nuisance? He adores her, his youngest and most charming sister.

Henry rubs his face and mutters something under his breath. Then he says more loudly, "What do you want? I have had a long day."

"I want my needle back."

"Are you going to use it to destroy my belongings?"

She chews on her bottom lip.

"I thought as much," he says, and pockets the needle.

Two chairs are arranged next to the grandest of the windows, and beside them a platter of marchpane and two fine vases of wine sit on a table. Henry takes one seat and invites her to take the other.

"How can you have anything of his in your rooms?" she says. The chair is comfortable, and she makes a show of making herself comfortable in it, leaning back, crossing her ankles and propping them up on the table. Henry's expression tightens.

"It was a long time ago, Cecilia. Why can't you let it go?"

Why can't she let it go? There are a hundred answers she could show him, dotted across her skin, but he does not deserve any of them. Instead, she takes his right hand and turns it over so that the inside of his wrist is visible. And there it is, the thin ridge of a scar, easily dismissed as a natural wrinkle rather than a puckered mending from a seventeen-year-old's knife.

She presses the line so his skin blanches. Henry stares at the scar. She cannot read his thoughts as she once could. His eyes are more lidded than they used to be, the lines beneath them deeper.

"You are tired, brother," she says.

"I . . ." He swallows. Then he extricates himself from her grasp, leans forward and rests his head in his hands. Cecilia draws back, her hands hovering near him. Her brother has never done this before. She has never seen him unsure. Weak. She is reminded, briefly, of Florin crawling along the floor, worm-like, and she has to stop her lip from curling.

"When Father told me . . ." he begins again. Cecilia stills. She knows what he is thinking of – the night, a little while after Arthur died, when Henry came to her sobbing and apologising, though he would not tell her for what he was sorry.

"We are in the right," he says. "Father explained it all. If we were not in the right, our god would not have triumphed over *her*."

Cecilia nods, reaches for his hand. In truth, she doesn't understand all of this wretched introspection and doubt. What does it matter who is "right"? What does "right" signify? What value does it have?

"You told me that you would be better to me, and to Aragon, than Arthur was," she reminds him.

"And I have been. I have taken care of all of you."

Her stomach clenches. For the first time, she thinks: *You married me off to a foreign king. You took care of yourself and your alliances, not me.* But that is soft, weak thinking. She has spent too much time with Seymour, who does not understand how monarchs must act.

"What do you want from me, Cecilia?"

She licks her lips. What *does* she want? Her brother. More. Brandon as a gift, chained to her bed. The queendom she was promised.

"Will you hold me, as you used to?" is what she says.

Almost imperceptibly, he recoils. "We are not children any more. Arthur isn't here."

A shiver runs all the way up her arms and neck. A voice, not her own, whispers, *Oh, but he is.*

"Please?"

It's disgusting, the way she has reverted to pleading. Those moons in captivity turned Cecilia from queen to supplicant. Another thing that is Seymour's fault – Seymour and her panther. But when Henry opens his arms, she climbs into his lap and curls up there. Their old ritual, when they were both at High Hall and Arthur was on one of his rampages. Henry would hold her, and soothe her, and she would fall asleep understanding safety.

She is too grown to fit as she once did. His arms are bulky, not wiry. The divine power cools her skin. She is too old, and she has seen too much. She closes her eyes tight. Tudors do not weep.

"Did you really come here to destroy the book, sister?" Henry says. His voice vibrates through his chest. He chuckles. "You can see it's empty. The knives and scalds were smelted long ago."

How can she explain that the book's very presence in his rooms is an ill omen? *His* shadow is cast across the whole space, as if that empty book had expanded and filled the room with all the horrors it once contained.

"I know," she says.

She wants to ask him what is happening to More. She wants to ask him – *what is happening to her?* – to show mercy to his queens. She almost does ask him.

The divine power flickers down his arm. There is something irrefutably *goddess* about the playfulness of that strength. How did she never see and question it before? She holds out her hand, wondering whether the power might jump to her. Henry shifts. Her body hollows out. Though he tried to mask it, she knows – he does not want her near his stolen power. He does not want her near him.

CHAPTER SIXTY-ONE

Cleves

They travel in near silence, joining the large groups making their way to High Hall for the festivities. The journey is more muted than Cleves remembers from previous years. This will be her sixth Moon Ball. Despite her determination to never be too impressed by her new country, she still remembers the feelings of awe inspired by every one. The Elbenese may be a strange people, but she cannot deny that they understand pomp, especially when it comes to their monarchs. Even the most committed enemy of Elben could not fail to by moved by the Moon Balls' spectacle.

None of them compared to last year's, and Boleyn's daring display of truth. In that moment, she understood why Seymour loved the woman. She understood that she herself could be more than simply the Queen of Cnothan. She was seduced by both idea and ideal. Fool that she was. Is.

Cleves also knows that when a monarch is threatened, they will do their utmost to give the impression of ultimate power. So it is with this year's Moon Ball. Despite the anxiety that hangs over those travelling to High Hall, from the nobility with their trains of carts, to the hired performers and the cooks and salesmen hawking their wares, it becomes clear that this ball is going to be the greatest in Elben's history.

And if Cleves and the queens have their say, then it will be the most memorable. Possibly even the last.

For the first time in her life, Cleves does not enjoy her solitude during the journey. With Lelij stowed safely back at Mathmas in the care of Parr's household, she is truly alone for the first time in her life. It had never occurred to her before that she was not a recluse by nature. She had merely replaced people with animals.

They stop on the outskirts of the palace's grounds, in sight of Cleves's own old wing, which is just visible above the manicured orchards of her gardens. Here there is a makeshift village set up next to a small fishing lake, where aspiring performers prepare. Beside the tents, people take turns bathing in large wooden butts filled with warm water boiled from a local stream. She washes herself in one such bath, then – while the rest of the makeshift camp sleeps – she lights a candle and sets to work on herself.

Her glasses are put to one side. She warms curling irons on the candle and sets her hair into waves. Her telltale Ezzonid blouse is folded away in a bag and she dresses in Elben's more fashionable full gown and sleeves. When she has finished, she sits back and stares at herself in the hand mirror, her face clouded.

"There," she says. "You do not look like yourself at all."

Does she feel like herself? She no longer knows. The Cleves who was a fixed point would not be in this position. She once prided herself on being unapologetic. Yet – was that her, or was it her armour? Is this Cleves, the one who feels so raw, so open and so wounded – was this the real Cleves all along?

There is one more thing she must do.

Seymour's tent is on the other side of the encampment, and there is still a candle burning inside. Cleves stands outside it for what seems like an age, listening to the other woman moving around inside. It is only when the bells of High Hall toll midnight that Cleves summons the courage to approach.

"I hardly recognise you," Seymour says when she sees Cleves.

"I want to tell you something," Cleves says, her back stiff, her face stiffer.

Seymour moves aside for Cleves to enter. The tent is bare except for a travelling bag and a thin mattress that can be rolled up and secured on the back. A lone candle flickers in one corner.

"What do you wish to tell me?" Seymour says, securing the tent shut and sitting on one end of the mattress. There is space for Cleves on the other end, but she has not been given permission.

Cleves is used to saying whatever will swing the balance of power in her favour. She has a quip or a soft little barb for anything and anyone, king or commoner. But that's not what she must do here. If she wants Seymour – and oh, how she wants her – then she must hand that power over to her, willingly, in gilded paper.

"There is something that I did not tell the others at the Sanctuary of Litavis," she says.

"I know," Seymour replies. "You went to a memory, at the end, and your face shuttered."

Cleves's shoulders curve inwards.

"I have never spoken about this with anyone. Not even my siblings or my parents or Johana."

"I understand." Seymour is giving her permission to speak or be silent.

To speak would expose her soul, stabbed and bleeding, and invite further injuries. To be silent would strengthen the wall, fix her cement. Stand, or leap?

"One night during the *Tilhep*f, we were not quick enough to flee," she says. She holds Seymour's gaze; a reminder of why she is doing this. "The duke's soldiers came upon the house where we were staying and rounded up my family in the banqueting hall. I did not know it at the time, but my father's troops were on their way. He only needed to buy us time. The soldiers taunted him and Mother, telling them how they were going to kill my sister and me in front of them."

Seymour takes Cleves's hands and kisses her knuckles. Cleves wants her to tell her not to go on.

"My father laughed at them. He told them that my sister and I were worth nothing to him. My mother joined in, made some comment about having girls that made the soldiers laugh. Soon, they were exchanging quips – barbed, still dangerous, but the soldiers were less likely to kill us. They said they would wait for the duke to arrive and give them orders. It bought us enough time."

"So the soldiers did not . . .?"

"Not to me," Cleves says. She does not mention the other bargain her mother made with the soldiers, or the sounds Cleves was forced to hear from the antechamber next to the banqueting hall, and how she grew to understand what they meant as she learned about the different violences that people could enact upon one another. That is not Cleves's anguish to share.

"It was all a ploy, of course," Cleves says. "But it worked. My parents told us, once we were safe again, that it was an act. That act saved our lives that night. It was a lesson to me, and I have never forgotten it."

Seymour smooths a stray lock of hair away from Cleves's face. She kisses the teardrop clinging to Cleves's eyelash. "I am not a soldier," she whispers.

She kisses Cleves's cheek. "I am not going to hurt you."

She kisses Cleves's mouth, long and soft. "If you want me, I am yours. But if you want me, you must be mine too."

Cleves makes a sound in the back of her throat, her hands tightening around Seymour's waist. She starts to cry in earnest then, great wracking sobs that she cannot hide. Seymour cradles her head to her chest. Cleves is making Seymour's bodice wet, but she cannot stop. Twenty-five years of tears are pouring out of her, and she cannot find the right joke to make them subside. All she can do is bury her face against the woman she loves, like a drowning sailor clinging to driftwood.

Seymour lets her cry until she feels wrung out. When Cleves can command her words again, she wipes her nose on the back of her hand and says in a thick voice, "My apologies. I felt the lake outside was looking a little dry."

Seymour chuckles. "You are doing it again."

"Well, we cannot both be angry queens."

"Not all the time, no."

Cleves looks up at the woman who has endured so much hardship and yet is still able to hand her heart to another so freely, knowing that it might be crushed. Cleves runs a hand down Seymour's beautiful, beautiful cheek, her brown skin peppered with darker freckles.

"There is something else I came here to do," she says.

Seymour raises an eyebrow. "That is very forward of you."

"Not *that*."

Cleves dips a hand into her pocket and pulls out the little cushion Johana gave to her in his dying moments. The phoenix feathers that cap each dress pin glimmer in the candlelight.

"Do you know what these are?" she says.

Seymour shakes her head. Her hand hovers over the pins, not daring to touch them. "I saw them and knew they were precious, but you did not wish to talk about them."

Cleves tells Seymour about the phoenix, about the tradition of the royal family of Ezzonid, and how her sister Sybil was granted a single, priceless feather.

"I did not know what she had done with it until I saw these," Cleves explains. "I imagine it was my mother's idea. She always had a talent for making precious things appear worthless."

She and Seymour possess hundreds of dress pins, of course. Even the lowliest of nobles do. Even a peasant might own a dozen, for pinning coifs and hoods or securing belts. Those on the hunt for a feather of mighty power would look to brooches, or rings – not a common dress pin, intended to be invisible.

"Now I see where you get your own talent for disguise," Seymour says.

Cleves touches the tips of the phoenix feathers, feeling the warmth radiating from them. More than a decade separated from the bird, and they still have something of its heat.

"There is an old tale told about phoenix feathers, in my country," she says. "No one knows if it is true, of course. Probably it is not."

"Tell me."

"It is said that they who wear the feather of a phoenix in its entirety, freely given by bird or hand, shall never come to harm."

She tips the cushion into Seymour's palm. Seymour catches her breath.

"Cleves, no—"

"Your life is worth more to me than anything else."

The cushion lays there on Seymour's open palm, as though she is afraid to claim it.

"I have already lost one woman I loved," Seymour says. "And my love for her is nothing compared to my love for you. What would I do if . . .?"

Cleves wipes away her tears. "You will continue to shine, Seymour. You and your brightness. It blinds me."

Seymour rubs her cheek against Cleves's hand. "A sun cannot blind another sun."

Cleves's heart skips a beat.

"My angry queen. You could rip me to shreds."

Seymour claims her mouth, and there is no softness in it this time. This time, they are two dragons, marking their territory. Cleves tears at Seymour's bodice, then slips her hands beneath her shift and finds the spot that makes Seymour's legs buckle.

Seymour groans. "And you could burn me to ashes, my sunlit queen. Let us warm each other instead."

There are no more words. There is only their bodies. Parr was right. Boleyn was right. Sometimes, stepping over the cliff's edge is the only way to live.

CHAPTER SIXTY-TWO

Howard

Howard cannot remember the last time she said "no". She has acted "no" in myriad ways. She has spoken it with her body, with her eyes. But has she ever said it? She thinks not. It is a word of power.

The night before they make their final journey to High Hall, Howard finds herself wandering from room to room, staircase to staircase of the lodge where they are staying. She does not want to sleep. She wants to chase power. She needs to know she is capable before she sees Henry again.

Florin's room is at the very top of the lodge, beneath the eaves. When she knocks upon his door and he opens it, she can understand why he chose the space. It is a burrow, a cosy nook. It is safe. As far from the endless fury of the ocean, or a dowager queen, as can be.

"Katheryn?" he says, rubbing his eyes. "What is the matter?"

"We are not in love," she says, forcing the words out before she loses her nerve.

He stills. "No. We are not."

"But I find you attractive. And I feel safe around you."

The unspoken question hangs between them, until he steps back to allow her in. Florin closes the door softly, and softly he comes to her. Softly he traces her bare arm.

"You are safe, Katheryn. And I am safe with you."

"You are," she says.

She steps into his arms and cups his face. "Is this all right?" she asks.

"Yes." He leans towards her so that she can see his eyelashes. He pauses until she nods, and then his lips are against hers. He matches her but never escalates. *He is waiting for me,* she thinks, and a thrill runs through her. It might be lust, it might be the power of the goddess. She slips her tongue into his mouth and feels his hesitation. Although he says nothing to stop her, she recognises that tension. She pulls away.

"I am sorry. You are safe," she says.

Florin's eyes are wide. "I am sorry," he says. "I . . ."

"I know."

She moves away, ready to slip out of the room if he needs her to.

"Don't go, please," he says.

"I won't unless you want me to."

"Tell me what to do to please you," he says.

This is what Voda Kelaverinn meant, all those moons ago. Despite the lovers she took before she married, despite Henry's experience and Culpepper's confidence, no one has ever asked her that. They assumed things of her body, and she forced it to bend according to their pleasures. To bend until it cracked.

She laughs giddily. "I do not know," she says.

He understands sooner than most would. He smiles ruefully. "I do not know either."

They hold hands. Everything about the night is soft: the darkness, their skin, the pulsating power that is building between them.

"Tell me no, and I shall tell you no," she says. She kisses him again. It is the slowest, gentlest kiss she has ever experienced, and she feels as though she is melting into him. She wraps her arms around his neck, pulling him closer, wanting to share his warmth, his spirit. She thinks: *I have never kissed a boy my own age before.*

They kiss their way to the bed and sink onto it as one, cradling each other, neither one on top.

Usually, this would be the moment when her lovers would grow rougher. They would cover her, smother her, own her. She always thought it was a sign of their love, but Florin's tenderness is more potent. The way his hands stroke her whole body, not merely groping her breasts or buttocks, or pulling at her hair. She does not doubt his desire even though it is measured.

She has never been the one to instigate, but now she unbuttons his doublet and tugs at the shirt beneath so that she can feel his chest.

"Undress me," she says, relishing the command in her voice. She turns round, closing her eyes as his fingers go back and forth, loosening the strings. She steps out of her gown, dressed now only in her shift, and kisses him again. He sighs against her mouth, moaning as her hand dives inside his hose and takes hold of his manhood.

Something is wrong.

Her hand moves mechanically, as she was taught by her first lover when she was twelve. But in her head, all has gone still and silent.

"Howard, stop," Florin says. He pulls her hand out of his hose, then cocoons her in his arms. "Stop."

Feeling floods back, and with feeling, the shaking. She doesn't understand it. The last time she had this sensation was when Henry was on top of her, and she coped with it. She tries to take Florin in hand again. He will be angry with her if she stops. He will think her a prude, a temptress. She was the one who undressed him. How can she be so indecisive?

"You are safe, Howard," he whispers. "You are safe. You are safe."

She says, her voice very thin, "I'm sorry. I don't know . . . I just can't."

"Let us simply hold each other, if that is what you would prefer."

He pulls the blanket from the mattress and wraps it around her trembling shoulders. He kneels in front of her.

"You do not owe me anything, Katheryn, just as I owe you nothing but my respect. You can make all the promises in the world, but some promises must be broken."

Howard frowns. "It's not that I don't desire you. I do. I want to . . ." Warmth creeps up her neck. "I want to feel you inside me. But . . ."

"It is all right," he says again, smiling up at her. "We are safe together. You taught me that."

She holds up a hand, and Florin presses his palm against hers.

"Tell me again," she says.

"You are safe. You are safe. You are safe."

She kisses him again, shrugging the blanket from her shoulders so that he almost topples backwards. She straddles him as he kneels on the floor, tangling her hands in his lovely curls.

"Keep saying it," she whispers.

"You are safe, my queen."

Their words are not poetry, full of shifting meanings and hidden mires. Their language is solid; firm, open ground like the hills of

Plythe. She guides his hand to her breast, where his finger flicks across a nipple. Pleasure shoots through her, from breast to belly to groin.

"You are safe too," she says, running her hands over his chest.

"You are safe," he says, as she moves his hand down to dive beneath her shift. She does not want him to stop, but she must test him one last time. She must have one final proof that this night will not crack her further.

"No," she says, and he stops, his hand darting back immediately.

She moves his hose so she can see his hardness, and this time she locks eyes with him as she grasps him.

"You are safe," he says.

"And you are safe," she replies. They press their foreheads together as she guides him inside her. They stay still like that for a while, simply feeling the closeness of the other. As they begin to move, Howard marvels, light-headed. She never thought she could be aroused by a man who could control himself with her, but she has never been more aroused. *This*, she thinks, as she lets thought fly away, *is true coupling*. The night is full of the words of power. *No* and *yes* are handed back and forth between them like a needle, passing a thread through their wounds.

CHAPTER SIXTY-THREE

Cleves

They leave Seymour's tent at dawn, just as the rest of the camp is awakening. The first test will be whether the guards at High Hall's gates will permit them through. They go separately, so that if one of them is caught, the plan can continue. Guards line the perimeter walls, more than she has ever seen at High Hall.

Praying that Seymour manages to slip in behind her, Cleves makes her way towards the gate where the extra servants – those recruited outside High Hall to service the needs of the thousands of guests – are being given directions. A harried-looking man, officious but not unpleasant, stands on a podium clutching a long parchment and a quill, ticking off tasks as he assigns them. Cleves joins the queue of workers. Elben and its queues. She sighs. The person in front of her, a Feorwan sailor from the look of their cap and sandy hair, turns to her and grins. "What we do for a bit of coin, eh?" they say.

Cleves grunts in agreement, then chances a bit of conversation, masking her accent. "And a sight of the king, don't forget."

It is the Feorwan's turn to grunt now. They turn away, evidently deciding that someone loyal to the monarch of Elben is not worth further conversation. Cleves's heart beats with strange optimism. The Feorwans will make for good allies if they can be promised some independence. If Cleves harboured any doubts about weakening Elben's power in the wake of their presumed victory, those doubts are ebbing away. Theirs will be a different kind of might; one based in freedom, not control.

Oh no. She is becoming idealistic.

The Feorwan is assigned to latrine duty, and steps aside with a grimace. Cleves almost gives them a look of sympathy, for she has no doubt the task is mired in prejudice, but she cannot risk her own role. She bobs a curtsey to the foreman.

"What are your skills?" he says, peering at her over his glasses.

She bobs once more for good measure. "I can carry a good weight," she says.

"Hmm." He looks her over, his eyes lingering on the shadow of her arm muscles. The man nods. "Very well. Report to the kitchens."

Close enough. She will be able to slip into the maze of servant passageways easily from there, and they will be so busy that her absence should not be noticed for some time.

She keeps her eyes on the ground as she walks back along the line, only glancing up to note Seymour joining the back of the queue. Their eyes lock for the briefest of moments, and Cleves's hand brushes against Seymour's as she passes.

As she makes her way towards the door to the servants' entrance, she notes the colours of their tunics, indicating which queen they serve. Blue, white and gold. Aragon, Parr and Howard. They are all inside. The first part of their plan is in place.

The kitchens that serve the king and his guests stretch across the centre of the palace, with vents out to courtyards at each corner to allow smoke and smells to escape. The scent of roasting meat and bubbling gravy is overpowering. For the next few hours Cleves is occupied wholly in her new work, hefting bags of grain and fruit from pantries to the different cooks at their stations. She welcomes the distraction. As the light outside dims and the first fireworks are released, turning the night sky into a garden of many coloured blooms, the head cook shouts, "Places!" and the servants who will be ferrying dishes to the banqueting hall line up. Cleves ducks behind them and into one of the passageways leading to the wine cellars.

She has rehearsed the directions in her head a thousand times, but she still wishes she had Howard's memory as she makes her way through the twisting servants' staircases which lead up, up to the hall. When she hears the roar of the guests' conversation and the music of the entertainment, she breathes easily once more. She keeps her head down, stepping neatly to one side whenever she crosses paths with another servant, acting as though they are both far too busy with whatever work they are doing to question each other.

There is a nook at the top of the hall, behind and to one side of the minstrels' gallery, which is full of musicians. They play a royal tune: an Elbenese tune by an Elbenese composer. From this position, she can look down to the top table at the opposite end of the hall. There is Henry, sitting in the middle of a long line of subservient women. Cleves's eyes skate along them. At the last Moon Ball, each queen hosted her own table. This year Henry's dominance is asserted. There is Parr at one end, and Aragon at the other in her wheelchair, Princess Tudor by her side. Mary Boleyn is on Henry's right-hand side, Howard on his left with her little lapdragon, restored to his true colouring, draped around her shoulders, and Cecilia beside her. Cleves's hands clench in anticipation. There is nothing to suggest that their plan is going awry. All Cleves has to do is wait for the binding cloths to be produced, and then allow herself to be captured, if they have not already spotted her.

The eating is interminable. As she watches everyone stuff themselves, she begins to feel a little ill at the display of excess. Having so recently been near starving, the sight of so much food is revolting. By the time Henry raises a hand for silence, her legs are aching with the effort of standing still for so long. Cleves shakes some feeling back into them, and peers out once more to see if she can hear whatever lies her husband is going to use to manipulate his audience.

"My people," he says, standing up, his arms out. Cleves hates that when the room falls silent it is not because of any divine power, or his kingly birthright, but because of his natural charm. "My people," he says again, and his voice is quieter now, as though he is about to let them in on a secret. Even Aragon and Parr lean in.

"What a year we have endured," he says. He looks like a martyr. "Treason, heresy, our enemies amassing beyond and within our borders. I have tried to shoulder the burden of it all. I thank you for your faith in me." He pauses. Cleves's heart beats painfully. She has the strongest sense of being back in that castle, waiting for the men who had captured her family to decide their fates.

"The Moon Ball is a celebration of Elben's queens." Henry raises an eyebrow, and the hall titters. There are only four queens to celebrate, and it is clever of him to acknowledge the irony. It reflects his humiliation onto those who have humiliated him; onto the queens who as far as he knows remain faithful to him. Mary Boleyn smiles, attempting to share in the laughter. Aragon and Parr look stoically forward. Howard, though: Howard is watching their husband like a hawk. How could Cleves have ever thought her dull?

"Nay, nay," Henry continues. "We should celebrate our queens. And tonight we must celebrate them even more, for I have a great favour to ask of them. A favour that will secure them in history as the saviours of Elben."

The whisper that flows around the hall at this is an icy wind. None of the queens sitting at the high table betray any shock beyond a tensing of muscles. When Henry turns to them now, he holds each of their gazes one by one, testing their fealty.

Charles Brandon nods to one of Henry's men, and they duck out of the room. This is it. She tears herself away from her hiding spot and makes her way down the passageway.

She can hear Henry in the hall beyond, talking about loyalty, about the old edict of "humble, loyal and true" that has been used for centuries to deny the queens their own powers. By the time Cleves has secreted herself in a nook near the dais, Henry has come to his point. Cleves grips the wall, peering out, waiting for the moment when the box containing the binding cloths must be produced.

He turns to Howard, Mary, Parr and Aragon. Cleves's eyes are not drawn to them, though, but to his sister Cecilia. When Cleves met her, she was vibrant, taller than her natural height, vicious in a rather charming way. Now, though, she looks as if she is masking exhaustion. There is something brittle about her.

Cleves hears Seymour join her, delighting in the fact that she knew it was her from the softness of her movement. She is wearing a simple gown, the frontlet and headpiece secured with pins that gleam with tips of umber and gold. Cleves leans into her as they watch the proceedings. Seymour squeezes Cleves's waist.

Henry continues: "All know that the bordweal weakens thanks to the treachery of three of my queens. One of those queens is dead. The remaining two are living still."

He pauses, then turns to face her and Seymour, as though he has traced her journey from kitchens to gallery to dais all along. Perhaps he has. "And here they are," he says, holding a hand towards the two of them as if inviting them to a dance. She feels someone approach from behind, and pretends to attempt an escape. Charles Brandon catches her around the waist, and someone else takes Seymour.

So, let it begin.

CHAPTER SIXTY-FOUR

Howard

Howard schools her features as Cleves and Seymour are thrust, still struggling, before her table. She must be the rose without a thorn for a little longer. A smooth and pretty object with fragile petals. Something to be consumed, smelled, plucked and displayed. Something with no way to protect itself from such treatment. Something with no other purpose.

Henry struts towards the two captured queens. His limp is barely visible, the bandage that must be around his thigh covered with hose of gold velvet.

Lord Brandon pushes Cleves to her knees, and Henry stands over her.

"Queen Cleves, if I had known you could look like this . . ." He raises eyebrows at the assembled courtiers, enjoying their laughter. Their gaze rakes across Cleves's body. She holds her head high, and Howard tries not to let the pride show on her face.

Cleves smiles up at Henry. "Even if I had looked like this all along, I would still have found a way to avoid your touch, husband."

Henry flushes. Cleves does not need to detail her deceit on their wedding night. All she needs to do is sow questions in the guests' minds. Sometimes questions can be more destructive than answers.

"It matters not," Henry says, attempting to regain his audience. He has not even glanced at Seymour: she is beneath even his words.

Cromwell, at one corner of the hall, begins to clap. The sound catches, and soon every courtier is applauding the arrests of the two traitor queens. Howard joins in, clapping more loudly than anyone else. Henry bows. "Here is the start of the remedy!" he shouts. Quiet resumes.

"There is a way to bolster the bordweal. To ensure the survival of Elben and of our people. A way to end the unrest in our great kingdom. I have given all I can to protect you," Henry says. "Now it is time for my queens to do their duty."

Howard grips the arms of her chair, steadying herself.

"How may we serve you, Your Majesty?" Mary Boleyn says.

"Not me: Elben."

"My apologies."

Henry goes to her, kissing the back of her hand as a sign of his forgiveness for her error.

"I can be stronger," he says. "I can channel more of the divine power. But Cernunnos requires a sign of loyalty from my queens."

Here it is.

"The blood of a Queen of Elben, spilt upon the binding cloth that ties her to me, and thereby to Cernunnos, will multiply my power tenfold. A hundredfold. Elben will be invincible."

A stunned silence descends upon the hall. Not even Henry's most loyal advisors can look up from the floor. Howard glances across at his sister. Cecilia is very still. No one, no one apart from Henry, is enjoying this moment.

Henry looks to the dais where his loyal queens are seated. "You know I love you all, my darling wives. But I am a king first and foremost. It is my duty to love my country more than life itself. Will you make this greatest of sacrifices for our kingdom?"

The very floorboards seem to hold a breath. There is no air in the hall.

This is her moment.

Howard forces herself to her feet. "I will be glad to serve my country and my king, Your Majesty."

Parr stands next. "My life's work is to be useful in all that I do. What greater use can I offer than this?"

Aragon takes Princess Tudor's hand, gripping it tightly as she says from her seat, "As the first and most loyal of your queens, it is only right that I humble myself to further the glory of you and our country, my husband."

Howard looks to Mary Boleyn, the only one of them who has not prepared for this moment. Her sister was always the paler of them, but now Mary is ashen. She was always the more substantial of the sisters, but now she is ghostly. Her eyes flick from Henry to two children who stand among the guests, their fine cloth of gold garments marking them as royal children. Mary's children, from her first marriage, made royal through her second. At last, she stands. "Whatever you wish, Your Majesty," is all she is able to utter. What a price to pay for a few moons of queenship.

Howard is led into a line. Cleves is pushed to her right, Parr to her left. Lord Wolsey, old and shaking, emerges bearing a tray of six boxes. The boxes containing the binding cloths. Cleves cannot take her eyes off them, and Henry notices. He sneers, comes close to her so that only she and Howard can hear. "You thought you could steal yours, did you? I knew you would attempt it. Once again, I have outsmarted you, my lady. And the most delightful part of it is that your brother has washed his hands of you. Your death will not even be mourned in your own putrid country. My people will piss upon your grave, as they piss upon Isabet's."

Howard has to stop herself from laughing. Powerful men and their need to be right. It makes them so very short-sighted. Howard cannot quite believe that she once thought him the cleverest man in the world.

The boxes are opened, one by one, and the velvet binding cloths are pulled from their innards and tied around the queens' necks. Aragon's is so old that it bears almost no resemblance to the vivid purple of Mary Boleyn and Seymour's cloths.

In the rafters above them Goldfoot, set loose from his mistress, lets out a mournful cry. Howard does not dare look at him lest it betray their secret, but she takes comfort from Cleves's presence beside her. She thinks of their conversation at the last Moon Ball. Of the simple sentence that made Howard laugh delightedly.

Come, sister. Do not let them see that you are more than your beauty. It will confuse them.

She will not let them see. She is a little queen and a mighty songbird. She will keep her wings furled until the last moment.

Henry's eyes are wet. There is nothing performative about it. As they all realised long ago, he believes himself a loving husband. He believes that what he must do for the sake of the kingdom is his sacrifice as much as theirs.

Cromwell hands him a silver knife, the blade glinting in dragonlight. Henry holds it loosely, and Howard cannot work out whether he is genuinely doubting what he thinks he must do. Maybe even he knows that if he kills all his queens – including those who he believes to be faithful – he will never again be able to see himself as a good husband.

"Your Majesty, may I beg you to take me first?" Howard says. Her voice is tremulous, the perfect pitch of sweet and terrified. Men like Henry tend to fall in love with a voice like that. Henry looks at her in astonishment.

"My queen? You wish for this?" he says.

"I am ashamed to say it, my liege, but I am scared that if I am not first I will not hold my mettle. I will humiliate myself."

Keep those wings furled.

Henry nods, crying freely now. He kisses her, long and hungrily. Goldfoot caws from above.

"My rose without a thorn," he says. He holds the knife up to Howard's throat. Only Henry is close enough to hear Howard's next words.

"Maybe one."

Henry pauses. "What, my sweet?"

Howard puts her hands over his, smiling beatifically at him.

"I said, maybe just one thorn, Henry."

She looks to the ceiling and her wings unfurl. Her voice rings throughout the hall like the tolling of a bell. "Now, Goldfoot! Now!"

In the pause before Henry exhales, Aragon and Parr pull the binding cloths from where they are wrapped around their necks like lovers' hands, and toss them high into the air. The lapdragon's flame hits them at their zenith. The purple velvet catches light like a firework, the cloth brittle from their long residence in those little boxes.

In the seconds between Henry's confusion and his rage, Howard pulls at her cloth, and then Cleves's, while Parr tears at Seymour's. Henry roars, reaching for the fabric as it rises into the air. Goldfoot lets out another blast of flame, incinerating all of them.

The hall is full of noise, full of bodies rushing this way and that, full of orders being shouted and followed and ignored. Howard lifts her arm once more, calling Goldfoot back to her. He screeches, flitting like liquid through the air to his mistress's side.

Henry spins to face her. She has never seen hatred so potent. The divine power is leaving him, dissipating into the air like mist. But it is not gone yet, and she is too newly freed, too fluttery, to be able to command it as she should.

"Oh, little rose," he growls. "How I am going to rip your petals out."

The chaos narrows to him and her. The vestiges of the divine power gather in his hands. He will choose to use it all on her if he must, even if it means he has none left for anyone else. She cannot outrun him. But at least she sang, at the end, her very own song.

He thrusts his hands towards her, and the power flashes from him. Inescapable. She will not close her eyes. She can be brave, as Boleyn was brave.

There is a shriek, high and familiar. A whip of iridescent colour, fleeting towards her, quicker than magic.

Goldfoot somersaults through the air. He spreads his wings before her, and the power of a vengeful god smites him in his beautiful, brave little heart.

CHAPTER SIXTY-FIVE

Cecilia

He was such a sweet boy. This is all Cecilia can think as she witnesses Henry watching his youngest queen cradling the body of her lapdragon. That sneer, those red cheeks: they are not her brother's.

He was such a sweet boy, always protecting her and her sister.

She does not recognise the man before her.

Or she does. He has turned into the other brother. The one who was supposed to have died. And she does not know when the transformation began. She has never been the sort to freeze in the face of adversity, but she freezes now, only able to watch, while all around her is movement.

Mary Boleyn pulls the cloth from around her neck and rushes to her children, standing too close to the violence, and covers their eyes. Her binding cloth lies discarded on the floor, trampled beneath panicked feet. Aragon is wheeling herself towards the door while Princess Tudor and Queen Parr fumble to untie Seymour and Cleves's bindings.

Well, well, well. What clever women. Cecilia could never have conceived of so many of them conspiring. If she had a heart, she would find it touching.

Something of the old Cecilia winds through her. She has spent the last few days forgetting herself. It is time for Queen Cecilia to rise again.

Cromwell is directing soldiers to intercept Aragon, but Cecilia runs towards her brother. He has launched himself upon Howard, pinning her to the ground. The body of her pet lies beside her. Cecilia wonders why he does not use the divine power upon the little queen as he did her dragon. She is a mere chit, after all.

As she gets closer, she sees that they are tussling for the knife that should have already slit the girl's throat.

"Oh," she says, coming to a halt.

A thread of gold-pink-blue winds around the couple's hands. Yet the divine power is not aiding Henry. His eyes flicker between Howard and the threaded light, and sweat sheens upon his brow. The power is not helping him; it is helping her.

The hunger takes Cecilia.

"Brother, allow me," she says. She rips through their conjoined fingers, takes hold of the knife. Howard fumbles for the weapon, and Cecilia dances out of her reach.

"Give it to me, sister," Henry says, his eyes alight.

Cecilia spins the knife. It is very slender. Not so different from a needle.

She pounces. Howard screams as Cecilia pins her down with one arm and with the other holds the knife to her throat.

"Shall I do your blood ritual for you, brother?" she asks Henry.

He prowls. She and he are the same in so many ways. She does not know how to feel about that. It once would have thrilled her.

"He will never give you your crown," Howard says, struggling against Cecilia's grasp. No divine power surrounds her now. Cecilia glances around the hall. Most of the courtiers have scattered, blocking the entrance as they flee. Mary Boleyn and her children are nowhere to be seen. The remaining queens are surrounded by royal soldiers. Seymour stands before Cleves like a shield.

They should be on their knees, but there is no hint of surrender in their stances. Instead, they are surrounded by light. It gathers like a storm around them. It is the bordweal, flocking to protect its true mistresses.

"It is time," Henry says not to Cecilia, but to Charles Brandon, standing to her right.

Brandon grimaces. "Your Majesty, we have not—"

"It. Is. Time."

Henry flexes his fingers, and a little of his remaining power glows around his fists. Cromwell disappears through the door behind the dais.

"Even if you kill us, people know the truth now," Howard says.

Henry sneers at her. "An old truth is nothing. You want a new religion, little rose? Then I will give you one."

The doors behind the dais open. Cecilia spins around, bringing Howard with her, and witnesses the most monstrous being she has ever seen loping across the threshold, its eyes red, its teeth bright.

The beast is as big as two men, and though its shape is human, little else about it is. Its arms are too long for its body, and they end in claws sharp as knives. It is covered in rusty scales, patched and painful, raw as though it once had skin that has flaked away. Along its spine several horns erupt, bone-white and tipped with poisonous green. The face is the most unsettling part of it: it has the muzzle of a brute, but its ears are shell-like, human. It roars again, that same sound she heard the night More sacrificed himself. The roar of the crone.

She knows those eyes.

"What have you done?" Cecilia whispers.

They have forged a crone from the bones of the man she once adored. But this is a different kind of crone. They will need to find a new name for this horror.

"Kill the women," Henry shouts. Not the queens. The women.

The beast that was More surveys its targets, its eyes coming to rest upon Cecilia and Howard. The creature bares its teeth and snarls.

In some part of her, Cecilia has known how this will end since the day she found Arthur's book – with the space inside for his favourite instruments of torture – inside Henry's rooms. She knows what she must do.

She pushes Howard away and flings herself at her brother. They topple together to the floor.

It is not Henry she grapples with. Not the beloved brother who protected her, day after day. It is the other one, the older one. The one who liked to pull her hair out and burn her toys.

Their tussle is frantic. All around them courtiers flee the monster that was Bishop More, and the plight of their king is lost in the pursuit of their own survival. If she tries hard, she can imagine they are children once more, play-fighting in the nurseries of High Hall.

He bears down on her, his mouth pursed with effort. His hand closes around her wrist and slams it against the oak floor. Pain shoots up her arm, but she does not let go of the knife. She knows pain, and she can bear it. She is a woman, after all.

She brings her leg up hard against his groin.

His weight slacks, and she uses the momentum to swivel them over, so she is on top. She kneels upon his chest. It is obscene. She likes that. She likes that this final humiliation should be so shocking.

"Sister," he says. She pauses. Is her Henry returned? But no – from the corner of her eye, she spies him reaching for a cudgel, dropped by some panicked guard.

He thinks to use her heart against her? Oh, what a foolish boy he is.

The knife slides into his neck, between his spine and the tender hardness of his gullet. For a fleeting moment, she sees the boy he once was. Then he is gone, and all she sees is Arthur's hatred.

"Goodbye, brother," she whispers, kissing him on the lips as the strength ebbs from him.

She stands and raises the bloody knife. "The king is dead!" she shouts.

Time itself seems to pause. The chaos of the hall ebbs.

She addresses the beast, its claws hanging with gore. "Stop, More. Come to me now. I am the Tudor line."

She is beautiful. She is magnificent. She shall be king and queen both. She wields the knife as she would a needle.

Why is the beast not obeying her? Why are Cromwell and Wolsey and Brandon – especially Brandon, who she could make her consort if he plays his cards right – exchanging glances? As though they have a secret that she does not.

"Someone bring me Mary Boleyn," she says. If she gives enough orders, they will accept her as their leader. She will kill Mary Boleyn, and take the Palace of Brynd for herself, and from there work out how to expand her control over the rest of the island. Now she has saved Howard, the other queens will have to accept her.

As one, the men shrug off their robes. Cromwell does so willingly; Wolsey is slowest of all.

Cecilia stamps her foot. "Why are you not listening to me?" she shouts.

Brandon rips his shirt down the front, revealing a stomach taut from long hours in the saddle and in bed. "I am sorry, my lady," he says.

The men curl inwards. They convulse. They grow, like smoke and rage, welts wriggling across their backs. When they stand, there is not one beast, but four in the banqueting hall. Their scaled bodies reek of musk. Their eyes are the only remnants of the humans they once were.

"Brandon," she says, keeping her voice steady. "Brandon, I order you—"

The creature springs towards her, fixing his jaws around her waist. His teeth puncture her beautiful gown, ruining the embroidery she laboured so long over. Pearls scatter across the floor as he shakes.

Don't they understand? She is a queen, goddamn them. She is a queen.

CHAPTER SIXTY-SIX

Cleves

Keep running, Johana had told her. *Keep running.* All she has ever done is run, even when she thought she was a bastion. She runs now, keeping low as she dodges between soldiers and courtiers, monsters and men, trying to reach the far side of High Hall's vast banqueting hall, and the great doors that lead to safety.

In the midst of it, she spies Howard gather Goldfoot's body to her chest and crawl away from the siblings as they battle for control of a country that was never truly theirs. She feints to one side as Brandon turns into a monster, his tale lashing dangerously close. She reaches Seymour as Cecilia's body is flung, doll-like, across the hall. She lands, eyes open, in front of Cleves and Seymour.

At the sight of the monsters and their dead monarch, courtiers and soldiers alike scatter, discarding their weapons and rushing for the doors. Cleves cranes her head above them all, looking for the others.

"Howard needs us," Seymour says, able to see far more easily than Cleves.

They join hands and run for their young sister. Everywhere she looks there is spattered blood, for the rage is upon the monsters. All she can hear is the drumbeat of boots and her childhood, looming, looming. Through it all, she thinks: where is my power? No light flickers across her skin. No phoenix-warmth spreads through her veins.

Howard is edging around the side of the hall, but she has not escaped the creatures' notice. The one that was More turns towards her. Cleves has never trusted the influence wielded by mortal men who pledged themselves to Cernunnos, even before she knew the truth. He towers over Howard now, the very embodiment of that influence. Such men get too much satisfaction from putting women in their place. And Howard is all alone.

Not alone. Aragon and Parr, on the other side of the hall, are racing towards her. They reach her at the same time as Cleves and Seymour. Five queens, tired and bloodied, together.

The banqueting hall falls eerily quiet.

They are hemmed in. The ancient stone wall of the original palace on one side, and four monsters between them and the great doors.

The only noise is the rasping breath of the beasts.

"Why do we not have the divine power?" Parr is saying. "I thought it would be ours to command."

"I had it momentarily," Howard says. Her face is streaked with dirt and tears. She is still clutching Goldfoot. "But I could not keep it."

Aragon hits the wall with her fist. "It is a godly power. Just because it is now ours does not mean we will be able to command it easily. We must master it over time, as with any skill."

Cleves stands before them, her arms spread like a shield, as the monsters gather. "Well, that is inconvenient," she says. "I rather think we might need it to get out of here alive."

Keep running, cousin.

It comes to her then. The impossibility of her being both castle and runner. She has been doing it all wrong, all these years, building walls around herself to run away.

"What do we do?" Seymour whispers.

Cleves closes her eyes. Seymour's breath is on her shoulder, as real as her own heartbeat. Beneath it, she feels something else: Cnothan. Home. Her link to it is stronger than ever; the divine bond that had been poisoned by Henry for so long, now renewed. It calls to her like a child cries for its nurse.

She does not need to look, or to hear her fellow queens' gasps, to know that light is consuming her body.

Cleves whirls round, taking in her companions. She crushes Howard to her chest and whispers into her hair, "You have nothing left to prove, but I ask you one final favour, little sister. Protect Seymour for me."

"What?" Howard says, pulling away, frowning.

"Promise me, sister."

Something settles in Howard's expression. She understands. "I promise," she says.

Cleves kisses Seymour. "Go. I will hold them off for a little while."

"Cleves—"

"Go!"

Cleves turns to the gathering beasts, the divine power flickering brightly across her body, telling her that she is precisely where she ought to be, and precisely who she was always, always supposed to be.

She clenches her fists before her, steadying herself for what is to come. Light pools inside her hands. She thinks of a wall, thick and strong like marble, and she opens her hands.

From her palms erupts a wall of light that shimmers from pearlescent to the purple-black of a jay's feathers. The bordweal light, as it was always intended to be. It stems from the part of her that longs for home, whether that is Cnothan, or Ezzonid, or the woman she adores.

She can barely see the monsters, but can feel them prowling beyond the power's wall. One of them lunges at it, and is rebuffed. She feels the attack as a crush, deep in her belly, as though something is inside her, eviscerating her gut.

The light wavers, but holds.

She moves with the other queens, holding back the monsters, until they reach the doors of the banqueting hall. She can smell the roses and the light, fresh air of High Hall's gardens beyond.

"Come, Cleves!" Aragon calls.

She glances back. All of them are through the doors. Seymour is reaching for her. Howard, keeping her promise, has one hand upon Seymour's arm. She alone of them understands what is about to happen. She nods at Cleves, a little lift of the chin that says, *Well fought, sister.*

There is another lurch in her stomach. The monsters are attacking once more. She will not be able to keep this wall up for much longer. And when it comes down, there will be nothing preventing them from following the others. She must buy them more time.

She probably should have kept Johana's gift, but perhaps it will keep Seymour safe through the war that is to come. Yes. That is as it is meant to be.

She has sought safety above all ever since the soldiers. Safety above happiness, safety above companionship, safety above love.

"Come on!" Seymour says.

Cleves smiles at her, and says what she has never said before: "I love you."

Seymour launches herself towards Cleves, even as Howard and Parr seize her round the waist.

"I love you," Cleves says again, her throat thick with it. With one hand, she heaves the doors of the banqueting hall shut.

The sound of Seymour's screams dims, leaving only the sound of the *tap tap* of the creatures' claws on the flagstones.

Slowly, Cleves turns, wielding the fading power of a goddess newly risen. All four beasts are bearing down upon her now. There is only them, the bodies of the foolish dowager queen and her upstart brother, and Cleves. All else is still. All else is calm.

"No more running," she says, lifting her chin, stilling her trembling hands.

Her chest grows hot as the monsters strike.

No more running.

CHAPTER SIXTY-SEVEN

Howard

Howard made a promise, and she intends to keep it. She and Parr heave upon a feral Seymour, entreating her to come with them. Howard blocks out the sound of the creatures beyond the doors. The sound of claws upon stone, of teeth against flesh.

The night air is cool and busy. Courtiers are scattered across the grounds, like sheep stranded on a mountainside. Some of them, incapable of accepting what is happening, attempt to continue the festivities, picking at the exotic fruits hanging from fake trees, or dipping goblets into canals of wine. Others scramble to find carriages. Howard even spies some scurrying from the queens' wings with stolen silverware and candlesticks. She can hardly blame them. They all may need a little extra wealth in the turmoil to come, for even Howard can see that the monsters that were More, Cromwell, Wolsey and Brandon will not permit the queens to assume the rule of Elben without a battle. Perhaps one day, perhaps soon, she will learn how to wield the divine power properly, and alongside her sisters will crush the beasts utterly. But not now.

Their carriages are waiting in the same courtyard from which Boleyn had fled High Hall – Howard's courtyard. The drivers are fending off courtiers jostling to commission them.

Ursula looks down from her place on top of the foremost carriage.

"Move aside!" she says, kicking a nobleman as she jumps down. She pushes through the crowd to Howard and Seymour, her eyes taking in the lack and looking to Howard for the answer.

"She stayed," Seymour sobs.

"She gave us a little time, but not much," Howard adds.

Ursula hustles Seymour into the carriage. Princess Tudor leaps out of the second vehicle and helps her mother in.

"Wait," Seymour says, her arms braced against the open door of the carriage.

"We cannot wait," Howard says.

"*Wait.*" It is a command as if from Hyde itself. Seymour ignores the chaos around her, her eyes fixed upon the doors into High Hall.

In the palace, there is a great wrenching of metal and wood, and the roars of four beasts who were men echo into the night. Howard swings herself up into the carriage, sitting next to Ursula. She made a promise to Cleves, but she will not sacrifice herself to it. She no longer has anything left to prove, to them or to herself. She has lost her best friend, her little loyal dragon. She will not lose herself as well. Not again.

Seymour is frozen, listening to those roars. They all know what it must mean.

"I gave them back," Seymour says. Her stiff arms wilt. "I gave them back," she says again.

Parr steps out of the second carriage and catches Seymour neatly as she crumples. Without a word, she lifts Seymour bodily into the carriage and closes the door upon her wails. She looks up at Howard and Ursula. "Drive," she says.

The carriages spring away down the long road towards the coast. Howard will take Seymour to Plythe. Parr will go to Mathmas, and Aragon from there to Daven. While they may not have been able to take High Hall immediately, there is now no longer a living Tudor male. The queens have demonstrated their power. The truth will spread. It cannot be stopped. And while there will be battles ahead, she can see her way to winning the war.

She thinks of the bordweal flowing into her as Henry grappled with her body. She was equal to him. Of course she was.

Dawn breaks over Elben as Ursula urges the horses onwards, towards the blistering gold. Howard looks to the sky. The bordweal is barely visible, still muted grey. The dawn has not touched it yet. When it does, she thinks it will be the colour of Cleves's power. A tribute.

Something moves in that grey. For a moment her heart soars, for the movement is so akin to Goldfoot's flight that she thinks it must be him, that the goddess has brought him back to her. But it is no dragon. It is a murmuration.

The swallows twist like ribbons in the cool air of a new day. They soar, rising points and falling waves. Her chest opens, and the little bird inside flies free to join them.

EPILOGUE

The dream takes the queens one by one, creeping across Elben like a cloud's shadow. It takes Aragon in her royal sheets, and she cries out, waking Princess Tudor who has been slumbering on a cot at the foot of the bed. Parr is thrown from deep dreams of movement in shadows into the tempest of the nightmare. Seymour, curled in her grief, eyes and heart raw, falls from doze into the vision. Howard, cocooned in Florin's arms, the wash of the Kyttle Falls outside her window, twitches. And in a darkened dungeon, cold and shivering, a lonely woman, gown studded with priceless pins, thinks she has passed from waking nightmare into insanity.

This is what they see.

The procession is maudlin as it trundles inevitably up the icy mountain paths and comes to a stop outside the royal baths. Cloaked figures emerge from the bath house as though they have been expecting the procession's arrival. The large, low carriage at the centre of the train is secured, and six men in the cambric of minor courtiers scuffle to pull something from inside. Cromwell, his skin covered in the scars of welts, barks orders. Wolsey, huddled in large fur coats and looking very, very ill, says nothing but only watches through pale eyes.

A stretcher carrying a large bulk swaddled in velvets and silks is conveyed into the bath house. It is unmoving, but the queens have a sense of malice rearing from that bulk, that prone shape. Howard thinks of stifled songbirds; Seymour of her dying and desperate brother. The prisoner thinks of the soldiers' drumbeat. Aragon thinks of her first husband, the cruel boy and his stonelike father; Parr is reminded of nothing so tangible, only the sickbeds of her first two spouses, and the knowledge of the mercy of their deaths.

The dream takes them into the baths, where the steam whirls and eddies around so many shapes. Cromwell talks in a low voice to the keeper of the baths, a short, austere man wearing the headdress of Cernunnos. They look together at the nuns, all six of them in their doe-inspired hoods and simple gowns of white linen.

Charles Brandon bends over the bundle on its stretcher, and pulls back the covers.

In her sleep, Howard reaches for Florin's hand, clinging to him.

Henry, the king that was, lies pale, his skin blotched and blue, on the stretcher. The wound at his neck, the one inflicted by his sister, is a strike of scarlet that is almost black in that dim light.

There is a commotion, like a fluttering of butterfly wings, and the six does step forward to look upon Henry's body. Their faces are blank. Parr recognises the expressions, even in her sleep, as the result of drugs. Perhaps the flower of Esphagia, which makes one suggestible.

The keeper of the baths leaves, and returns momentarily with a bundle of fabric. He opens it to reveal six golden knives, each one sharp as midwinter. Aragon has the strangest sensation of inevitability. Seymour does not wish to see what happens next. She knows she dreams. She knows she must wake, and yet whatever power is showing her this vision will not release her.

The keeper's voice is hoarse, unused to speaking loudly, but it grows in confidence as his words pour forth: "Oh Highfather, on this, the mountain where you declared victory over the heathen goddess, we offer you blood freely given. Blood humble and loyal and true. We invite you, we beg you, oh Highfather, to bestow your presence upon our most worthy king."

As one, the does raise their golden knives. As one, they draw the blades across their necks, their white gowns turning red. They do not utter a sound as they bleed out upon Henry's corpse. Even their death fall is delicate, muffled by the steam.

Wolsey surveys them in horror, but the rest are stoic. This must be done. This is war. There will be blood and suffering.

The keeper raises his hands once more. "Bless us, oh Highfather! Bless us, and bless our martyred king, who died in pursuit of your glory!"

He pants with the passion of his words, perhaps more overcome by the death of his companions than he might like to admit. The steam of the baths swirls, flickering strangely in the dimness.

Then, one by one, the candles lighting the space go out.

In the hush that follows, there is a sense of impending thunder.

There is a shifting sound in the darkness. Moving, shaking and then an awful cracking, like bones being broken. *Crack crack crack crack crack.*

"My lord?" Wolsey's voice says, tremulous.

One by one, the candles flicker back on. At first, the queens can see nothing through the thickened steam. Cromwell frowns, also peering through the fog. Then the keeper starts back, pointing at the stretcher.

It is now empty, and of the bodies of the six does of the baths, little remains but their discarded gowns, still red with their spilled lifeblood.

The men spin round, and their faces fill with wonder and horror and everything in between. Cromwell is the first to kneel.

Towering over them, rising from the water of the baths, which bubbles red, is Henry. Yet this is not the Henry who wed Howard and Seymour, Parr and Aragon. He is handsome still, in form very much the same man, but he is taller, stronger, his muscles bulging from his naked body as though they have a life of their own. Aragon feels the loss the most – she still remembers the loving boy who rode to her from his father's deathbed to ask her to marry him. There is no vestige of that boy left in the king who stands now in the baths. His eyes are smaller than they were before, his mouth a mean little line. No human words come from that mouth, only a godly roar as two horns, like the horns of a stag, erupt from his forehead and branch out like spiders' legs. The horns are like no stag horn known on Elben. They are made of human bones, delicate and strong. The bones of the women who sacrificed themselves to bring him to the mortal realm.

Cernunnos-who-was-Henry looks up at the ceiling of the baths, and it is only then that the queens see he has been crouching. With one hand he pulls down the roof of the baths, tearing apart the rock and ice as though it were nothing. He stands fully upright, the height of two men now, and surveys those kneeling at his feet.

"Oh Highfather," Cromwell says. "We serve you and your cause."

Cernunnos surveys the land beyond the baths, and Howard shivers in her sleep, as if feeling his gaze come to rest upon Plythe and the treacherous women sleeping therein.

Cernunnos, Henry, roars once more, then looks down at his servants. "Rise," he says, in a voice unused to worldly speech. "Rise, and let us crush the heathen woman once and for all."

"Your will," the men say. Their heads touch the ground, and their bodies begin to bubble and morph. Far above them, the inky sky flickers, for a breathless moment, in shades of dawn.

ACKNOWLEDGEMENTS

This book gave me major second-book syndrome, and I'm not sure I'd have finished it without the support of many, many people.

My first thanks must go to my agent, Zoë Plant, who is an amazing advocate, cheerleader and (at times) counsellor, and to my Orbit UK editor, Nadia Saward, who is seemingly effortlessly able to hold all the many facets of publishing (editorial, marketing, sales, strategy . . .) in their head at once, gives the best notes and also knows how to perfectly time an announcement at a launch party.

My thanks also to the rest of the teams at the Bent Agency – particularly Martha Perotto-Wills, Emma Lagarde, Aminah Amjad, Molly Ker Hawn, Victoria Cappello and Jenny Bent – and Orbit UK and US – particularly my US editor Brit Hvide, as well as Nazia Khatun, Anna Jackson, Emily Byron, Serena Savini, Joanna Kramer, Ellen Wright, Aimee Kitson and many more! Thank you to Niall Grant for creating yet another stunning cover, and to Olivia Dowd for her incredible audiobook narration.

Thank you to those publishers who are translating my books into other languages, and to the agents and translators who made those editions happen. A special hat-tip to Benjamine, Janis and Laura at Sabran in France – you know how to show a girl a good time!

My friends and family are everything to me, and I'm so appreciative of the coffees and baked goods, the chats, the pre-panel dinners and the post-panel drinks, the wild swims and walks, the camaraderie and disagreements, the offers of playdates so I could write . . . There are genuinely too many of you to list here, and I'm terrified to attempt it because I will absolutely forget someone. However, I would like to give a little shout out to my fellow 2025 Orbit debuts Modupe Ayinde and Annabel Campbell. It's been wonderful riding this publishing train alongside you both.

To my parents, Louette and Bob, to my husband Alex and my daughter Ada: I love you all beyond belief. You are all of the heart, all of the good, in this trilogy. I hope you know that.

Finally, thank you so much to the booksellers and readers who have read and yelled about *Six Wild Crowns*. Your advocacy and messages over the last year have meant so much – I hope that you love Cleves and Howard and Cecilia as much as you loved Boleyn and Seymour!

ABOUT THE AUTHOR

Holly Race is a writer and script editor, and has worked for companies including Working Title Films, Aardman Animations and Red Planet Pictures. She is a Faber Academy graduate, and her YA urban fantasy trilogy, *Midnight's Twins, A Gathering Midnight* and A *Midnight Dark and Golden,* was published by Hot Key Books (2020–22). She lives in Cambridge.

Find out more about Holly Race and other Orbit authors by registering for the free monthly newsletter at orbit-books.co.uk.

RAISING READERS
Books Build Bright Futures

Dear Reader,

We'd love your attention for one more page to tell you about the crisis in children's reading, and what we can all do.

Studies have shown that reading for fun is the **single biggest predictor of a child's future life chances** – more than family circumstance, parents' educational background or income. It improves academic results, mental health, wealth, communication skills, ambition and happiness.[1]

The number of children reading for fun is in rapid decline. Young people have a lot of competition for their time. In 2024, 1 in 10 children and young people in the UK aged 5 to 18 did not own a single book at home.[2]

Hachette works extensively with schools, libraries and literacy charities, but here are some ways we can all raise more readers:

- Reading to children for just 10 minutes a day makes a difference
- Don't give up if children aren't regular readers – there will be books for them!
- Visit bookshops and libraries to get recommendations
- Encourage them to listen to audiobooks
- Support school libraries
- Give books as gifts

There's a lot more information about how to encourage children to read on our website: **www.RaisingReaders.co.uk**

Thank you for reading.

hachette UK

[1] OECD, '21st-Century Readers: Developing Literacy Skills in a Digital World', 2021, https://www.oecd.org/en/publications/21st-century-readers_a83d84cb-en.html

[2] National Literacy Trust, 'Book Ownership in 2024', November 2024, https://literacytrust.org.uk/research-services/research-reports/book-ownership-in-2024